How to Tell Toledo from the Night Sky

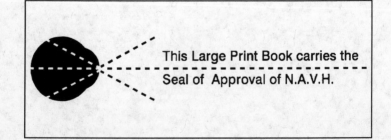

This Large Print Book carries the
Seal of Approval of N.A.V.H.

How to Tell Toledo from the Night Sky

Lydia Netzer

THORNDIKE PRESS
A part of Gale, Cengage Learning

Farmington Hills, Mich • San Francisco • New York • Waterville, Maine
Meriden, Conn • Mason, Ohio • Chicago

GALE
CENGAGE Learning°

LIBRARY OF CONGRESS CATALOGING-IN-PUBLICATION DATA

Netzer, Lydia.
　How to tell Toledo from the night sky / Lydia Netzer. — Large print edition.
　　pages cm. — (Thorndike Press large print peer picks)
　　ISBN 978-1-4104-7257-1 (hardcover) — ISBN 1-4104-7257-4 (hardcover)
　　1. Large type books. I. Title.
PS3614.E528H69 2014b
813'.6—dc23　　　　　　　　　　　　　　　　2014023896

Published in 2014 by arrangement with St. Martin's Press, LLC

Printed in Mexico
1 2 3 4 5 6 7 18 17 16 15 14

FOR JOSHILYN AND SUSANNAH,
MY SISTERS

"A CRADLE SONG"

The angels are stooping
Above your bed;
They weary of trooping
With the whimpering dead.

God's laughing in Heaven
To see you so good;
The Sailing Seven
Are gay with His mood.

I sigh that kiss you,
For I must own
That I shall miss you
When you have grown.

—William Butler Yeats

A test field in the form of an initially uniform train of waves propagating into a Kerr-Newman black hole has its crests crowded together and magnified by gravitational and Doppler blueshifts that grow without bound at the Cauchy horizon. Such perturbative results suggest (though they do not prove) that inside a black hole formed in a generic collapse, an observer falling toward the inner horizon should be engulfed in a wall of (classically) infinite density immediately after seeing the entire future history of the outer universe pass before his eyes in a flash.

— E. Poisson and W. Israel, "Inner-Horizon Instability and Mass Inflation in Black Holes" (*Physical Review Letters,* volume 63, pages 1663–66, 1989)

PROLOGUE

On the night when George and Irene were born, the sun set in a boil of red-orange ribbons across the Ohio sky. The people of Toledo looked out their western-facing windows at the night, buttoned the collars of their pajamas against the cold, and closed the blinds as darkness fell. They lay down flat in their beds and began to sleep. Some turned over on their sides, first some punched their pillows, and some sighed. But sleep came for them all, one by one, and they slid under it willingly. No one fought. No one refused. Sleeping, they lost track of what was going on. They were no longer in Toledo, but in Paris or in the past, on the moon or in a book they'd read. Behind closed eyes and sleeping faces, they were gone.

Into what deep well did they all fall, single file? On what small ledge did each waver, and then drop down from waking into dreaming, down from life to death? A man who falls asleep is like a diver who slips from the air into the water. Yet through it all, the sleeping man's body stays put, under a thin sheet, straight and flat. You could put his whole body in a box. You could put the box into the ground.

Sleep is a shallow death we practice every night. City after city, as the earth turns and rolls around the sun, we lie down and close our eyes. We try out this thing, death, for an eight-hour stretch. New York, Toledo, Dallas, Los Angeles: we all go down. Our sleeping minds blur the boundaries between our bodies and our idea of the world into what would otherwise be madness. In sleep we have no senses but imagined senses, no grasp on fate except a lunatic's idea of control. Being crazy is like being asleep, and being asleep is like dying. It's just like dying, because the body needs to do it. It has no choice.

By the time the people of Toledo actually die, they will have practiced it thousands of times. The sense of going under will be familiar. The sense of slipping loose from sanity will be no stranger. They will be very good at dying, by the time they get to do it. So good, it will be absolutely irreversible. To everyone, this seems like a good idea.

On the night that George and Irene were born, the city was silenced by the effort of sleep, and all the astronomers and astrologers, and all the preachers and historians, and all the girls and boys had gone into the dark.

There was one hospital in the city of Toledo, a box of light and nervous energy in the sleeping world. Inside, the people were wide awake. In the maternity ward, two mothers pushed and strained to give birth. There was a lot of grunting, a few tense moments, several people counted to ten, and then the babies emerged, full of love and covered in blood. The mothers that birthed them smiled at each other. These births had been carefully arranged.

George and Irene were born to be together.

The night sky was dark and windy from the stars exploding. But when the babies came out, they were perfect: a boy and a girl. The wide-awake nurses even said how beautiful and big and healthy they were. George and Irene didn't look alike. Nor do gods look like humans, or heaven like the earth. They were the same age, exactly. Not an older and a younger twin, but the same twin repeated. It's very difficult to produce twin souls. It's not just a matter of double strollers and mega–diaper packs. There are subtleties and manipulations, and there are moments of distress, when it all seems like it won't work out correctly. When you think about it, how many times have twin souls been successfully created? Look at Antony and Cleopatra. Now there was a botched project.

Look at Castor and Pollux; they ate each other in the end. At least, people think they did. But maybe they sat down together on an unmade bed, and began to kiss, and covered each other's mouths with their mouths, and began to breathe, in and out, holding each other around the neck, and taking each other's carbon dioxide, until their eyes bugged out and they were gone.

As for the twin souls of George and Irene, this is their story. How they met on earth, and how they slept and practiced for their deaths, night after night, and met in certain dreams, and came to love and lose each other, and live on.

1

At the time her mother fell down the stairs to her death in Toledo, Irene was far away in Pittsburgh, working in a lab. As her mother bounced down a flight of stairs in a bright city on the sparkling shore of Lake Erie, Irene sat in a dark room, in the basement of an ugly building, in a drab university, in an abandoned steel town. Irene's mother was named Bernice. They had not spoken to each other in years.

Irene pulled her lab coat around her and stared intently into a small glass window on a large metal apparatus. She wasn't thinking about her mother at all. In fact, all she was thinking about was her work. As her mother landed at the bottom of the stairs, arms and legs cracking, Irene concentrated only on recording the data from her machine. All of her recent days had been spent alone, just like this, compressed into the space in her own head. Yes, she had a boyfriend, a mother, a boss. But there was her and there was everything else. There was her and there was the world. She had a reason for this. It wasn't only vanity.

As her mother's limbs banged and broke and settled into place around her on the floor, Irene peered again into the window in the middle of her machine. It was as big as the whole room, and had the shape of an 8, made of bright metal. She leaned over it and looked down into it, where the two sides of the 8 connected. The machine buzzed under her hand. Inside, the little particles were whirring around. She was an astrophysicist, attempting to observe a black hole by exciting the particles in the machine. It was all she had been doing and trying and thinking about for months: proving that there are black holes all around us, and we have been walking through them all our lives. It was her work, and her entire focus was there.

In Toledo, Bernice's spinal fluid leaked into the tissue around her cervical vertebrae, and there was thick blood coming out her ear. In Pittsburgh, Irene concentrated on turning a little numbered dial, click by click. Although her eyes were heavy and she was tired, she would not quit.

She adjusted a different knob on the

control panel and flicked a switch. She adjusted and peered, over and over. There are a lot of fractions between zero and one. There are a lot of sort-ofs between off and on. She had to test everything. For an almost innumerable number of failures, she had continued. She had to assume that this day would be no different, but she would carry on anyway.

Never once had she felt the desire to hit the machine, to jostle it, berate it. But she had considered what it would feel like to slide it gently into the water, where the two rivers of Pittsburgh converged, then jump in after it. She would ride it down to the sea, like a barrel over the falls. Then, sleeping peacefully, they would drift out on the waves. These things had occurred to her. She had stood for panting, tense minutes at the railing of the George Westinghouse Bridge, glaring down at the train tracks below, flanked by green, thinking of jumping.

In Toledo, her mother was finally dying, and one last breath came out. Irene did not know the fight her mother was having, right at that exact moment.

Outside Pittsburgh, there was a green forest to hike in, with rivers and bald eagles. Inside the city, there were buildings you could look at, visit, and enjoy. A funicular went up and down, up and down, but Irene had never been in it. Irene didn't care about all that. She just leaned over the experiment, her back bent. There are elements common to all cities. University laboratories, suicide bridges, small apartments to live in, boyfriends to have.

Irene kept her face steady, her eyes open, pointed at the machine. If she worked until her face melted into the detector, if her brain fell down into the path of the accelerator, if it was penetrated by pions and if a small black hole was created in her skull, then at least she would have finished all the data for this set. She blinked her eyes to wake herself up, clicked the knob, and peered into the machine, like every time before. But her mother had nothing left with which to blink herself awake. She could not stop.

Far away, her mother died.

And this time, when Irene looked into that little window, she saw something completely different. This time, even before her forehead pressed against the humming steel, she saw a tiny purple glow. A little bit of light came out the window she had been looking in. Light that had not been there before.

Her stomach dropped. Her brain woke up. She took a deep breath in, and she felt her heart tremble and thump against her ribs. The lab was perfectly quiet, a heavy door blocking out any sounds of the hallway. There was no window and no potted plant, no ticking clock, no stars marching across the firmament, no heavenly witnesses. Irene sat frozen, vibrating, the purple glow from the apparatus window lighting up her eyes. At that moment, she almost couldn't look. It was too much to take.

As the person who had been standing in the upstairs hallway in her mother's house came slowly down the stairs, step by step, toward the body, Irene pressed her face up to the experiment one final time in faith, opened her eyes wide, and stared at the evidence.

For the first time, it was there. More beautiful than she had ever imagined. A tiny pinprick in space, absorbing and draining particles, leaking radiation that came to her as light through the detector she had made. It flared up from a deep violet to the fiercest lavender and back again, the size of a speck of dust, as far as her human eye could tell. Her breath came faster. Her eyes did not want to pull away, did not want to leave the window, and the purple light bathed the sharp lines of her face, her pointed chin, tired eyelids, the pencil forgotten in her ear. Her finger pushed a button and recorded an image. Another image.

Then in a mist of lavender, it was gone. She blinked. Her heart surged and hurt against the back of her sternum. She felt prickles of adrenaline rippling down her limbs. Her hand reached into her lap and fished around in her lab coat, picked up a pencil. The hand felt the distance between the coils and the other edge of the notebook, felt its way halfway down the page, and then while her face was still glued to the machine, she wrote.

Irradiated Argon. Polarization 60%. Frequency 16 PHz. Wavelength 47nm. Visible Hawking radiation from possible black hole. Estimated mass, 1 ng. Estimated radius of anomaly, 0 nm. Estimated density, infinite. Halflife

She stopped writing. Had it lived for two breaths? Three seconds? Had she been watching for an hour? She leaned back over the machine and looked into the detector. The particles continued to whirr through the collider. Soon, there would be another one. Now she had no trouble staying awake.

One hour passed. Two hours more, and she was still looking. She saw one more, two more, but it was not enough for her. She was hungry for these results. *Just one more,* her brain said. *Show me one more. Then I'll sleep.* "More gas," her hand now wrote. *A purer substrate. Try protons, for a perfect leptonic decay. The color of irises in spring.*

When she finally pulled away from the machine, a visor shape was marked into the pale skin of her face by the pressure of her observation. She waved her hand through the air in front of her body and smiled.

Black holes had formed and decayed, without taking the universe or even Pittsburgh with them. Each left a puff of radiation, just like it was supposed to, and then was gone. A leak of energy that could be measured, documented, graphed, applied to paper, faxed, e-mailed, and reported to the world. The smallest collision, the smallest suction of mass into a singularity, the quickest fade, the sweetest moment of bright purple light in dissolution, like a shallow breath let out quickly. Because of her design, it had been visible. She had seen X-rays it emitted, like no one else on earth had ever done. All around the earth in space, these tiny collisions were happening all the time. Matter rippling like a puddle in a rainstorm. Irene felt better than she had ever felt in her entire life. If she had known a song, she might have sung it. If there had been someone there, she probably would have spoken to them in an elevated tone. She might have even let that person clasp her hand in congratulations.

Her phone rang.

She walked on stiff legs to her desk and picked up the phone from where she had set it down what seemed like years ago. A glance at the time surprised her. So much of it had passed. She slid the phone on and clicked to answer.

"Sparks," she said.

Irene was a small girl with a face like a trapezoid. Her smile, when it appeared, could have been called winning, but her voice was not charming. It grated, and was not pretty. At times, she cultivated this ugliness. She tried for a caustic manner. *Small women have to do this,* she had told herself often. *It's bad enough I have to be short. At least I don't have to be cute.*

"Irene? Is that you?" The voice on the phone had the unmistakable buttery tone of her mother's pastor.

"Hello, Father Allen," said Irene. Why was he calling? She had not talked to him since the last time her mother had an episode.

Inside her happiness, a tiny speck of doubt took hold, spiraled around, and sent a plume of anxiety through her body.

"Honey," said Blake Allen, his voice sounding like a waterfall of olive oil. "Are you alone? Are you with someone?"

"Yes." She walked back over to the machine and leaned her face on the metal. It was cool on her forehead. She felt her breath start to come out fast. She felt the blood coursing through the arteries in her head. Something deep inside her chest sent out a little pain. Something bad was about to happen.

"Okay, Irene, I'm with your mom."

"Where is she?"

"She's here at home, Irene. I'm at her home right now, and I'm sorry, but she has passed away."

"What? What are you talking about?" This was not what Irene had expected him to say. Passed out, maybe. Past hope. But not away.

"I'm so, so sorry, Irene. I hate to have to tell you this. But she has passed."

"Where is she? Where are you?" Irene's voice scraped along her throat, tears starting up in her eyes.

"She's here in her home, and I'm with her. Honey, she appears to have fallen down the stairs."

"Are you sure she is dead? Did somebody really check? She can be — a deep sleeper," said Irene. Her tears were now making her face wet. Irene used her hand to swab her eyes. She used her lab coat, leaving a rumpled wet patch on it. She began to flick switches on the control panel, powering down, shutting everything off. She was thinking off, off, off as she clicked the metal switches.

"Yes, I'm sorry. It seems that —" Here he coughed. Blake Allen was pastor of the Unitarian Church. Her mother attended weekly, prayed with a prayer circle, knitted shawls for the bereaved. Of course, she also practiced palm reading, tarot, and other astrological divinations. The recitation of liturgy, the meditative chants, altar clothes, tie-dye with bells, a crystal ball, a chalice. All the accoutrements of firm belief. "It seems that the neighbor came by to see her. I guess they usually had afternoon tea together. Anyway, she found her."

"Are you telling me she's lying on the floor at the bottom of the stairs?"

"Yes, but the coroner will take her away soon. I want you to know that I'm going to take care of whatever needs to be taken care of here. Don't worry about anything like that."

Irene paused. She felt like there was too much oxygen in the room. Her lungs just kept filling up and replenishing her oxygen supply and then going back, inexorably, for more oxygen. It was like the damn brooms at the well. She could see her mother, curled innocently on the floor next to the bottom step, one hand closed under her chin, one fist open, palm exposed, as if to say, "Come with me."

"Is she broken? Did she break —" Irene began to cough.

"We don't know the cause of death. She may have had a stroke at the top of the stairs, a heart attack, we just don't know."

There were times when her mother would say, *I'm dying. I need to get a haircut and make a will.* Irene would just roll her eyes at that. That was before Irene had said, *I am leaving Toledo and I will never come back. I will never speak to you again.*

"I'm so, so sorry. I know you and your mom were not close," said the rector.

"We *were* close," said Irene. She choked back a sob.

"Of course, of course. She spoke of you so often."

The rector said a few words to someone else in the room there in her mother's house in Toledo. She imagined him stepping

25

nimbly over the corpse of her mother, trotting adroitly over to the front door, stepping out onto the porch. She could hear traffic sounds. He was probably wearing a bespoke suit. He was such a natty dresser.

"I don't want to come home," said Irene stupidly. She didn't know what else to say.

"Really?" Blake Allen wanted to know. "Your mother always said it was your dream to come back to Toledo."

Her dream was to come back to Toledo, and work at the Toledo Institute of Astronomy. But it was not something she could ever do while her mother was there, or while her experiment was unsuccessful. But now . . .

"I don't —" Irene began.

"Irene, excuse me for one moment," said Blake Allen. He put his hand over the phone and Irene waited, listening to the silence on the line, feeling her heart tap against her ribs in an irregular rhythm. *I need to sit down,* she thought. *I'm going to have a heart attack, too. I'm going to fall down some stairs.*

"Irene, I've just talked to the coroner. From what he was able to determine, sweetie, there was no suffering in the end."

"Was she just tired or was she confused or was she —" Irene wanted to say drunk, but that was not something she would ever say

26

out loud. Still, her mind would not comply: Was she blasted? Wasted? Hammered? Was she? Was she like, "Whee! Down we go!"

"Sweetie, we just don't know. We don't know. Listen, I need to speak to some people here that have just arrived. I will call you again later."

Irene turned the phone off and put it down. There was a dense, strange feeling in her chest, like the residual joy at having successfully observed results in her experiments had collided with the grotesque horror of having her mother die of a broken neck, and a black hole had been created in the center of her chest, sucking in all her feelings and her will. She began to cry. She sat down in her chair and put her hands in her lap, coughing and sobbing.

Does death always make you feel sad? What do you do when someone dies? What if the person was a terrible and unsolvable lifelong problem for you? What if the person was your mother?

Irene cried and cried, in spite of herself. Her mother had been a bad mother, yet she was sad anyway. She couldn't make the sadness stop, just because it was reasonable to feel relief. She tried to figure out what she would say to someone else in this situation. Maybe the years of awfulness dissolve, when a bad mother dies, so that all you really have to feel is sadness. Or maybe Irene would say to the person, "I'm sorry for your loss," and that would be the end of it.

Exhausted from her tears, Irene finally looked up and saw her gleaming machine. She remembered the good thing that had happened to her, and what she must now do. Then she gathered her backpack and keys and went outside the lab and up the stairs. She did not fall. She did not die. She locked the door.

Outside, she saw it was midafternoon. The blue autumn sky seemed to hover just above the colorless buildings. The breeze felt cool but there was warmth radiating off the pavement all around. She felt sure it was a Monday. A rumbling of shouts came from the stadium, and she knew there was a sports practice going on there. A group of men shouting rhythmically as they ran forward, sideways, backward, or hunched in squats. Irene opened her phone and placed a call to the Toledo Institute of Astronomy. On the phone, her tone was full of spirit.

2

The Toledo Institute of Astronomy was founded in 1837 as the Stickney Library of Almanacs (or al-manakhs) by Angelica Stickney, whose family's fortune had been made in shipping, and whose lifelong passion was observing the night sky. She employed two full-time academics in her library. The more elderly of them, Dr. Claude Pooley, had been hired to study and catalog the information in Mrs. Stickney's astonishing collection of almanacs, from a tablet of Sumerian origin depicting planetary movements to a document from the sixteenth century that was believed to have been penned by Francis Bacon. The other scientist in her employ, self-taught female prodigy Esther Birchard, was charged with studying stars and weather patterns in order to better inform the decisions made by the Stickney family's transportation business, which operated largely on the Miami and

Erie Canal and its Wabash extension. Birchard's husband was an elevator man. He was a naturally suspicious person.

Pooley, the librarian, enlightened by the study of ancient texts and tables, became involved in light experiments postulating the chemical composition of the sun. He had such success with his observations that he began to publish his work and bring in other researchers to work with him. On the other side of this dual operation, Stickney Carriers laid unfortunate claim to the record for most vessels lost in the river to storms, mechanical failures, and crime. Esther Birchard, whose job it was to advise the captains of these boats, grew more and more reclusive, as her predictions increasingly failed. Year by year, she found herself relying less on her anemometer and more on fervent prayer to improve the fates of the company. Eventually, she lost her job. When pressed to account for this, Angelica Stickney calmly explained that Esther Birchard was a weather witch, and had accordingly been banished from the company. Her husband almost immediately fell down an elevator shaft and died, leaving behind a curt note to his children that his wife was not to blame. Esther Birchard was not seen or heard from again.

Angelica's son Harold Stickney, a prescient man who anticipated both the decline of canals and the importance of the scientific work being done at the library, wisely sold off the family's interest in the shipping industry and poured the family's fortune into establishing a college of science in the swampy country north of the river. He dreamed of founding a mecca of learning and culture to rival the East Coast universities. They had a two-hundred-year jump on him, but no more zeal for learning and truth. His motto was *Scientia vincere tenebras,* or "Conquering the darkness through science," and at this humble academic outpost on the Maumee River, Stickney and Poole planted a flag for reason. Deep in the woods, Esther Birchard whistled up a wind.

Almost two hundred years later, the Toledo Institute of Astronomy had fully emerged as the epicenter of knowledge and research that its founders had imagined. Its lecture halls and laboratories were well funded by interested corporations, its trust well endowed by generous individuals, its campus a glorious example of frontier classicism, and in 1992 its reach even extended into space, as the first *Toledo Space Telescope* had been launched into orbit via space shuttle. The city of Toledo was proud

31

of its astronomers, proud of its status, standing shoulder to shoulder with Brussels or Shanghai or Sydney in the quest to unlock the secrets of the universe and plumb the depths of the history of stars.

George Dermont, third-year postdoctoral research fellow and favorite instructor of most female undergraduates at the Toledo Institute of Astronomy, stopped in a stairwell of Stickney Center, looking for a vending machine that would take his dollar. George had a headache. A bad one. It felt as though the fibers of his brain were full of ice, and every thump of his heart was a hammer, shattering them over and over. It felt bad.

From the vending machine, he could get some headache pills. He could get some caffeine gels. At the Toledo Institute of Astronomy, the vending machines were stocked with sundries geared specifically to the young scientist. One could find lens cleaner, superglue, clamps, Altoids, and rubbing alcohol. One could certainly find migraine medication: vasoconstrictors, sumatriptan, even opium nasal spray. But George's dollar was so wrinkled and old that it seemed he might try all the vending machines on campus and have no luck. The dollar kept coming back out.

George left the stairwell and turned down the corridor toward the lecture hall. He had five minutes to get to class and look over his notes from last semester, to try to remember what he was going to say to the new students. He pushed through the double doors and the class hushed their chatter. He pulled his notes out of his briefcase and pretended to look at them while he casually closed his eyes. It was the beginning of September. There was no need to panic.

He opened his eyes, turned his head to the left and right, and smiled down on the class. This is what they had come for. To learn the history of astronomy. And he would teach it to them, by the book this time: Ptolemy, Copernicus, Galileo, and the rest.

At times he tried to show his students extra stuff about the universe and give them a peek at what the Toledo Institute of Astronomy really had to offer. Then they would squint, shuffle their feet, cock their heads to the side. As if that lecture was not something they wanted to hear. As if it would slide off their brains at an angle, leaving a scuff mark. He knew that if he went off book too much, it would get harder and harder to get back to the textbook's comforting pages. He would end up standing in a corner, facing the wall, ranting and raving at nothing. George Dermont was the bright young star of the cosmology department, the "it boy" for concerns of the whole universe and beyond. But if he ever really told them what was in his mind? If he ever fully expressed the depth of his beliefs? Would they keep on smiling, winking, waving? Or would they say to him, "Now what the fuck is that all about?" and denounce him as a fraud?

George began his lecture, and the students learned. They nodded their heads. Twenty minutes in, George eyed a girl in the third row in a tank top and khaki shorts, looking like a young Lara Croft from Tomb Raider, minus the pistols and with double the braids. There was one ropey braid on each side of her head, each draping down to decorate one bulbous breast. George almost thought he had seen her before. There was something about the braids that looked familiar. The way her eyes met his. The way she held his gaze. And just like that, George found he had departed from his lecture script. He had limbered up. He had remembered exactly what he had to say, and from an introduction to the first six constellations, George took a sharp turn.

"Remember the Assyrians?" he said. "They were the ones that came down like a wolf on the fold. They had gods. So did the Babylonians. The Greeks also had gods: commonly seen wearing white and having really smooth brows. Romans had gods. Hell, yes, everyone had them."

The students nodded and chuckled. They remembered. This was something in the history of astronomy that they could comprehend: humans having gods. "Nowadays we assume there are pretty much three gods. Ours and the ones in other people's religions."

George smiled through the pounding in his skull. Lara Croft the freshman was tickling the tops of her breasts with one braid. The other hand was resting on her laptop, but she wasn't typing. George looked at her, but found himself unmoved. Years ago, he might have let a girl like this come chasing after him with her braids knocking into her tits, might have thrown her down on a cascade of throw pillows, might have thought, "We're in Toledo; what could go wrong?"

"Three gods. The world population is pretty much agreed on this fact, with the exception of Hindus, who remain belligerently polytheistic and Buddhists, who don't even really have gods."

George waited. The students still watched him, waiting for him to get back to chapter 1, "The Ancients," and the book. Lara Croft nodded too slowly, like she was saying yes to a different question. Then, strangely, she began to glow. Her face blurred for a moment as George's head contracted into stabbing pain, and then it reformed with redder lips and darker eyes. George blinked and squinted. Her hair grew down until her braids were coiled around her feet, and her limbs stretched and curved into pinup proportions. Now George saw she was wearing not a tank top and shorts but a bustier and a type of undergarment that George had once referred to as "spanking panties."

"No one worships, for example, Zeus anymore," he went on bravely, closing his eyes against the sight of her. "Or Ra. So where did all those other gods go?"

One of the young men in the class raised his hand.

"Yes," said George. "Your name?"

"It's David," said the boy. "What page are we on?"

"Where did they go?" George pressed on. "Are they sitting somewhere in a retirement home for aging deities? Sipping tea and asking for their sons, who they know are coming to visit them today? Asking every day until the nurses must dress someone up as a son and make the fake son visit all the rooms? And the gods don't even notice the difference? Because they are in their dotage?"

The braided vixen before him was rising into the air now, shaking her head as if to say, no, no, no!

George got louder, "Does the fact that they did not survive mean that they were not real? Greta, do you think the gods were never real?"

"Well —" began a girl in the front row. She shook her head. Seemed about to say her name was not Greta.

"It's too horrible to imagine." He interrupted her. "Gods don't die — they don't just disappear. They can't do that."

Now the gorgeous, glowing creature in the air of the lecture hall was nodding, nodding, her sweet curves dancing a slow dance for him. This was the thing he could not tell anyone, in the lecture hall, in the office, in his weekly report to the chair of the department at their meeting in his office: "Hi, Dr. Sanji. My work on the latest astrometric project proceeds apace, and, oh, also I see gods floating around sometimes. I yield the floor to Dr. Jones."

Religion is private. It's a private matter between you and the dozen or so deities who visit you at the most inopportune moments.

George grasped the podium with both hands and squinched his eyes very tight. Then he looked around again at the class. They were sitting up straight, their eyes lit up, on full alert. Something was happening — they had figured out. A real astronomer was now speaking to them, here at the Toledo Institute of Astronomy, where they had come to be educated by real astronomers. They leaned forward, eager to hear what he would say next. George looked all around the room, everywhere else except her curves and colors. "If they fall into disrepair, do we have to retroactively call ourselves unbelievers? Are we stupid? Are we duped? If it happened to Ra, it could happen to anyone! Ra was an ass kicker. Ra was the sun god! How could this happen to Ra?"

No one raised a hand. The girl who looked like Lara Croft had now fully changed into the brilliant, irresistible form of a goddess with whom he was quite familiar. She had appeared to him before, but never at work. Now she climbed astride the long fluorescent light fixture near the ceiling, swinging from side to side, using her long braids like fishing lines to dangle in front of unsuspecting students. She laughed silently, but George could hear her, could remember her voice, telling him exactly what to do. The goddess of sex. American pantheon. Contemporary era. His head creaked in pain and he smelled cinnamon, like a very strong exotic tea.

"Maybe —" George paused. He began to move around on the stage, back and forth, trying not to gaze into the space above their heads. The god of sex swung her legs gleefully, biting her lower lip and waving at him. *Hi, George,* she seemed to be communicating. *I'm up here.*

"Maybe Ra was sucked into a wormhole," George said. "Or maybe he just went back willingly into the wormhole from whence he originally came. Something has to happen at the other end of a wormhole, otherwise where the hell is your conservation of matter and energy? Nowhere, that's where!"

Students were nodding. The girls were smiling. Someone's book fell onto the floor and it wasn't retrieved. A boy in the back row chewed a pencil between his teeth. "Could you believe that a wormhole might end in an ancient ziggurat?" George continued. "A cathedral in France? A human uterus? Maybe I'm asking for a looser interpretation of matter conservation than the one you're willing to give."

George was pacing faster now, and the sex goddess was swinging faster, his long limbs eating up the stage at the front of the hall, her body flowing over the light fixture and dripping onto the floor below. The students peered at him wide-eyed. Some of them had their mouths open. He would push the idea into the mouth, close the chin, stroke the throat. Even if the idea was blatant lunacy, they would try to swallow. He had that going for him: a certain charisma, a magnetic charm. But if he said, "Observe, above your heads: a modern deity. Observe." Would they look up? Would they nod and smile, and write down points? He brushed his hair out of his face and turned a winning smile on them. He spread his hands out, long arms wide, a crisp white shirt illuminated in the stage lights over his khakis and loafers.

"George!" called the goddess from the ceiling. He ignored her. He tried to ignore the idea of her. "Tell them!"

"Maybe I'm asking you to believe in the conservation of gods and godliness. Is that too altogether impossible to believe?"

The class waited.

"Think about it. Nothing comes from nothing!" George implored.

The class tilted their heads to the right.

"There has to be a doorway from which they all crawled out, and then into which they all crawl back. There is a supermassive black hole at the center of our galaxy, kids. What's it doing over there, just killing time chewing up asteroids? It's flaring. X-ray flashes: do you know what makes them? NASA doesn't. I don't."

The rows of eyes were all locked on him, each little light devouring his words, none of them drooping down to look at laptops or checking out the other students in the next row. Was it his smile, his apple cheeks, the curve of dark hair on his noble brow? Was it the god above, directing the traffic between their ears? George was the tallest astronomer in Toledo. He was broad-boned and firm as a rock. He returned to the center of the stage. The words came out of his mouth without his intervention. He felt the odd but familiar sensation that he was talking for the goddess, that she was now putting words in his throat for sport, and then pulling them out on a string.

The door at the back of the lecture hall banged open and George could see, standing there, one of the older professors, his boss. Why was he here? To observe the class? To fire George? To find out if George was just a mouthpiece for a god?

"Who sang before the angels sang? In what shape did the stars align themselves, before they took the shape of Greek prophets, Roman warriors, and such? Where did the first flint-reaping knife drop from a weathered hand, so the hand could take a copper idol? Who built the temple of Eridu?"

What the hell is Eridu? thought George. He felt the panic coming on. He felt his brain was not his own. He would lose his job. He would lose his mind. This lecture had gone completely off the rails. The sexy goddess on the light fixture shrugged at him and made a kissy face. George took himself back behind the podium, put his fingertips together lightly and inclined his head, as if to say, Namaste. Good-bye. He gave a weak smile to the professor at the door. But the class breathed in, breathed out, waiting for him to finish. They wanted him to say one more thing. But what would it be? What could it be?

He opened his mouth and out came, "What is history but a list of kings?" He decided that was the end of the lecture. It wasn't safe to say any more. He gave a final

42

emphatic nod.

Silence hung in the room. The students picked up their books and left, whispering to each other, glancing back at George in amazement. The History of Astronomy class at the Toledo Institute of Astronomy was required for all incoming students. He was its most popular teacher, and this fall was his sixth time teaching it. Usually on the first day, there were no gods in attendance. Usually he stayed in control of his language. And his head didn't hurt as much.

"You're wasting your talents there," his mother had said. "Take a hundred dollars. Get a haircut."

His mother didn't like him spending his time teaching freshmen. She didn't like his car. She didn't like the girls he typically pursued. His mother actually wanted him to leave Toledo entirely.

"You're not happy here, George, and you never have been."

"But I will be," he would say.

"But you aren't," she'd respond. "I just need to point that out."

His mother was a lawyer. Pointing things out was her specialty. But George knew she was wrong. He would be happy.

The professor at the back of the room strode quickly up to the podium, as the students filed out.

"Dr. Bryant," said George, by way of greeting. What more could he say?

Dr. Bryant had been much published, quoted, and admired. Dr. Bryant had never been asked to teach the undergraduate History of Astronomy class, or lecture from a textbook, or speak to freshmen. He never would have done it, either. But now the older astronomer was panting, sweating, and rushing down the aisle.

"George, she did it." Dr. Bryant gasped.

"Really, well, here's to another happy twenty-five years then, sir. That's —"

"No, no, no," he stammered on. "I'm talking about that strange young woman in Pittsburgh. Irene Sparks."

"Oh, yes," said George. "As I recall, she was determined there are black holes in tea." George began to pack up his bag.

"That's right. That's her," said Dr. Bryant. "Not tea, though. She was here for an interview, years ago. She had schematics for a micro-collider."

"Well? Has she collided something?"

"George, she has. She's got — you know — what you might call black holes. In a collider she fabricated in Pittsburgh, can you imagine? The whole experiment is the size of a small truck! Hawking radiation, detectable with a human retina. Apparently . . . it actually glowed."

"That's not possible," said George. He picked up his briefcase and made for the door, his office, his pain medication. But Dr. Bryant followed him.

"She's got numbers. The radiation loss has been charted. And I've seen an image. With my own eyes."

George frowned. He stopped short of the door. "So what does this mean for . . . downstairs?" He dropped his voice to a whisper and pointed toward the floor. Dr. Bryant came close.

"I think we're going to be able to get her here, George. She could be the crown jewel of the whole project!"

"I see," said George. "So, is she going to be teaching?"

"Who cares about that?" Dr. Bryant said. "Teaching? What does that even mean? We were the first call she made, George. That's something, isn't it?"

"Interesting," said George.

"Oh, wait until you see it," Dr. Bryant said. "I want to get her here before . . . Discover . . . Time . . . you know what a frenzy this will cause. When she talks to the media."

George put his hand on Dr. Bryant's

shoulder. The old man seemed about to keel over.

"Are you alright?" he said. "You seem . . . crazy."

"I'm going down to admin," he said. "I'm going to put in a proposal right now, this minute. I'm going to have her here by the end of tomorrow," said Dr. Bryant. "It's imperative. How could we have been such fools to let her slip away?" He was looking at George as if he could hardly remember George's name.

"OK, doc," he called after him. "If you say so. Just don't give her my office, alright?"

"Oh, George," Dr. Bryant turned and called back. "I can't believe I forgot — that's what I really needed to see you about. We are giving her your lab. And you'll need to be out of there by tomorrow. Thanks for understanding."

As he watched Dr. Bryant bustle out into the hallway and away, the pain in his head almost forced George's right eyelid to close, and George could suddenly think of nothing else but to get to his office, turn out the light, and die. But then he had a sudden thought. A different thought, and his hand shot out to push the door open so he could call down the hall.

"Dr. Bryant?" George bellowed. "What color hair does she have?"

"Hair?" said the older man. "Hair? It's brown, I think. Brown hair. How can it possibly matter?"

And then he was gone, leaving George to wonder if it could.

3

Irene walked home. She felt light, strange, evacuated, like she was already having her breakthrough article translated into Czechoslovakian. When she had sent her data to Toledo, they'd asked her to come immediately. Looking at her numbers, they were already sure, like a coroner standing over a broken neck, sure it was broken.

What would her mother have said about this, had she not fallen down the stairs and died this afternoon? What would her mother have said if Irene had turned up on her doorstep. *Oh, Irene,* she might have said. *You're back in Toledo. It's everything I ever wanted.* Would she even have been able to go to Toledo, if her mother had never fallen in the first place? If she had never wandered out into the upstairs hall, taken a misstep, taken a tumble.

She opened the front door to her apartment and a rush of cool air escaped. Irene's apartment was spare. There were no house-plants; there were no Parisian advertise-ments on the wall. Irene was not a decora-tor. She was not a homemaker, nor was she a person who was comfortable in rooms that were collected into an idea called: home.

Irene tossed her backpack on the kitchen counter, picked up a plastic cup, and drew a pint of water from the fridge door. She drank, and let guilt wash into her. She should have stayed with her mother so that her mother was not alone. No one should die alone, not even drunks. She set the empty cup down on the counter. "Come back," her mother had said, on a postcard that Irene had thrown into the trash. Be-cause she knew that if she did come back, it would be, "Welcome backits beautiful beau-tiful beautifulbyerful," and when the words all ran together in her mother's mouth, Irene would have to fall off a bridge. Some-times you just have to keep away from the things that are trying to kill you, even if they're the same thing that gave birth to you. Sometimes those two things are the same, and their name is mother.

She left the kitchen and went back through the apartment into the back room, where the lights were dim and her boyfriend, Be-lion, was hunched over his keyboard. There were three monitors spread out before him, and his giant hands tapped aggressively. Belion was huge, both in literal frame and in personal aspect, the kind of person who sends out ripples into the room, seeming to bump into the walls even when they're in the center. He had long, curly black hair that lay over his bulky shoulders like an animal. His hand shot out and moved the mouse around, clicked three times.

"What the hell, Irene," Belion growled.

"What the hell, babe," she returned. She walked over to him and leaned against the vastness of his back. It hulked up over the back of his rolling office chair.

"What the hell, for real, though," he said. "This person is driving me batshit."

"Where?" said Irene, looking around.

"In the game," said Belion.

Belion was a game designer and coder for an online fantasy role-playing game. The name which his mother had given to him when he was born was Arturo, but he had it legally changed to Belion. His online name was Belion, Archmage of the Underdark, but he had not changed his legal name all the way to that.

Irene lifted up one of his arms and crawled under it and into his lap. She sat on one thigh, her arm around his collar, hand threaded through under the fall of his hair. She rested her head against his cheek. She pressed her forehead into the firm shape of his jaw.

"Dammit," he muttered. "There she goes again. Somebody's renaming all the bears around my L-shaped cottage. They're all 'Good-bye Silvergirl' or 'Farewell Silvergirl' or 'So long Silvergirl.' "

"Rude."

"Yeah, rude."

"Bears should just be called 'a bear.' "

"Yeah, you know what, I'm lifting the rename command from players, unless the animal is a pet."

"At least until this Silvergirl person kills herself and her account goes dead. Sounds like it might be any minute."

This made Belion turn his big head around and frown at Irene. She shrugged, "It does!"

"Can't have the fucking bears around my L-shaped cottage all wandering around like a pack of greeting cards or something."

"What does she look like? This Silvergirl?"

"I don't know. Never seen her."

Irene began to cry again. Still in the circle of his arms, she put her hands in her lap and tears fell down her face.

"Hey, what's wrong, babe?" Belion's

prodigious brow was now furrowed with concern. "Are you OK? Are you sick?"

"My mother fell down the stairs," she said. "And died."

"What? She fell down the stairs? Where?"

"In her house. Belion, I have to move to Toledo now."

"Why Toledo, though?" His face still pointed at the computer screen, and now he was looking at code.

"That's where she lived, asshole, do you have any idea what I'm talking about right now? She lived in Toledo, and I was born in Toledo."

"Yes. Yes, I knew that. Wow, I'm really sorry."

He turned his eyes to her, and she saw his unibrow, his large brown eyes underneath it, large nose, large chin, large everything, like he could swallow the whole world. She told him about the whole day: the black hole in the collider, the neighbor's discovery, the call to the Toledo Institute of Astronomy, the impending funeral, the house.

"I'll kill that bastard neighbor for you," said Belion, his voice rumbling deep inside him. "If you need. It's always the neighbor. He probably killed her."

"The neighbor is female."

"Girls can be bastards, too. It's science."

"You're not listening," said Irene. "I have a chance to study and work and teach at the Toledo Institute of Astronomy. This is something that most physicists only dream of."

"I don't want you to go. You already work at a cool university, and it has the added benefit of being right here."

"It's not the same," said Irene.

"It has a Cathedral of Learning, for Christ's sake. How can Toledo compete with that?"

"For one thing, the Cathedral of Learning is at U Pitt, not Carnegie Mellon. But let's leave the fact that you don't even know what university pays me. It's not just the job. There's my mother's house to deal with, which is mine now."

"Nuke it from space," said Belion, the side of his face lit from the glow on his monitor.

"Yeah, no," said Irene. "That's not something people actually do."

"That sucks. Wasn't, she, like, married?"

"BELION! Are you serious right now?"

"I can't remember! I'm sorry! Hey, you never talk about her. I didn't even know she existed!"

Irene got up from his lap, climbing out from under his arm and replacing his hand on the keyboard.

53

"No, she's not married. Wasn't married."

"Oh. Sorry about the bastard comment earlier. I didn't know you were —"

"A bastard?"

"Yeah, to put it, like, all Tudory."

"Well, whatever. I need to go sleep. I'm exhausted. I think I've been at work for two days, and my mother —" Irene gritted her teeth together, afraid to start crying again.

"You want company?" he asked. He turned to her and held out a hand, beseeching, but Irene shook her head and walked away.

She took off her tank top and draped it over the bedpost, left her jeans on the mat next to her side of the bed. Pulling back the comforter and sheet, she slid into the coolness beneath them and lay flat. She pulled her hair out of the ponytail and flipped the rubber band off her finger toward the dresser.

She closed her eyes and exhaled, then her eyes popped open. She jumped out of bed and locked the door before lying down again. This was private. Like praying. If she had prayed, she would not have let anyone see her do that either. If you had asked her, "Irene, do you meditate or anything?" she would have said, "No." She probably would have added, "And all that is crap."

Irene was an empiricist. She believed in science, and math, and numbers. She did not believe in love, or any god. She did not believe, "Someday you will be happy." She was opposed to novels, most poetry, and dance of any kind. However, she was also a lucid dreamer. She could control her dreams. It was because her mother had been such a dedicated hippie, astrologer, mind reader, tea drinker, nutcase, and had pressed the lucid dreaming on Irene before life had taught her suspicion.

It started with dispelling nightmares, the same way any mother teaches any child to take control of a dream and turn it away from horrors. But Bernice hadn't left it there. She'd shown Irene how to make her body fall asleep and keep her mind awake, how to travel, unencumbered, in a lonely world behind the waking one. She hadn't gone there in years, had sworn she was never going again. But now she had to go, to know for sure if her mother was really, really gone.

Irene blinked three times and closed her eyes. She said the words, "I'm dreaming and I'm aware," three times under her breath, and then she began to regulate and count her breathing. In her mind's eye she was focusing on a little curio shelf in her mother's house. This was her old way in, like a portal. Just one shelf, dark wood, stuck to the wall in her mother's house in Toledo, and lined with bells. She went down the row of bells, ringing each one in her mind. The small dark bell from a sheep. The little gold bell that was a souvenir from Galveston. The silver bell from a wedding reception. The crappy, bulbous one that child Irene had made in a pottery class. The porcelain one in the shape of a cat entangled in yarn. A blue bell commemorating America's bicentennial.

She knew that before she reached the bell on the end, which was bejeweled and had no ringer, her body would be asleep, but her mind would be awake. She would be in the place she and her mother called the Hinterland, and dreaming. And her mother, her mother might be there, too. She had to go and see.

When I pick up the final bell and ring it, I hear a ringing sound. The sound tells me I am dreaming and aware. I walk away from the shelf of bells, and out of my mother's house.

Astrology is the mad mother of astronomy. My mother is a predictive astrologer, and also a psychic. She does it all: tea leaves, wrinkles in your hand, whatever seems to make you trust her. I have watched her clients sit there on the sofa, stretch out their necks, and tilt their heads, all earnestly listening like so many fools. All her magic comes down to advice a good professional organizer could give them. *It's always easier to see someone else's problems,* she would say. *I can clean your house better than I can clean my own.* Then she would take a sip of gin. A swallow of gin. A glass tumbler of gin, full to the brim.

Mother and I have a complicated relationship. Outside the Hinterland, she is a drunk and I am ashamed and afraid. Inside the Hinterland, she is always sober. So here I come, to find her. I miss her. I can't help myself. Even now, when her body is dead, I wonder if her mind is here still. Maybe in death she has entered a final dream. Maybe here I will retrieve her from the alcohol. The Hinterland is bleak and spare. I make it this way. I have never allowed it to become elaborately decorated because that's foolish and a waste of time. So there are very few things, besides her house, the gray dust of the earth and the gray rim of the sky. There is only one other structure. I call it Dark House. From the outside, it's a Victorian mansion of three stories.

When I first dreamed into Dark House I was very young, dreaming of exploring an old house, opening room after room. At the center of it, between all the rooms, with a rim of broken beams and torn wires around it, I came upon a whistling chasm in the floor. I almost fell in, and it scared me, sent me skittering backward, a cold wind in my face. I could not even look into it. That was the first time.

After that I ended up in Dark House again and again in my dreams, always coming in from a different direction but headed for the same sinking center, back to the same bad place. Putting it inside the Hinterland, giving it walls and some exterior structure, let me have some control over that awful hole. I have never been sucked into the center of Dark House. Monsters, grief, immolation are there. Always right there at the edge. Sometimes I dream I am clever and free, but I wind up in the Dark House anyway, teetering on the edge of the blackness. A good dream is when I can get out without falling into the black. So they are all good dreams, so far.

When I was six, my mother burned our house down. Not a dream house; a real house. Down to the ground. I don't remember anything before that. She wants to rebuild the house in the Hinterland, keep it forever, but I won't let her.

"You make something then," mother once told me.

"I did," I said. "I made this." This is a horror. But she doesn't mention it.

I hurry now through all of the safe rooms until I am out of breath and I am still absolutely alone. I am out of places to look. "Mother!" I scream. She has to be here. I point my face into the center of the house and call again, "Mother!"

A bit of movement pulls at the corner of my eye. Is it she? I quickly turn to see a tall form step away and then recede behind a broken wall. That is not my mother. That is someone else. My mother is a small person with long hair. This stranger is a tall person and the hair is short. Someone else inside the Hinterland. Looking for me, for my mother, for the center of Dark House? My nightmare: someone's come to push me in.

4

George had seen a picture of himself when he was two. He was a fat baby with a bubble pipe clutched in one hand. The camera captured him in the act of running, with a free hand up to catch the bubbles. What interested George in this picture was not himself. It was his mother and father in the background of the shot, which must have been taken by a friend or a neighbor, because it showed the whole family. His mother was young, with her blond hair down and long. His father looked happy, and his face was shaved. His mother was sitting on his father's knee and grabbing his neck with her elbow, pulling him into her chest, and his father had a goofy look on his face. His mother's teeth were incredibly wonky. They were all showing.

George's mother was a tall person with smooth long limbs, like a model's. In her youth, she'd had long blond hair, and her teeth had been horsey and huge. When she got some money, she had them fixed, and now they were normal, and she was a perfect-looking fifty-year-old woman. Wise, sure, with ashy short hair and dove-gray scarves to tie around her throat. For George, looking at his mother with these awful teeth was touching. Especially the fact that she was grinning like an ape, and clearly didn't care.

George drove down I-75 toward Bowling Green, a college town just south of Toledo. He was going to retrieve his mother from the courthouse there. She had punched a client and broken his nose.

On the phone, his mother had said, "He was being an idiot. Had you done the same, I would have punched you, too. Everyone knows he deserved it. They're just being careful because he's a student. They all need punching."

"Mom," George said. "Please don't punch anyone else."

"I'm not making any promises," she said.

"Do you want me to tell Dad?" George wanted to know.

"Don't tell your father anything. In fact, go and lock my house so he can't get in there until I get back."

"Mom, I can be there in twenty minutes."

"Don't rush. I pick up clients when I have to stay in jail."

Then someone had said, "Come on, lady. Let's go." And the phone went dead.

If George had to pin down the moment when his mother changed from the carefree woman with long hair and snaggle teeth to the woman she was now, so firm and sensible, brusque and put together, he would have to say it began when he was about six years old.

When he was very small, he remembered his mother walking with him through the woods, her huge long legs making whishing tracks through the brush and bramble, with him on her shoulders, and she'd sing "I got a brand new pair of roller skates," and George could touch the treetops, he felt like. The mother of his youngest days was a beautiful, sweet, idyllic mother. He remembered a striped poncho she used to wear, and how they would eat peanuts in the car and throw the shells into the backseat, laughing.

She read to him from a book of Irish poetry every night. His favorite was written by Yeats, "The Stolen Child." It was a song about the faeries enticing a small child away from the world he knew. Which seemed a bit sinister, at the end, but also beautiful. The faeries came, young George understood, and transported this lucky golden child to a land of enchantment, where there was magic and singing.

Sometimes he was allowed out of the house by himself, and he would run around out in a small dark wood, near where they lived out west of the city, by Lake Sawyer. George could remember sitting in a clearing in the woods, hypnotically entranced, to the point where he could hear the flapping herons and the drowsy water rats from the poem, and feel his lips upon the ears of sleeping trout, and know that he was sitting on that leafy island, leaving his mother and father behind. If he concentrated, George could remember a time when he had played with a faery, and he wanted to get back to that good feeling. He felt sure that the faery would come for him again out of the woods, and take him by the hand to lead him off. He could see the strange shape of her faery face from his memory. It was beautiful.

George's car was a Volvo wagon. His mother had bought it for him when he graduated from college, hoping he would stay in New England or move to California, or anywhere really, the hell away from Toledo.

"I miss Toledo," George had said. "I want to study at the institute."

"Don't come back," his mother had said. But George had come back anyway. What happened to turn that laughing mother into the mother he had now? George often wondered. What happened, what happened? Now his mother was always certain of everything, and often angry. She referred to his childhood faery dreams as "that crazy crap." She was hard on George's father, hard on George.

The wagon rolled down the long flat stretch between Toledo and Bowling Green. It was late, late summer, and the sky was deeper blue than it had been all year, the rows of corn tall and brittle. The roadside swaths of grass were brown and the wildflowers waved on dry stalks. Northwest Ohio crunched under the foot of an encroaching fall. As an academic, George was disconnected from the planting and harvest cycles on earth, but he knew how to look up and tell what time it was at night. In the late summer he could see Sagittarius, the archer, Babylonian god of war, his bow cocked and arrow aimed straight for the heart of the scorpion twenty-eight degrees northeast.

By the age of nine, George became gangly, not so fat around the wrists and ankles anymore. He knew the faeries would no longer see him as some great prize to be lured away. Frustrated and crying in his room one night, with the lights off, he saw his mother and father both come to the door. She was working her way through the ranks at her firm at this time, trying to make partner, trying to make money. His father was painting, having art shows, traveling. He wanted to tell them, very privately, that he was sorry the faeries hadn't stolen him away yet, and he was becoming afraid that it would never happen.

But when he opened his mouth to say it, he did not. Instead these words came out: "I miss her." And when he said them, he knew that it was what he meant to say in the first place.

"I miss her," he said again, more firmly, and then he began to cry. "I want her back."

His mother came over and climbed into the bed with him, kicking off her shoes and pulling her long legs in nylons under the quilts. She held his arms close to his sides while he cried to her. His father sat at the bedside, silent.

"Who do you miss, baby?" she said. "Who is it that you miss?"

"There was a faery I knew," he sobbed. "I knew her. I miss her."

"You were dreaming," said his mother. "There was no one. No one. It was a dream."

"Oh, Mommy," he cried. "What if I've been badful, badful, and she never comes back?"

"George, are you looking for lost faeries?" said his father. George nodded.

"Stop it, Dean," said his mother. "How could he possibly? Miss her? How?"

His father raised a long arm to point to the window, where the night sky was stretched.

"There are faeries up there, George," he said, "Look, you can see them."

George pulled off the interstate and onto the highway. His mother would be waiting, netbook case under her arm, toe tapping. As he turned on his signal to get in the left lane, he glanced into the backseat and saw another goddess.

She was sitting behind the passenger seat on the leather backseat. Her legs were splayed open and her arms were crossed loosely across her chest. She wore white running shorts, a tank top, a pair of Nikes with ankle socks, and a terry cloth headband. Her taut mouth worked a stick of gum, and George could smell it. Spearmint? Eucalyptus? Ambrosia? When he saw her he immediately slowed, pulled off the road, stopped on the shoulder. The goddess looked out the window, eyes squinting, chin sharp. She uncrossed her arms and drummed her fingers on the armrest.

"Go, go, go," she said.

"Nah, it's kinda bad to drive when you're around," said George. He tapped on the side of his head, as if to explain.

"I'm not a hallucination," said the goddess. "I'm a goddess. Go. Go fast."

"You're the goddess of —" George squinted and peered off into the fields.

"The race, the race!" she said. "America, present tense, you, me. Hurry. Go. They're beating you. They're winning. I'm here to tell you. You need to hurry. You don't have a lot of time."

Her eyes flashed silver and steel, and when they met his, he felt his head go cold inside, felt his brain contract.

"Who's winning and beating me?"

"All those other physicists, George. They're winning! We gave you a vision. Can you not bring it to the world?"

She waved her hand around fiercely, punctuating her questions with hard gestures while the other hand kept drumming, drumming on the armrest, like a cantering horse.

"I'm capable. I'm capable," said George. He rubbed his hand across his eyes. He turned in his seat so that he could look at her better, see her. "I'm just having a problem defining the axis of the gate. Every time I begin to map it, something doesn't fit. I've got computers working on it right now. Eventually —"

"The gate was explained to you already," snapped the goddess. She chewed her gum with her mouth open, the lines around her jaw jerking in and out of relief. Her skin was flawless. The veins popped out across the muscles of her arms and legs, rippled across her when she moved.

"Explained by the goddess of love, though," he pointed out. "So, yes, but she's so vague on the actual numbers, the figures, you know, the physicists like to see data. It's kind of their thing."

George had begun to have visions of gods when he was entering puberty. As soon as his mother had money enough, she moved

68

to the city and bought a condo. They kept the house in the woods for his father, but his mother never went out there much. She had gone from loving it to hating it in a nanosecond, leaving George's head spinning. He felt unmoored. "But I still love *you,* baby," she said. "Come to the city with me." George liked to sit quietly in the clearing, just as in the old days but now occasionally smoking pot, having visitations from what he first thought were the promised "faeries in the stars." They told him they were gods and goddesses, and introduced each other to him, told him about themselves. He liked that.

When the old gods spoke to him it was with mist and fire. But when the new gods came and spoke they appeared in person, wearing clothes, sometimes earbuds, carrying diaper bags or modern weapons, sometimes preoccupied with their phones. They helped him understand the history of space, the things Pythagoras had seen, the movement of the crystal spheres, and how things on earth decay and in heaven they don't. When they showed him, finally, a plane of symmetry on which the universe could fold and duplicate itself, they said, "This is important. This is something that no one else knows."

"OK," George said. He heard their voices layered over each other, and when he looked into the sky he could see the stars, static, unforgiving, speaking to him.

"There is a gate on which the universe can bend, one side to another, an axis on which it is replicated, transformed."

"Transformed," said George.

"Bring this message to the world," said the gods.

"It's there," said the goddess of love, suddenly next to him on the grass, looking like a movie star, in a silk dress. "Believe it. On this side, one thing. On the other side, the same thing. Everything passes through the gate. Tell them. The answer isn't symmetry. It's asymmetry." He knew that it was insane for him to see gods or hear them or be aware of them at all, so he must never ever talk about it. But he didn't want to stop seeing them. They kept him from being so unendurably alone.

"The Gateway of God" became George's research project. It was a sexy concept: There exists somewhere in the universe a plane of symmetry, so that galaxies and nebulae can be mapped back and forth across it in predictable measures. The reason this plane of symmetry had never been noticed, George now posited, was that it was not actually a plane of symmetry but a plane of asymmetry, and the relationship between the stars on one side and the stars on the other could be defined not by a simple equality but by an equation of some complexity. There was a relationship of one side to the other that was not simply one to one. Maybe a constant was involved. Maybe an exponent. He would figure it out, given enough time.

He told everyone about the gate. It exploded his career as a physicist. The only person he ever told about seeing the gods was his father, and then only once. George was a teenager, and Dean was in between trips to New York City, meeting with clients and gallery curators, and he and George were out for a hike in the woods.

"I had a chat with Athena," George said casually, stomping along.

"Ticks out here," said Dean. "Keep an eye."

"I had a chat with Athena, Dad, and I'm pretty sure it was her. Really her."

Dean stopped walking and put his hand up against a tree, wiped his forehead off on his rolled-up sleeve.

"I think I understand you, George," said Dean. "I think I understand what you mean when you say this, but don't go totally fucking nuts on me, son. I love you. Don't want them to put you in an asylum."

"I'm not nuts," George said.

Dean got the look on his face like when he stood considering a painting, brush dripping paint onto the floor, jaw locked, breath coming fast.

"Don't talk about this to anyone else," his father finally said. "It sounds too crazy."

"I'm your son," said George, trying to laugh off the moment. "Right?"

"Don't forget it," said Dean.

So George kept on seeing gods, but through the visitations and the messages, he never told anyone. And he also never forgot about that one first visitor he still thought of as a faery, the one he felt he was always missing, that he had known and then lost.

He had her as a haunting memory, like a remembered dream. He felt a presence, like a shadow on the other side of the plane of symmetry, a shadow not replicated but the same. He knew it was she. If he was a star on one side of the gate, then she was a star on the other side, her position determined by the application of an equation he had not yet written. He knew that once she had been there, that he had known her, touched her, felt her, and now she was not. In his sleep, in his imagination, he would often find himself saying, "I miss her, I miss her, I miss her." There was another side to his equation. There was another hand reaching out to his, from beyond.

George's mother became a successful attorney and had money, and his father became a successful painter and had fame. George had access to every privilege and every advantage. He was handsome, and life was easy. As a teen, he began to have sex with pretty girls who wrapped their limbs around him in a way that was comforting. They would smile and guide him straight into themselves, and that was very inviting. None of them were the one — how could they be?

In George's mind, the faery grew up, as he did. And in the midst of sex, with the rhythm of going in and out quite overcoming any other thoughts in his head, he felt he was always pushing through to her, to the one he was missing. Each dewy sternum under his chest, each firm pair of legs tucked around his waist, each hot envelope he pushed himself into, a little better, a little better. Sometimes he bit at them with his teeth, sometimes he pushed himself in so slow and so deep that the girls would cry, *Don't stop, don't ever ever stop.* But he was always trying to make these bodies fall away, trying to pin that one transcendent spot.

And when it eluded him, he began to pursue another girl, a different girl. All he had to say was "Mom, I miss her," and any obstacle that could be toppled with money immediately vanished. His mother gave him everything she could give him. He became the most eligible bachelor in Toledo. Yet he was always scraping away, chafing against the lack, against the wanting, and never quite sinking in.

Was he his father's son? Did he have his mother's blood? Or did he not belong to another partnership, a past-life twin, a different scheme of things, beyond the predictable sequence of genealogy. Was he crazy? Were the gods real? Should he ever, ever tell? By the time he got back to Toledo to teach and work at the Institute of Astronomy, he was still empty. Still lost. Maybe the other side of his partnership was still out there. Perhaps it was purely hypothetical, like a plane of symmetry in the universe, or the density of a black hole, or love.

George addressed the goddess of the race, sitting in his Volvo on the side of the highway. He chose his words carefully. She seemed on edge.

"I don't want to disappoint you, but I'm working as fast as I can."

"That is something that everyone says," she quipped. "It's never been more false."

"Can you tell me where the Gateway is then?"

"I can't," she said. "I don't know."

She almost smiled.

George's head began to pound.

"I have to go pick up my mother," he said to the goddess of the race. "She's waiting at the jail."

"I'm not leaving," said the goddess. "I don't have to and I'm not. And when you turn around, and you see me, you'll know that I'm saying go. You haven't got a lot of time."

When he pulled up outside the jail, his mother was chatting with one of the cops. As she pulled away from the conversation, she left her card in his palm, curled his fingers shut around it, and patted him on the shoulder. *Good to meet you,* she would be saying. She tapped across the pavement to George's car, slid the door open, and dropped into the front seat.

"Alright?" he asked. He looked nervously over his shoulder and the goddess of the race mimicked him silently, "Alright?"

5

Belion was in the apartment. Irene had gone. He was deciding whether he would join her in Toledo. He felt that he probably would. On the other hand, maybe he wouldn't. While he looked forward to the strenuous physical work of moving, he did not look forward to change. He sat in his chair at his terminal and played his game and worked. In the absence of Irene, not a lot had changed. In some ways, it was like she had never been there at all.

Over the twenty-four hours after Irene left for Toledo, it became hard for Belion to deny the fact that he was stalking Silvergirl, the player who had renamed the bears on his game. He didn't want to be stalking her. That was stupid. At first he told himself that he was acting responsibly as a game administrator, keeping watch over a player who was possibly unstable or suicidal. But the reality was that he was not the kind of admin who had any reason to be in touch with players at all.

He was a world creator, not an interactive deity. However, there was something about Silvergirl that had provoked his slumbering sensibilities. She was plaintive; she was sorrowful, and somehow seductive. At first he felt angry, because he had never known anyone to leave such strange and illogical marks on his world. Renaming bears. Leaving unexplained piles of fish arranged like standing stones. Putting mulberries into the pockets of every goblin in the forest. He began looking for her signatures, blaming her whenever anything was out of order, whether she had been there or not. There was a bag abandoned in a mine shaft. It contained only silver coins. Was it hers?

With each new discovery, he became more interested. He, Belion, Archmage of the Underdark, found himself tracking the movements of a midlevel player, her stats and position filling him with excitement. Every time he learned something new, he would shut his screen down, turn away from the monitors, and lift some weights on his bench. At first he only did what he could do behind the scenes. He only looked at data he could read in his coding language, interpret according to the meanings he knew.

Then, late at night, he found he had been drinking a lot of pink lemonade. While Irene was living there, she drank it all the time. He had not drunk any pink lemonade in front of her. In fact, when she offered it to him, he had said, "Irene, that's kind of a woman drink." But he was wanting some, even as the words of refusal came out his mouth. Once she was gone, there was no reason not to drink it, and he found it went down so easily, he could drink the entire gallon she had left in the fridge without stopping to breathe. So late that night, in a cloud of pink sugar, he remembered Irene having asked about Silvergirl's looks. "What does she look like?" Irene had said.

If Irene suggested it, he should do it. Irene might want to know, next time they talked. So he searched for her name in a different interface, and her avatar came up on his screen. Silvergirl was long and lean like almost every other pretend woman in this virtual world. But she was covered head to toe in a metallic slip, pointy on her head and draping over her toes. With a flick of his mouse, he could remove this metallic slip and look at her character's naked body, but that would have been pointless. They all look basically the same. Did she choose darker nipples or lighter? Did she place her belly button nearer to her rib cage or her hips? If he wanted to spend all day looking at players' avatars without their clothes, he could, but that was stupid. He wouldn't do that. For one thing, he could be fired.

Belion had not really said to himself, "My girlfriend and I broke up." He had not addressed the fact that Irene had gone to live in another state. For one thing, Irene hadn't really wanted to talk about it. Several times she said, "You can do what you want." If that meant coming to Toledo, she did not specify that this would be wrong or unwelcome.

Belion took a long, refreshing pull of pink lemonade straight from the jug. He took off Silvergirl's metallic slip. Peach nipples, small. Round breasts, flat hips. Surprise, there was no belly button at all. As Silvergirl stood there on a dais in the creation screen in front of him, he turned her left and right and looked over her in every position. With her hood off, he could see she had long dark hair, standard for a druid. No tattoos or piercings. He told himself not to be such a dirndl. Silvergirl could be the avatar of a three-hundred-pound male, or a thirteen-year-old girl, or a golden retriever.

He did not have access to the real-life details in her character file.

Belion spent long, thoughtful minutes looking at Silvergirl naked on his screen. He thought of the bag of silver coins, the bear named Good-bye Silvergirl, and the other enigmatic offerings. He wondered if he should interact with her, in the game. He could animate one of the computer-controlled characters sitting around on benches, and she would know it was something special. He could lead her down to the duck pond, by the willows, and say, "Why are you saying good-bye?" What would she say? Would she say, "I can explain, but first let me fellate you until your eyes pop out." Belion had never cheated in real life on a real-life girlfriend. But he had cheated on all his girlfriends online. He could never explain what he was doing or why. He only wanted to know that his virtual cock was getting reliable attention. If there was another reason to have a virtual cock, Belion didn't know what it was.

Belion was not introspective. His behaviors came from an immediate place of desire and fulfillment, about an eighth of an inch under his skin. In life, he was faithful. In pretend, he was a whore. But what god isn't? He could possess the body of the stalwart warrior-guard outside the city gates, express an arrogant but urgent love for a passing maiden, and before he knew it he was sneaking with her into the robing room of the monastery chapel across the street, and she was ripping off her jerkin and yanking down her leggings, touching her pixelated hands to her pixelated crotch, drawing him between her legs, pulling him down by the neck. Women love special attention from gods. They never know who they're fucking, they don't really care, and it has been this way since the beginning of time. Ask Leda. Ask any of them. Let a god come down in the shape of a mortal, and see if you can keep your legs together.

Two days after Irene went to Toledo, Silvergirl went into a cave and stopped moving. Belion became concerned. Maybe real-life Silvergirl had shoved her head into an oven and turned on the gas. That would be a giant bummer. He wanted more time to lay in wait for her, stalk her, seduce her, push himself into a fold in her silver slip. Belion broke down and hacked open her account information. When he saw that the log-in from her last session was from Toledo, he slid backward from the keyboard, stunned. An idea entered his mind and lodged there.

Silvergirl was Irene. He scanned her logs and saw that she rarely spoke, had joined no guild, and had no allies. He was convinced. Was she spying on him? But why? Was she trying to tell him something?

It was morning in Pittsburgh. He had been up all night. He was eating some fresh salsa from a plastic container, chewing down whole-grain corn chips, shoveling the tomato squares and onion bits into his mouth. He was nervous and upset. Without Irene present to soothe him, he felt his brow must form a permanent furrow. It's not that he missed their conversations, because they didn't have them, or their love, because she had never loved him. It's not that he missed the sight of Irene's naked body, because, honestly, he had never been allowed to see it. Light or dark nipples, belly button, he had no idea. Was she showing herself to him online, through this avatar? Was he to unlock this puzzle she had set for him? How?

There were times when Belion, frustrated and cantankerous, would rise from his office chair and go to Irene, where she was sitting at the kitchen table, hunched over her laptop. He would stand next to her, and put his big hand on her head. He might say, "Hey." She would turn and look at the top of his pants. She would unbutton the button. Unzipping him, she would reach inside with her soft hand, ease him out of his underwear, and bring his balls along, too. The balls would hang out over the zipper, at first uncomfortably and then not. She would take him in her mouth and swallow everything in turns, and put her hand around to the back of his legs, to bring him in tight to her face. It was decisive.

From the moment she unzipped his pants until he was shaking, his broad hip locked in her arm, life was a blur. He could put his hands around a beam in the ceiling of the kitchen and rock against her biting mouth. Then he would stagger off. Looking back, if he did look back, he could see her spit into a paper towel. Wipe her mouth off on it carefully. Stretch her lips into a smile. Turn her face back to the glow of the laptop. Then the typing, tapping would begin again. Was it a lonely operation if it made Belion feel so damn much better? What is loneliness? How long would it take him to drive to Toledo?

He decided to go to the cave. Maybe Irene would allow him, in a virtual cave, to do what Irene, in an actual bedroom, had never allowed: to see her naked, touch her with his hands, or be near her with his face. He had always been longing to do it, and he had earnestly tried. She had rebuffed him. There was no ire in it. But still, it was a rebuff. And if there's anything Belion knew about women, it was that when rebuffed, one had to withdraw, even if you were withdrawing your face from a crotch belonging to someone who should by all rights allow you to put your face right in it. What does the word boyfriend mean anyway, he thought.

Belion, Archmage of the Underdark, was a huge man, part ogre and part water buffalo, clad in black leather with a long sweep of a cape clasped around his neck. He wore a leather helmet shaped to his buffalo head with horns that draped down over his shoulders. He wore heavy boots, held an iron cudgel, and had no upper limit on his carrying capacity. If he had wanted, he could have picked up the whole world. If he had wanted, he could fly. Everything and anything was open to him in this world, all commands, all powers, everything. There was nothing he could not test or try.

Belion teleported himself to the grassy area outside the cave, and he marched straight in, ignoring whoever was standing around. His animated legs carried him along. He touched a button on the keyboard and changed from an aerial view to a first-person view, so that he looked at his screen as if through the eyes of his avatar. Had Zeus enjoyed this capability? Had Apollo been able to summon any item, any character, any object to his hand? Probably.

The cave was deep but lit with wall torches. Belion knew exactly where Silvergirl was hiding in this cave and exactly how to get there. He marched through the dim cave, his boots making sounds he could hear through his monitor. When he was around the corner from her, he hesitated, and his avatar sat down on a crate to think. Irene was not likely to have sex with him in a cave, with a buffalo head. She wouldn't even have sex with him in a bed, with his regular head. "I'm a virgin from the neck down," she would say. "Let's keep that dream alive." His avatar stood up. The cave lights flickered. He decided that he would try. Pittsburgh is a long way from Toledo. He got up and marched around the corner to confront her directly. His pulse elevated. His brow a Gordian knot.

She sat on an outcropping of rock above his head, her silver slip folded against the dark gray of the cave wall. She was halfway up to the ceiling. His avatar had to look up to see her. She sat with her hands in her lap, in repose. Long bare feet hung down. Irene's real feet don't look like this, thought Belion. Irene wears a five and a half. For a few minutes, he waited for her to say something, but she didn't.

"Silvergirl," said Belion. He used a special communication channel that sent a message to a player on their phone or computer even if they were away from the game screen. "Silvergirl," he repeated. "I'm here. I found you. I got your message." She stayed still.

Belion's hand dropped to his groin. He was wearing very large athletic shorts, cotton knit, the kind with two layers of fabric. Under the inner layer, he was rising against the seam. He looked at the silver slip she was wearing, remembered the peach nipples she had, remembered her round breasts. He rubbed himself with one hand, as if scratching an itch. He was all alone in his apartment, and it was morning, and he was tired. But he could not sleep. He could not go to sleep without something happening. If something didn't happen, he would just stay awake, keep working, keep trying. He shifted a little and loosened his shorts around his balls, but he did not put his hand inside.

After a few moments, Silvergirl's eyes opened. The player had returned to the game. He put both his hands on the key-board.

"Hello," he said. "Irene?"

Silvergirl shook her head, hopped down from the ledge, and began to walk across the cave, farther toward the back, away from him. He had no choice but to follow, or let her go.

"I'm not Irene," she said as they walked.

"You are Irene. You're Irene, Silvergirl."

"You found my messages. That's good."

Whatever game she was playing, whatever she was trying to teach him, he didn't understand. Would she let him pull the slip over her head? Would she stand next to him, not wearing any clothes? Would his water buffalo head see what his human head could not?

"How are things in Toledo?" He asked. The words appeared in a bubble over his character's head.

She halted. "How do you know I am in Toledo?"

"I know everything; I'm an admin."

"I don't know who you are."

"I'm Belion, Archmage of the Under-dark."

She turned and murmured an incantation, her pixel hands waving in two little circles. Part of the cave wall fell away, and she

87

opened a small door set into the rock. Behind it was a passage that was unfamiliar to him. He felt frustrated, and he wanted to stand up, grab onto the kitchen beam, and put himself straight into the throat of someone small and willing. I miss my girlfriend, he thought. I miss her! I should go to Toledo. This is stupid. Putting your dick in someone is enough. It doesn't have to be in someone's vagina.

"Go through this door," she said.

"OK, OK," he said, and tried to duck through the door. But it was too small. His character was extralarge size. He couldn't get through the door.

"Shrinking spell?" she suggested.

"I'm an admin, I said, for chrissake," said Belion. "I can shrink myself if I want to, but for what?" He would never shrink this avatar down. Not for some chick. Please.

"I need help," she said.

"Are you Irene? Irene? Is that you? I think I miss you. I want to come to Toledo."

Silvergirl went through the door. She left it open behind her, but he did not follow. Then he was alone in the cave, with nothing. It made him angry. It made him writhe in frustration. In his tired mind, he was rubbing up and down against the silken silvery folds of Silvergirl's robe, and all of the silver was tugging at him. He pushed against the keyboard tray, his eyes closed. Her hands around him, slipping in between the fabric layers of his shorts, her eyes turned down to look at him, the way she spun around on the avatar pedestal, one hand curled into the perfect shape to hold him. In and out he went, feeling it just ahead of him, through the layers, getting warmer and falling through, until he was finally deep, deep inside, where the girl was.

6

While the Toledo Institute of Astronomy took root and flourished as an academic center through the second half of the nineteenth century, bringing about an international renaissance of star science, there was a strange sister renaissance flourishing in the shadows of the institute's shiny new buildings: a rebirth of the art and science of astrology. Perhaps the new astrology's lineage could be traced to that original witch, Esther Birchard, evicted from her position as chief weather scientist to the Stickney Carriers fleet. Perhaps it was a natural balance to all the strictly scientific behavior going on behind the walls of the institute proper. Whatever the cause, the symptoms were spreading: holy groves emerging in the gardens of the library. Prayer flags draping arrays of satellite receivers. Swamp voodoo huts popping up along the banks of the Maumee River in the dark, while everyone was looking up.

The first quantifiable development to emerge from the concentrated research efforts of astrologers and mystics in northwest Ohio was the practice of overlaying the lens of a telescope with the elements of a Native American medicine wheel, so that the degrees of a circle became merged with the white, black, red, and yellow quadrants and the thirty-six points: snow goose, west, illumination, mother earth, etc. This evolution of star-chart interpretation was attributed to no one and claimed by none, in contrast to the patents and named star clusters rolling out of the Institute of Astronomy at a rate of several per week. Yet the chart was widely adopted, as were several other effective practices blending scientific instruments with spiritual symbols.

Before the sun was identified as just another star, astrologers had sat cheek by jowl with academics in medicine and physics. Now astrology had long been relegated to the realm of pseudoscience; some even called it a religion. But in Ohio the seers and the predictive astrologers, the psychics and the strangers, taught and learned exacting principles, and apprenticeships were formalized, curricula laid down. No, there was no manual for wise men, no instructional video for understanding the philosophical underpinnings of an astrological practice. People couldn't even really agree on whether philosophical underpinnings existed or should be set down in writing if they did. Yet as their methods became increasingly scientific and exact, with chicken bones measured in nanometers and tea leaves subjected to mass spectrometers, the star gazers of Toledo worked toward a common disciplinary matrix of theory and application, symbols, interpretations, and tools. And this is why aspiring astrologers came to Toledo. Despite their lack of leadership, hierarchy, or any overt organization, Toledo managed to turn the direction of the art.

There is no evidence or proof of the legitimacy of any theories or principles of astrology. There is no reason to believe that stars and planets or their movement could have any influence whatsoever on the lives of human beings or the countries of the earth. Neither is there any empirical evidence to show that true love is anything but a construct created by humans to solidify a family unit based on monogamy and a strong, diverse lineage for the species. No evidence of any true god. And yet we watch the stars, we fall in love, we pray. Therefore scholars of astrology, love, and religion have been forced to accept that something can be real, even if it is not true. Scientists, obviously, acknowledge no such paradox.

Irene came back to Toledo from the south, crossing the Maumee River on Interstate 75. The railroad terminal lay down on her right and beyond that were the glittering spires of the city central. Late afternoon sun slanted across the buildings and towers, sparking a red-orange glow on the shining facets of the "glass city." She craned her neck toward the west to see the tallest tower of the Toledo Institute of Astronomy rising out of the farmland, safely outside the glow of city lights. Its central spire was crowned with a magnificent observatory. But she couldn't see it. It was too far.

The house that burned had been in the historic district, but now her mother lived, or had recently lived, in a little house on West Bancroft close to the hospital, where the ambulances went up and down. Every time an ambulance passed, she would say, "Bless him, Mother, for he is your child." Or she might say "Bless her . . ." instead. She said she always knew if it was a male or female in the ambulance.

"What if the ambulance is empty?" Irene

asked once. "Stands to reason it must be, half the time."

"There's always someone driving, Irene," her mother had argued.

She pulled her little gray Fiat off the freeway on Bancroft Street and joined the flow of traffic. Little had changed in Toledo that she could see. The same minimarts, the same storefronts, the boxy kit houses and the lawns tired from a summer of heat and wind. Her mother hadn't lived in the good part of Toledo. This was the seedy part.

"It's OK," she could hear her mother say. "Seedy is good. Half of my clients are paying me with their rent money. It's more important to them to know what the stars say than to have a new car."

"Rent money doesn't buy a new car," Irene would challenge. "It buys rent. Do the stars say they will be homeless?"

"Irene, stop," her mother would have said. "Don't be so literal. Not every word means what you think it means."

Irene's tongue was wide in her mouth, and her lungs felt too large for her chest. Her heart skipped, pushing against her heavy ribs, rapping on the wall of her body. Maybe her mother had a heart condition. Maybe a heart attack pushed her down the stairs. Was Irene cursed with it now? At what point does the mother's heart beat in the daughter's body? She was driving and not thinking. She was prickling in her rib cage. The thought of her mother's house, empty. The thought of her mother, dead.

In a long row of shabby homes, her mother's house was beautifully kept, and her lawn, among all the drab ones, was emerald green. A tidy rose garden sent shoots up over the porch railing and two urns full of petunias overflowed next to the steps. In the window a sign hung, dark now, that said PSYCHIC and had a wide eye beneath. When her mother was home, the eye was lit and would blink open and shut. Now it was dark. *I don't want to go in,* thought Irene. *I don't want to see.*

She parked on the street and shimmied out of the car, keeping the door tight to the car to avoid traffic. Keys in hand, she walked up on the porch. The mailbox, nailed to the wall, was full to bursting with flyers, envelopes, catalogs. Irene pulled the stuff out of the box automatically, as she always did for her mother. The box was always overflowing, so this in itself did not mean that someone had died. It was no different from any other day. She looked down at the shoe rack next to the door. No different: flip-flops, sandals, ballet flats, and tennis shoes. Bernice believed that shoes belonged outside the house.

Irene put her key in the lock and stood for a minute. She opened the door, keeping the gap narrow and tight again, shimmied inside. Everything looked the same as she remembered.

Except on the floor at the bottom of the stairs there was a place where her mother had lain down and died. There was no blood, no mark or shocking indentation. There was only smooth linoleum beside a carpeted staircase, and that was it. The house was unbearably silent, smelled of incense, and felt unaccountably damp. Irene drew some long breaths, felt her heart racing. She set her keys down on the banister, as always.

The foyer and the front room were for the clients. Tie-dyed scarves, fringed window treatments, and beaded curtains covered the walls and windows. A tall red shaded lamp stood in the corner. A long dark sofa stretched low under the window, and a red velvet armchair sat near it, where her mother would sit for consultations. On the coffee table Irene saw the accoutrements of Bernice's trade: the crystal ball, the tarot, bones in a little cup. There were books for consulting sky maps and charts. An old tape recorder in a leather case, which Bernice used to record all of her sessions, just in case she forgot something later. Irene walked across the room and picked up a large wooden box engraved with a picture of a bird with no beak. It was locked. There was a new foot-stool, embroidered in heavy thread with trees and vines.

Irene sat on the sofa and looked around. She was overwhelmed by the new absence in her mother's house, yet she was also overwhelmed by the way it was exactly the same.

There was a knock at the door.

Irene went and opened it, and found the neighbor, Mrs. Betty, standing there.

"Oh, honey," said Mrs. Betty. "I'm so sorry."

"Thanks," said Irene.

"I just miss her so much," Mrs. Betty went on. "She was an angel, an angel."

Mrs. Betty reached out one arm as if she was going to hug Irene, but when Irene didn't come forward, she ended up just patting her on the shoulder.

"Thank you," said Irene.

"When I saw her, I just cried," she said. "Your sweet, sweet mother and all the troubles and trials she had in this life, and all the good she did for other people, and all the people who loved her, and —"

"That must have been awful for you — finding her," said Irene. "Dead."

"Oh, I'm more sorry for you, honey. With you so far away when it happened."

"Thank you," said Irene again. "Well, I'll be sure and let you know, if there is a funeral. When it is."

Mrs. Betty hesitated on the threshhold.

"There was something I wanted to tell you," she said.

"What?" Irene asked.

"She had a client that day." Mrs. Betty looked at Irene with an eyebrow raised. "Right before."

"Really?" said Irene. "She must have had clients all the time —"

"Yes, well," said Mrs. Betty. "This client would have been the last — to see her. But I don't know who it was."

Irene swallowed hard, and frowned at Mrs. Betty. She didn't care about her mother's clients. The neighbor caught her mouth in her hand and said, "I'm sorry, I've upset you. I'll go."

"It's OK," Irene started to say, but she was thankful Mrs. Betty was turning to leave.

"And if you need anything else, please —"

"I'll be sure and call," said Irene.

"You can come over for dinner," added Mrs. Betty. "Just come on over; you don't have to let me know."

Irene walked back through the beaded curtain and into the kitchen, the area of the house where clients were never invited. Irene stood next to the garbage can looking at dishes in the sink: a large mug with two tea-bag strings wrapped around the handle, tea bags inside. A large spoon. A plate, previous contents unknown. A glass, containing about half an inch of water. Near the faucet was a toothbrush and a tube of toothpaste. Apparently her mother had been sleeping downstairs. On the windowsill was a hairbrush, full of hair. She should pull out all that hair and throw it away, or she should keep it forever, in case her mother could be cloned. She should never clone her mother. She should clone her mother, and raise her as her own, parent her right, make things turn out differently for her poor, poor mother. Irene felt her heart scrabbling in her chest like a squirrel climbing around and around one of her ribs. She put her fingers on her wrist and took her pulse. Fast. She didn't wait to count the beats against her watch. She could feel them pounding behind her eyes. Slow down, heart.

Next to the sink, on the drainer, there was a red bowl and a few pieces of silverware, a frying pan, a couple of small plates, and a cleaned container of cottage cheese, ready to reuse. She should just throw that away. No one reuses cottage cheese containers. The sight of this irritated her, especially since for years she had given her mother Tupperware and other containers to try and get her to stop reusing plastic containers from deli meat, cheeses, yogurts, and more.

"It's disposable, mother," she had said.

"Nonsense, it's perfectly good," her mother had asked. "Just look at it. Who would throw that away?"

Irene picked up the cottage cheese container and opened the garbage can. It was half full. She considered digging through her mother's trash to re-create the last few days before she died. What had she eaten? What else had she thrown away? Obviously not any mail. It was scattered all over the dining room table.

Her mother never threw mail away. She never threw anything away. The half-full garbage was probably at least a week's worth of trash and only things she couldn't find a way to put in a box, preserve, bag up, or rinse out. Coffee grounds, tea bags, some old lettuce. An empty bag of oatmeal. And something at the bottom that was clunking, clunking. Reaching down through all the trash she pulled out a long shape wrapped in many plastic grocery bags. Irene took her hand away and let the bottle fall back down in.

She shut the lid on the garbage can. She sat down at the table in her mother's little living area, where her mother had her computer, her television, her own private space. The enormity of the task at hand felt crushing to Irene. The house had to be emptied. Or she could live in it just the way it was. Her mother's affairs had to be put in order. Or she could wait until someone came knocking at the door, or shut off the gas, or approached the house with a bulldozer.

Maybe she did want Belion to come.

If she said, "Empty the house, Belion," then Belion would trudge in and out of the house carrying armload after armload of her mother's possessions, inexorably, into a Dumpster that she could surely call and get, and then all of the stuff would be gone. Belion would do this for her without questioning, without analyzing what he was carrying, without balking at the strain. She should call him. But then she would have to explain about her mother, and she never explained her mother to people. If people couldn't figure it out on their own, then they were too stupid to know the truth. Really, her whole life she had been wondering, how can people not know? How can they not figure it out? And really, what must they all think of her, the bad daughter, all this time? Because her mother kept everything hidden.

Irene stood up and began to go through the cabinets in the TV stand. She opened every drawer in the kitchen, pulling out piles of dishcloths, many unopened packages of plastic cups, bags of napkins, boxes of plastic silverware, endless saved Cool Whip containers, ant traps, roach spray, extra coffee filters, many cookie cutters, and a thousand plastic grocery bags. She threw phone books on the floor, phone books from every year since they had moved to this house. She dislodged a pile of crime thrillers, and several spiral notebooks.

She knew that what she was looking for would be downstairs, but where? In the powder room she found a drawer full of wine corks. Now we're getting somewhere, she thought. Then, at the bottom of an antique copper basin full of extra toilet paper, she found the bottle, half full.

"Gin," she said out loud. "There you are."

Had she landed at the bottom of the stairs with a bottle in her hand, half empty, half splashed across her legs, then that would be something new. But instead it was the same as it ever had been, not an act of sudden heroism or decision, but a slow and silent death, cup by cup, pint by pint, measured into drinking glasses and nips from under the countertop.

Irene began to cry. She went back to the trash and pulled out the thing that was at the bottom. She tore off the grocery bags in chunks, flung them into the trash, and then she was holding an identical gin bottle, but this one was empty. She sobbed and blinked her eyes, and then she made herself stop sobbing. Each hand held a gin bottle. Irene could feel her face taking its traditional shape to match her place in this house. The face was blank. It had no reaction. Because the other person who lived in this house was too drunk to interpret a face having a reaction, and too drunk to care if it did.

"You did this," she said. "You did this to me. You are a coward, a coward, a coward."

She did not say, *You left me, and now I am all alone. I should have been young, and happy, and proud, but now I am here with your gin bottle in my hand, and the only choice that matters is if I take a drink or not, if I sleep in your bed or in your chair, if I wear your clothes or burn them.*

This was true, but it was not true. Irene was sitting with a gin bottle in her hand. But there was no one to take it away from and no place to hide it. She was lost, and she was alone, but she knew that she would never, ever, ever drink that gin.

7

Three years before Irene came back to Toledo, George had gone to visit an astrologer. As an astronomer, a doctor of science, shuffling down the street after a late dinner on a lonely barstool, he had every reason to sneer and shake his head at the astrologer's studio, advertised with a neon blinking eye. But instead, George had stopped and stumbled up the sidewalk.

The psychic had met him at the door to her house, a silk skirt swirling around her legs, a silk scarf wrapped around her head, and a crust of rings over her fingers. He felt immediately that she knew him, and was happy to see him. It was a powerful feeling he did not question. George was not a man to question the existence of things that were strange. He had reasons for this. It wasn't just lunacy.

"George, come in," she had said. "Your name is George, isn't it?"

"It is," said George, impressed. "It is George. I am George."

She pulled him in by the arm. She seemed excited, and treated him as if he were a marvel. The astrologer's house from the outside was unremarkable. It wasn't decked in improbable palm trees, or sporting a gold sidewalk. It had none of the ostentatious decorations commonly found on other astrologers' places of business in the city. But it had the advantage of being between the office he was returning to and the restaurant where he had just been dining.

George had been a little bit drunk earlier in the evening. He had been a little heart-broken, saying good-bye to the most recent girl. He was not too heartbroken over this particular girl, but just a little heartbroken about the state of things. It doesn't really matter, he told himself, walking back to his office, where he'd left his car. She wasn't the one. So a little drunk and a little sad, he had seen the psychic's neon light blinking from her window: a brightly lashed eye going open, closed. And he knocked.

The psychic helped him sit. While she was holding onto his elbow, she seemed to wobble on her legs a bit. It struck him, sinking down into the psychic's sofa, that she might be a little drunk, too. Maybe they

106

were both drunk. Hey, why not? If the other fellows at the institute found out he'd been here, he'd need a good excuse. "I was drunk," he could say. "It doesn't mean much. It doesn't reflect my core beliefs or anything."

"Tell me what you want to know," she said to him. "Ask me anything."

"I don't know," he said. "I don't know what I want to know. I guess I'm looking for someone. A woman."

"Do you believe in love?" she asked him. She took his hands in hers. Her rings were warm; the metal touched his hands, and she stopped his arms from moving all around.

"Of course," he said. "I mean, not in a Huey Lewis way, but yes."

"And are you prepared to give yourself up to love?" said the psychic. She was letting her head knock back and forth in a very convincing fashion, dangly earrings falling against alternating sides of her neck. He felt, in his mild intoxication, that she was pretty rad. Like authentic.

"Yes, I am prepared to give myself up for love. To love. Over love. Whatever."

The psychic stopped rocking back and forth and her fingernails bit into George's palm.

"What does your mother think about this?"

George pulled back. "Are you seeing something, about my mother? Are you reading something there?"

The psychic resumed her rocking. "I see your mother. She is standing in the canyon, and her body becomes a wall, becomes a wall hard and high, and the canyon is dry and parched, waiting for water, but the water is behind the wall of your mother, and she is holding it away from you."

"She's holding water away from me?"

"Water is love," said the psychic curtly. "In this story water is love."

"What can I do?" asked George. "Do I need to perforate her in some way? Dig under her? What?"

The psychic dropped his hands.

"Do you want me to look into my crystal ball?"

"You can do that? I mean, that's a real thing?"

"Yes, of course it is a real thing," said the psychic. "You don't believe in it?"

"I believe, I believe," said George. "It's just my canyon-wall mother, she thinks this kind of thing is all ridiculous."

"But you don't think it's ridiculous?" she asked him.

"I believe in everything," said George. "I can't deny much. I probably have crystals in my pocket right now. I talk to cloud formations. I'm like, your ultimate demographic. Trust me."

The psychic rose, and in a swish of silk she settled into a chair across the low table from George. She took a deep breath and smiled at him. Her face was sad, ruined by wrinkles. The silk wrap distorted the sides of it, pulled the skin back from the bones. Her eyes watered. She put her hands on both sides of the crystal ball and began to turn it, rotate it, twist it back and forth. Finally she left it alone and stared into it, only her fingertips touching it, her nose inches away from it.

"I see her," she said at last.

"You see who?" George practically leaped across the table.

"I see your love. She is here in the ball. I see her."

"What does she look like?" George asked. "Does she see you? Can she see me?"

"She is beautiful. George, I cannot help but love her, too."

"I need details," said George. "How can I find her?"

"She has brown hair," said the psychic. "Beautiful brown hair."

"OK," said George, "That's helpful. That's actually very helpful. Thank you. I need more though."

"You will find her in Toledo," said the psychic.

"Good, also good," said George. "I am in Toledo right now. So that is very convenient. Do you —"

"She is a dreamer," said the psychic. "A dreamer of dreams."

"Great," said George. "I love that, because a dreamer of dreams is so much better than a dreamer of, like, roadside fruit markets. No quality girl would ever dream a —"

"She is an astronomer," said the psychic.

"NO," said George, suddenly finely attuned. He leaned in close, as if he could look into the crystal ball, too. "An astronomer, you say? But that's — did you know that I'm an astronomer?"

"That is all," said the psychic. "That's all I can tell you. I can see her plain as day. And she will find you. She will. I believe. Do you?"

George nodded emphatically. "Well, let's just say I will find HER. I'll find HER. Do you have any idea when I'll find her?"

"I don't see," said the psychic, "But I can tell you what I feel. You will be young together, you will be loved, and it will be more beautiful than either of you could have imagined. Because this is the least that she deserves. Do you see this? The least that she deserves."

George stumbled to his feet. He felt moved, on the spot, with an urgency he could only partially attribute to the liquor he had ingested, to find the girl and to experience the beauty that he himself and now the psychic also knew to be waiting for him.

"What do I owe you?" said George, suddenly anxious to leave. "Do I cross your palm with silver? I've always wanted to do that."

"You don't owe me anything, George," said the psychic. "I have seen that we will meet again. Your debt will not be to me, but to the stars. They don't need your money. They want your spirit. Are you ready to give it?"

This was exactly the kind of hokey bullshit that made his mother snort with contempt.

"Go easy on your mother," said the psychic sharply. "She's often wrong, but she loves you."

George had made it safely back to campus, back to his lab, where he slept off his liquor on a fine leather sofa and woke refreshed.

Ever since that night, in his mind the girls

of Toledo were arranged in the shape of a target. On the outside ring, girls in Toledo. Next ring, girls in Toledo who had brown hair. Inside that, the rings got more and more specific until at the very center there was a spot so dear that his dart would not stick in the board, but would fly straight through and never stop flying, until the end of the universe. George had thrown a lot of darts since that morning he awoke in his lab, ready to hunt, but had never struck the middle.

After class on the second day of the semester, George packed up his lecture notes and swung out through the doors of the lecture hall without glancing up at the ceiling at all. No sex goddess. A boring lecture on the Egyptians, another headache, and that's all.

A friendly grad student approached him on the sidewalk outside the building, but he swung his light backpack onto his other shoulder, grinned, waved, and kept moving.

"Hi, George! What are you doing? Teaching?"

"Hey, Lucy! Great! See you later!"

Lucy was blond.

George believed, since that visit to the psychic, that true love was waiting for him here in Toledo. One by one he had narrowed down the field, and all the brown-haired astronomers who could reasonably be described as dreamers were tested and tried. His hopes were, like a photon traveling out of a gravitational sphere, growing dimmer.

He was still searching for love. But he had not yet found it.

Then, last spring, just when it seemed he had worked his way through all the likely candidates and there were no more girls within range, he met Kate Oakenshield. She was a brunette, obviously, an astronomer of the highest order, and a dreamer, one would hope. He had been after her all summer, and he was still after her. He intended now to go up to her office and make himself very charming. *Are you the one?* he would ask. Kate Oakenshield might respond, audibly, *I am.*

But maybe not. Because Kate Oakenshield had been raised a mute. She had only been allowed to hear musical sounds until she was five years old, at which point the state intervened and took her away from her insane father. As a result of her limited exposure to language, she had become a math genius, just as her father had planned. She did not respond to George's advances like other girls did, but, if anything, this made him more convinced that she must be the one, the center of the target.

Part of Kate Oakenshield's difficult childhood was that she had been locked up on her father's rural estate. George had sometimes fantasized about bursting into a tower room, lit with the sun's afternoon rays, where a little girl was chirping out the window to a sparrow or some other more colorful bird that chirps. He would ask her name, and she would turn, bemused but friendly, suddenly twenty years old, and warble a tune in her throat. He would scoop her up and gallop down the stairs, past the father who would be in the process of being arrested by the police and out into what would have become suddenly night. Then he would commence teaching her to talk.

She had, of course, been rescued and taught to talk already. Kate Oakenshield, though raised a mute, could talk alright given the circumstances. She could also do math like nobody's business. She must have had an amazing brain, all untainted by nursery rhymes and reprimands and television. The mind that fugues built, said *Psychology Today*. Science loved her, and George thought he might, too.

So far, he had managed to make her officially his girlfriend, at least as far as he could tell. At least he had told her she was, several times, and she had seemed to hear him. Next, he would get her in bed. This wasn't the way things usually went for George, but Kate Oakenshield had been raised mute, and things were different when she was involved. George took it as a promising sign.

Another colleague approached him as he took the stone stairs up to Herschel Hall. The guy was coming down the stairs and George almost knocked into him.

"Hi, George," said the guy. "Did you, ah, get a chance to look at the numbers on that new lens?"

"Sure, Ken." George waved him off and galloped on up the stairs. "I'll absolutely take a look at those numbers on that new lens as soon as I get back to my office. Great work. Great times."

"It's Frank," said the guy. But George pulled the door open and entered the building.

Herschel Hall was a four-story building with an enormous atrium in front. The entranceway dazzled visitors with a giant oak door, marble pillars, and a thick chandelier. Farther on, huge arches of windows stretched to the back, and a vaulted ceiling claimed its shape in the pointed roof. Around the walls, under the windows, a giant mosaic-tile mural portrayed a colorful solar system, with comets and quasars whishing about. The floor was stone, and couches and tables were scattered about artfully among varied greenery, potted palms and fig trees for the most part. A fountain tinkled in the middle of the room, which took up the whole building. The fountain was a rough human form intended to be Hesiod, the Greek astronomer. Water came out of the top of his head in a gentle spray.

Upstairs, Kate's office was a mess of potted plants, and a birdcage in the corner housed a pack of finches. George breathed in deeply a couple of times. Was it pollen making his skull ache so much? The floor of her office was covered with a reed mat, and as he poked his head in the door, wearing his most radiant grin, he heard the sound of a flute. He saw that she was sitting in the open window, her legs outside, playing it.

She was a tall girl, and willowy. She had long dark hair flat to her head and wore long fitted skirts that forced her to take small steps on her platform shoes. George felt immediate fear that she would fall out the window. George looked at the thin long fingers holding the flute. Her eyes were closed. She seemed far away.

"Kate!" said George, "Kate Oakenshield!

It's nice to see you!"

It was hard for George not to add "the girl who was raised a mute" to her name. But he refrained. For her.

She jolted, and for a moment he thought she really was going to fall out the window. But then she hesitated, put the flute in her lap, and leaned her shoulder against the frame.

"George," said Kate. She said everything emphatically. Not like a foreign person. But with decisive pronunciation. George figured that the emphaticness was the only way she could talk in English instead of trilling a sonata or something.

George came into the office, stepping onto the reed mat. "Hey!" said George. "Why not come back in the window? That'd be better, right?"

Then he leaned against the wall, relaxed and unthreatening. Certainly not alarming enough to shock someone out a window. How many meters would it take her to reach terminal velocity, if she were to fall?

"Hello, George," she said.

"I came up to see you," said George.

Kate Oakenshield nodded emphatically.

"That's a great flute. Great song. Would you like to read some of my new article? I wrote it for the *Dark Star Review.* I mean,

I'm writing it. This is a draft, do you want to read it?"

George pulled out a piece of paper from his pants pocket and unfolded it. It was one sheet, with small letters on the front.

"Put it on the desk," she said.

"You don't have to read it now," said George.

Kate Oakenshield barked at him, sort of a comforting shushing bark down in her vocal cords, and he understood that she really wanted to get back to playing the flute while hanging half out the window. Maybe in her brain she was calculating the mass of a neutron star.

"Do you want to go to dinner?" he pressed. "Or something? A walk?"

Kate Oakenshield coughed or hummed and shook her head. Dinner or a walk would be torment, he knew, for both of them. Him straining and trying to make her talk, her perplexed and frustrated with talking. He felt like that guy with the grapes in the water, where the grapes were a pretty girl who happened to be insane, and the water was his burning desire to make her fall in love with him. Or something.

"Wait a second," said George, "Maybe you could write back to me? Instead of talk! I mean, if it's not too much trouble to write?

You could show me, at dinner, your answer. We could write, back and forth, on paper!"

Dear Kate, he thought of writing. *Do you like me? Circle yes or no. Thanks, George.* But she frowned. George dragged his fingers through his hair. Of course. Calling attention to her weakness like that had been a mistake. She was probably angry or sad, and would now go and cry over her computer, making whuffling sounds like a clarinet with a wet cotton ball in its mouthpiece. Now she was opening and closing her eyes rapidly. He didn't want to be responsible for her having some kind of medical setback.

Then the blinking stopped and he heard her call to him, loudly, and she was singing the whole sentence.

"I am studying black hole accretion," she sang, "It is Dr. Bryant's main focus now."

George knew this. To him, black hole accretion had always sounded like pooping. But this was the longest thing she had ever communicated to him. Which made it very exciting, in terms of the seduction.

"I have always been profoundly interested in black hole accretion myself," he sang. He tried to sound like he was in an opera, the way they sort of sing without having a reason. And the lines kind of go up at the end. "My-SELF!"

Kate Oakenshield writhed her way backward out of the window, somehow without showing a peep of her leg, and when she had gotten her feet on the floor she approached him, smiling. She put her hand on his chest, and through the crisp white shirt she pushed him backward. Would she drive him to the ground, mount him like a vulture, tear him to pieces, squawking and squawking? But she was pushing him out the door. The last thing he saw, before the door closed between them, was her teeth.

In this manner, they had been going on for weeks, Kate making strange noises in her throat and George wanting to get her into bed, both working hard at the Toledo Institute of Astronomy, waiting for a breakthrough. George wondered, in his heart, if she could really be for him. But categorically, given the words of the psychic, how could it be otherwise?

8

The avenue that led into the campus of the Toledo Institute of Astronomy was flanked with tall cedar trees interspersed with statuary representing the world's famed telescopes and cameras, both orbital and terrestrial. Irene drove down its wide expanse with a faculty parking pass hanging from her rearview mirror for the first time. Inside the Fiat, the air-conditioning was on. She could not hear any sounds. She had turned the radio off. She was counting her breaths, marking the stabs of her heart against her rib cage, and how her organs turned inside her like marmots struggling to get out. On the seat beside her were some papers, all the materials she had printed off from the joyful e-mails the institute had sent her. There was a temporary ID card, a map of the campus, boat tickets for a cruise on the Maumee River for two, and a page of interview questions for the campus newspaper. Someone was writing an article about her.

How did she feel when she first saw the black holes? Excited. How long had she been working with this experiment? Months. Who had designed the microcollider? She had. Who had built it. A fabricator. What were her plans for the future? To make black holes in Toledo. Apart from that, her plans were indeterminate.

Don't put this on Twitter, they said. Come to Toledo, and all will be explained.

Driving down this treelined avenue with a faculty parking pass, she felt like she was leading a parade with brass bands and people marching in big head costumes. There might as well have been screaming fans packing the curbs, hanging from the trees, pelting her with roses.

This is it, she thought. *This is me. I am here. I have not failed. I have done the opposite.*

Alone in the cool silence of the Fiat, on the treelined avenue, she could be triumphant. It was finally all happening, and she forced herself to enjoy it. Many beautiful things were gone in an instant. A feeling, a memory, a black hole brightly glowing in a jar.

Irene parked the Fiat and got out into the

September heat. She walked across the sunny parking lot, breathing in that hot Ohio air. Her heart had yet to establish its own steady rhythm. It still beat and skipped and raced to find her mother's heart beating. Walking up the sidewalk, she clutched her laptop bag to her chest. She read the names of the outlying buildings on their brass plaques: COPERNICUS POWER CENTER, THE PLANCK FOUNDATION, GALILEO HEALTH ATRIUM.

She walked past three enormous animated metal sculptures and remembered learning about each one when she had visited the campus in elementary school. There was a gyroscope, spinning sedately on its axis. Next to that, two synchronized pendulums swung in a frame. Then there was the Tusi couple, a huge circle with a circle half its size inside it. The inner circle rolled around inside the larger one, and a black spot on its perimeter moved up and down, up and down in a line. She remembered her teacher explaining the function of these sculptures with a laser pointer. Now she was no longer a child on a field trip, or a tourist or a job applicant, hopeful and nervous, but faculty, on her way to examine her appointed laboratory for the first time. If she needed something, she could ask. She was even going to have an assistant.

Irene approached the enormous wrought iron gate that stopped people from entering the institute without permission. There was a brick wall around the older part of the college, ten feet high, topped with crenellations and bird-repelling spikes. Beside the ornamental gate, which would open for cars, was a smaller door to the gatehouse. She put her hand on the door handle. It was silver and it felt smooth under her hand. She smelled the burnt grass smell of fall in Ohio, the smell of hard dirt and hot roads, and she heard the noise of a thousand insects in the fields and woods around the institute, humming.

Inside, there was a man in the uniform of a security guard. The insignia of the Toledo Institute of Astronomy was emblazoned on his lapel. He reached out his hand for her temporary ID card, and then he waved her through. She turned to the second door, on the other side of the gatehouse, and opened it. She was inside.

Irene remembered the last time she had stood here, after her college graduation. She had come for an interview with the Toledo Institute of Astronomy, and, having opened this door, she turned directly to the right and vomited into a bush. She had found the appointed room for her interview, and then had so utterly shit the bed on all the questions that the professor conducting the interview looked at her almost kindly.

"Do you really want this position?" said the professor. "You seem a little undone."

The night before that interview, Irene had stood in her mother's kitchen, holding her car keys and her purse. She was exhausted from the drive, but she was never allowed to fly home to visit, because Bernice had seen a vision that she would die in a plane crash, so begged and demanded Irene would stay out of them. Cried. Cajoled. Irene had conceded the point, conceded air travel entirely. Bernice was holding Irene's face in one hand, and kind of hurting it. The words she made sounded like "told you, toldyer, tole," and Irene wondered: How can this person have a life, and friends, and answer the phone, and not have anyone know that she is the town drunk, in a silvery gray cardigan, and Birkenstocks, and a fog of lavender oil, and dead sea salt, and jazz? Irene hated jazz. Hated everything about it.

"Look," her mother had said, "I made it. I bumped it over. I bumped. I buh." Her mother smiled apologetically and shrugged her shoulders. "I can't put my sentence in order!" she said. There were two bright spots of red on her cheeks, and her eyes were watery. "I'm so happy you're here," said her mother. "I bumped up a dinner. Bumped. Buh." Her mother's shaky hand lifted the lid from a huge oval Crock-Pot that was plugged into the wall. Inside were some gray things and some brown. "Root vegetables," said her mother. "Buff. I can't say it. Beef tenderloin. That's what it is. Now I cooked it a long time. And then. Well. You get a plate. I'll get you a plate. Sit down in the other room."

It wasn't funny to Irene. At all. It's not funny when it is your own mother.

Her mother's television had been tuned to the Food Network. Bobby Flay was auditioning some chefs who were making canapés from ingredients found in the wild. Wild Indian cucumber. Wild coconut. Wild blackberries. The chefs were winded, fraught, red in the face. Her mother brought out a plate that was a paper plate wedged into a smaller ceramic plate. On the plate was a piece of meat that was beef. There were also cubes of vegetables and runny juice pooling under all the food and in between the pieces were thick wedges of mushrooms that looked like they had been in the back of her mother's fridge for a while.

Her mother had said, repeatedly, that if something was cooked long enough, it was fine. *Ishfine. No, it's not. Ishfine. It's a freezer, Mom, not a cryogenic chamber. Ishfine.*

"I don't eat mushrooms, Mom," said Irene. "I don't like mushrooms."

"Oh, well if you can pick that out. Those are turnips. This is beef. You want soup? I also made soup, from celery, and it's in the car. It's in the freezer. It'll taste ahhh."

"I don't want any soup," said Irene.

She peeled a shred of beef tenderloin off the chunk and put it in her mouth. When she was a child, she remembered eating watery lasagna, peanut soup with beet greens, flatbread, undercooked and wet, smeared with soy sauce. Irene had never developed a taste for food. She had always regarded it as a dull necessity.

"Aren't you going to eat anything?" she asked her mother. "Aren't you going to have some?"

"No," said her mother. "I am not hungry. Now I just already ate mine, and it's gone."

Her mother sat down heavily on the red stuffed chair, watched the television while Irene ate. She ate the turnips and the parsnip, but the meat tasted as if it had been boiled in parsnip juice. She shredded the meat and then decided to leave it on the plate. When she turned to look at her mother, Bernice had fallen asleep on her chair. Irene went up to bed, and hunched over her laptop, and studied. The interview committee might ask her to name a thousand stars. They might ask her to explain the Aristotelian disunion between the perfect sky and the rotting earth, the spirit and the self, the stars and the man. They might ask her to define loyalty, or explore in an essay why a young, intelligent woman would want to come back to live at home with her mother, when her mother was likely to boil turnips in beef slag and then leave it on the counter for days, still eating away at it. The answer to every question might be, "Guilt." Who discovered Saturn's rings? Guilt. Who delivered Pythagoras's pizza? Guilt. What made Irene try coming back to Toledo? Guilt.

Sitting upstairs from her passed-out mother, looking at science things on the laptop: this was a moment when Irene felt a sharp urge to find a tall, tall bridge over a deep river. The Anthony Wayne Bridge was Toledo's suicide hotspot. Someone had even started a Tumblr, to darkly document the slippage of humans into the river from this bridge. *It is a terrible way to die!* The author of the Tumblr wanted people to know. *Like being hit by a car, but then you drown!* What was keeping her from slipping over the edge of this bridge, Irene wondered. What was keeping her awake? Guilt, guilt, guilt.

That night, laptop shut, sheets flat, Toledo drifting into unconsciousness all around her, she dreamed herself into the Hinterland. Lucid dreaming always came easiest in her mother's home, where Irene could so well remember her early lessons in the practice. In her mother's house, she didn't even need the trick with ringing the bells on the shelf, because she was already home. She almost felt her mother's fingers on her forehead, her voice chanting the words, talking Irene into dreaming, helping her stay under it. I want you safe in your own head, her mother would say. I always want you to be able to find me, no matter what happens.

If sleeping is like dying, her mother had taught her, then dreaming is like heaven. If dreaming is like heaven, then you can build your own heaven, if you know how. Or you can build your own hell, a massive Victorian monstrosity with eleven rambling wings connected by a whistling ruin that wants to annihilate you. Irene had decided maybe dreaming is a preview for the afterlife, a directionless meander through our finest wishes, our most compelling fears, our wretched secret sexual urges, our basic confusion. Like life, like memory, most of which we will experience deeply and not remember at all. She knew that science could tell her almost nothing about dreams. And almost nothing about death. The most important things are mysteries: the universe, and the way we die.

Asleep, she sat on the porch of her mother's house and stared at the bleak Hinterland. Irene put her teeth together and kept all the guilt inside her mouth, where it piled up on her tongue and made her sick. When her mother came out of the house, at last, she went and sat on the porch rail. She pulled a stem of the climbing rosebush that had wrapped itself around the railing through her hand. It didn't hurt her. In the dreamworld, there are no thorns on roses. If you count your fingers, you will find the wrong number. If you pull your hair out, it will be daisies. If your drunk mother talks to you, it will make sense.

"I'm sorry, Irene," said her mother.

"It's OK," said Irene.

"No, I'm really sorry," her mother insisted. "Here you are, home for the first time in a year, and I feed you mushrooms. That is just a mistake I will not forgive myself."

Her mother did not say, *I'm sorry for being drunk. I'm sorry for being incomprehensible. I'm sorry for nearly burning you to death. I'm sorry for giving birth to you. I'm sorry for delivering you from wherever you were before you were born. I'm sorry.*

"It's OK," said Irene again.

"Did you pick them out?" said her mother.

"Yes, I picked them out."

"And ate the beef?"

"Mmmm," said Irene.

"When I wake up, I probably won't remember," said her mother. "So if you tell a lie, I'm at your mercy. But you'll always know."

"I'm sure I will," said Irene.

"What do you want to do?" said her mother.

"I want to talk about my interview," said Irene. "I don't want to come across as desperate. But I think I am desperate."

"You are."

"Yes, I'm desperate to go there."

"Did you pull it up out of the well? Did the well show you this fellowship, Irene? Or did you try to stuff it down the well yourself?"

In the center of the square of the Hinterland there was a well. An old stone well that was deep and had no bottom. When she had been learning lucid dreaming from her mother, as a child, her mother had used this well as a trick for her mind, to let her access her subconscious. So she might say, *Well, show me something pretty.* Then she would reach in and pull up a gardenia bush. *Well, show me what I should wear to the prince's ball.* She would reach in and pull up an outfit. Now that she had better control of her dreaming mind, she didn't use the well as much. But when her mother said, "pull it out of the well," she was asking if Irene really wanted it, or if it was something she was only trying to want.

"Mom, I would be a janitor there, and I would be happy to get that job. A grad student, fine. I'll pay to go. A research assistant, great. Give me a job. A fellow, my god. Could I ever deserve that?"

"You deserve everything," said her mother. "You're the smartest person in the whole world and I'm so proud of you."

Irene relaxed. She put her head in her mother's lap. She drifted farther into sleep. She left the Hinterland without stepping foot into Dark House. It was a beautiful dream.

■ ■ ■ ■

In the morning, her mother would not get out of bed.

"How did you get in bed," said Irene. "How did you get yourself up the stairs?"

Her mother lay in the bed with the covers pulled up to her chin, one arm thrown over her face, her nose buried in the back of her elbow. Her bedroom was quaint and quiet, white walls and carpet, an iron floor lamp with a toile shade, lace around the Victorian patchwork quilt on the bed. Many throw pillows, also edged in lace. "I have a head-ache," said her mother. "I am not getting out of bed."

"My interview isn't until eleven," said Irene. "Can I bring you anything? Tea? Pills?"

"Tea and pills," said her mother.

In the kitchen, Irene pulled three tea bags out of the canister and flooded the cup with boiling water. She wrapped the strings around the handle, tore the foil off two sinus pills, and trudged back up the stairs.

"Just leave it on the nightstand," said her mother, who had not moved.

"Mom, what's that smell?" Irene smelled something sharp.

"I had a problem," said her mother from under her elbow. Her lips were terse, wired together.

Irene set the tea and pills down on the nightstand as directed. She walked into the bathroom and began to fill the clawfoot tub. It was wide and deep, dramatic. Irene squirted lavender bath gel into the water under the running tap, and it began to foam up. When it was steaming and full, Irene went back into the bedroom. Her mother was sitting up and had taken the pills with the boiling tea.

"Go get in the tub," said Irene. "Throw your clothes outside the door when they're off."

The stain in the bed was orange, a deep vibrant orange. It was large. Irene swept the fluffy quilt back, stripped off the white sheet and the mattress pad. Irene felt a mad, animal urge to run away from that stain in the bed, from a mother who puts stains in her bed. But she picked up her mother's clothes off the floor in the hallway, bundled them into the sheet, and hauled the armful down to the laundry room. Standing in the kitchen, listening to the washing machine fill, she felt a drip of water on her head. She looked up and saw a water stain darkening on the kitchen's drop ceiling, and raced for the stairs. Her mother had let the water of the tub overflow. Had she drowned? Was she dead? How was she able to sustain life in this state?

It's not good when your mother pisses herself in her bed. It's like you're the one doing it, and you feel sorry. But you're also the one seeing it, so you feel rage. There was too much of her mother in Irene for her to feel completely safe from pissing her own bed, and no matter what tourniquet she tied around her neck, she could not guarantee that her body would effectively die, that her belly button would effectively disappear, that she would separate, be just a head, her own head apart from her mother's.

She found her mother dozing with the faucet still spraying, the water in the tub spilling over gently onto the floor. Irene switched off the water and began to cry. Later that day she drove to the Toledo Institute of Astronomy, parked in the visitors' lot, barfed in a bush, blew up her interview, and accepted an offer in Pittsburgh instead. Pittsburgh had a bridge 240 feet above the Allegheny River. It would do.

But before she left for Pittsburgh, she had one more conversation with Bernice. When she got home from the ruined interview, her mother sat in a rocking chair in her bed-room, her mouth flattened into a line. The graying hands in her lap clasped each other urgently, as soon as Irene said, "Mother, I'm leaving. So we need to talk."

When the words were out of her mouth, Irene almost wanted to call them back.

"I know about your drinking. I know you drink. It's not sinus, or an ulcer, or anything like that. You're drinking too much. And you have been forever." She sat next to her mother on the ground, in a supplicating pose, took her hand, held it. She wanted to go back to not having said those words out loud in the world, when she could just dream about it and then get through the waking hours as if they were a dream.

"I'm not going to visit you anymore, once I get to Pittsburgh," said Irene. "Unless you stop drinking. Then I will."

"I don't know what you're talking about," her mother had said. She was sitting in a rocking chair, and her face was drawn and tight, her mouth suddenly small and pinched. "The doctor recommended I drink a glass of wine a day," said her mother. "For my health. But I'll stop. I'll stop. If you say I have to."

"That doctor doesn't know how much you drink."

"It was a different doctor a long time ago," said her mother. "I have a heart condition."

Irene paused. She wished she had never brought it up.

"Mother, I know you pissed your bed this morning, because your liver is failing, because you drink so much gin. You think you are fooling everyone you know, but you're not."

"No one knows. It's none of their business what I do."

"They know, mother. They can smell it."

But did they know? No one seemed to know. How did they not know, when she sometimes answered the phone by saying nothing at all?

"It's odorless," her mother said. "It doesn't smell like anything."

Irene remembered a time when she and her mother had been arguing. Her mother had sunk her fingernails into Irene's arm, face close enough for spit flecks to fall from her mouth to Irene's cheek, and had said, "You're a hateful child. A child of the devil. You're an ungrateful, hateful devil child." The cold stones in her mother's eyes had flashed completely sober, and Irene had found herself, in that moment, impatient for her mother to get that drink inside her, to become tolerable, to fall asleep, to go away.

But now Bernice's face didn't move. It stayed taut and she kept staring away from Irene, over Irene's head.

"You'll see me in your dreams," said Bernice. "Like we always have done."

"No," Irene said. "I won't be joining you there either. You must stop drinking, mother. You're going to die."

"I don't even drink that much," said Bernice. "You're exaggerating."

"Mom, I know you're trying to kill yourself," Irene had choked out. "I understand that you are."

"No, I'm not," Bernice snapped.

"The only sad thing," said Irene, "is watching it take so long. It's taking too long, Mom. Killing yourself this way is taking too damn long."

Irene had gone to Pittsburgh. And her mother lived and lived, and tried to write and call, but there wasn't enough guilt to bring Irene back: not to the Hinterland and not to Toledo. Then she died, and Irene came. And went back to the Toledo Institute of Astronomy, this time in triumph. It was hard not to connect the dots, and make a constellation: it would be a flame, a twisted, tangled flame. And above the flame would be not a phoenix, not a bird at all, but a girl all alone.

9

Irene's phone barked in her pocket. She fished it out and looked at the number.

"Hello?" she said. "Sparks."

She crossed a two-lane street decorated with hanging baskets of geraniums, and she was standing at the head of the main quad.

"Hello," said Belion. "Belion."

"Oh, hi, babe," said Irene. She looked down the quad at the glistening arcs and spires of the university's buildings. "I'm in Toledo."

"Yes, I know," he said.

"I'm on campus," said Irene. "Right now."

"What's it like?" Belion wanted to know.

"It's nice," said Irene. She walked straight down the quad, across the grass and the criss-crossing sidewalk squares. She passed a tall, stately marble building on the left, and on the right a smaller one, capped with a dome and surrounded by a portico. The style of the buildings was Greek revival, because obviously, Pythagoras and everything. Yet the tallest building, the one at the end of the quad, was different. Its roofs more Persian, its spires twisted and eastern, its doorways arched. And at the top, a layered series of rectangles, each one smaller, until on the last was mounted a long dome, the only elliptical observatory in the world.

"I'm coming up there," said Belion. "I just wanted to let you know."

"But why are you coming?" Irene asked.

"I'm just coming. I thought I was supposed to come."

Irene identified Herschel Hall and shoved the map into her laptop bag. She took the phone in her hand.

"You don't have to, though. What about work?"

"Work?" Belion sounded confused.

"Or the apartment?"

"I'll sublet it. Craigslist."

"Well, great. You should come then. Come then."

"Oh, I am coming."

"Great, come."

"And I mean that as a double entendre, where you say one thing and mean not only that thing but an additional thing."

"I get it."

"A sexual thing."

"Right."

"Let's just say I'm dying to know what's behind that door, but I don't want to have to shrink myself to get through."

"I'm entering a building, Belion. My reception may become sketchy."

"What building could be inside that cave, Irene?"

"It's not a cave, Belion, it's an internationally renowned school of science and math."

"I'm coming up there," said Belion. "And we're going to straighten out all this funny business."

"Enjoy," said Irene. "I left you my mother's address. That's where I'm staying."

"I can find it," Belion said. "I'll see you in a while."

Irene pushed the END CALL button on her phone. She opened the doorway to Herschel Hall and found the building directory between the gleaming elevators. There was her name, right beside the number 201. So, second floor. Upstairs. There might even be windows.

She stepped into the elevator alone, but once inside she was joined by a tall woman with bare feet and long brown hair. The woman hummed to herself as the elevator rose to the second floor, making no eye contact with Irene. When the car stopped, she drifted out between the opening doors and was gone. Irene got off the elevator and found a steel door marked 201. She swung the door open.

Her new lab was huge. Her heart skipped and jumped. There was a wall of windows but flat slats of metal made up shades that locked out all the light. Irene let the door swing shut behind her, and it clicked tightly. The lab was dim. Granite tables flanked one wall, and her microcollider, brought on a truck from the basement at Carnegie Mellon, sat disassembled in the middle of the room. Once, it was the shiniest thing. Now it almost appeared to have shrunk. On the far wall there was a desk, and on the desk was the only source of light: a laptop. Behind the laptop sat a girl.

"Hello," said the girl. "So you're here. Let the party begin."

The girl's voice was dry, her inflection sour.

"Who are you?" asked Irene.

"I'm Sam Beth," said the girl.

Irene reached out to the wall and flicked on a light. Fluorescent bulbs overhead came to life, and the room was bright.

"Ugh, switch to LED, for the love of god,"

said the girl without raising her face from the computer screen.

"What?"

"It's the switch on the left," she said. "So move your hand a bit to the left, and there it will be. Or, you can read the label. It's spelled L-E-D."

Irene switched the LED lights on and the fluorescent ones off. Then she frowned and wished she hadn't been so obedient. So automatically compliant.

"Who are you?" asked Irene again.

"I'm Sam Beth," said the girl again. Irene set her laptop bag on a table and walked toward the girl. She was Korean. Her hair was braided up into a bun on the top of her head. She wore a tracksuit — blue with white stripes running up the arms and legs.

"Yes, but who are you, what is your capacity here, what are you doing in my lab?"

"I'm your RA," said Sam Beth. "Your graduate student."

"Oh," said Irene. "I thought I would be able to interview for an assistant."

"Not assistant. Research assistant."

"Still, I should be able to interview —"

"Trust me, there's no one better," said Sam Beth. She looked up from the laptop finally, and stared down Irene. "That's why you got me."

"Oh, I see," said Irene. She noticed, seeing Sam Beth full on, that the girl had tattoos or face paint under her eyes, three red dots marking each cheekbone.

Sam Beth rolled her eyes and went back to her laptop.

Irene continued her inspection of the room. The tables were clean and bare, but there were holes drilled in a circle in the floor, holes that appeared to have been recently vacated, as if the room had been recently rearranged and something had been taken out.

"What was here?" Irene asked.

"Oh, the universe," said Sam Beth.

"What universe?"

"This one," said Sam Beth. "A model. The best model we could make anyway. It rotated. It had axes."

"Where is it now?" Irene asked.

"It's getting set up in his new lab. In the basement. It barely fits."

The sourness of Sam Beth's tone folded in on itself and became hatred.

"Whose lab was this?"

"George Dermont," said Sam Beth. "My old boss. He was a physicist. You've heard of him?"

"Yes, yes," Irene said. "My mother sent me clippings. I know who he is."

"Awww, that's cute," said Sam Beth. "Your mother sent you clippings out to Mississippi, so you could read about real astronomers and what they do? Your mother must be a nice lady."

"She's dead," said Irene, biting the word off tight and savoring it in her mouth, like a cherry.

Sam Beth snapped her laptop shut. "Oh, sorry," she said.

"You can go," said Irene. "You won't work. I'll interview for an assistant."

"So emotional," said Sam Beth on her way out the door. "Did you get to be a big important scientist like that? I doubt it."

The door closed behind her. Irene switched back to fluorescent lights. "This is how we do it in the basement," she muttered.

Irene had not gotten to be a big important scientist by being emotional. Nor by opening doors smoothly on their hinges, walking through those openings, head held high. Rather, she had got in by chewing relentlessly at the place where the wall met the floor, chewing from the outside always in the dark, chewing and chewing while the spit ran down her chin, until there was a hole big enough to pry at, and then prying relentlessly until she could squeeze inside.

It was relentless, what she did.

She walked around the lab, circling the holes in the floor. She imagined a body outlined in the center, sketched in with masking tape. Outside the body and inside the circle of holes, there would be words where someone had scribbled, "Mysterious body found on this spot. Cause of death unknown." The scientist who had worked in this lab, did he feel defeated and wronged? Did he feel like, *Fuck it, I'll never get it right.* Or was he right on the verge of something, too?

Probably Sam Beth would go and tell him now what a bitch she was. Irene should have been more authoritative.

"You'll never make friends by being such a smart-ass, Irene," her mother had said. "Be lovable. Be small. You're so small, you're barely alive. Can you stand to be nice to someone at some point in your life, just to be nice?"

Irene rewound the conversation with Sam Beth in her head. She imagined how the conversation would have gone if her mother's body inhabited the imagined masking-tape outline on the floor in the center of the universe.

"Hello, who are you?" Irene would have said.

147

"Oh my god, it's a body!" Sam Beth would have said.

Not better, just different, thought Irene. *She still runs from the room, and I am still here alone.*

"I'm sorry," said Sam Beth from the doorway.

"For what?" Irene asked.

"For being bad," said Sam Beth. "It's just that I'd rather work for George."

"That's fine," said Irene. "I'm not bothered."

"If you weren't here, he would be," said Sam Beth. She threw one booted leg up on the door frame and pushed at it, her back pushing against the other side.

"Yeah? Hey, it says here on this sheet that I'm supposed to work with an RA called Patrice."

"That's me," said Sam Beth.

"Your name is Patrice?"

"My name is Sam Beth. That's my Chaldean name."

Irene looked up at her with a measured stare.

"Chaldean?"

"Babylon. The Persian Sibyl? Don't you know anything about the Daughters of Babylon?"

"No," said Irene. "Do they all have eye dots?"

Sam Beth did not get angry. "If you read those articles your mother sent you, and the work of Dr. Dermont" — she coughed a little bit — "of George, you would know about the whirlwind, and the stormwind, and the significance of the mystic called Sambethe to the room you are standing in, the universe you are inhabiting."

She pulled the hood of her tracksuit around her face as if it were a monastic cowl. Irene put it together then. This nut-bag Dermont, whom her mother kept trying to impress her with, had grand ideas about the shape of the universe as defined by ancient concepts of transformative symmetry. It was stupid stuff, the kind of thing that gets lapped up by pop culture magazines and young people who don't really understand math.

"Doesn't he believe that Toledo is built on the ruins of ancient Babylon or something? Like, the Maumee River is the Euphrates?" Irene asked with a gentle sneer.

"The Maumee River is the Tigris," said Sam Beth. "On an axis of asymmetry defined by the prime meridian, Toledo and Babylon are phenomenological twins."

"That is just utter bullshit," said Irene,

looking at the paperwork in front of her. "Utter and complete drivel. We need a scouring pad and a bucket, right away. I can smell the ridicule of such a nutty idea still bouncing around in here."

"It's OK," Sam Beth purred. "I know it's hard to understand. Maybe when you meet him, you'll discover —"

"Wow, so this is what sycophantic opportunism looks like from the front," said Irene, staring down Sam Beth who was still standing in the doorway.

"I will always take care of him," Sam Beth replied. "But how will I take care of you?"

When Irene got back to her mother's house, Belion was already there, sitting on the sofa, his laptop on his knee.

"I went ahead and set up a hotspot," he said. "Your mom didn't have Wi-Fi."

Later, the lights were out, but the street-light sent an orange glow into her mother's bedroom. Irene had changed the sheets, had changed the pillowcases, but the laundry soap was lavender, the fabric softener lavender, and lavender permeated the room. Irene shut the door and closed the blinds. Belion was naked on the bed. His huge bulk sank into the center of this bed, made of high-density foam, conforming to his irregular contours, embracing him. Irene walked over to the bed. She slipped a ponytail holder around her hair and pulled it high and tight on her skull.

"Is it too soon?" he asked her. His words sounded like a prayer, thin and hopeful.

Irene didn't respond, but climbed onto the foot of the bed and approached him on her knees. She smacked her left hand onto one meaty thigh, her right hand onto the other thigh, and pushed his legs apart sharply. She hooked her elbows under his knees.

"Oh, God," said Belion. His hand shot out and grabbed a lacy pillow, pressed it against his face.

"Go ahead and yell," said Irene, making words against his skin. "Alarm the neighbors."

He stiffened under her, this huge block of flesh that was following her around. If she was being cruel, driving into him only to pull herself away, she felt it was justified, with him being so bold. He brought himself here with his legs wide open, her mother not even buried. So she was cold with him, pulling back just when he needed her most, but in the end she became merciful and sweet. She felt herself unspool inside, a warmth emerging, a generosity of spirit, and she got softer, she let her understanding take over. Then her hesitation wasn't mean but thoughtful, her mouth not full of teeth but full of tongues.

Why not? She felt herself standing on the side of the bridge, her hair blowing this way and that, looking at the water. Why not unloose her tongue, let it wrap around the first thing that could save it?

"This is all about control with you," one guy had said, who wanted to feel her breasts against him while they slept.

"Why don't you shut the fuck up," she had said. And then she'd dumped him for a guy with a little less enthusiasm for introspection and analysis.

When she was done with Belion, she left him sprawled on the bed and went to the bathroom to clean up. Irene had a saying about mouthwash: "Know Listerine, know oral sex. No Listerine, no oral sex." It wasn't snappy, and it wouldn't fit on a bumper sticker, but it went through her head every time she spilled the burning liquid into her mouth and imagined all the little germs popping like balloons. She could hold Listerine in her mouth forever. But then she spit it out. It was full of alcohol.

Irene loosed her ponytail, washed her face, and went back to bed. When she saw Be-

lion, he had pulled the sheet up. She thought
he was asleep, and tucked herself as quietly
as possible into a corner of the bed. But he
was not asleep.

"Babe please, can I feel inside you?"

"No," said Irene. She imagined a large,
blunt finger scrubbing around in her underwear. Pushing itself against her pubic bone.
Thumping away at her.

"I'll make you feel better, I promise," said
Belion.

"I don't feel bad," said Irene. "I feel glad."

In the morning, when Irene opened her
eyes, he was still there. That night, at a
welcome banquet for new faculty and students, he would be her date. The institute
would announce her addition to the staff,
welcome freshmen and new graduate students. She was content with taking Belion
as her date. With him in town, she felt more
like herself. She was Irene Sparks, girlfriend
of Belion, virgin from the neck down, scrap-
per, chewer, magic bean eschewer.

She got up, opened the blinds. Belion lay
inert on the bed.

"Get up, Belion! Time to wake up!"

Irene stepped into the bathroom and
turned on the shower, then began to count
in her head as she brushed her teeth. Irene

finished brushing her teeth and put her hand against the glass shower door. It was still cold.

Belion had rolled over to her side of the bed and had buried his face in her pillow, her mother's pillow.

"You know what's funny," he said. He rolled over again and was lying on his back. "Is when people say, like, 'He took it in the shorts' or 'I stabbed you in the shorts.' "

"Those aren't real phrases," said Irene.

"Yes, they are," said Belion. "You know, 'He took it in the shorts.' "

Irene stopped fiddling with things on the sink and stood with her hand on the shower stall's glass pane. Just waiting for it to heat up so she could get inside. Belion giggled to himself. She could see his balls, so ponderous, lolling against his thigh.

"Belion," she said, "there is no such phrase."

"There is so," he said belligerently.

"No, there's not," she said.

"Fine," said Belion, "let's do a search on 'took it in the shorts.' "

Belion reached his hand over to the floor and pulled his laptop up onto the bed. He rolled over onto his stomach, so she could see his furred butt and the broad expanse of his back as he typed into the tiny machine. One thing about Belion: for a big fat guy, he was really very lithe.

Irene felt the glass get hot. She shed her robe and slipped into the shower. She could no longer see him.

"Here it is," hollered Belion. "Listen to this: 'As a consequence, I think the foxes kind of took it in the shorts. They ended up getting persecuted by coyotes.' And that's on the PBS Web site!"

Irene poured shampoo into her hand. "You're making that up!" she said.

"Here's another one," he called to her. " 'Needless to say, fame was not to knock this time around, and the boys took it in the shorts!' Two is proof! Your rule!"

There was a pause. "OK, well, I must have made up 'stabbed you in the shorts' because there's nothing on that. But it would be funny, if there was."

Irene rolled her eyes.

"Baby, can I take a shower with you?"

Irene said nothing.

Scrabbling through her mother's desk, looking for the keys to the garage, she found this poem:

How did I get you? I'll tell you.
    I bought an old crock at an auction, a

155

brown crock marked with a five, for five gallons. I paid twelve dollars for the crock. The crock was dusty inside with cobwebs and plaster, and I reached in, down deep inside, and I felt you in there. You were warm and dry, curled in the bottom. My hand touched your back. I wanted to see what was in there, and so I found you. Dust in your eyelashes and spider web sticking your eyes shut tight.

I knit you out of my own hair. I made you out of three hundred daisies strung together. I collected your pieces for years, and then put you together, click by click, until you suddenly cried.

Out on a farm there is a long line of sunken spots where an underground spring runs down the hill underneath the grass and topsoil. In the middle of summer, I found deep holes in some of the spots, damp and mossy — not animal holes. And I lay down on the grass, and stuck my arm down deep inside, to see if I could touch the water. But I touched your hair, stuck with earth to your head, and you were damp, and when I brought you out, there was water on your face that looked like dew.

That's how I found you.

Irene looked at the artifact in her hand and found herself wondering who the woman was who had written this poem, and for what child it had been written. Even as she wondered, she knew: it was written by her mother for her. Death is final, and there is no going back to ask questions. Her mother was gone from the world and gone from the dreamworld. But Irene had questions, questions she could never ask the drunk woman who was her mother, but maybe when she was dead, and they were both just dead people on equal footing, Irene would be able to ask all the questions: *Why set a fire, and burn down our house? Why have a baby, if you didn't want one?*

What is my emotional connection to the dead person that was my mother? Irene wanted to know.

She picked up her own keys and drove to her favorite bridge for the first time since her return to Toledo. Maybe standing on the bridge, in the quiet space before the fall, everything would make sense.

Toledo's Anthony Wayne Bridge is blue and white and wide. Two tall towers are draped with huge suspension cables, and the bridge rises in a high arc over the Maumee River. It is ninety years old. In Pittsburgh, Irene had spent many moments on the George Westinghouse Bridge, an arch bridge made of concrete, staring down at where the train tracks crossed the brown water of Turtle Creek.

Now Irene parked her car in a back corner of the Owens Corning lot and walked up the bridge's long ramp toward the river. Cars went whizzing past her, decelerating as they left the bridge, and Irene felt her body relax a bit. On the Anthony Wayne Bridge, there is a tall cyclone fence along the walkway. This fence is too high to climb without attracting attention and curves inward at the top for extra safety. Irene always found it funny that when you get farther along and the bridge is over water, this fence just stops. Between the two towers, you can lean over the railing as far as you like. If you lean far enough, you can fall right in. It is as if the people who define the safety regulations for bridges did not consider the idea that a person would ever go near the railing of a bridge over water, that they would only be in danger of spilling off a bridge over land.

Irene knew that Bernice had killed herself — maybe not through a tumble down some stairs, but through an intentional consumption of a poisonous amount of alcohol, over days, hours, or years. She knew the impulse that led her mother down to death. Or did she? Where did it start? With the fire? With the birth of her daughter? What was the moment that led to the rest of her life, and how could Irene steer past that moment, guide herself to safety?

Suicide has an event horizon, Irene thought. *Death does not.* Death can take you quickly, and you are gone, but suicide has a slow approach. It takes years sometimes, or it takes a whole lifetime. But there must be some pivotal moment, a moment that goes by as quickly as any other in your life. A point of no return: the trigger is pulled, the body tips forward or backward off the bridge, the chair is kicked. After this moment has passed, you keep on living, but it's a different kind of life. A life in which nothing you decide or think or do can change what is happening. Time stretches, as you pass through it. Some say you see your life pass before your eyes. That would take a long time. Longer than the four seconds it takes to fall from a bridge and be crushed on the water's surface. But because of the special behavior of light and time around the singularity of a death, there is enough time. There is unlimited time. And then you are dead.

If you crossed the event horizon of an actual black hole, and your friend was standing safely outside the event horizon, watching you, it would be the same. You pass an invisible threshold. You cannot tell when you are beyond hope. There's no signpost. You might be saying something, like, "I can't handle this pain anymore. I want to die." To you, traveling toward the singularity, the words would come out like normal, and you would hear them coming out of your mouth one after the other, a perfectly rational explanation for what you were doing. But to your friend, outside the accretion disk, the words would come at increasingly perplexing intervals. The gaps between the words would stretch and stretch, until years passed between "I" and "want" and then decades until "to," and maybe your friend would age and sicken and die herself before the word "die" managed to reach her. At which point she would have already found out what you wanted to do.

Some physicists had written about how a person entering a black hole might experience the entire future history of the universe, wrapped around that endless last moment of life. Irene just wanted to know . . . when did her mother begin to want to die?

"I see you falling," Irene's mother had told her. "I see you falling to your death. It's happening, almost every time I close my eyes." This was when she had forbidden Irene to travel by air, insisted Irene drive everywhere, never visit Europe. They had been to South America by boat. "Airplanes are not for you," her mother said. "Trust me." And while Irene had nodded and complied, she had privately thought it was all part of the same bullshit. And yet when your mother tells you you are going to die, and how, can she really be ignored? What kind of mother tells her daughter this, and then dies falling down the stairs?

I don't miss you at all, Irene thought to her mother. *Whenever I start to think I'm missing you, I remind myself that it is nonsense.*

Irene passed the first high tower, and a jogger went huffing past her, going toward the center of the bridge. She slowed and watched him go, and then she went up there herself, stood in the middle, where the suspension cables dip down to the bridge's deck. From here you can hoist yourself up onto the main cable, and using the guide wires you can walk your way up it right to the top of the tower. Most jumpers think they have to climb these cables to get high enough to die, but Irene knew that this was not the case. You could die just as well from the drop at the center of the bridge. Everyone knew that climbers didn't really jump, and real jumpers didn't climb. Irene stood there at the center of the bridge, listening to the cars hissing past behind her. A whiff of the harbor reached her nose as she leaned on the railing, her body pressing out into the air, probing for the transition between standing and falling, the point at which impact becomes inevitable.

She looked down at the shallow water on the west side of the river, where a pair of fishermen had managed to upend their boat. They struggled with it, sinking into the sand, trying to get it right.

10

The Max Planck Memorial Ballroom was sponsored by the Hamburg Plancks, in honor of their progenitor's contribution to the world of science. It inhabited its own gorgeous building at the Toledo Institute of Astronomy, and on this night it was lit up like the Horsehead Nebula on the Fourth of July. Chandeliers sparkled in the lobby, leaded glass windows glittered up and down the façade, and a stunning brass astrolabe decorated the lobby, surrounded by cocktail waitresses spinning in a bright, bubbling orbit. The night of the annual welcome banquet was truly a night of a thousand stars, and the party was thrown in honor of the glamorous new acquisitions the institute could boast about in brochures and the incoming students, who dreamed of becoming such celebrated guests.

George and Kate Oakenshield emerged from his wagon, and George tossed the keys to the valet along with a twenty-dollar bill. He wore gray jeans, a white shirt he'd already opened at the throat, and a gray striped tie he'd already untied. When he got out of his car, a couple of undergraduates fluttered to the sidewalk and then shyly hid under a tree as he came around the vehicle, collected Kate Oakenshield on his arm, and strode into the building. No, he was not the star of the evening, nor was he even any longer the brilliant ingenue. He needed a breakthrough, and he needed it soon. But he still commanded a modicum of respect among the gentlemen, and the ladies still found he brought color to their cheeks. Kate drifted along beside him, in a droopy and romantic lemon chiffon.

Inside the lobby, George immediately spotted Father Oakenshield, wearing a clerical collar and pacing thoughtfully up and down one wall.

He called, "Mr. Oakenshield!"

Kate corrected him quietly and immediately. "Father."

"OK," said George aside to her. "But he doesn't have a parish. He's never preached a sermon. Father of what? Why does he wear that outfit?"

Kate said, "Father of me."

They reached him. George and Father

Oakenshield shook hands. Father Oakenshield maintained a certain ascetic distance from his surroundings. His face was pinched and disapproving, his aspect removed. His eyebrows said he was aghast. His hands spread apart, as if to say, "What can I do? Here I am. I participate." He had served his prison sentence and emerged unapologetic, and since Kate had turned eighteen, he was allowed to be near her again, by her choice.

"George, how are you?" he said, and then he turned and warbled something to Kate.

She warbled something back. She wouldn't speak in English when her father was around. Her voice sounded to George like a wood thrush at dusk. Vaguely chorded, pretty, but incomprehensible.

"Well, that's just great," said George, as if to a passing waiter. "Great evening. OK!"

George saw his mother and father coming in the door from outside. Sally wore a stylish camel-colored evening gown and the soft stretchy wrap she'd gotten in Panama last year. Her hair was blown back and restrained, her diamond earrings flashing. George's father walked a step behind her, and off to her side. He had been stuffed into a tuxedo and had a hunted air. His hands floated around, unanchored. George saw Sally take him firmly by the arm and propel him toward the ballroom entrance.

"Hey, hey, Mom," he called. George interrupted their progress and called them over to join him, Kate, and Father Oakenshield.

"Dad! Here we are."

He clapped his father on both biceps, convivially. He kissed Sally on the cheek.

"Mom, you look beautiful. Dad, thanks for coming. You look . . . in attendance."

"Well," said his father, "your mother said I can't eat in the house anymore if I don't start behaving like a human being."

At this, Dean stretched his arms out as if to demonstrate that he had, in fact, taken the shape of a human man. When he smiled, George thought he was being very charming. He dropped an exaggerated wink on Kate. Sally beamed at George, unperturbed.

"Good job, Dad," said George. "Dad, Mom, you know Kate. And this is Father Oakenshield."

"Ah, yes, the jailer!" Sally said. "Well met, Father. How is the tallest tower, now the princess has flown away?"

Father Oakenshield gazed scornfully at Sally, and licked his lips.

"I don't expect you to understand my daughter," said Father Oakenshield, taking Kate's hand away from Sally.

"Her I understand just fine," said Sally,

taking Kate's hand back with firmness. "It's you I'd like to beat with a stick, buddy."

"You and I will have to accept our differences, Sally, if our children are going to marry."

Sally balked.

"Who said anything about marrying?" she asked.

"I have seen it in her computations," said her father. "A new candor. A new simplicity. She is in love."

Sally pinched George on the arm. "What, with HIM?"

"George understands her," Father Oakenshield elaborated. "I always knew she would marry a mathematician. No one else could appreciate the subtleties of her training."

"Bullshit," said Sally, not quietly.

"Mom," George began.

"Yeah, I give it six months," she said. "Here's a clue, Padre. He only seduced your little chickadee because he thought he couldn't do it. Now that it's done, it's done, you know what I mean?"

"Not done," George interjected. He shook his head at Kate's father. "Not done in any sense of the word. Not done. Did not do."

"I do not see what you mean in the slightest," Oakenshield said to Sally. And then, without warning, Sally pulled back her smooth, toned arm and punched Father Oakenshield right in the nose.

Inside the ballroom, wall sconces shed a warm glow on a rich red carpet, black wood trim, and round tables spread with bright white clothes, dappled with glittering cutlery and crystal plates. The parquet floor was inlaid with deep hardwoods, glorious chandeliers blossomed from the carved ceiling, and paneled walls were hung with oil paintings of popular constellations. A podium at the front of the room was flanked by two tables, and rows of chairs faced the podium. At the back of the room the caterers' tables were set up with hors d'oeuvres. Among other things, there was a chocolate fountain and a champagne pyramid, ready to be filled.

Academics milled around, finding their places with their wives, their children, their grandchildren in some cases. Dean and Sally, Kate and George, and Father Oakenshield were supposed to sit together at a table, according to cards on the plates, but Father Oakenshield lingered behind, leaving one seat open at their table. When a large man entered the ballroom, clearly late and looking for a place to sit, George saw an opportunity to remove Father Oakenshield from his mother's arm's length, and motioned the man to come and sit with them at their table.

"Belion," said the big man. He shook hands with George and sat down daintily on a folding chair. He looked like an elephant on a Victorian footstool. Sally's eyes widened and she placed a hand on his arm, taking to him immediately.

"Hello," she said, in hushed tones, for the program was beginning on the dais.

"Belion," said Belion, and stuck out his hand.

"Well, don't you look dashing and debonair?"

"I wore a tuxedo," said Belion, to explain. His tuxedo was immaculate, and his hair was neatly brushed.

"My husband, Dean," said Sally, pointing to George's father, "and my son, George."

Belion nodded blithely, and Sally turned to George.

"You've got to get rid of that girl, son. It's just getting ridiculous."

"Now, Mother." George adopted a calming tone. "I told you last year what the astrologer down on Bancroft said. Brown hair, astronomer, Toledo. There are only so many, you know."

"But that's so limiting. Only astronomers?"

"Mother, come now. You don't want to go against the psychic, do you? Against fate?"

"No," said Sally wryly. "No, I wouldn't want to go against her."

"There you are," said George, patting her arm. "You know best."

At the front of the ballroom, the scientists and guests were taking their places at the head table. The microphone had been checked, a glass of water had been installed near it, and now as the others were seated, Dr. Bryant stepped up to the podium. The lights in the ballroom got a bit dimmer, except for those trained on the stage. The chandeliers above the assembled crowd twinkled warmly but were muted now, their false candlesticks playing in hushed light against their brass ligatures. George pinched his forehead between both his thumbs and exhaled.

"Good evening," said Dr. Bryant. "Welcome to our favorite annual event. Welcome to our new faculty and their families, welcome to our patrons, our friends, to my colleagues, to the future of astronomy."

Everyone applauded. George applauded. Oakenshield, in the back, dabbed his nose with a cloth napkin. The waiters surrounded the tables and ladled bisque into bowls, the top layer of flatware and cutlery assembled before all the diners. Sally picked up her spoon and expertly dipped it into the soup, delivering it neatly to her lower lip. Belion dandled his spoon in his soup bowl, pushing a cheese crouton around. George trained his eyes on the floor, suddenly feeling dizzy. If he looked at his soup a wave of nausea might surprise him into puking in it. There on the carpet was a rich pattern of curling vines and leaves, a baroque array of ornaments in large circular arrangements. And cherubs.

And then the cherubs were moving.

Dr. Bryant continued, "Our work, here at the institute, and around the world in other ivory towers, or rather aluminum domes, often goes unnoticed, except when we have enough beautiful pictures to warrant a coffee table publication, or when Hollywood decides to make two asteroid movies in the space of a summer."

There was a polite chuckle. Dean coughed out a loud laugh, but no one looked over. George was watching the rug very carefully now, his brow furrowed. The cherubs that had been so still, clinging to vines along the very predictable columns woven into the rug, had swung down off the vines and were clambering over the columns and other greenery — woven into the rug in muted tones of gold — and headed toward the head table and the dais.

"We know, as scientists, as mathematicians, that recognition will be interspersed with long intervals of quiet, solitude, in the shadow of the world's attention. We all need the courage to be ignored."

The audience nodded, spooned up their soup.

"Of course, we also hope, on behalf of ourselves, our students, and the institute itself, to draw the world's eye back to astronomy on occasion. Not because the world is about to end, of course, but because we have unlocked another secret, another mystery."

Dr. Bryant waved affectionately toward the new faculty on his right. George looked up, squinting, and when he looked back down at the rug, the cherubs had all congregated in front of the microphone and were now pointing excitedly at it, as if to say, "Look, George!"

"Perhaps one of these, the new additions to the TIA family of scientists and scholars, could be the next one to put the stars back on the front page."

Applause sounded in the room. The rug

cherubs clapped and turned somersaults. Several marble gargoyles from around the edge of the ceiling now appeared to creep across to where Dr. Bryant was standing and aligned themselves behind him in a bunch. Were they muttering to each other? Were they nodding? Were the columns painted into the walls now hiding flocks of naiads who were peeking around at George, giggling, tugging at each other, and gesturing to him?

"Now without any more pontification on my part," he went on, clearing his throat, "Let me introduce our featured speaker this evening, one of our new fellows . . . joining us from Carnegie Mellon University, with a brand new Ph.D. in computational astrophysics and a two-page spread in *USA Today* coming out tomorrow, covering her groundbreaking research in the genesis of black holes, Dr. Irene Sparks."

A small dark-haired woman rose from her seat at the head table and went to the podium. She shook hands graciously with Dr. Bryant. He bent down, removed a small block of wood from inside the podium and set it there for her on the floor, and she took a step up on it to stand behind the microphone. She faced her audience, politely smiling. George strained to see better. This woman was the one who'd taken his office and his assistant.

They were probably fifty feet away from each other. How far is fifty feet? To the top of the tallest tree? From one lip of a volcano to the other? As far as a man can go in ten seconds, striding briskly? As far as a man can go in five seconds, falling over himself in enthusiasm? Irene Sparks surveyed the room with a wide smile on her face, as if public speaking classes had encouraged her to make eye contact with the audience.

When she looked at him, George felt himself rising, involuntarily, from his seat. She did not continue showing her friendly smile to the room. She looked straight at him and she halted. From behind the columns painted to the walls, the naiads pointed their fingers. From the cherubs pulling eagerly on vines in the rug, from the gargoyles flocked against the ceiling, all the demigodly fingers were pointing, as if in a giant circle radiating inward, and telling him: her.

It's not like time stopped for George, or like the stars suddenly shone brighter. It's not like there were fireworks, or avalanches, or that the woodpecker drilling a hole in the side of his head paused to say, "Wow, she's a looker." It's more like every electron in every atom in the universe paused, breathed in deeply, assessed the situation, and then reversed its course, spinning backward, or the other way, which was the right way all along. And afterward, the universe was exactly the same, but infinitely more right.

"It's you," said George. And his mother, next to him, grabbed him by the back of the pants and pulled him down into his seat.

Irene's jaw dropped. He saw her falter. He felt the moments ticking by, moments where she wasn't saying anything.

"It's her, Mom," said George, pushing his mother's arm away. "She's right there." He said it loudly enough for the room to hear.

"George, sit down, and take some medicine," said Sally, reaching in her bag for a prescription bottle. "Here, have a pain pill."

For George it was as though a seed that had been sitting in his brain for twenty years had now opened, sprouted, and flowered in a moment. As though his ears had just popped or he'd just been plunged into water and a whole new layer of sound and feeling was available to him.

He looked at Irene on the podium, blinking stupidly. She obviously couldn't remember what she was going to say. George beamed stupidly back at her. He felt she knew him. He felt she heard him say, "I missed you. I'm so glad you're here."

Everyone else assumed it was stage fright. Irene picked up the water glass and took an indelicate chug. She pressed her lips together.

"Thank you," she said. George heard her make the words with her mouth. He took in the way she made the words, the way she moved her mouth, the way her hand went up to poke at her hair, the way one foot went sideways, scraping the side of her heel against the podium. It was all so admirable. He admired it.

"Thank you," she said again. "I want to thank my new colleagues at the institute for choosing me to receive this position."

The people in the room nodded at each other. It was alright. She was going to be OK.

Irene took a couple of deep breaths and looked up at the ceiling. *Look at me,* thought George. *Look at me, I'm right here. I want you to look at ME.*

"You know, when I told my boyfriend I was going to create a black hole in my laboratory, he was like, 'Wow, I hope you have a really excellent copper casing and a very accurate calibrator for your magnetic containment field!' "

Boyfriend, thought George. But the word

didn't really mean anything. She laughed nervously. The rest of the room was silent. "No, actually he didn't say that. But, obviously, since the earth and all matter didn't collapse into my work space, I must have had the thing calibrated pretty well."

Irene glanced around the room. It seemed like she was purposefully avoiding looking at George. The cherubs laughed. The naiads slapped their naked thighs. The gargoyles were pulling the petals out of the ornamental daisies on the stone decorations. She loves him. She loves him not.

"Little did I know the attention my experiment would receive. I'm just so humbled, and grateful, to be here. With all of you . . ."

Irene's eyes locked onto George's again, and he felt the sensation of being plunged underwater, feeling lighter, looser, more fish-like.

"I haven't been able to understand exactly why I was a scientist," said Irene to George, "until now. Have I? Have I been able to?"

George nodded his head vigorously. He had not been listening to the words she was saying, but he felt sure any question she asked must be answered with "Yes."

"But now I do," she said. "Thank you."

Dr. Bryant stood up and began to applaud, gesturing to the audience to do the same. He took Irene by the arm and gently led her to her seat. She shook her head. She seemed to be still talking. But the audience was enthusiastic. They clapped and clapped.

I'm having a heart attack, thought Irene. *I'm dying, I'm dying, I'm dying. This is it.*

Death does have an event horizon, she realized in that moment. Surely this must explain why she could still hear the reception going on around her, still smell the lobster ravioli on the plate next to her, still hear the band, a couple of Bolivians with acoustic guitars and a Latin drum kit crooning. Maybe she would remember everything that happened before the fire. Maybe her life would parade before her eyes as her heart clutched and cramped, her brain failed from oxygen deficiency, her eyes closed. To everyone around her, it would seem that she fell straight to the floor. But to her, a lifetime of movement and memory would pass between the heart attack and the death. Time to think of everything. She waited for the slide-show to begin.

Some of the astronomers and their rich enablers were taking a spin around the dance floor, trying to samba or just shake it.

"I need a drink," said Irene aloud to no

one in particular, and she stood up. With her legs under her, her heart raced and skipped, but she was able to walk. She wasn't looking for the man at the table with Belion. But there he was, beside her, at the table where drinks were being served. She asked for a ginger ale. He was so familiar and so attractive, but she had never met him before. She wanted to say, *How are you? How have you been?*

A past life maybe, said her mother's dreamy voice in her ear. *In a past life, you were lovers.*

"Who are you?" she said. "Do I know you?"

"I'm George," he said. "George Dermont."

He was tall, smiling. He looked so glad to see her. She felt she might put her arms back around him, press her face into his ribs. *I missed you,* she might say. Or some stupid thing that one of her mother's clients would come up with. We were Scottish lords and ladies together. We were locked in a pyramid together. We were climbing the Andes together. Whatever. *Where have you been?*

"Oh, right, Dermont." She felt a twinge of surprise that this man and the man she'd taken her office from would be the same.

"You're sort of . . . religious, is that right? And I've got your lab and assistant now. How you must hate me."

"No, no!" he said, grinning. He seemed incapable of controlling his hands, switching his drink from one to the other, leaning on the table, fussing with his collar. She could not help but imagine those hands touching her hair, pulling at it, lodging themselves in it. There was some force pulling her ribs to his, her internal organs to his. As if she could never be warm again, without the warmth in his torso, without her face in his neck.

"I really like you," he said. "I mean, I'm not religious. You'll see, once you get to know me."

"I think you dabbled with one of my friends at the University of Toledo, years ago," said Irene. She felt herself scrabbling backward from him and this attraction, like she was cutting off tentacles of herself as they reached out for him, freezing them off, cauterizing the stumps.

"Probably not," he said. "Well, was she an astronomer? I —"

Irene picked up the ginger ale that the man in the jacket had set down for her.

"And you believe the stars are God's daisy chain or something like that . . . I actually read your abstract for that piece in the *Dark Star Review*."

Irene wanted to leave and go back to the dais and safety, but she could not. She was looking at his face, his pink cheeks, the dark curve of his brow, his square chin. There was something about her body that was saying to her brain that he was already hers. She recognized him, and she couldn't turn away from him. She wanted to go toward him, to slip her hand inside the button placket of his shirt, and touch his skin, and feel his heartbeat with her hand. It was a palpable want. She felt that if possible she should be very mean to him. As a precaution.

"You read that?" said George.

"My mother sends me clippings sometimes . . . you know, she doesn't know a lot about real astronomy. She's an astrologer."

"How strange. My mother used to be an astrologer, too."

"Really," said Irene. She took a deep pull of her ginger ale, suddenly feeling so dry.

"I mean, not a professional one. Just an amateur one."

"Mmm," she said. There was a flush creeping over his throat. His eyes kept darting back and forth from her to the rug. He seemed on edge, excited.

"I'm a — oh what can I say —"

"Are those your parents?" said Irene, pointing over to the table where George had been sitting.

"Yes," said George. "Those are my parents. Right over there."

"We should go over," said Irene. "I think your parents are devouring my boyfriend by inches."

"Is that your boyfriend? Well, I hope they came hungry," said George quickly, and then his jaw dropped and he stared at her, stricken. "Did I just say that? I'm so sorry."

"That was not kind," she said to him. But she found she was smiling. And she recognized also, in that second, that her heart had slowed to a reasonable pace, and she was no longer dying. But she did not slip her hand into his. She did not nudge him with her shoulder. She was in control of her body.

"Sorry, it's just — you're so beautiful. I didn't think he could be your boyfriend. I'm sorry, I'm sure he's really . . . smart?"

Irene picked up her drink and walked off to the table, glancing backward to George in what she meant to be a reproving glare, before she sat down decisively on Belion's lap. But had she winked at him instead? Had that happened to her face?

"Hello," said the man George introduced as his father. "I'm Dean. So nice to meet you."

"Dean," said Irene. "I'm Irene. And this is my boyfriend, Belion."

"Belion was just telling us about how he is an immortal in a role-playing game. That must be very exciting," said the woman George introduced as his mother. "Being an immortal."

"I don't play," said Irene.

"It is," said Belion. "Very."

"Reminds me of good old Uncle Ray," said Dean. "He thought he was an immortal, too."

"Uncle Ray!" said George, joining the table but standing awkwardly behind Kate Oakenshield's chair. "Yes, in a way. He was perfectly immortal, right up until the time he shot himself playing Russian roulette."

"Wow, really?" said Belion. "I didn't even think that game was real."

"It's not necessary to go into all this," said Sally.

"Uncle Ray!" Dean went on, entertaining the table. "Yes, he was the finest of uncles. He escaped from prison once on a cow."

"What?" said Belion, profoundly interested.

"It was a low-security prison," said

George. "He used the cow to swim across a river. True story."

"This is not appropriate," Sally said. "I don't think we need to talk about Uncle Ray anymore. You're making him sound like Paul Bunyan or something."

"Paul Bunyan," said Belion with arch solemnity. "Was my father."

Dean laughed long and loud. "I like you, Belion," he said to Belion. "You are not so bad."

"Belion," said Irene. "I'm tired. I think we need to go. Goodnight, all. Goodnight, George."

Outside the ballroom, locusts whirred in the branches of the maple trees, and the occasional breeze set the leaves stirring and rippling. Couples and groups meandered down the street or popped into cars the valets were bringing around. Irene and Belion had gone home, with Belion packed into her little car and Irene driving. George stood by himself on the sidewalk, just thinking about her, and wondering how soon he could get her into his orbit again.

There was a noise at his elbow and he looked over and it was Kate Oakenshield, the girl who was raised mute.

"Oh, hey," he said. "There you are."

184

She said, "I want to go home with Dad."

"What, back to his house?" George asked. He saw her father coming close, and his own parents right behind.

"Yes, to my house," said Kate. Her face was wounded, as if she knew she was no longer in the target position. George softened. Poor thing. She wasn't Irene, but who could be Irene? No one. There was only one Irene.

"That's not a good idea, Kate," he said.

His mother interjected. "Let her go."

"Yes, do," said her father.

Kate warbled, "Broodle bree, deedoodle! Deeedoo!"

George wavered. On the one hand, there was the fact that Kate should not be in her father's house. On the other hand, there was the fact that Irene said goodnight to him in such a charming way, almost as if to give him a secret signal that she was about to ditch Belion and swing back around to pick him up instead.

"OK," said George. He bit his lip and put his hand protectively on Kate Oakenshield's arm. "If you need anything, you call me. Or my mom. If I'm out. Or busy."

"Push off, Dermont," said her father, the heel of his shoe striking angrily against the sidewalk and echoing in the stillness against the other buildings.

Sally brandished her fist, "Hey, are you looking for more love, Padre?"

"You stay away from me," said Father Oakenshield, shepherding Kate away from them. "You're a monster."

"You're the monster," jeered Sally. "Freak."

Father Oakenshield and Kate, wrapped in her shawl, huddled off down the sidewalk toward the parking lot, tweeting and twittering at each other and producing rapid arpeggios. George turned to his mother and took her by the elbows.

"Mom," he said. "Listen!"

"I know, I'm sorry, I'm sorry. I get so excited. I sound like a twelve-year-old."

George said, "No, I don't even care about that."

Sally pulled her wrap around her arms more firmly, and a valet popped up at George's arm, ready to retrieve his car. George produced a ticket and handed it to the man.

"Really," Sally said. "Hmm? What then, darling?"

"It's that girl! The black hole girl."

Sally frowned, her finger tapping on her cheek, "Hmm . . . Irene Sparks . . ."

"Come on, Mom, isn't she gorgeous?

She's not even very, ah, scientific looking. More like, oh, I don't know, Aphrodite? Helen of Troy?"

"George, my son, my son," said his mother, as her face pulled into a wry smile. "Has your attention really been captured by that little black cloud in a dress?"

"I can't stop thinking about her."

"How interesting. I don't see it happening, George," she said coldly. "But it is so interesting."

"Do we know her, Mother?" said George.

"What? No, of course we don't."

"Because when I see her," he went on, as if she hadn't answered no, "I don't miss anyone. I just feel happy that she's near."

"Speaking of near," said his mother. "Where has your father wandered off to?"

They both recalled the existence of Dean, and looked around to discover that he had climbed a tree.

"Good grief," said Sally, but with warmth and affection that made George happy. "I can't take my eyes off him for a second."

11

When Sally and Bernice were children, they were best friends. They met on a playground.

"Push me," Sally had said to Bernice, who was just getting her own swing started. "Push me and then I'll push you."

Sally had long legs, and Bernice was smaller. Bernice was new to the school, but Sally had been there from kindergarten. They were in fifth grade, when the other girls were starting to say that swings were for babies. But Bernice had come to play on the swings because she saw Sally sitting there, ineffectually kicking those long legs around in the sand under her swing. Bernice hopped down and came to stand behind Sally. She put her hands on both sides of the hard rubber swing and pulled back, back, as far as she could go, scrambling for purchase with her heels on the scrubby grass beside the sandy pits. When she had lifted Sally as far as she could, she let go. Sally stuck her legs out and pumped, grabbing the swing chain hard and pulling against it. When she came back toward Bernice the smaller girl had to step out of the way fast as Sally's big feet came toward her, clad in massive clogs. When she went whooshing forward again, Sally leaned back far, so her blond hair was streaming, and she laughed a big horsey laugh, her eyes squinched together, her body arcing and bucking with laughing.

"I love the swing!" said Sally.

"Me too," said Bernice.

"I'm never giving it up!" Sally trumpeted.

"Okay," said Bernice, although she was privately afraid of heights.

"I don't give a FUCK what anyone says," said Sally, her face turned deliberately toward a group of girls who were clustered around the monkey bars, their pleated skirts chastely clustered around their knees.

Bernice had no response to that.

That afternoon they started the playground club. The purpose of the club was to ritually perform all playground activities each recess period. They'd start with the swings on their long chains, always, Bernice giving Sally an enormous push and then jumping into her own swing to catch up.

Then they'd leap from the swings and hit the ground running, and race to the slide. Sally usually got there first, with her long legs flying, unless she fell, which was frequently, and then Bernice grabbed the slide first. She pulled herself up the steep steps and flung herself onto the smooth metal, hurtling down and racing back around. Bernice found that in the company of Sally, she could grit her teeth and power through her fear, put aside the premonition that a fall was imminent, and just keep going.

Everything was a thrill for them: the bang of the teeter-totter, the dizzying whirl of the merry-go-round. The game always ended up near the monkey bars, where they would hang upside down on increasingly higher bars, grabbing on with their hands and then flipping off backward at increasingly greater risk to their ankles and heads. It was never fast enough, high enough, or hard enough for Sally, whose loud laugh rang across the playground even when she hit the gravel, or spun into a tree. Bernice met challenge after terrifying challenge with her teeth bared, her will determined. Sally was so uncoordinated, so gangly and unaccustomed to a body so rapidly growing, anyone would have thought it would be Sally that took a serious tumble and ended the game.

But instead it was Bernice. They were standing on top of the jungle gym that was shaped like a spidery dome. It had taken weeks for Sally to coax Bernice up to the top, and finally she had agreed. Now their feet were braced against each other and their hands were clasped together, and they leaned back against the connection. Sally was chuckling, trying to stare Bernice down, and make her laugh, make her forget she was so high up. Then somehow their hands separated, and Bernice went down through the bars, cracking her head on the metal pipe as she fell backward and passed through. Her hands seemed surprised to be empty, as if her very cells believed they were still connected to Sally, still holding hands on top of the gym. As the dull pain entered the back of her head and the lights went out on her consciousness, she found herself still reaching, grasping for Sally.

When she opened her eyes she was on the pavement under the jungle gym, and Sally was saying "Oh, no, no, my little purple bag!" Bernice was wearing purple overalls that day, and Sally had been teasing her, laughing as they rode the merry-go-round. Bernice blinked her eyes and looked up into Sally's face, the big teeth hidden, the eyes full of tears. She had never seen Sally look this way before.

"It's OK," she croaked. "I didn't die."

"Where's the teacher?" Sally barked at the crowd that was gathering around them. "Oh, for Pete's sake!"

With that Sally slid her arms under Bernice's legs and shoulders and lifted her. She cradled her tightly and said, "Don't worry, purple bag. We'll get you inside."

Bernice closed her eyes and her brain went swimming away. She felt Sally holding her, threading her through the triangle shape of the jungle-gym openings, was aware of her jostling stride as Sally ran up to the school, banged through the door, and hollered, "NURSE!"

Bernice had a concussion and was out of school for three days. When she returned, Sally decreed, "No more playground club."

"No," said Bernice. "It's OK. I can do it now. I knew that was going to happen. And I lived. It's fine."

"Are you kidding me? You knew that was going to happen? What are you, psychic?"

"No," said Bernice. "I'm not."

"Well, I don't care," Sally said. "Let the little kids break their necks on that shit. I'm done with it."

That day Sally started a mystics club during recess with a smuggled-in Ouija board and some dice, with which she loudly stated she was going to nose out any psychic ability that Bernice might possess. They never went near the jungle gym again. The following year they went to middle school, and Sally was able to get her physical energy out of her system by playing basketball, softball, and field hockey. She was terrible at each and every sport, and spent at least a few minutes of every game laid out on the field. Bernice sat on the sidelines, feeling every trip, every slam, her body tense and shifting left and right as Sally ran from left to right in front of her, slapping her hand against her face when something went wrong. But Sally was always up again, laughing, smiling with all her crooked teeth, running again. And that made Bernice smile, too.

In seventh grade, both of the girls' parents got divorced. Sally's mother suspected her husband of cheating on her during his business trips, laid a trap, and caught him at it. Bernice's mother, who had been in the Far East doing historical research, sent word that she would not be returning and that her husband was free to pursue other interests. Sally and Bernice were twelve.

It was during a meeting of the mystics club that they revealed the news about their parents to each other. The mystics club had been sustained by several minor moments that Sally claimed confirmed Bernice's psychic powers, and now had seven members, four or five of whom were in attendance at any given meeting. Their usual pastime was to test each other for psychic abilities with playing cards, tell stories about the witches of the Toledo swamps, and talk about boys. They met before school, in a remote section of the gym, climbing up to perch atop a folded-up section of bleachers. On this day, there happened to be only one other girl sitting up there, some sixth grader hoping to be included, so they told her to get lost, and then it was just the two of them.

Bernice held a deck of tarot cards, shuffling them halfheartedly, looking at each one as it came to the top of the deck.

"What's wrong?" asked Sally.

"My mother's not coming back from Thailand," Bernice said.

"Not coming back at all?"

"Right."

"Well, is your father going over there? Are you moving?"

Bernice turned to look at her friend. "Nope," she said. "They're done. Quits. *Finis.*"

Sally leaned back against the wall and

looked up at the ceiling for a few seconds, then began to smile.

"My parents are done, too," she said. "Apparently Dad got his dick wet in Albuquerque, and this is the fallout."

"Wow," said Bernice. "You're tough."

"Yeah."

"Where are the tears and the dissolution of your identity?"

"Where are yours?" said Sally. Bernice saw that Sally was actually crying and that made her cry, too.

"OK, I admit it, I'm actually sad," she said.

For a few minutes they sat there, and Bernice continued to shuffle the cards.

"Maybe they weren't meant for each other," said Sally. "You know, maybe it wasn't true love."

"Come on." Bernice rolled her eyes and banged her heels against the bleachers. Someone had turned the lights on in the gym. "Are you stupid?"

"Well, maybe it wasn't!"

"You know that's just bullshit, right?" Bernice asked.

"You're the one with tarot cards in your hand," said Sally.

"Yeah, bullshit tarot cards," Bernice said.

"Yeah," said Sally. She let out a sigh that

made Bernice feel terrible. That small puff of air had such finality, as if something permanent was falling away.

"Screw them," said Bernice. "It'll be different for us, you know."

"Different how? Sam Thomas asked me to the mixer, and then not only did he take Rachel Crumbley instead, he didn't even have the balls to tell me."

"I know," said Bernice, who had refused to even consider attending.

"So I got ready, got dressed, for nothing!"

"I know," Bernice repeated.

"My dad even took time out from running around on my mom to take a picture of me! Waiting and waiting for Sam Thomas, who was already at the dance with —"

"With Rachel, yes," Bernice intoned.

"OK, maybe it won't be different for us."

"Fuck," said Sally. "We need arranged marriages. You know, like they did in India. You pick your kid's husband, wife, whatever, and that's it. Their divorce rate is like nothing."

"Who would arrange our marriages?" snorted Bernice. "Our parents are too busy divorcing each other."

"Just imagine," said Sally. "Say you knew, when your kid was born, who they were going to marry? Think what you could do for them, to make that marriage awesome."

"Like what?"

"I don't know, like everything!" Sally spread her hands out in front of her. A clump of kids walked by under their feet, on the way to the band room. "You could just raise them to be together. Same ideas, same experiences, but enough different to make it interesting. Make them compatible, make them perfect for each other. This one plays the cello, that one plays the violin. This one loves mountain climbing, that one loves rappelling. You get it."

"Science."

"What?"

"It's like science. It's like what the swamp witches do."

Sally frowned. "Swamp witches? That's not science."

"Sure it is," said Bernice. "They're shuffling the cards, but they're reading the faces. They're putting protractors to the constellations and then naming them after gods. Like your idea with the arranged marriages — it's actually so Toledo. Soulmates in a test tube."

"Exactly. It's so Toledo."

The girls sat silently for a while, each thinking. Then the first bell rang.

"Fuck our parents," said Sally.

"Obviously."

A boy walked past with a trombone in a case, letting it bang rhythmically into the bleachers with each step.

"We could do better," said Sally.

Bernice gathered her things, put the tarot cards in her backpack.

"Our kids get married," she went on. "It's me and you at Christmas and Thanksgiving, how cool would that be?"

"Cool," said Bernice, zipping her backpack shut.

"I mean, having in-laws that get along is probably half the battle of having a happy marriage," said Sally.

"That and keeping your pants on when you travel on business."

"But don't you see?" Sally caught Bernice by the arm. "We can make them do that. We can train them to do that."

"What are you going to do, introduce electric shock whenever the kid hears the word adultery?"

"I don't know," said Sally. "I don't know."

For the rest of the year, during the mess of the divorces, they comforted themselves with their scheme. While Bernice's father was mourning, forgetting to pay bills, sinking into silences that lasted a week. While Sally's mother was engaged in her revenge affair with a neighbor's husband.

"We could teach her to knit, right?" Sally would say, as they sat huddled in the back of the classroom during social studies, not working on their group project. "And then we could knit him a really special hat or something, pillow, scarf, something. Then we take it away and he loses it. Then when they get together, she happens to find exactly that pattern, and knits it for him again — boom, that's love."

"That's science," Bernice would correct her.

"That's love," Sally would say.

It was in high school that Sally kissed her first boy and Bernice took her first drink. The boy was a neighborhood friend she had trick-or-treated with as a toddler. The liquor was pilfered from Sally's mother's cabinet. It was a Friday night, and the girls were in Sally's room. Bernice lay under Sally's bright blue sheets, watching Sally's Hitachi TV.

"You should come with," said Sally, who was spreading Nair on her legs.

"That smells terrible," said Bernice. "It smells like an old lady."

"Why don't you come with?" Sally insisted. "We can get Roger to come along for you. Or Chris."

Sally knew everyone on every sports team, and they were all her buddies. They would no more date Sally, Bernice thought, than they would date their sisters. She was safe from them. But there were other boys, like this neighborhood boy, or boys from other social spheres: the science kids, the poets, the musicians. She still had them to worry about.

"I don't want to come with," said Bernice. She sat up and reached over the foot of the bed to change the channel on the TV. "I'm going to stay here with Ponch and Jon."

"Will you be here when I get back?"

"I already told my dad I'm sleeping over. So it's either stay here and wait for you to get home or else embark on a life of crime."

"Are you ever going to double-date with me?" Sally asked. "Promise me you will."

"I already promised I'd marry my kid off to your kid," said Bernice. "Doesn't that count?"

"Maybe," said Sally. "Will we double-date first? Will we have double husbands?"

"Sure, I see it all now," said Bernice, pretending to wave her hands over a crystal ball on the bed. She made her voice wobble and wiggle like a witch in a trance. "We're living together, with our toddlers who are someday to marry."

"Oh, good," said Sally, drying her hair on a towel. "And mine is a boy. Come on, I want the boy."

"Of course, sure, yours is the boy," said Bernice in her normal voice. Then she resumed the act: "The babies are sitting in their high chairs, eating applesauce that we made from the apples in our own orchard, which we tend with hankerchiefs over our hair. And we're washing up the pots and the apple grinder."

"And our double husbands," Sally reminded her. "Don't forget that part."

"Yes, now I see," said Bernice, covering her eyes with one hand and reaching in front of her with her other arm. "Your husband comes in the room, just as we were laughing about something, and we stop laughing, and we look around at him, and he's like, 'What, me? Brave, handsome me?' and he swings his arms out —"

"His strong, manly arms," Sally put in. "What does he look like anyway?"

"Like an idiot. He knocks over the crockery on the countertop, and it shatters all over the floor. What a thug. I hate him already."

Sally laughed. She spread the cream above her knees, up onto her long thighs.

"You don't even have hair up there," said Bernice, flopping back down onto the pillow and pulling the sheet and quilt up around her. "You're just removing hair from nothing."

"You're just removing hair from nothing," Sally pretended to shout at the lotion on her legs. "Oh, my god! Stop removing hair from nothing."

Bernice sat back up and waved a threatening fist. "I would throw a pillow at you," said Bernice. "But you would just remove hair from it."

"Probably," said Sally, yawning. "Probably I would."

Bernice leaned up on her knees to turn the sound up on the television, then flopped back on the pillows.

"Hey," said Sally, "I'm going to write that shit down in my journal, you know? So we can check back. Were you seeing that? Or like *seeing* that?"

"What do you mean?"

"Like, were you seeing it for real?"

"I don't see things that way," Bernice said.

"You do, though," said Sally. "You do, and you know you do."

Bernice just shrugged and rolled her eyes. Did she see things? Did she know things? No, it was perception, not prescience. The safety of analytical deduction, not the madness of some second sight. If she could see the future, she would certainly not see Sally married to some arm-swinging oaf.

Sally went out the front door punching her date on the arm, falling off her high-heeled sandals, tugging her cutoffs down over her butt. Her long blond hair was pulled into a ponytail, and her fingertips had been carefully polished by Bernice: petal pink. Bernice shut the door behind her. And then silently crossed to the window to watch them down to the guy's stupid car. A Gremlin. As it pulled away it made an awful grinding noise before it puttered off. Bernice looked at her watch. Sally's curfew was 11 P.M., but her mother was out, possibly until morning.

Bernice stood at the window watching the dark street, and then turned to the liquor cabinet and took out the first thing she saw that was clear. She knew enough about high school drinking to understand how to cover her tracks by refilling a bottle with water. Bernice sat down on a black leather ottoman and uncapped the gin. She took a deep swallow. It burned, but not too much. She had imagined liquor would be harder on her throat. Her second thought was to throw up, but she breathed shallowly, and got through it. By the time Sally got home, Bernice was asleep, and nobody ever found out about that. There was no comical scene. There was no hysteria. There was just a mild swimminess, and then lights-out.

The next night, she pressed Sally to try it, but Sally wouldn't.

"I'm an athlete," said Sally. "I don't put poison in the instrument."

"I'm a chemist," returned Bernice. "I do."

High school was almost over. Bernice was headed to Bowling Green to be a chemistry major, and Sally to the University of Michigan on a basketball scholarship. Through dogged determination and a cheerful willingness to throw fouls, she'd been able to get pretty good at the sport, and at a long, lanky 5'11", she looked made to play. It was not a full scholarship, but Sally's father was happy to make up the difference. He could afford it, and he wanted to see his daughter playing NCAA.

Bernice felt at home in the chemistry lab, among scientists who were not prone to ask her how she was feeling, or whether she had good thoughts or bad thoughts, or whether the vomiting was flu or something more sinister. Bernice accepted the separation from her friend. In fact, Sally's acceptance letter with a scholarship, from the University of Michigan, had been a seed that bloomed into a strong sapling of despair that felt inevitable. Maybe it was rooted in that first night when Sally's wobbly sandals had carried her down the sidewalk with her first boyfriend on her first real date. It's when tragedy was born in Bernice's heart, and never did it leave. In that moment, she saw Sally's trajectory, and she saw her own, and she saw how they did and didn't intersect. Everything that mattered to her was clear. And it never got better, all through her whole life.

But Sally wouldn't submit to the separation. She insisted on calling Bernice every day from the pay phone in her dorm's lobby, using quarters and dimes by the handful. She took a class, her freshman year, for a humanities elective called The History of Astrology. Topics covered included ancient gods, the birth of constellations, the overlap of the faith of astrology with the science of astronomy. The teacher, a graduate student, was a professed clairvoyant, an astral projector, a mystic.

"Go to the island," he would say at the end of every class, his way of signing off on his lecture. "There you will find me."

It didn't take long for Sally to stay after

class and ask what island he was talking about in central Michigan, and from there it was but a short step to them lying in bed next to each other, his hand on her wrist, taking her pulse, his voice in her ear, coaching her.

"I'm dreaming, I am aware; I'm dreaming, I am aware; I'm dreaming, I am aware," he said.

She repeated it.

"There is an island in water so blue, it's like emerald."

"Emeralds are green," whispered Sally. "Is it green water?"

"Okay, like a sapphire," continued Dean, without breaking his tone.

"That's better," Sally said, giggling.

"Shhhhh," Dean urged her. "Let your mind become quiet. Let your mouth become quiet."

"My mouth has a harder time than my mind," she whispered.

"You don't have to whisper; there's no one else here," he said in a normal tone.

"I'm sorry," said Sally. "It's just . . . show me again."

Sally stretched her long body next to his and then really tried to still it and settle down. She was so restless, even in bed. Even after what he'd called tantric sex.

"There is an island in water so blue it's like a sapphire," he began again. "The island has palms waving in a light warm breeze, and a sandy beach as white as snow."

"Or pearl," Sally whispered. "To continue the gemstone theme."

"Relax your mouth," said Dean.

"OK."

"Relax it so much that words stop coming out of it."

"Maybe we better tantric again," said Sally. "I don't think I'm getting it."

With Dean, she never did get it. But the idea took root, and she brought it to Bernice.

"I miss you!" she said to Bernice on the phone.

"You don't have a boyfriend?" asked Bernice.

"Well, I do have a boyfriend."

"Is he boring and stupid?"

"No," said Sally. "He's actually pretty wonderful. As a professor, I mean."

"Naughty," said Bernice without inflection. "I suppose that makes it hot."

"Well, he has all kinds of strange ideas."

"Like having sex with a nineteen-year-old girl?"

"He's not that old. He's twenty-three."

"So he's a lecturer, not a professor."

"He's my teacher."

"I see. Glad you went to college so you could learn to sleep with older men."

"Not that kind of teacher! He's teaching me the history of astrology. And astral projection. And he does have this thing he does, tantricness, where the guy doesn't even ejaculate, just goes and goes on and on forever."

"Forever?"

"He's had a ten-hour orgasm before," said Sally. "Because nothing ever comes out, so it's never really over."

"You are attending the University of Michigan, are you not? Haven't transferred to the Edgar Cayce School or the New School for the Education of Nascent Prostitutes without telling me or your parents?"

"Astral projection could mean we could see each other."

"We'll see each other at Thanksgiving."

"No, I mean see each other all the time. Like tonight. In an astral plane."

Bernice stalled.

"Are you there?"

"Yes," she said.

"I miss you, my little purple bag. I just want to try this. Come on, I miss you so much. I just want to see you."

Bernice swallowed. "OK, what do I have

to do? Burn incense? Ingest substances?"

"No," Sally continued joyfully, her laugh booming across the phone lines. "It's all in your mind! I know we can do this! Listen to how it works." And she proceeded to relay Dean's explanation of lucid dreaming word for word, although all her attempts at sharing dreams with Dean had failed.

It didn't work for them either at first. They spent a whole month falling asleep in their separate states, meditating on their intention to join on a subconscious plane that manifested itself as a basketball court. Dean's tropical island felt too cliché, and anyway Dean might be there. The basketball court was a place with which they were both familiar — Sally as a player and Bernice as a spectator. Bernice visualized taking her place in the stands, looking up, and seeing Sally practicing free throws from the line. Sally visualized dribbling down the court, turning her head to the left, and seeing Bernice in the bleachers.

It was something they both tried very hard to do, while chanting "I'm dreaming, I'm aware, I'm dreaming, I'm aware." Sally had them doing other ridiculous things like counting their fingers whenever the clock was on :00 or :20 or :40. The idea was that if finger counting became a habit in waking hours, it would pop up in dreamland, too, and in dreams you never get ten fingers or toes. Observing this weirdness is a way to alert your brain you're dreaming. Then you're dreaming and you're aware.

At Thanksgiving the girls met back in Toledo, fully awake. They laughed about astrology and the stuff they were working on, but Sally had a stack of books on various mystical topics for Bernice to read, checked out from the University of Michigan library and not due back until after winter break. With Bernice's father traveling, they had Thanksgiving dinner at Sally's, and then went to bed under Sally's bright blue sheets in the bed where they'd had so many sleepovers, in a time that now seemed long ago.

Sally had a hard time falling asleep, and kicked her feet around petulantly, trying to get comfortable.

"Quit it," said Bernice. "You're going to bounce me out of this thing."

"Tell me a story," said Sally. "Make it good. I can't keep my legs still."

"OK," said Bernice. "But you have to close your eyes. And if you kick while I'm telling the story, I'm quitting."

Sally obediently closed her eyes and crossed her ankles over each other, to keep them quiet.

"Once upon a time," began Bernice, tracing Sally's eyebrow with one finger, first the left one, and then the right one, "there was a man. His wife of many years had died and left him and his three sons to fend for themselves in a harsh world of commerce and sport. He was a builder of buildings, and a strong, tall man with curly godlike hair . . ." Here Bernice let her finger slip along Sally's hairline, smoothing back the little hairs that curled there, like on a baby's forehead. "But he was sad because he was all alone."

Sally let out a great sigh and rolled onto her stomach. Bernice knew this meant she was almost ready to go to sleep.

"Scratch my back," Sally suggested.

Bernice dragged her fingernails down Sally's back through the T-shirt. Then she worked her nails back up to her friend's shoulder in little spirals, then back down the other side.

"Story," said Sally drowsily.

"Somewhere in another part of town, there was a woman with three beautiful daughters. They all had lovely golden hair. Their father, the woman's husband, had also died, leaving her lonely and sad as well."

"Great story," murmured Sally. "I think I

want to kill myself."

"Well, one day, the lonely woman ran into this lonely guy, this *fellow,* let's call him, probably in the supermarket," Bernice went on, her fingertips contracting and spreading slowly over Sally's spine, up and down from her neck to the waistband of her shorts. "And they immediately knew that this was much more . . . than a hunch."

"You ass," Sally said.

"That this group must somehow form a family," Bernice went on, louder, starting to bounce on the bed rhythmically with the theme song she was now singing.

"THE BRADY BUNCH!" hollered Sally into her pillow.

"The Brady Bunch!" both girls sang together, now yelling so that the veins were sticking out on the sides of their faces.

"Bernice!" yelled Sally. A dog was barking in the neighbor's yard. Sally always pronounced her name with an emphasis on the first syllable, like BERN-iss, when she was joking around like she was angry. "Bernice, this is unacceptable. Now put on a blue dress and your whitest apron, and sweep up this mess."

Bernice was laughing so hard, her stomach was in spasm.

When they settled down, Sally said, "Now

I'm all riled up again. You're going to have to scratch a lot more, and probably sing, too, but no more TV theme songs. I want Compton and Batteau. And hum the violin parts. You owe me. Hey, when we have our kids, we should teach them all about Compton and Batteau. It's such an obscure act, when they find out they both know the songs, they'll feel it's fate for sure."

When she was finally asleep, Bernice leaned over to look at Sally's face. The wide mouth was open, a bit of drool descending onto the pillow. The eyelashes were pressed against her cheek like little marks left by a stylus. The eyelids fluttered as if something beneath them was held in captivity. Bernice wanted nothing more than to press her lips to Sally's temple, feel the vein that pulsed there, blue and deep, and press their warmth together while her friend slept. It would have been a violation, she thought. It would have been a sin. So Bernice left Sally unkissed, and curled back around into the space in the small of Sally's back, and went to sleep.

Later that night, Bernice was dreaming. She was in a mall, but an ugly one, and she was passing by a men's clothing store. Inside the store, Bernice could sense a problem, like you do in dreams. She knew instinctively that something bad was happening. Then she herself was inside the store, moving through the aisles. She saw a woman, standing next to a display of brightly colored shirts, and the woman was naked. The woman was embarrassed, but nobody was really noticing her, so Bernice wanted to tell her it didn't matter. The woman turned and Bernice knew that it was Sally. Then she saw, like a hammer to the head, that it really was Sally. Not a dream Sally, but Sally having a dream.

"Sally," she said. "It's OK, you're dreaming."

Sally looked toward Bernice, but it was clear she didn't really see her. She picked up a shirt from the table and held it against herself, as if she was thinking it could cover her, front to back.

"Sally," said Bernice. "You're dreaming. Hey."

Bernice had to concentrate hard to stay in the room, in the clothing store, with Sally. She knew from reading the books that the hardest part of lucid dreaming was staying in the dream once you'd realized it was, in fact, a dream. Everyone knows what it's like to figure out you're dreaming. It's what you do with the information that matters. Usually you slide away, or just wake up. Bernice forced herself to stay put, and kept calling through the dense underwater audio of the dream, calling to Sally. Sally only pressed her legs together, pressing up against the table, looking back and forth.

Of all the checks you can perform to let your mind know you're dreaming, being naked should be the easiest. You might not remember to count your fingers, or look at a calendar, or check a watch. But you should be aware that if you've let yourself go out in public without pants, what you're experiencing is not real. However, most everybody in dreams, Sally included, finds themselves in public with no clothes on, and seeks no explanation — only a solution.

Bernice told Sally what the books said. "Take control. It's your dream. You can put clothes on. Just dream them on."

Sally turned toward her then, but still appeared confused, as if Bernice was a person she could not clearly see.

So Bernice did the only other thing she could think of to save Sally from the embarrassment of the naked dream, and that was to reach up to her throat and pull her own clothes off. Dreaming, she didn't bother with zippers and buttons, but just tugged the clothes off like they had already dissolved. Then Bernice was standing there in the clothing store, naked, too. Sally could see her now, though the other patrons still remained gauzily indifferent.

"Bernice," said Sally.

"It's OK," said Bernice. "See? We're only dreaming."

12

Irene saw George sitting in the dark. It was the back of his head that she saw first — a man's head, boxy and large. She came into the room through the back door, and it was him that she saw right away. Something about the way his shoulders lay back against the seat, or the way his chin was tilted to the side, looking up, made her say, "Mine." Something in this man her heart recognized. Or, not her heart but her throat. Not her throat but something else, something that might live inside you but not be made of blood and flesh. If there was such a thing available for people to have, Irene hadn't known about it until last night, when hers had jumped and strained, yearning for George. It was disorienting. Like being sick.

She had come to hear a lecture from a visiting professor. The room was dark, and the star machine was on. Irene didn't like that.

George turned to look back, and saw her. He waved vigorously, and motioned that she should come over. George had left a seat for her right on the aisle. She sat down next to him and leaned over without looking at him to get her laptop out of its bag.

"Hi!" he said. He put one hand on her knee.

"Hello," she said into her lap, still reaching into her bag.

"It's great to see you, Dr. Irene Sparks," said George.

She sat up with the machine, opened it, and said, "It's great to be seen, Dr. George Dermont."

"Do you have any gum?" he asked.

"No," she said. "I don't like gum. After all, what's the point of it?"

"It's for chewing," said George.

"I don't like chewing," said Irene.

George took his hand back and fiddled around with the notebook on his lap, curling and uncurling one side of the paper. Irene switched her laptop on.

"So how was your day?" he asked. When she turned to face him, she noted his gaze was hovering down around her collarbone.

"Fine," said Irene. "Assistant is a bit irritable. You know her, I guess."

"Yeah, Patrice."

"Sam Beth, she corrected me."

"Yeah, she's a . . . um . . . Daughter of Babylon. So they're big on their ancient names. But for paperwork, it's Patrice."

"Yes, I've heard a bit about that," said Irene. "The Daughters of Babylon, huh?"

"Some kind of Internet cult," said George cautiously. "Astronomer priestesses."

"But I guess you know her pretty well?"

"She told you?"

"She did."

Sam Beth had approached Irene at the banquet, just as she was trying to leave. Her face was flushed, and her eyes cut back toward George's table, George's parents. "I've had sex with Gilgamesh," she said urgently, clutching a wineglass. Irene had continued piloting Belion toward the door, but Sam Beth caught her by the arm.

"Sorry?" Irene had asked. "What did you need?"

"With George," said Sam Beth. "He's looking for his Inanna."

"I don't get it," Irene prompted. But this explained the way Sam Beth had behaved in the office. Something inside Irene felt disappointed, and a little sad.

"He's slept with almost everyone around here who has brown hair," Sam Beth explained impatiently. "Fuck and run."

"How odd," said Irene. "Well, that has nothing to do with me."

"That's right, but your hair *is* brown," Sam Beth said. "Not a good boyfriend for you. Look away. Walk away."

"Well, I appreciate you trying to look out for me," Irene began.

"No, I mean really, walk away, walk away from me, right now, don't talk anymore."

Irene had walked away, but when she got home and to her computer, in the back room of her mother's little house, she did a little research and found a few strange Web sites with wall-to-wall text and exclamation points that described Babylon as the "mother of harlots." Girls in graduate school will believe anything.

"Oh," said George, in the planetarium. "Those other girls —"

"George, I have a boyfriend, and you . . . well, you know. All the harlots."

Irene turned back to her laptop. She felt each breath coming quickly into her lungs, as much as she was trying to control it. She opened a new document and typed "September 5th. Guest Lecture. Nathaniel Lebernov."

"Who's Nathaniel Lebernov?" George asked.

Irene turned to face him and said, "The

Lebernov differential? You don't know him? Are you serious?"

She typed the equation on her laptop, her wrists snapping and fingers twisting into shape to make the special characters and punctuation.

"That's the Lebernov equation." She typed underneath it. "Did you not read 'The Spectronometric Analysis of the Geomagnetic Particular Radius of Dectrite Gas Molecules' in last fall's *International Journal of Physics*?"

George looked at her.

"Are you only here to pick up chicks?" she asked him sternly, out loud.

"Actually, I'm here because of you. I knew you'd be here, and I wanted to see you."

Irene blinked very fast, forced her chest to stop convulsing. She felt unhinged and didn't like it at all. She made her feet touch each other at the heels and imagined those heels on the edge of a building, forty stories up. She had to calm her blood down. She took a sideways glance at George, and he was lying back in his seat, looking straight up, utterly relaxed.

"Good afternoon," said Dr. Miller, taking the podium. "I will waste no time in presenting our speaker for this morning, whose work you all know has been so important to our field. He is a friend of mine, and as such he has agreed to leave his work at the University of St. Petersburg to come and stay with us for a few days, expound on his work, and enlighten us as to his current research. Please welcome Dr. Nathaniel Lebernov."

Everyone clapped.

Dr. Lebernov took the podium and waved off Dr. Miller, who sat down in the front and leaned way back, rolling his eyes up toward the ceiling. George did the same. Irene sat up straighter, her hands on the keyboard. Then Dr. Lebernov himself raised his eyes upward to the sky, taking in a big breath.

"The universe, my friends, is spinning. Spinning fast, beyond our control," he said. "We look up at the stars, we see them flare and fade, and we are afraid."

"He's talking about you guys, not him," said Dr. Miller, calling out without a microphone, "He's not afraid."

Dr. Lebernov made a shushing gesture with his hands and continued.

"My friends, we are all afraid of what we do not know. We are afraid of what we cannot clearly see. Of uncertainty, and chaos, and unexpected things we had no chance to predict. Chance collisions scare us, and explosions in our backyards, our heads being torn off our bodies by a sudden gust of stellar wind. What might happen to us in the future? What rock might plummet from the sky? How might we change, in an instant, forever, only because of chance? There is nothing we can do about it. No way to protect ourselves. As long as we have only these" — and he pointed to his eyes — "which are all most people have."

"They have their eyes, and they can stare up into the sky. They know now that the stars are distant. They have a vague idea that the universe is large. They know that giant clouds of gas are burning, that rocks the size of Belgium hurtle around like bullets, and they know that they are tiny, and everything else is big, and that's scary.

"Sometimes I wish," he went on, "that people would still believe the earth is flat, the sun is a lightbulb behind some paper board, the stars gods."

"Some people do," whispered George to Irene. His breath in her ear.

"Wouldn't that be easier?" said Dr. Lebernov. "Chaos is the most frightening phenomenon. Order, even malicious order, is at the least predictable. But the cruelty of chaos is murky, malignant in its expanse. Reason may be harsh, and difficult, but it is defensible. So in the absence of agency we create agency, in the absence of information we create myth, and we created gods to rule the heavens so that we know what is there."

Irene snuck a glance at George and noticed he was listening to the lecture. He still had his head thrown back in a posture of disregard, but his eyes were open. He was still awake.

"But then the astronomers came and put the gods out of business. Set the sun aflame, scattered the stars across the universe, made the earth into a ball. In this crusade, we have one friend. This is mathematics."

George leaned over and put his fingers on Irene's laptop and typed the words "this is crap" before she pushed his hands away. "Don't do that again," she typed back. His fingers were long, his knuckles reddened and rough, as if he were a longshoreman instead of a physicist. Those hands felt strong when she pushed on them, and in a comforting way: they were warm and tough. She wished that he would put them back. She wanted to watch them flicking over the keys of her laptop, writing more letters, more words to her.

"Math dispels ignorance. Math conquers discord, and anarchy, and revolution. It is math that says 6.3184 times ten to the third.

Math will see us through."

George made gagging noises in his throat and shut his eyes. She felt free, with his eyes shut, to look at him, to think about touching him, about tearing at him, about striking her hands against his wide collarbones, being encircled in his long arms. *I want to take my clothes off,* she thought. *I want to be naked for him, press up on him, naked as a clam. I want this.* She had never, ever wanted this before. And this was why she couldn't stop looking at George, all through the lecture. She was surprised to be wanting him. It wasn't like expecting a red circle and finding a blue one. It was more like unfolding an envelope and finding water. Looking into a hole and seeing the sky. She didn't know when she had been so surprised.

After it was over, she snapped her laptop shut and said, "Well, Dr. Dermont, thanks to you my notes for today consist of the word 'crap.' And here I thought you would only impede my work if I dated you."

"You could have taken notes," he said. He stood up.

"That's true," she said, relenting. "And anyway, I probably wouldn't have taken notes. Most of that lecture is in his published work, here and there, if you piece it

225

together. If you take the spirit of the thing."

"I thought we weren't supposed to take the spirit of the thing. I thought we were to singe the spirit into a blackened pile of ash and then count every molecule in the pile and call that the answer. Isn't that what he just said?"

"George, you're a dreamer, I'm afraid," she said, throwing her laptop bag over her shoulder and letting him out of the row of seats. She gave him a smile. She reached out and took his hand. It was almost as if her body acted on its own, and before she knew it she was holding one big hand of his in both of hers, and the bones inside it were moving around, pulled and pressed by all his soft tissue, and she grabbed it, and held it, and then dropped it as if it had become too hot.

"I said you're a dreamer," she repeated snappishly, and stalked off.

He followed her out into the hallway and down the stairs.

"Where are you going?" asked George.

"My office," she said. *Now is when he will say something about liking my skirt and wanting to talk me out of it,* she thought. *It will happen right now.*

"Do you want to come out on my boat sometime?"

226

"Your boat? What are you, rich?"

"Yes," he said. "It's new money, though, so I don't have an attitude yet. I'm all bewildered and charming about it."

There were still people walking around in the building, waiting to have their moment with the great scientist. *Can I have your autograph? I just love your equation,* they would say. She planned to send an e-mail later. *I am Dr. Irene Sparks of the Toledo Institute of Astronomy. I have read your book,* it would say. *I have these comments about your lecture.*

Stiff, dry, intelligent. Just the kind of person you would want to send a stiff, dry, intelligent e-mail back to.

"What would you say to Lebernov after this evening," she said to George, letting him walk her down the sidewalk.

"I'd tell him he had no soul."

"You would not."

"Dare me?" George stopped on the sidewalk. "Because we can go back in there right now."

"George!" she said, and pulled him by the elbow so that they were walking again. Her hand stayed on his elbow, that wonderfully working hinge that connected the upper part of his arm to the bottom part. And they were walking along the sidewalk with her hand inside his elbow, her knuckles bumping up against his ribs. She had to reach up to hold on to him. He didn't seem to notice.

"I'm surprised Miller didn't stand up and bash his skull in with a chair leg," said George. "I know he doesn't buy into all that age of enlightenment claptrap."

"Claptrap? Did you really just use the word 'claptrap'?"

George growled at her and smiled. She liked the look of his face. She didn't know which direction he had chosen to walk in, but she didn't care. She kept looking up, seeing his face outlined against the night trees and the orange glow of street lamps. *Fuck and run,* she thought. *Might not be so bad.*

"You know," said George, sort of wistfully, "everyone takes an astronomy course in college because looking at the stars is so cool and romantic. They get taught the constellations and everything, and how this used to be thought and that used to be believed. And then we get into calculating the distance in light-years from here to there, and everyone quits because they don't like the math. I mean forget parallax."

"It's parsecs," she said quietly.

"Right, parsecs, yes. But you don't get

what I'm saying. I don't like the math. But I stayed with it. The math is a necessary evil, but the stars are still stars. It's still cool and romantic."

She looked over at him again, and he had a little smile on his face.

"Did you want to be an astronaut when you were little?" she said.

"No," he said seriously, "always an astronomer."

They were nearing the west edge of campus, where the reproduction of the ancient temple ruins were. Now George reached out to her, and took her by the hand, and led her through some of the rocks, and she let him because she actually was small and genuinely did need help over the climbing parts. For a while they were just climbing. There was a path around on the other side, but they didn't use it. Then they were standing in the middle of the temple where the pillars were still in a rectangle, a dais at one end.

George pointed up to the night sky. It was really beautiful, the dark sky and all the stars, outlined by the stones and nothing else around.

"A star is being born right now," he said.

"Stars aren't born, George. And they don't die. Lithium, hydrogen, fusion: that's not birth. Just call it what it is. Don't engage in that stupid anthropomorphizing garbage."

"I like thinking about it that way," said George.

"But I always thought," said Irene, "that it was stupid to wander around and write poetry and sing. Elves do it. Not astronomers."

"Really? You never read poetry?"

"Sometimes," Irene admitted. "My mother read it to me."

"Bless her. I like her already," said George.

They stood under the bright sky, and she felt small next to the big columns, and the ruined room with no ceiling framed the stars. George was just standing there looking up. Maybe some people don't feel scared when they think about comets and supernovas. Maybe they think it is wonderful.

"So do you want to?" said George.

"No!" she said automatically, and in an instant she was brought back out of the heavens, into her skin and her brain, which was wondering how many girls George had plundered on that dais. How many girls had he had under these clouds, being a poet like he wanted to be, shunning convention, throwing out math with a dramatic, sexy flourish? He would say, *Look, Cassiopeia, isn't it beautiful,* and the girl would swoon, and he would put the moves on. His rough hand on her back, his face drawing down to hers, the warmth of his chest against her breasts.

"I mean go out on the boat," he said. She stared at him.

"Um, I don't know," she said. She thought about how it would be. Bright sun. Sparkling smile. Probably wine. Wind. Freshness. "My mother just died."

"Then we should go right away," he said, "for best stargazing. I can go so far into Lake Erie, we may be able to still see her, up in the sky."

"Wow," she said, "That's not what I was thinking at all."

That morning, she had gone to an appointment at the funeral home.

Bernice's body had been taken to the default funeral home for people whose bodies landed in the city morgue. Irene didn't know whether to feel bad about this or not. The funeral home was called Metropolitan Funeral Home. It had a generic flavor. A redbrick building in the shape of an H, and in the center a glassy lobby. One branch held a large chapel and one branch held administrative offices. One branch held the coffin showroom (there was a brochure titled "Merchandise"), and the other branch was entirely closed off. *That's where the bodies are,* thought Irene, taking note of the way the building was mapped. *That's where my mother is. Back there in that part, next to where I parked. She's inside, and she's about to be lit on fire. As soon as I sign the paperwork, she will burn.*

Irene was met by a smiling man in a black suit, who guided her to a luxurious-looking seat in the hallway between the offices and the chapel. There she waited for her consultant.

"I don't want to buy a casket," she had said earlier to Belion, who had called the funeral home on the phone for her. "I don't want to buy an urn."

"She doesn't want to buy a casket or an urn," Belion had reported into the phone. "She will come in and just sign papers. That's all she wants to do."

Belion had waited, his listening face on.

"Don't you have something lying around to put the ashes in? Something regular?"

Irene felt she should have known which funeral home had exsanguinated generations of Sparks women, should have recognized the very building where they had lain in state. But she really had no idea what had happened to all the other generations of Sparks women. There was no record. Irene might be able to turn up something in her mother's attic, but right here, right now, the Metropolitan Funeral Home, with all its easy-to-vacuum carpet and all its posh-looking chairs that you could wipe up with a paper towel, had been chosen for her.

There was a large flat-screen TV on the wall. On the screen, there were pictures of dead people in rotation, displayed with information on their funerals and snippets of quotations from their families. Irene sat in horror that her mother might come up in the rotation, smiling patiently, next to a blank space, or worse, a note that read, "Bernice Sparks, survived by her daughter, who declined a funeral, declined an urn, declined to give us anything with which to fill this space. Will she be missed?"

A half door swung open and a young woman called out, "For Bernice Sparks?" Irene came to the half door, and beyond it she could see a very pedestrian sort of office, with filing cabinets and rolling office chairs, just the sort of place where accounting is done or billing is accomplished. She received some forms on a clipboard and retrieved a check for several thousand dollars from her purse. The transaction was made over the half door, Irene never stepping inside onto the vinyl tile, and the billing person never stepping outside onto the appropriately colored carpet.

"Thank you," said the woman in a hushed voice. "You're all set."

"All set for what?" said Irene. Beside her on the flat screen, the parade of dead people continued in silence. They were all so old. Most had tubes coming out of their faces, or wisps of white hair falling into their eyes.

"You're all set."

"Are they going to —" Irene felt tears coming into her eyes. She pushed her mouth shut.

"They will cremate your mother and go ahead with the death certificate, as you specified."

"When?"

"We do our cremations at night, ma'am," said the young woman. "So, probably tonight."

Irene hesitated.

"Did you need to view the charging?"

"No," she said quickly. She wiped at her eyes. "No, I just wanted to know when."

Irene knew from the Metropolitan Funeral Home Web site that the inside of a crematorium is called a retort. What a strange word for it. She lingered by the half door.

"Did you want to look at an urn?"

Irene turned and walked back to the lobby, pushed the door open, and walked out to her car. She went to work at the institute. The weather was beautiful, the roads clear of traffic, and she felt, looking around, as if the world was showing her what a good thing it was to be alive. All the fall-blue sky, all the sparkling windows and the dark taut wires criss-crossing the air between her and space. In the coldest branch of the letter H, her mother lay dead in a refrigerator, and soon she would be all burned up in a fire. Burned the rest of the way. Her first burning had happened many years ago. It had not killed Bernice. But you might argue that it had killed her daughter.

13

Fire is an astronomical necessity. On stars, everything burns.

When Irene was six years old, her mother burned their house down. It was not an accident, but it was not suicide. The difference between an accident and a suicide is that someone dies. So the fire was not a suicide because Bernice did not die. Had she died, it would have been full-on suicide, because the fire was absolutely set by her. Much time was spent among neighbors, discussing whether the fire was set by her on purpose. It was actually caused by drunken mishandling of a smudging stick, and a profusion of oil-soaked silk scarves.

Was it a suicide? What death is not a suicide? What choices does a human really make, and where does the fault lie? When you have determined what constitutes "on purpose," then you will know.

The police had questioned everyone, and

no one knew what happened. Bernice did not know. She was screaming when she woke up, screaming louder than anyone had ever screamed. At the time the fire started, she was unconscious. She had been drinking. She had been smudging. That's all they knew. Whether she purposefully laid down a smoldering smudge stick on a pile of oil-soaked scarves, or whether she had genuinely fallen asleep with a smudge stick in her hand and cascaded over herself onto the scarves, or whether the scarves and the smudge stick had not been involved at all was unclear. You could say that when you take that first big gulp of liquor, the rest is like falling off a log.

Irene did not remember waking up that night, but the smoke was probably making her choke. She most likely fell out of bed coughing, her eyes bleeding tears. Taught by her schoolteacher to crawl along the floor in the event of a fire, she stayed on her knees and crawled. This is what they learned from the bruises on her knees: she crawled fast. Irene did not remember crawling out. She must have crawled down the stairs, maybe calling "Mommy, mommy!" or maybe just trying to breathe. It doesn't matter what was poignant or what was real. It only matters that Irene went down the stairs and, finding her mother lying there, on fire, she had begun to kick her and pull her burning hair. What was known for sure was that Irene had kicked and dragged and prodded and forced her mother out onto the porch, where the firefighters were arriving. And they saved Bernice and Irene from that fire.

It's not possible for a six-year-old to carry a woman out of a burning house, whether or not the woman is on fire. Therefore, Bernice must have saved herself. Even if she didn't remember. Even if she never meant to. What the firefighters and neighbors saw coming out of the door, along with belching smoke and hot air, was a woman crawling and a child kicking the woman and pulling at her burning hair. The child was shouting angrily, "You don't die! No, you don't die! You don't die!" If you're dying in a fire, sometimes the best thing for you is a person who will stand there kicking you, telling you not to.

The only remnants of the fire on Bernice were the bubbles of scars on her neck and back. Her dreadlocked hair burned all away, leaving wounds on her head that were awful to see, but some hair grew back. Who knows what really happened, in that burning house? Irene's memories began the following day. She could not remember the fire or anything that came before. She had learned to get by with something adjacent to forgiveness: forgetting. She tried to forget that her mother had burned them up in a fire. But she could never, ever forgive.

On the weekend visits during college, Bernice and Sally studied astrology together. Sally was enamored of it — soon they were both doing star charts and reading Manly Hall. Sally learned the art and philosophy of it, Bernice the science. Sally said her dream was to return to Toledo and open a psychic shop with Bernice. They could do a radio show. They could write a book. Summer of sophomore year, they apprenticed themselves to the infamous "Witch of Toledo," an ancient woman rumored to have descended from Esther Birchard, who lived on a creek offshoot of the river in Maumee and took in clients for psychic readings, curses, cures, and charms. So many people had crashed in cars on the road beside her house that there were hexes and wards hung from the trees, yes hexes and wards even in a highly sophisticated scientific center like Toledo. After all, she called herself a witch. Never mind it was a blind curve with no guardrail.

Sally and Bernice worked for her for free

through the summer of '82, cleaning her house, ordering her appointments, and being allowed to listen in on client visits. Sally learned how to talk about the way the winds move through time, and Bernice learned how to apply statistics to an individual, so that holding a client's hand and gazing at her palm became a riddle of mathematics, a rigid flowchart of possibilities. Sally got really good at talking and believing, and Bernice got really good at tricking and pretending, until together they could captivate anyone they practiced on. By the summer of '83, she was allowing them to practice on clients and giving them a cut of the fee. By the summer of '84, before their senior year, they were practically running the place, and Witch told them she would give them half her business, were they to set up shop on their own.

"I'm done," said Witch sadly. "All these people are wearing me out."

In their senior year, Sally got engaged to Dean. She did try dating other people, but then she would get back together with him in a mad, tantric affair. Bernice said it was like she kept getting on lifeboat after lifeboat, but then when the lifeboats got too far away from the ship, she had a panic that she would never find land, yanked the oars away from whoever was rowing, and paddled right back to the sinking vessel. Bernice didn't care for Dean much. But Sally couldn't live without him.

As Sally approached graduation, Dean switched from the philosophy department to visual arts. He painted large canvases with scenes part science fiction and part mythology. His form was graphic and dark, like a comic book in paint.

"I love him," said Sally. "I know it's crazy. I mean, he's an artist. But I love him. And you know what? I think he's really talented. He dazzles me."

"That's stupid," said Bernice. It was the weekend of the first basketball game of Sally's senior season, and Bernice was in Ann Arbor to see it. Sally and Dean had a place off campus, a little half house that Sally's mother had insisted on purchasing and furnishing. "You're just drunk on fucking him. Tantric this, tantric that. That's no reason to marry the guy."

Bernice was living in her parents' old house in Toledo while finishing her degree at Bowling Green. Her father had been only too happy to give her the house, as if her graduation from high school had been some kind of finish line that he was eager to cross.

He also bought Bernice a car, and she could drive to Ann Arbor to visit Sally whenever she wanted. This was good, because the only way they could dream together was if they were in the same city. It still worked best in Toledo. Sally said it was because the energy was right. Bernice wouldn't have said, "Sally, it's because you suck at lucid dreaming." But it was true. Sally would lie down and hope for magic every time, where Bernice was learning exactly what physical behaviors would contribute to maintaining control of her dreams. "Just put your body to sleep, but keep your mind awake. It's not mystical. It's not even difficult," said Bernice. But Sally struggled, and could only dream with Bernice if Bernice would come and find her in one of her own dreams. Sally always had trouble sleeping. It was something that troubled her all of her life.

"I thought it was stupid at first, too, this art thing," said Sally, throwing herself down on the leather sofa her mom had gotten from Finland.

"But then you took him to bed," said Bernice. "And then it didn't seem so stupid."

"Hey, shut up," Sally said. "You should try it sometime. You might like it."

But Bernice had actually had sexual

encounters with several girls. Her thin dreadlocks, her porcelain skin and large gray eyes, her tiny frame made it easy to pull in someone whose warm mouth would bump against her crotch enough times to forestall the aching need there. Whose fingers would slide around in a pleasing way, soothing her. She did like it. But she was a greedy lover, uninterested in giving back what was given to her, and sometimes she slapped her girlfriends, so she didn't have a lot of repeat customers. This didn't bother her. She didn't want a lot of love.

"You're leaving disappointed," she would say to these girls, and then blame it on the liquor. "You shouldn't have let me get so drunk." The booze she could leave in Ohio long enough to visit Sally for one day, two days, and then she would be driving south on 75, back to the comfort of gin, back to pushing her crotch into the face of some sad soul who didn't mind keeping her pants on, who didn't mind having her hair pulled a little, just to be in company for the night. She wouldn't say, "Sorry." She certainly wouldn't say, "I apologize, but I'm in love with my best friend. And when your tongue is on me, I'm pretending it is hers. And that's the reason I have such a longing for your tongue."

"Hey," said Sally. "I have something to show you. Look in that envelope on the counter and pull out what's inside."

Bernice reached over and slid a manila envelope close to her, reached inside and slipped out a bundle of stapled papers and some photographs.

"What do you think? This is the place I picked out. You know. For the astrology studio. When we take over from Witch."

Bernice spread the pictures out on the counter and looked them over. They showed a strange little farmhouse and some wooded land. Yes, they could appoint this place with all the trappings of a gypsy's lair. It already had an old well, a busted-down split-rail fence, and plenty of odd outbuildings.

"We could make it really arty and interesting," said Sally. "Kind of like Witch's house but even more so. So it's a real experience, not some tawdry affair in a strip mall in the suburbs or glassy storefront downtown, like next to the cheese store. Or the magazine rack. Let them feel the magic of it."

Bernice glanced at the map, the survey. She said, "From here we could see the stars. Witch's house is too close to the city. This place would be perfect."

"Exactly," said Sally. "You get it."

"But what about Dean?" Bernice asked.

Sally rose from the sofa and came over to the counter. She leaned over Bernice and pulled aside one of the photos. It showed a little shack, maybe what used to be an old sheep barn.

"This," she said, "will be his art studio."

"What about his degree? Won't he be staying here?"

"Well, he'll have to come back up, you know, on weekdays or sometimes," Sally explained. "But of course he'll be there, I mean, I can't leave him. I need him, Bernice. This will be our house, mine and Dean's. We'll live there," Sally said slowly. "We'll live there. You'll keep living at your house, of course."

"Oh, of course."

"I mean, you don't want to live with us, do you? I just assumed you wouldn't. I mean, that would be kind of awkward. We're in love."

"Of course."

Sally laughed suddenly. "Whoa, that could have been super uncomfortable!" She tossed her long body onto the other barstool and leaned against the counter.

"Don't be dumb," said Bernice. "I think the farmhouse idea is perfect."

That night, Sally scored twenty-nine points and her team won. Bernice sat in the stands, watched her friend going left and right, left and right, twitching the basketball jersey forward on her shoulders, folding her waistband over, pushing down her socks. Three months later, Sally missed her period. It was early February, midseason for basketball. Sally took a pregnancy test, and it was positive. She spent an hour crying in the bathroom in the dark, and a day in near silence. Then she called Bernice.

"BER-niss," she said. "BER-niss, what I have to say to you is very SERI-iss."

"OK," said Bernice. She closed the book she had been reading and switched on the television. *Laverne and Shirley.* They both had boyfriends, equally distasteful and equally serviceable. Maybe if there was another Dean, she would, too. Would she, if there was another Dean?

"I'm pregnant," said Sally. Then she coughed or sobbed. "I'm pregnant; I just found out."

"Oh, no," said Bernice. "How did this happen? How did you let this happen?"

"I'm not even sure," Sally said, not offended. "He's not even sure. I don't know how it could have happened. You know how his big sex thing is that he shoots it right back into his balls."

"Maybe he got distracted."

"Maybe! I don't know! Anyway, I'm pregnant; I had like multiple tests and everything."

There was a pause. Bernice didn't know how to react.

"Are we like happy?" asked Bernice. "Are you going to keep it?"

"Bernice," Sally said, skipping over the question. "Do you know what this baby's due date is? Do you know — can you figure it out?"

"Can't the doctor figure that out?" asked Bernice. Meanwhile, Laverne answered the door. It was her boss. She clapped her hand to her head and bowed at the knees.

"Yes, yes, I know," said Sally. "I'm saying, do you know? Never mind. I'll tell you. It's November eleventh!"

"Eleven eleven?"

"I know!" Sally gasped.

"That's auspicious."

"Auspicious for twinning. For twinning souls."

"I mean, who knows if the baby will even come on its due date, though . . . sometimes they —"

"Listen," Sally jumped in. "Remember when we were kids, and our parents got divorced, and I had that stupid crush on

Sam Thomas —"

"He said you wore him out," Bernice reminded her.

"Yes, exactly, and we were like, bah, boo on love, boo on romance, who needs it?"

"Who needs boys!" said Bernice.

"Do you remember, though, the conversations we used to have about arranged marriage? I mean, really, we were like twelve or something when we thought of it. When did we get so smart?"

"Of course I remember that," said Bernice. It had been a few years since they'd talked about it. Bernice thought Sally had forgotten. Laverne was putting on her coat and hat and grabbing her purse in a very purposeful manner. She had a ritual for these things — a way to put on the hat, the coat, to clothe herself for the world outside the apartment set.

"Do you remember what we talked about —"

"Oh, no, Sally. No, hold on —" Bernice got up and began to walk toward the front door.

"We wanted to have two babies," Sally repeated. "And like we would raise them, and then separate them —"

"Yeah, I remember those conversations." She found herself in the kitchen, pulled out a sauce pan, and slammed it down on the stove.

"And they would love each other. They could marry each other, be perfect for each other —"

"Sally!"

"And now," Sally went on, breathless and sniffing up her tears, "Look at this? I'm pregnant and due November eleventh! Bernice, we can do it! We can make that happen!"

"No," Bernice had now filled every burner with a different cooking pot, all empty. Finally, she reached into the pantry, behind the flour and sugar, and pulled out a bottle of gin.

"What?" Sally sounded distracted, like she couldn't believe what she was hearing.

"No! That was all purely hypothetical." Bernice drank from the bottle.

"Listen," said Sally. "All we need to do is get you pregnant right away. No problem, right?"

"But my due date won't be the same as yours. You'll be —"

"Doesn't matter, Dean says," said Sally. "We can still go into labor on the same night. You just take the herbs or whatever."

"What?" Bernice scoffed. "Dean says?"

"I told him all about it. He thinks it is a

wonderful idea."

"Wait, does Dean know you're talking to me right now? Does Dean even know you're having a baby?"

"Say you'll do it. We even have an idea for who we can get to make you pregnant."

Bernice drank again from the bottle. "We?"

"I need to know if you're in this with me or not," Sally said.

"I can be in it with you, but I'm not getting pregnant beside you, Sally. You have to see this is crazy."

"I can't be all by myself!"

"But you have Dean! Right? You're in love," Bernice snapped. Then she felt sorry about it, sorry she had sounded so mean.

"Please, Bernice, just think about it. Can you just do a reading? Just look at tea, or dream about it, or something. Please. You know you can see what's right for us. I'll trust you; just say you're with me!"

"No. I can't see things in tea."

There was a long pause.

"You can live at the farm with us. I mean, considering everything, and Dean driving up to Michigan all the time, I really do need someone with me. Please. It'll be just the two of us. No Dean, like most of the time, anyway. Just you and me."

Sally vomited into a snowbank on the way in to Bernice's house. There was no warning. First she was smiling, then bending, and the vomit came out her face, with barely enough time to lean over. Bernice watched from the window, then opened the door for her and handed her a tissue. When she marched inside saying, "I'm fine. I'm just sick," Bernice had said, "No, you're pregnant."

Sally pulled off her coat and flopped into a chair. "Oh, shit," she said. "I might barf again. Seriously. This is pregnancy? I feel like I'm about to die."

Bernice stood behind the chair and put one finger on each of Sally's temples and began to press and release, press and release. She closed her eyes and hummed softly.

"Shouldn't you have your hands down here?" Sally asked, pointing to her stomach.

"The baby's not there yet," said Bernice. "Anyway I can't read him yet. I can only read you."

"Ah, but you know it's a him," Sally pointed out.

"Because I'm already reading you. Be quiet." Bernice resumed her humming a little louder. Sally closed her eyes.

After a few minutes, the teakettle boiled.

"You already have the tea on," said Sally. "Thank you, thank you, thank you. I know you can do it, Bernice, and I'll do whatever you say. Whatever you see, we'll do it."

"I don't see," said Bernice.

Sally opened her eyes and looked around, and then again without warning she quickly sat up and unleashed a thin stream of vomit into a spider plant beside the chair, barely leaning over in time to keep it from going down the front of her shirt. Bernice went for the teakettle, and for a handful of paper towels. Sally began to cry. Sally rarely cried. Once, on the basketball court, she had taken a vicious kick to the knee that ended in torn ligaments and six months in a metal brace, and never shed a tear. But now, her eyes were brimming.

Bernice fussed with the tea, came back over with two mugs steaming in her hand. She handed Sally a mug, and Sally saw there was a metal tea ball filled with loose leaves sitting down at the bottom. Bernice sat down on the coffee table next to Sally, and held her mug up to her face, blowing on the water.

"Think and drink," she said. Bernice had said this exact thing to a hundred clients before. As for the practice of reading leaves, she had learned just how to do it, from books and from her training — how to interpret an arrow as anything from an impending miscarriage to the location of a lost dog. Sally put her hand on her belly and opened her mouth to speak but Bernice shushed her. She allowed no talking while the tea was being drunk. Sally drank hers as quickly as she could cool it off, and when she had drained the liquid down to the top of the metal ball, she set the cup down on the low table and said, "Ready."

Bernice opened the ball of tea and shook the loose leaves into the cup, and began to swirl them.

"We ask a question," she said. Sally opened her mouth again but Bernice shook her head. "Shhh."

Bernice swirled and swirled the tea leaves in the dregs of Sally's tea, and then dumped the rest of the tea out into the saucer, leaving the leaves and twigs stuck around the bottom of the white cup. She watched the leaves and sticks settle and stop in the shapes they would take, and stared into the mug.

"The tortoise. Patience. A long plan," she said.

"Nine months long," muttered Sally.

"I think," said Bernice, "that you are going to have a son."

"You said that already," said Sally.

Bernice frowned. She saw a very distinct shape in the tea, one she was not familiar with.

"Look at this," she told Sally.

"What?" Sally demanded. She sat upright in her chair.

"Look here. Looks like . . ."

"Looks like a barbell," said Sally. "There is a barbell right there. What does that mean? I've never seen that symbol before."

"I don't know," said Bernice. "Have to get the book out."

She crossed to the bookshelf and put her finger down the spines of several books, then pulled out a slim one and opened it up.

Sally covered the teacup with her hand, coughed.

Bernice read the words next to the symbol that matched the one in the teacup. The book said, "Broken soul. Danger. Death."

Sally read her face, snatched the book away, and glared at the entry for barbell.

"Are you serious? What a shitty, shitty thing to say."

"Wait," Bernice told her, picking up the mug again. "Is that a rainbow, though?

Maybe it looks like a rainbow."

"It's a fucking barbell," said Sally. "Broken soul. What the fuck does that even mean."

Bernice shrugged and sat down on the coffee table again. She felt sad and sorry. She felt that Sally should not have to survive this pregnancy alone, not have to survive being married to Dean alone. What if the baby did have a broken soul? What if Sally got sick every day, had to be helped to the bathroom, helped back to bed?

"Maybe we can save him, though, don't worry," said Bernice.

"What breaks a soul?" Sally said.

"Love," said Bernice. "Gambling?"

"Love can literally kill him? Like with literal death? The book says death."

"Maybe that's metaphor," said Bernice softly. "They're only tea leaves."

Sally lay back in her chair, and ground her teeth together. The tears came out the corner of her eyes and dropped into her hair, her ears.

"What can I do," Sally said, enunciating each word very clearly. "What steps must I take to fix this? How can I help this boy?"

She sat up and glared at Bernice, as if her body was on fire, and she couldn't stand it. Bernice looked in Sally's face and saw a raw edge there that she had not seen before. And her heart was pounding, so full of love. It was just a clump of tea in a porcelain mug. But look at the spirit. Look at the flesh.

"How can we help?" Bernice corrected her. "I'll help you. I will."

14

"Here we are. Frankie's diner. Diners," said George, "are the best places to have arguments."

"No argument," said Irene. "I've been waiting to go to Frankie's since I crossed the border into Ohio."

Frankie's was attached to a nightclub, and George and Irene had waded through a band unloading instruments and amplifiers into the club side on the sidewalk. George took Irene's elbow, guided her through, but he was nervous to touch her, as if she would evaporate like a smoke golem, disappear into the ether again. When they got into the restaurant they were almost alone. The vinyl seats in the tight booths had been patched with duct tape, but a small brave pink carnation mounted a defense against dinginess in a miniature crystal vase on each table.

"Astronomers don't normally go here,"

said George.

"Good, then we won't see any of your ex-girlfriends," said Irene.

"Touché," George said. He picked up a menu and perused it, but Irene didn't touch hers.

"I'm eating fish tacos," said Irene. "Be warned."

"First date, and you're having fish tacos. That is bravery. You are an innovator."

"This isn't a first date," Irene corrected him. "I have a boyfriend. You have . . . some kind of girlfriend, right?"

"Some kind of. Yes. And you have some kind of boyfriend. Wizard is he? Hill troll? Batman?"

"He's into role-playing games. You know, online ones. He's made quite a lot of money designing scripts and things for them, thanks."

"Dungeons and Dragons, that sort of thing?"

Irene said, "Look, I'm here to discuss work. My work and your work."

"Our work," said George.

"We don't have 'our' work," said Irene. "I'm pretty sure we might even cancel each other out."

George said, "Let's discuss my work then. Speaking of poems, once upon a time, when

I was a little boy, my mother read to me a poem about how the faeries would sometimes come and take little boys away to play with them forever on their island."

"I know the poem," said Irene.

"Do you?" said George, incredulous.

"Yeah, it's Yeats. It's just . . . a regular poem. Lots of people know it."

George felt the Yeats was a cosmic signal, more than a happy accident. "Well, my mother was an astrologer, and she taught me that there were gods in the stars."

"Lots of people do that, too, and it's called church." Irene rearranged the sugar packets in the ceramic container, ordering them pink, yellow, blue. She took the white ones out and made a separate pile.

"Well, I believed it," said George. "So do you want to put rulers and calculators through all my internal organs?"

"Alright."

"You have killed me with calculus."

Irene smiled, looking at him through her eyelashes. He moved his feet carefully under the table, not wanting his long legs to kick her.

"That's so weird that our mothers were both astrologers," Irene said, turning the labels of the hot sauce and ketchup bottles forward. "Your mother didn't really look like an astrologer to me."

"Yes, well my mother doesn't do it anymore. She changed."

"Neither does mine. Maybe we have the same mother."

"Probably. Because the only thing worse than meeting you when you obviously have already found the love of your life" — George gestured with his arms to indicate Belion's largeness — "is meeting you and finding out you're actually my sister."

An old woman approached the table. She didn't wear a uniform or carry an order pad, but she asked, "What you guys like to eat?"

"Fish tacos, please. And chili. And Fortuna? Rip the roof off on the peppers, OK? I want to leave here without a lining in my stomach."

George raised his eyebrows. "Same," he said.

"Careful," said Irene. "We used to come here all the time in high school. I know what I'm dealing with. You've been sheltered. You've been protected from fish tacos and the fire they represent."

"Well," said George, "I know they're messy and spicy and come with beans. You're breaking all the rules of date food. You care nothing for me. This is proof."

"When I'm choking, flatulating, and dripping fish from my seared-off lips, you'll be able to see the beauty of my calculations instead of the asymmetry of my eyes."

"Probably not," said George. "I will never forget the asymmetry of your eyes. It is transformative symmetry. It is the best symmetry. It is the symmetry that is beauty."

Outside, it was late. She got into her car and started it. "Come on," she yelled to him. He got into the car, and as soon as he opened the door, he could hear music. A soaring violin part and a man's deep voice singing a song from the seventies. This freaked him out. No one else should have known this folk song — the band was so obscure and weird: Compton and Batteau. He had never met anyone before in his life that knew this music.

"How do you know this band?" he asked her.

"My mother again," said Irene.

"Was she a violinist?" he asked. He wanted to know all about her. Every year, every hour. What she liked for breakfast, whether she liked her pillows hard or soft. "And what do you like for breakfast?"

"Just get in," said Irene. "Before we get to breakfast, I want to hear all about your 'plane of symmetry' thing."

261

"Are you sure?" George asked.

"Sure, but I might have to tell you why it's not going to work."

George buckled his seat belt. "Please do. I've been waiting for this all day. Without this information, I may stumble through tomorrow thinking I have a future in science."

"If such a thing were to exist, it would have been found by now."

"Not true. The more we work with the *Toledo Space Telescope,* the more we find all kinds of things we didn't know existed."

"But what you're talking about, this axis of the universe, this gateway, it cannot possibly be known, even if it were to exist. Not for thousands of years, maybe. We just don't have the instruments. We cannot measure this."

"Who cares what you can measure? If you can think about it, it could be real."

"It's not religion, George. It's measurements. It's math, whether you like it or not."

"You know, religion and astronomy and astrology all used to be the same thing," George reminded her.

"Well, they're not anymore," said Irene. She waved her hand around next to George's head. "Religion, astrology, hokey schmokey over here." Then she slammed her hand into the steering wheel. "Astronomy, math, rulers over here."

"My side of the car is more fun," said George.

"Your side of the car isn't even a car! Just saying something doesn't make it real."

George sat silently. He was watching her hands gripping the wheel. He couldn't help smiling.

"How can you be like this when you're working on the *Toledo Space Telescope*?" she asked. "Astrometry isn't about guessing, or writing poetry, or whatever."

"Yes, yes, I know. But the box I was working on is at JPL right now. Undergoing thermal testing. I don't have to think about it for a few months. I have the semester off thinking about it."

"Oh, dear, you've finished with the TST, and your little side project isn't going so well either, is it? Maybe I could talk to someone at the institute for you. You've only lost your office, your lab space, your assistant, and most of your funding. I'm sure they can find something for you to do, though. Maybe you can come and work for me."

She flashed him a wicked little smile and his heart contracted. "OK, can you just point the car and drive?" he said.

"Back across the bridge?" said Irene.

"Yeah, downtown. We need to get up very high so I can show you what I need to show you."

Irene frowned. "High? Are we going to One Seagate?"

"That's right," said George. In all the glass spires of Toledo, one lone "skyscraper" dominated the skyline. One Seagate was a thirty-two-story building with an exterior made all of glass. The tallest building in Toledo.

George and Irene stood next to each other in a glittering elevator booth, going up. His elbow touching her shoulder, carefully touching it, not pushing it. They were absolutely silent. George watched her pulse beating at her throat, and wondered what she thought of him.

When the door opened at the penthouse, a uniformed security guard at a small podium nodded dispassionately at George and waved them inside.

"Come on," said George. "This is my mother's office."

George took Irene by the elbow and pulled her on past the granite reception desk and down the hallway. The office was beautifully appointed and lit for overnight from dim canisters in the ceiling. The carpet was rich and dense, Dean's paintings on the wall looking strangely bold for such a conservative office.

"My father's art," George tossed to Irene as he swept her on toward the back of the suite, flipping on light switches as he went. She stopped in front of a painting, and he frowned. The last thing he needed was for her to dutifully inspect his father's work and feel she had to say something horrific like, "They're nice" or "I don't get it."

"My god," said Irene, staring at the canvas. "I think my mother has one of his paintings hanging in her house."

"Well, he's kind of famous," said George. "But whatever. That's cool. Come on. There's something I want to show you."

They emerged onto the deck, and the city lay before them in lights. The patio was broad, running the length of One Seagate, and there were plants and trees up here, rooted into pots or huge dirt-filled holes in the floor.

"Trees," said Irene.

"I do her gardening," said George. "It's part of why I get paid my exorbitant salary as son."

Irene went straight to the edge. For a second, George had the terrible impression that she was going to go straight over, and fall to her death. He almost reached out to touch her, grasp her around the waist, pull her back into him, wrap her up tight. But she stood, instead, gripping the railing. When her face turned back to look at him, it was clouded. Her eyes looked wet, as if she were about to cry, or had just stopped herself from crying.

He went over to her and put his hand in the middle of her back.

"Are you afraid of heights?" he said.

"No," said Irene. She bit her lip. George imagined her biting his lip. He wanted to kiss her, feel her teeth pressing against his mouth, her wide lips on his.

"Did you know," he said, "that a fear of heights is actually not a fear that you'll accidentally fall, but that you'll be possessed by the desire to fall on purpose?"

Irene was silent, then pulled at a vine from a nearby pot and said briskly, "How do you maintain it? I mean, this vine here, it's got to be some sort of jungle species. Surely it can't survive out here in the winter?"

"We've got walls. Retractable walls. In the winter it becomes a sort of terrarium."

Irene leaned dangerously far out over the rail, the vines and branches of the trees waving alongside her in the high breeze.

"It's like the hanging gardens of —"

"Wait," he interrupted her. "Really, to understand this properly, you have to close your eyes, at this height, and imagine this is still Mesopotamia. This is still Babylon. The sand, the oppression. Forget the space shuttle and satellite telescopes. This is like *old*. Irrigation is brand new here."

"Babylon, you say?"

He waved his arms. "The Tigris River. The Euphrates."

George pointed to the west, to show her where the Toledo Institute of Astronomy lay inside its brick wall, inside its gates.

"There's the ziggurat at the institute, see it?"

Irene nodded.

"But that one's just a model," said George. "You are standing on the site of the ziggurat that Hammurabi built. That Nebuchadnezzar used to climb on a Saturday morning, with his hot cup of tea and bagel sandwich. Prototype for the Tower of Babel. Eighty thousand steps up or something ridiculous like that."

"Right, something ridiculous," she said drily.

"And you look down, over the side, Nebuchadnezzar," he went on, "and there's the world, spread out below you. Babylon.

Toledo. All these sparkling lights from the windows of your citizens, and the roads they use to travel by, and the corners of the world. And you look up, and there are the stars, sparkling and marking out the corners of the sky."

Irene sighed. "It feels like falling," she said.

"You know you can point the orbiting telescopes out to count the stars and measure space. But you can also point them in, you know? And sometimes at night the earth looks almost just the same. The stars out there, the people and cities down here."

Irene laughed. "Somebody told me you believe Toledo is built on the ruins of ancient Babylon, and I thought they were shitting me. Is this all to say that I'm standing on some kind of tomb?"

George shook his head. "The ziggurat was not a tomb. It was a temple. So, you're standing on a kind of altar. A very tall one. This is where it would have been. By the river."

"Comforting," she said. "Like blankets and hot tea, but warmer and safer."

"I'm about to tell you the best part. This is the reason I brought you up here."

"Oh, good," said Irene. "I was beginning to think this nutburger you were feeding me about the Tigris and Euphrates was the point."

"See the Maumee River? That's the Tigris."

"Oh, dang, it is the point," sighed Irene. But she smiled at him, as if it were all OK.

"So where's the Euphrates?" George pressed on. "Where do you think?"

"I'm pretty sure it's in Iraq, with the rest of ancient Persia."

"Nope. It's here, too. You just can't see it."

"Do tell," said Irene.

"Have you noticed," George began, feeling like a proud parent on Christmas morning, about to rip the paper off a shiny bicycle, "that lots of people at the institute whisper about what's 'downstairs' and then maybe they point down sort of suggestively like there's something underground that they're being very secretive about?"

"No," said Irene. "I've noticed you doing that, but not everyone doing that."

"Well, there is something underground that we're being very secretive about, but since I believe you're about to be asked to be pretty much in charge of it, I think the time has come for you to know it exists."

"What?" Irene was now interested.

He pointed, and she turned to look west

toward where the sun had set, toward the institute. He moved to stand behind her, so that the light breeze blew her ponytail back to brush against his shirt front.

"It starts over there," he said. "And it comes this way, that way, this way, down to here." He traced a path with his finger. "And then crosses under the Tigris, and goes back up that way, that way, and up to there."

"But that's a circle. You're telling me this thing is actually following the path of an ancient river?"

"An ellipse actually. But never mind."

"Rivers aren't circles."

"Yes, I know, but this is a supercollider. It's only called the Euphrates because we already have a Tigris. It's metaphor. Like poetry is. Like music. Sing it. The Euphrates!" He sang.

She was glaring intently at the place where he'd gestured, and he could see her mentally calculating.

"It's eighty-seven kilometers," he said. "The beams intersect in six places, with six different detectors. I'm sorry, five. They're waiting for one more. I think you have it in your lab. It might be attached to a figure-eight-shaped device at the moment, but I'm sure it can be fitted to the river."

"The river," said Irene slowly.

George put his arm more securely around her. He started to say something: "I'm so —" But he stopped. They stood there together silently for several minutes. It was as if his entire life had led up to that point and she had been there the whole time, just quiet. She fit so perfectly into his arm, and there was no bumping of hip bones or awkward dangling of arms. She was exactly the perfect size.

"Since our mothers were astrologers, I have to ask you, what's your sign?"

"Scorpio," she murmured without hesitation.

"Really?" he said. "Me too. What day?"

"The eleventh."

"What?" he said. "That's my birthday, too!"

He spun her around to face him, holding her now by both arms.

"You know what? I have to go," she said. She sprang away from him and marched back to the patio door, threw it open, and went inside. He chased her.

He caught up to her next to the elevator, mashing on the DOWN button with an angry little finger.

"We can be birthday buddies! Let's do a joint party. Let's see, what could the theme be? I know — nebulas! You could dress like the reflection nebula, you know, all shimmery, and I could go as a horse head."

Irene stared at the crease in the elevator door. After pursing her lips together for a few seconds, waiting for the elevator car to come, she spat out, "I'm leaving."

George laughed. "I see that. Making the elevator come usually leads to leaving."

There was a ding, and the doors slid open. Irene turned to look at him. "Well, bye," she said. She slipped into the elevator and began to mash the CLOSE DOOR button. But George followed her in.

"I'm leaving, too," he explained.

As the digital numbers descended 10, 9, 8, 7 . . . she finally spoke: "How old are you?"

George said, "Twenty-nine."

"You are not," said Irene.

"Yeah, I am," said George. "Are you?"

He felt his stomach contract. He actually felt nervous. "Move," said his stomach. "Move, move, move. Act, act, act." At the first floor, Irene raced him to her car.

"But if we were born on the same day," he said, rushing along behind her, "then Irene, we're not just birthday buddies. Don't you get it? This is why we know the

272

same poetry. This is why we know the same songs."

"I don't know those songs. I don't like that poetry. Don't be weird," said Irene.

She had her car door unlocked when she was ten cars away. It beeped and blinked at her, and George skipped ahead, getting between her and the door before she could reach for the handle.

"Toledo General? Toledo General? Come on, were you born at Toledo General?"

"I'm sure not. No, I don't —"

"Then where?" said George. "Where? We're twin souls, Irene! Twin souls."

His back was against her car and he was braced there, against it; she could not open it. She came toward him, as if she might attack him or climb him or shout at him. But then she pressed her body up against the front of him and put one hand across his mouth.

"I don't want you to go home," he said through her hand. "I'm sorry. I'll stop talking, but —"

"George, shut up," she said. She put her hand behind his neck and kissed him. He stood up from the car, and she came up with him, his hands under her butt, lifting her, catching her to him, and she clung now, her hands around his shoulders, mouth still touching, now opening, a small soft tongue brushing against his lips. He felt her mouth touch his, causing a long, slow, swell of happiness that started from where the rough denim of her jeans pressed against his khakis, continuing up to where her hips lay against his belt, her breasts pressing against his chest, and all of her warmth and anger spilling out of her like a fountain. Her fingernails were in his hair when she pulled her face back.

He spoke first. "OK, forget whatever I was just saying. I have nothing else to say."

"Really? Because you had so much to say, thirty seconds ago."

"I was stupid then. I can't even remember what I was thinking about."

He went in for another kiss, but she turned her head to the side.

"You can put me down," she said quietly. He set her back on the sidewalk. She put her hand on the car door again.

"Let's get a grip here, George," she said.

"No," he said. "Marry me."

It was all he could do to keep his hands from plunging in between the buttons of her little button-down shirt, shedding it from her, putting his mouth over her collar bone, her breast, her hip bone, yanking off her pants.

"We have obligations," she was saying. "It's probably not even legal for us to date. We could get fired."

"What?" he asked. "Do I have a job? I feel like I'm one-minute old."

"You need to understand something." Irene put her hands up to her face, covering her eyes. George remembered that her mother had just died. And here he was, being the asshole. How could he make her cry?

"I'm sorry," he said. "I'll stop. I'll go away."

"No," she said, and she took her hands down and showed him that she was laughing.

"What is going on?" he said, almost laughing, too. "Are you going nuts on me?"

"I want to have sex with you," she said, laughing to the point she was crying, and then wiping away the tears. She punched him in the chest. "Sex! I want to have sex!"

"Good!" said George. "That is super good because I want to do that, too!"

"No, you don't understand," she said, sniffing and pulling herself together, wiping her eyes. "I mean I want to have sex like in my vagina." She pointed at his zipper. "That going in there," and she pointed at her crotch. This sent her off into another gale of laughter.

"That's great, because that's exactly how sex is done. Exactly that way." He was confused a little by her behavior, but in his mind the fact that she was talking and pointing at his crotch was enough to distract him from analysis.

"This is going to be OK, Irene," he said. "This is going to be great."

"I don't normally feel like this," said Irene. "I don't. This is weird."

George put his arms around her again, so in love with the feeling of her against him, as if they were two pieces of a two-piece puzzle, and they just wanted to make the picture work.

"We need to go to a place," said George. "I know the place."

"What kind of place?" she said.

"Don't worry," he said. "It's a good kind of place. It's a nightclub for astronomers. You'll feel right at home."

15

They decided to do it at Bernice's house. That way she would be the most comfortable, Sally pointed out.

"I'll need at least a shot," said Bernice. "I don't think anyone here would begrudge me a shot. Would they?"

The girls sat in the living room on the wood-frame love seat that was hung, charmingly, from the ceiling. A thick braided rug took up half the floor in a room stuffed with antiques and furniture that Bernice's father had made long ago. Her mother had wanted a porch swing she could use all year. So this was it. It hadn't worked out for her father, making that porch swing. He had still ended up alone.

"Maybe we should do it on the kitchen table," said Bernice. There was a large wasp's nest there currently, defunct and used as a centerpiece, augmented visually with several tiny quilted muslin rabbits.

"This is not an operation," said Sally. "We do not need a table."

"It's an insemination. Same thing," said Bernice.

Bernice made a show of retrieving two ice cubes from the fridge and placing them in a short glass, going to her father's bar, which was now her bar. She pulled out the whiskey and poured it into the glass. She took a swig, grimaced, lifted the wasp's nest with the other hand and set it on the counter.

"Right here," she said, patting the table. She swept the quilted rabbits onto the floor.

The table was the kind made from a crosscut of a tree. Its surface was irregular.

"No," said Sally. "Come on, don't be so nervous. It's just sex. We'll do it in your bed."

"Not in my bed. Not upstairs," said Bernice, draining her glass. "I don't want that thing going upstairs."

"What, Ray's dick?" She teased. "His love wand? His trouser pickle?"

"Ray's anything. Ray."

Bernice refilled her glass.

"Don't get drunk," said Sally. "Probably inhibits —"

"What, inhibits the egg from opening its legs for a suitable sperm? I would think the opposite would be true."

278

Sally began to move around the down-stairs, pushing her hands into chairs and the cushions of the small sofa, testing surfaces. She moved into the dining room.

"After tonight you can't drink anyway," she called. "Pregnant, and all. I don't drink."

"Bullshit, I'm drinking right up until I see that positive test. If I even see it. Which I probably won't."

Sally stopped. "This is perfect," she said. She was standing in the office, and when Bernice came through the foyer to see what she was talking about, she saw that Sally was sitting on the Victorian fainting couch, which had once been one of her mother's prize possessions. When acquired, it had been upholstered in horsehair, but her mother had redone it in red corduroy, with gold upholstery tacks.

"It squeaks," said Bernice.

"I didn't think you drank that much anyway, that it would be such a big deal to give it up," said Sally.

"I don't," said Bernice. "But why is this perfect? This of all things?"

"Because of the elevation," Sally explained. She lay down with her head at the foot of the fainting couch and her feet on the headrest. It was a gentle slope up, and when she scooted up until her ass was just at the edge of the top, it was about waist high.

"This is the best way to get knocked up," Sally said. "Because of gravity!"

She demonstrated by holding her knees, and her jeans stretched tight over her crotch. She pointed to the X where the seams met. "See, the sperm just sinks happily down right into the egg; it's not even work! It's just falling — that's not even hard."

Bernice raised her eyebrows.

"You don't want him sweating away on top of you, do you?" Sally asked. "This way, he can just stand up."

There was a knock at the side door. On the way through to let her caller in, Bernice did another quick shot of whiskey. Then just one more for safety.

Though Sally's arrangement was scientifically sound, Bernice was too short. With her ass scooted to the high end of the fainting couch, her head was upside down, and it was hard to stay up there, hard to smile with the blood all rushing to her head.

"This is stupid," Ray said. "Let's flip her around."

Ray had been presented by Dean and selected by Sally based on his astrological pedigree, his willingness to have sex with a girl casually, forsaking any resulting child, and his geographical accessibility. Basically, Ray was chosen because his driver's license said he was born on the right day, he was kind of an asshole, and he was around. While this made the perfect sperm donor for Sally's agenda, it made a rather lousy sex partner for Bernice's first foray into heterosexual intercourse. By the time he had been at the seduction for five minutes, Bernice was in tears, Ray was sulking, and nothing had even come close to being inserted into anything else.

Bernice lay on the fainting couch, head on the headrest. She was wearing a short skirt with an elastic waist, which was pushed up over her hips, and her dingy pubic triangle was huddled there between her pale legs, exposed. She was also wearing a turtleneck, a cardigan, and a linen scarf. It's chilly in Toledo in March.

"I think I know what's wrong," said Sally suddenly. "Ray, can you give us a minute? Like, go smoke on the back porch or something. OK?"

Ray sighed and rolled his eyes and pulled his jeans back up, snapped them shut, and slouched off to have a cigarette outside.

"I'm sorry," said Bernice. "I'm sorry that

I can't do it."

"Wait," said Sally, tugging Bernice's skirt back down and patting it into place. She sat down on the edge of the couch and took Bernice's hand. It was almost like being in a hospital bed. Bernice had almost died of being penetrated by a stranger. Sally was visiting her.

"I have to ask you something now, we never really talked about," said Sally.

Now Bernice felt a flutter in her lungs, and the tears rolled again.

"Are you a virgin? Because, that can make it hard. I understand if you are, I mean, I think it's totally cool, but you really should have told me."

"I'm not," said Bernice.

Sally was gazing down at her, seeming so kind, looking so thoughtful.

"There's a membrane, you know, it's —"

"I'm not a virgin!" Bernice snapped. How many fingers, how many vibrators, how many dildos ripping up through her? Not a virgin.

"Really?" said Sally, her voice changing, suddenly gossipy. "Who did you sleep with? I'm trying to think —"

"Get him back in here," Bernice growled. "I'm ready."

"Are you sure?"

"Ray!" Bernice called. "We're done talking!"

Ray came in, flicking his cigarette butt into the darkness. He pulled his jeans open again and his heavy hands pushed Bernice's skirt up around her hips again. He kneeled over her and began to push himself around on her, grabbing his dick around its base and pushing it into the side of her thighs, first one and then the other.

Sally had moved up to a spot beside Bernice's head and was chastely looking out the window, but she snuck a look back and said flatly, "Ray, that's all you've got? Seriously?"

"Shut up," Ray grunted. "Open up her legs. I can't get anywhere."

Bernice pulled her knees up and put her legs on each side of Ray's, and he began to press his half-soft dick against her pubic hair. It was soft against soft.

"Again I say, Ray, is that it?" Sally questioned.

"I gotta see something, come on," complained Ray. "She's buttoned up like a nun!"

"Take your clothes off, Bernice," Sally sighed.

Ray pulled back, and Bernice sat up to take off her scarf, her cardigan, and her turtleneck, which left some static crackles on her dreadlocks, and only her little bra around her chest.

Ray nodded appreciatively and said, "Good, that's better. But when are you getting naked, Sally? I mean, let's get this party started."

Bernice glared at Sally. "What did you tell him?"

"I'm sorry!" Sally said. "I might have told him it was a twofer! I mean, I knew I wanted to stay in the room with you, right? So it's kinda a twofer?"

Ray stood up and kicked off his jeans, pulled off his sweatshirt. His underwear sagged around his hips, and then he pulled that off, too, and was completely naked. He had a stocky body and a smooth chest, like a wrestler or a shot-putter. He pointed at Sally. "Your turn?" he said. Sally pulled off her top and dropped it on the floor.

"Sorry," she said to Bernice. "Let's just get this over with."

"Thanks," said Ray sarcastically. His face was nice enough, but it was a face that kind of said, "I don't give a shit."

"Oooh, baby," cooed Sally, her mouth making an oval kiss shape. "Give it to her. Give her what you've got."

Sally sat back down next to Bernice and held her hand. Bernice tried to relax her legs as Ray's hand began to probe around. She focused on the curve of Sally's tit, the one that was nearest her. The warm roundness of it, the nipple so pale it was almost translucent. She could imagine reaching out to that perfect skin, tracing a circle around it. But when Ray reached out with his other hand to touch it, Sally slapped his hand, hard.

"No," she said sharply. "You're a bad man. No touching!" But it seemed to have the opposite effect that she intended.

"I'm getting somewhere, now I'm getting somewhere," he said, letting his breath out with a groan. Bernice could feel him now pressing up against her. She closed her eyes. She tried to think of every girl she'd ever let explore down there, every set of teeth that scraped across her lips, every fingertip that went inside, every tongue like velvet. She felt Ray's finger prying.

"Oh, come on," said Ray, "She's dry as a bone. Is this some kind of joke?"

"I'm OK," said Bernice, eyes still closed. "I'm OK." She reached her hand down to separate herself, try to make the way for him easier.

"You know what helps me sometimes," Sally whispered to Bernice, close to her face. She realized Sally was kneeling on the ground next to the couch. "Is when Dean sucks on my breast, when he's inside me. It's crazy good, right?"

"OK," said Bernice. She felt Sally's hand unclip her bra in the center, and those feathery fingers push it to the side, slipping across her nipple. Her eyes were shut tight. She would not open them.

"Come on, Ray," said Sally. "Do it. Here it is. Suck on her."

Bernice felt his body move, his chest lay low against hers, the heat of him.

"I can't, Sal. She's too short. I can't reach my face down to it and still keep my stick in her."

"OK, I'll do it," Sally's voice was low and determined. And then Sally's mouth was on her breast, and the heat of it charged through her, and arced down to her crotch, and with a rush he was inside her, and as long as that mouth was attached to her, it was good. She felt him surge and pull away, and surge again, and his hand came down beside her head, and his other hand grabbed her thigh and pushed it up. The pressure on her breast and the electricity running between Sally's mouth and Ray's cock in her was excruciating and the tears rolled.

"Mmmm," Sally's mouth against her skin was vibrating. And Bernice felt her mouth buzzing and realized she was saying, "Mmm hmmm!" She let her hand stroke Sally's hair. Ran her fingers down over Sally's back. Now Ray had grabbed her by the hips and was going faster, and Sally pulled away to murmur, "I think I'm going to do the other one."

Her breast, wet, was cold, and then Sally laid her own against it to put her teeth around the other, and then Ray was pressing suddenly very deep, and he said "Oh, god, yeah" because having sex with a virgin isn't just fun because of the idea of it, or the way you enforce your will onto another person. It's fun because that extra ring of skin feels really good. And then she was tearing, and hurting a little bit, and she thought to herself, "I really was a virgin, how funny." But Ray had blown his wad deep inside her. And he was panting as he pulled himself away.

"You guys turned out to be hot," he said.

Before Bernice was able to feel chilly, Sally was pulling her shirt back on. As she tossed Bernice her cardigan, she gave her a thumbs-up, like good job. Big smile. All the crooked teeth.

"Now you want a cigarette and a beer," she said to Ray. "You can find both at Frankie's. You should go there. And if you say a fucking word about this, I'll tell your entire lacrosse team your dick erect is the size of a kalamata olive. And I wouldn't even be lying too much."

When Sally had shown him out, she came back to the room where Bernice was still lying on the fainting couch, having remembered and turned the other way around to elevate her hips.

"You did awesome," said Sally in the doorway. "I am so proud of you. I'm sorry he was so dumb, but you know, a smart guy after that kinda lay would never let you go."

Bernice smiled. "Never let us go," she said.

"Ha!" Sally barked out a laugh. "Yeah, I guess you're right."

Bernice slept on the fainting couch that night, doing her best to keep her hips higher than her head. Sally slept in Bernice's bed. There were no lucid dreams.

Sally and Bernice moved in together, to the cottage in the swamp.

Sally was blond. Blue eyes. Wide face with pink cheeks, tiny gold cross around her neck, just for style. Sally wore faded jeans and industrial-strength sandals and beads and was beautiful. She had long arms and used them for hugging people in sweet, clinical hugs, like other people shake hands.

Not gushy or cloying. She was a big smiler and had a big smile with lots of teeth. She liked to eat candy.

Bernice was pale, small, pointy. She had an army jacket that she wore for intimidation purposes, but it was too clean to have much of the desired effect. She was not a candle burner or a picture hanger, but she did keep cards in her file of pictures she might have hung or people she might have thought about dangling over a candle flame. She was a keeper of mementos, and a little bit furtive.

She was closed, to Sally's open. Dark to Sally's light. Lingering resentment to Sally's effusive forgiveness. Bitter truth to Sally's grand statement. Smirk to Sally's horse laugh. Fuck to Sally's kiss. Love to Sally's love.

Had they found love? Can anyone ever find it? You may say that it's worse now, but in 1984, it was already pretty bad. Religion had crashed, science was on fire, and the ideologies of governments around the world wore thin and tattered, turned old in one day. No monolithic monologues, no true truths, no classic classics. And the hardest of these to fall, the towering construct that cratered out bigger than god, democracy, and penicillin, was true love.

What an idiotic notion.

All the love stories had their clothes yanked off. Penelope: a trollop, feverishly quilting her chaste little heart out, waiting for her man. Wouldn't that be just the thing you'd want in an absent wife. Abelard lost his balls; they were hacked off right before his lover joined a convent. Is this what you meant by beautiful? Tristan and Isolt died before even making it into the sack, poor fools, and Guinevere was an old hag before Lancelot ever got up the sack to bed her. Is it really even a pity? Alexandra ate her young while Nicholas watched, aghast. Think of any story people bring up to illustrate great love through the ages. Invented stories, morality plays, or subversive texts, scribed by manipulators to trap you into this or that tenet or belief. Every author was just trying to make a point. What is your love story? Is it so epic?

Romantic love in its heavenly attire and all the light and beauty around the concept — a creation of the government and the church, to stop young people from falling into bed with whomever they pleased. Love in a teddy, in a titty bar, in a G-string, passionate love — a symbol of sexual defiance against the church and government, "amor" and "Roma" being orthographically and theoretically opposite. Which proved it! There were wheels within wheels. Nothing was as it seemed. You think you're going to run into that special someone just by chance, walking around in the same space you are, looking for a special someone, too? What exactly are you smoking?

Imagine Sally and Bernice sitting under a tree in the yard in the night, with the tattered remains of love falling around them like leaves. They don't want to be duped. They don't want to be stupid. If falling in love is something ridiculous that only morons do because they don't know any better, then it isn't for them.

At the same time, who can truly despair of love? Who can look at herself and deny she is a creature made for it? It is hard, like growing up a born-again Christian, threatened by the fires of hell and promised the golden streets of heaven, and then reading Karl Marx. Your brain says, "I no longer believe." But you still look at every cloud break like it is the rapture, and you still find yourself wondering, "Will I go to hell?" Prayer is almost a guilty pleasure. So it was with thoughts of romance for Sally and Bernice.

They knew what they were supposed to think. And they knew what they wanted to believe. So the scheme to make their babies fall in love was born of this compromise: Make love from science. Plan for happenstance. And ultimately, believe. Faith has to be taken on faith. You have to have it before you can take it. Likewise love. It seems stupid unless you're in it. But do you really want to be so cool and mature that you turn your back on love, when you might have found it just next week, perfect, beautiful love like you'd never even imagined could exist? What would have happened if Sally and Bernice had had a love story of their own?

16

Toledo comes alive at night. It really does. While the city sleeps and dreams and dies a thousand deaths, the young and intelligent people come out to play, like constellations bursting out in the darkness of the black sky.

Irene remembered being a teenager, sneaking out of her house, and meeting up with kids from her school in the city. Toledo was like a university town on steroids, where tourists had animated conversations about quasars and tall hotels filled up with guests hoping to hear a lecture from an aging astronomy superstar or visiting mathematician. Tourists flocked the marina at Summit Street to do a night cruise of the Maumee River and Lake Erie. Restaurants overflowed with stargazers smoking long cigarettes and eating dumplings. Toledo isn't big, but it can hold everyone interesting in the world of astronomy at the same time. It is a gathering place for people who want to know what's out there. It's a home for rocket scientists and numerologists. For people who see a face on Mars and people who want to analyze Martian soil with an alpha proton X-ray spectrometer. All those people, together, make Toledo great.

The river cruise was popular because at certain points on the map there were nighttime blackout laws in effect to protect the institute's stargazers from the distractions of ambient light. The boats would head south through the lights and sounds of the city and the harbor, and then suddenly the banks and the boats would both go dark, sending travelers slipping up the river to loop around the Audubon Islands State Nature Preserve and loop back. Irene could remember sliding by the murmuring darkness outside town and then stepping back out of the yacht at the Summit Street Marina, back into the lights and noise of the city. The feeling of urgency from the tourists, the excitement of being downtown with honking car horns and radios leaking out of buildings, the chance of spotting a higher-up at NASA or one of the program directors from the launch facility in Dayton. The endless SETI@home frequency-time-power graph on an LED billboard on Madison and

Superior. She hadn't realized she missed it, but being there brought back memories that weren't entirely terrible.

Teenage Irene would sneak out just to sneak out, not to drink or party or rebel, but just to be away. And did it really even count as sneaking, if her mother was passed out in her bed with her arm crooked over her eyes, saying she had a sinus headache, falling asleep in the middle of the sentence?

"I have a sinus." And that was the end.

Irene could sneak out the front door, clomping along in her rough-shod boots, hitching a backpack full of booze on her shoulder for everyone else to drink. Bernice's supply would intoxicate the world, and Irene knew all the hiding places, all the secrets of the stash. If a few were missing, would Bernice even care? And what would she say, if she figured it out? "I'm sorry, but have you seen several pints of gin that I don't drink and wasn't hiding in the brick cavity behind the laundry room garbage bin?"

No, they never talked about the drinking. And they never talked about the fire. Everything else in the world was OK to talk about but never seemed as interesting as those two things, or as deadly. If something's not likely to kill you, why mention it at all?

■ ■ ■ ■

By the time Irene and George arrived at the nightclub, it was two o'clock in the morning.

"It's here? Where should we park?" she asked him. "On the street?"

"Valet, baby," said George.

Irene pulled up to the curb in front of the door, and a man in a black jumpsuit vaulted over the car's hood and opened the door for her. She put the keys into his hand. The valet gave her a hand out, and she stood up into the street. Looking down at herself, she realized she was wearing her black jeans and a button-down shirt, work boots. The man in the black jumpsuit drove away with her car after handing her a plastic ticket, which she stuck into her backpack.

"Come on," George called. He was looking at her as if she were a knife. Or a sandwich. Or a knife about to cut open a sandwich. She liked the way he was looking at her. He motioned for her to follow him, and she said, "Am I dressed for this? When you said, 'nightclub for astronomers' I thought you were kidding. I thought it was some back room at the institute."

"Why?" said George.

"Because it sounds like something that wouldn't be real!" Irene said. She smoothed her shirt and kicked the dirt off her boots.

Then she was standing on the sidewalk, and there was George, big and tall, with a questioning look on his face, like what the hell is wrong with you, lady? And then he was shaking his head. He said, "Are you kidding? You are perfect. Just like you are."

George's hand wrapped around her arm and she was pulled out of the street. The astronomers' club had no name on the front. They stepped through an iris door into an airlock, and the door closed behind them. There was a hiss of silence and frozen air, and cold steam surrounded them. Quiet.

"Couldn't they give it a name? Like The Comet or The Milky Way or . . ."

"Or The Black Hole?"

"Yeah."

The cold steam hissed again. She could barely see George. She shivered. The silence, after the noise on the street, was weird.

"That's what the gay secret astronomers' club is called."

Irene said nothing.

"Because of the gayness," George explained.

"I get it," said Irene.

"I bet people kiss in here sometimes," said

George.

Then his hand was on her shoulder, and she felt his thumb hard against her collar bone. What strange energy was in his hands, she did not know, but it made her feel as if he was leaving fingerprints on her, marking her, turning little parts of her alive at a time, wherever he touched. She heard his breath in the cold steam.

"You bet or you know?" said Irene.

Then he was kissing her again, and she felt herself rising up off the floor to meet him, like she was inhaling through his face, one long breath in. He put his hands in her ponytail and tugged the scarf away that was holding it, shook out her hair behind her head, pulled two handfuls of it up beside her face, grinning.

"Now you look more like a scientist," he said.

"George, that thing doesn't actually work where the boy pulls the girl's hair out of a ponytail and she shakes it out and she's magically transformed into hotness."

"Actually it's pretty reliable," said George. "You were hot before, but you should see yourself now."

The second door of the airlock swooshed open, and George and Irene spilled into the room. It was cavernous and dark, with a blues band taking up the stage. A singer in white was bathed in a spotlight, crooning at the microphone. Tables and chairs were scattered around the place, and there was a dance floor, where several couples were standing.

"I look too much like a scientist," said Irene.

George waved at people who were calling to him from the bar. There were astronomers of both genders draped around the place, locked in conversation, moving to the slow jam, or showing off big smiles.

"Let's get a drink," said George.

"I don't drink," said Irene.

"You'll drink this," said George.

He led her to the bar and motioned to the bartender, who turned around and started mixing.

"Uh oh, I think our favorite Daughter of Babylon is here," George said into her ear. The proximity of his mouth to her ear made her body tighten up into a spiral. When he said, "Over there," his lips brushed against her earlobe and a passing group of guys pushed her into him. His rib cage was broad and strong, his shoulders wide. He caught her up and held onto her. She raised her face to him, wanting just to kiss him and not to think about it, but he was pointing.

Sam Beth wore a long white dress, flowing and puddling on the floor. Her pigtails were drawn up fiercely into two buns, one on each side of her head, her arms were wrapped with gold bracelets, and under each eye the three dots glowed a bright white. It seemed like there were stripes in her hair. She approached them sedately.

"Princess Leia," said Irene.

"Nice boots," said Sam Beth.

"Thanks, Patrice," said Irene pointedly.

"Are you here together?" asked Sam Beth, motioning to George.

"Have you been drinking?"

"The Daughters of Babylon do not drink alcohol," said Sam Beth, but she took a crystal atomizer from the bar and gave herself a brisk shot in the face. Her eyes widened.

"What is that stuff?"

"What is that stuff?" Sam Beth imitated her.

With a rustle of fabric and a slow nod, she moved on through the club, and then the bartender was ready with the drinks and George was leaning over the bar. His shirt came untucked. She saw the waistband of his khakis and underneath the waistband of his underwear, heather gray. What was it about this man that made her feel so possessive, as if she should reach out and tug that shirt down into place or slide her hand under it. He turned and smiled at her, holding a blue drink in a tall glass. Inside the drink was a flutter of white blobs, floating between the surface and the bottom and then back again, like a lava lamp.

"I said I don't drink," said Irene.

"This isn't alcoholic," said George.

Irene took the drink out of his hand. It felt cool in the glass, but there were no condensation droplets around it.

"What's in it?"

George rolled his eyes. "Do you want a recipe? I can have someone print one out for you. Or you could just drink it. It's pretty good. If you don't like it, I'll get you something else."

"It's not alcoholic, really? I don't drink alcohol, like ever at all."

"Why?" asked George. "Why no drinking?" A simple question, asked in innocence. One she had never answered.

"My mother was an alcoholic," she said suddenly. She reached out for him and grabbed his hand. The air went whooshing out of her. She couldn't believe she had told him.

"I'm sorry," he said. "Well, I would never give you alcohol without telling you."

"I feel like you wouldn't," she said. "I believe you."

"But it's hard for you," George said. "I get it."

Irene took a deep breath and a little drink of the blue liquid. It tasted like raspberries and cucumbers. Very fresh. She let one of the white bubbles into her mouth and it burst with a little fizziness against the roof of her mouth. She felt a tickle in the back of her throat, and then she seemed more able to breathe than she had been before. The band finished their song and set down their instruments to take a break. New music came through the speakers, some kind of strange world house music or something. It thumped in the bar. She looked up to see that George was watching her. She had told him about her mother. And nothing bad had happened.

"You look beautiful," he said. "Will you marry me?"

"I've only known you for three days," said Irene. "I'm not going to marry you."

"You will," said George.

"Whatever," said Irene.

"Tell me everything about yourself. Favorite color, favorite food, what you want from life, what you want from me."

"Black, don't have one, some sort of

publication like everyone else, and —" Irene stopped.

"I want publication, too," said George. "You see, we're not so different."

"I want something from you," she went on, her breath coming fast.

"You told me," he said, smiling. "I mean —"

"I think I just want you to be real," said Irene. Whether it was the bubbly drink or the music thudding in her sternum or the proximity of George and the skin she wanted to touch, kiss, press against, she felt herself telling him something serious.

"I am real," said George. They were leaning against a column, George ducking down to hear her and speak into her ear, Irene clutching her drink, wanting to inhabit the space between his arms.

"But this is —" she began. "This can't be real. It's too silly."

"It's not silly! We are meant to be together. We're twin souls! I swear it on Compton and Batteau and Yeats and Toledo General."

"That's ridiculous."

"No, it's not."

"But George, you're a cosmetologist! You of all people should know."

"It's cosmologist, actually." George rolled his eyes, and smiled, all too familiar with

303

this intentional jibe on his branch of astronomy.

"You're a cosmetologist! The first axiom of cosmetology —"

"Cosmology!" George corrected her gently.

"Is that there are no special places. The universe is heterogeneous. This place" — here Irene pointed to her heart — "cannot be special. See?"

George shook his head.

"The second axiom of cosmology," she went on, "is that there are no special directions. So no special places, no special directions. No soulmates. No twin souls. Random intersection of lives, sexual attraction, mating. Just like lizards."

"Lizards don't have sexual attraction for each other."

"You don't know."

"So you admit you have sexual attraction for me."

"Do you need me to say it again?" said Irene.

"Come with me," shouted George into Irene's ear. "I need to take you in a special direction and show you a special place."

She followed him across the dance floor, where it was possible to feel the house music thumping through her feet.

"What is this music?" she shrieked up at him.

"Chaldean house music," he answered. "Base six or something. The DJ is a Ph.D. in anwa. You know what anwa is, right?"

Irene nodded but didn't.

"If you listen close, there's a sample of frequency in this song," George told her, "that comes from a black hole. You know, like the black hole is singing."

"Black holes don't sing," Irene shouted, over the buzz of the music. "It's periodic oscillation. That's not song!"

"You don't know," George grinned at her, pulling her by the hand. "You don't know everything."

She knew that every girl in the place was giving her a once-over and lots of people were calling out to George. People recognized them, maybe wondered why they were here together. Sometimes he shouted back random things like, "Hey!" or "Yeah!" Other times he appeared to be staring up into the rafters and then shaking his head. Irene followed him closely, and then the stairs opened up and they were headed down. Downstairs was quieter. There was a woman in the corner playing a mechanical harp. Dancers writhed in glass tubes.

"I want to get to the part where we're

alone," said Irene.

"Are you sure you want to?" said George.

"Yes," said Irene. "I'm sure." She felt herself begin to laugh or cry. Was this what sexual frustration felt like?

"OK," said George. "Right this way."

Down a hallway, down another flight of stairs, they came to a little room and went inside. It was paneled, like a sauna, but there was a cool breeze coming from a vent. She set her drink down on a little table. George shut the door, and Irene's heart raced. There was a desk in the corner, some papers, a laptop. A sofa pressed against the wall with a lamp on each side.

"Whose office is this?" she asked.

"The owner. Don't worry," he said. "No one will come."

For a moment she was shy. She couldn't look at his face. He was so near to her, so captured in this privacy, she wanted to take each breath from him, think about it, see it, experience it. When she did look at his face, he was looking at her. She saw the skin of his neck, so close, the blood vessels beneath it. His chin bent down close to her. She saw the muscles behind his ear. It didn't make her uncomfortable. It moved her. She felt a significant inner peace, inside some dark place of her body, cooling and spreading out, as if it was overtaking her with calm. She felt good.

"Are you claustrophobic?" he said.

She laughed. She touched one of his hands with hers and he clasped it, so they were holding hands. His face looked smooth and young, and she thought, *It's so improper. Me the damaged, soulless thing. Him this beautiful boy that everybody wants to be next to. Why is he here with me? Why is he holding my hand?* She could see something in him that was hers, something beckoning to her to find it, take it, use it. Irene watched him unbutton the collar of his shirt, and his hair fell down over his forehead, and she wanted to reach out for it, that piece of shirt, that curl of hair, to touch it and make sure that it was real. She felt that each of her breaths was fighting to leave her lungs. She felt her ribs fighting to pull the air back in. She sat back against the desk.

"Take off your clothes," said George. His hands on his own buttons.

A burst of fresh air came from the vent, smelling a little bit of cucumber, like the drink she'd barely touched. What was in her blood right now, making her lose her grip on twenty-nine years of keeping her legs crossed? Making her want to open them, tear off her shirt, spread her breasts across the room for him, feel the cucumber air make her shiver? George reached inside the collar of her shirt and touched her just above her heart. It was the simplest touch, not a stroke or a caress, or even really purposeful, but just a finger moving from up to down, touching a little stretch of her. Maybe he did not even notice it. She said nothing. But she knew that she would remember that touch forever, until the day of her death, as the moment she woke up. It was a moment of total danger and fear followed by a moment of complete surrender.

"I want you to take them off," he said. His voice was deep.

She knew in that moment there were two Georges: the wise-cracking, sunny-smiling George whom she could tease and ridicule over fish tacos, who made jokes and made things easy for her. And then there was another George, inside that George, that was darker, and more strange, and she felt in that one finger pulled down across her chest that the animal George inside had reached out through the human George and touched her.

All men are just this way, she thought. Until now she would have looked upon this animal with contempt or just disgust, with a glowering, impatient desire to bring out that animal and tame it and destroy it. But now Irene felt a new thing: a desire to meet that animal and to know it. Her own animal rising. This was the danger: the animal inside her, pushing to the front. This was the surrender: but she didn't care. She could growl and snap if she had to; she could wail and moan. He wasn't going to look on her with anything other than the best of love. He wasn't going to let her out of this room until she was done. This was where it was all going to come apart: here in safety, here with George. She put her hand over his heart, inside the collar of his shirt, and pressed her fingers into his skin. When she looked up at his face, it was her real face looking up, her animal face from dark inside, and his animal face responded.

He made a noise inside his chest, she felt that noise as a vibration in her hand, and it was the most powerful stimulant she had ever felt in her life.

Gone the snide remarks. Gone the lifetime of making men subservient before her. Gone the wide cracks in her, the bitterness with which she filled the cracks. She looked into his face and she knew him, and she let the cracks fall wide open. She began to undo his belt. He lifted her shirt up and pulled it over her head. She yanked the buttons of his shirt. He pulled her jeans to the floor. They moved like automatons, held in each other's notice, and frantic to get more close, more near.

Irene was naked now, the clothes gone. The light was bright, and she stood there in that little room, exposed and raw but closer, closer to him and his body. She wanted to be close. She could see all of him, open to her. He put his hands gently around her and she took in a deep breath. There was no place to go but onward. There was no reason to it, and no sense. Then he was moving her to the sofa, his hands fully locked around her rib cage, his mouth on her neck, and the feel of him was pure other-George, the George behind the sun, the dark animal she had felt moving the hand over her heart. She felt him so acutely that it made her cough. This black animal, grappling with her blackness. Bathed in the brightest light, naked to each other, locked in.

She felt the pressure as he pushed against her, heard a soft moan, was it him or her with mouth open, making sounds come out? And then he pushed on inside. It was so easy, and it was done. She lost herself immediately, her legs wrapped around his thighs, her belly against his, her breasts against him, hands raking along the cushions of the sofa to get herself closer and closer. She wanted to scream, *This is how a vagina should be! Full. How stupid I've been carrying around an empty one for all this time.*

"You can never take it out again," she said to the side of his face. "Just remember that. Never never. I never want to lose you again."

He began to move inside her in a way that was rhythmic and thrilling, and she felt her mind tripping away. She was spinning in this world, on the point of him in her, and as she felt herself joined up with him, there in her depths, in the geometric depths of her round cervix, her mind spun again, and she saw what was entirely mathematical. A vision before her face of a circle and a point and a line, and the way they moved together, up and down, back and forth. One circle inside another circle becomes a point that moves just up and down.

"It's the Tusi couple," she said to him. "It's the Tusi couple. It's happening inside me."

"Oh," he said. "Good. Can't talk now."

"It's the Tusi couple, George!" she said. "It's happening inside me!" Rolling around, rolling around. Up and down. He wouldn't tell her no, his forehead was pressed into the fabric, his hands around the back of her, and the feeling she was having inside her only grew.

"You know about the Tusi couple, George," said Irene. She was grasping, grasping to hold onto her words. "You know what it is."

"Shhh," said George. She glanced at him, her eyes open wide in the light. Was he smiling or was that a grimace? Was his head thrown back in laughter, or was it pain? What was happening inside her, between her legs, so sweet and urgent.

"Copernicus," she gasped. "This is Copernicus we're talking about! Copernicus!" How can Copernicus be wrong?

"Copernicus, shhh . . ." said George, his voice rough and low. His hands now found her breasts, and he rolled her nipples roughly between his fingers. He sank his teeth into her shoulder, his tongue following the line of her collarbone, and the firmness rubbing between her legs, shooting up into her and drawing down again, sending electric shocks out into her extremities, tunneling into her body and filling it with energy.

Then Irene found she couldn't talk either, and the Tusi coupling inside her found its own rolling rhythm, and she and George, pining for each other, and finding each other, pressed together on themselves. In the dark behind her eyelids, she lost track of who she was, and who was with her, and who was not her. She felt him through her body, inside her body, and she could feel the whole of him. And there, down inside, she met him, quiet and slow and dear.

"George, there's something wrong with you," said a voice inside them.

"No, there's not," said another voice.

"I can feel it. I can see it. I can't be this close and not see it. I can't be so near, and not feel it."

"No, there's nothing wrong with you."

"It's you, not me," said a third voice. "It's you there's something wrong with."

The Tusi couple went on spinning in itself, one circle rolling inside the other circle, the point on the line going up and down, up and down, and the deep conversation hovered on the edge of her consciousness, until she could hear that it was just repeating. When it was over, Irene locked her arms around him. "You can't take it out," she said again, her voice sounding strange to her now. "I already told you that." She felt likely to cry. She felt likely to shut off the lights, yank off her face, crawl under a rock. The fan blew its cucumber air. The sofa creaked behind her back. Had it always been creaking? "Please don't leave me," she cried. She calculated the effort it would take to pull her clothes back on, yank the door open, march back up through the club and out, give the ticket to the valet, get her car, drive to the Anthony Wayne Bridge, stop the car, get out, climb over the railing, jump off, and die. Or the effort it would take to stay here, entwined with this creature who was so strange and so familiar, whom she did not know she had been missing so much.

17

Belion stood on the other side of the small door. He had decided to shrink himself. He had already gone through the door. This was the only course of action he could pursue. He had now pursued it, and he was on the other side.

Silvergirl's avatar was nowhere on the regular map of the game. She was in a dark spot on his map, or to put it in coding terms she was in a set of numbers that had no definition. The game was coded in chunks, in blocks, and every space, every object, every creature had a number. The numbers she inhabited had not, it appeared, been assigned. They had been skipped.

It was as if when she passed through that door she went into another world — one that had ceased to exist or had not yet been created. Or had she given up on him, quit the game, deleted her character, ended her life? He had never been told by an administrator, "This player has committed suicide. Please erase her avatar and distribute her belongings among her friends." You couldn't kill yourself in the game universe. You fought for your life, because a fighter never quits. That was the whole idea. Stabbing yourself in the guts with a knife was an invalid operation. You could, however, inadvertently become a jumper. People did that all the time. Only to regenerate at the fountain in their hometowns, good as new.

On the other side of the door, he quickly made himself big again. He got back his water buffalo horns. He put back on his large-size armor. Enough of being small and going through stupid little doors. He was now gigantic again and a god. He followed a path out of the cave and through the dim forest, listening to repeated ambient noises of birdsong and the rustle of squirrels on a loop.

Belion, sitting in Toledo, turned to a different monitor and checked that he was still listed as online. He was. His character appeared in a dark part of the map. He could see Silvergirl there, too, but he couldn't see what was between him and her. Belion felt, for the first time in a long while, worried about his safety. He had no idea if he was still invincible. The thought that he could be killed or even hurt was new to him. But instead of unpacking the idea, he felt like throwing it down a well. Stupid idea.

He came to a grand gate in a stone wall. On each side of the gate were huge carved figures, like solemn pillars. They had cone-shaped beards made of regular stone curls, and they wore fez-shaped hats. Their round eyes regarded Belion without concern. Above them was a huge stone lintel, carved in pictures and angular marks. The gate was just an opening in the wall, and nothing was stopping Belion from going inside, so he did.

Before him the main causeway of the city was dusty and empty, lined on both sides by ancient buildings and rubble. He listened intently, but the ambient noises coded into this area were just a whistling breeze and the scratch of ragged linen on stone. He found himself checking his other screen for approaching PCs, but there was nothing to be seen. He could not tell if he was in danger or not. This was living. This was not spectating, orchestrating, or destroying. This was life.

He stood inside the gates of this dusty old city and surveyed the rough streets, crumbling red stone buildings. At the bottom of his screen, a text box informed him that he felt a thin breeze, and smelled something sour. A horned lizard watched him from the railing on one battered patio. Belion moved toward the first intersection, and almost immediately he was attacked. The thing came at him from the side: a woman with the body of a four-legged beast. It pounded at him with gnarled fists, licking its lips greedily. After the initial shock of seeing his own hit count go down for the first time in a year, he removed its head with one stroke of his club. When he clicked the command to search its corpse for valuables, he removed from it a lavender stone.

He crossed a bridge over a wide river. There were no boats on the river; nothing floated there. On his left he saw an official-looking building, and inside he opened a glass cabinet and withdrew a silver flute. He smashed a table and found nothing underneath. In a murky fountain he saw what he thought might be a rotted arm, but the graphics were so lame, he wasn't sure.

He turned down a side street, killed two more of the woman beasts, and came to an abandoned marketplace with tattered awnings stretched over dusty stalls. There were stalls that had held tapestries, stalls that had held furniture. In one stall he found something he could pick up — when he examined it, the game told him it was a chunk of venison. Venison. He shook his head and dropped it. He checked the map on his other screen and saw that he was coming near to the dot that marked Silvergirl's presence. She was alone at the edge of the city.

There were four watchtowers, one at each corner of the city wall. He thumped up a circular staircase, a squeeze for his wide shoulders. No more shrinking, thought Belion. This is it. Upstairs, he found a stone golem and the back of a girl. He saw the wrinkle of her silver cowl at her neck, and knew that it was she. Silvergirl sat in the window, her feet outside, the robe puddled on the sill around her buttocks. The world outside her window was blurry and incomplete. It had not been properly coded and the textures were rough, but she looked at it as if it were some kind of damned sparkling vista or something.

"Stand down," she said, and the golem, who was silently standing there, not looking at Belion or anything else, dropped his weapon and dissolved into dust, leaving a full set of mithril armor on the ground.

"Put it on," she said to Belion. "You're going to need it."

"I don't mind the lamia," said Belion. "I already killed five."

"You're going to kill something else," she said. "A beholder."

"Wait a minute, am I in Thalos? Where did you get the code for this area?"

"You're in Babylon," she said. "Think about it. Did you ever see a river in Thalos?"

With that she dropped out the window. Belion leaned out after her, aghast, and could see her down below, on the ground, collecting herself and walking away down the street. He rushed down the stairs to catch up to her.

The phone beside Belion's desk rang. He picked it up quickly, discovered it was not his phone, but rather the house phone at Irene's mother's house. Mentally staggering through layers of disorientation from coming out of gaming and into this unfamiliar house, he jabbed the wrong button and turned it off. He stared at the phone until it rang again.

"Hello?" He jabbed the right button. "Hello?"

"Belion?" It was Irene. On the screen in front of him, Silvergirl was passing him a smooth ball of quartz.

"Yeah?" Belion did not want to be interrupted.

"Belion, I need to break up with you."

"Yep, OK." He examined the ball of quartz in his inventory. A light source. He followed Silvergirl down a wide main street and saw a domed temple before him, rising up out of dried gardens, the desiccated vines and trees still climbing colonnades and statuary.

"I'm breaking up with you now," Irene was saying.

"Got it," said Belion. "Thanks."

He moved his avatar over to the doorway to the temple and angled himself to be able to peer inside, but it was dark. Silvergirl stood at the entrance to the temple, and she put out a hand to stop him from entering. She pulled back her cowl, showing her face to him, and then she leaned over and gave his avatar a kiss on the cheek.

"Belion," said Irene in his ear, "do you understand what I am saying to you? We are broken up. I had sex with another man. Penis sex. I am not your girlfriend as of now."

"Sad," said Belion. "Sorry. Miss you. Gotta go."

He pulled his broadsword out of its sheath and strode into the temple.

George and Irene sat in Irene's car in the

parking lot of the Metropolitan Funeral Home. They'd stopped at Frankie's to eat breakfast: jalapeño eggs for Irene and coffee for George. Then Irene had said she needed to run an errand.

"I hope you're not tired. Are you tired?" she asked. "I'm not tired a bit."

"Not tired," said George. He was not tired if tired meant she was going home without him. He would stay awake forever.

"Maybe you should go home," said Irene. "And get some sleep."

"No," said George.

George's head pounded. He palmed a small, flat vial out of his pocket and twisted the cap. Painkillers. The only way to get on with the day, sometimes. He stuck the cap in his nostril, squeezed the vial, and sniffed. Then he stretched his mouth open and gulped a little.

"What was that?"

"I'm fine," said George.

"I'm sure you are," said Irene. "But what did you just put in your nose?"

"I take medicine," said George. "Vitamins, really. For health purposes."

"Vitamins don't look like that. And you don't put them in your nose. What was that thing?"

"Irene, I love you," said George.

"Wow, that must be some interesting stuff, for you to deflect like that."

"Yeah, no, it's just a vitamin. But maybe we should go home. We." George emphasized the plural. "We should go home to my house together."

"Aren't you working today?"

"Not this morning," said George. "I don't have a lecture until three."

"Fine, then," she said. "We can squeeze in my errand. But we have to hurry."

"Here?" asked George groggily. He could feel the painkiller invading his skull from the top, like a dripping river of precious ice water numbing his head, making it all so much better.

"Yes, here," said Irene.

"But they don't open now," he said. The sky was barely pink, and it couldn't have been after seven.

"Now is the right time. They've burned her up, but they haven't opened for the day."

George put his hand on Irene's leg. Maybe she would crawl out from under the steering wheel and into his lap, and she would fold herself up under his chin and rest her head on his chest. He would put his arms around her, around all of her, her folded legs and her small back. He would lock her in, and they would fall asleep for a little while, her cheek against his throat, his cheek against her hair, just for an hour or two. It couldn't hurt.

"George," said Irene. He popped awake.

"Yes," he said.

"I told you my mother died three days ago, right?"

"Yes," he said.

"Well, I have to go get her, and I'm not filling out any forms or organizing any sort of meeting with any sort of undertaker. I've sat in that lobby once, and looked at that damn parade of mouth-breathing dead people on that monitor, I'm not doing it again."

"They're not open," George repeated. "And dead people —"

"George, if I go in there, and pick her up, and sign a form, then before I know it I'll be picking out an urn. And if I pick out an urn, then I'm arranging a service, and if I'm arranging a service, then I'm buying a dress, and making a list of people, and composing an ad to go in the paper, and opening the house for a condolence party with cream cheese and olive sandwiches and ginger ale and lilies. Don't you see I can't do that? Condolences? It's not even viable."

"Probably you should though," he said. She seemed so determined, and her adorable face was being very serious and fierce. He wanted to help her, even if it meant eating a dead person's breathing mouth on cream cheese.

"I'm asking you one more time what was in that little bottle," said Irene.

"Opiate," said George, too medicated not to be honest. "It's opiate. It's totally legal and a prescription. A pre-scrip-tion," he said slowly. "For me. Mine. My water buffalo. Mine."

"Oh my god," said Irene. She opened her mouth and shut it again. She started to laugh but then rolled her eyes instead. "At least you'll have plausible deniability," she said. "I'm sorry, officer, I was just helping my friend here steal her mother's ashes. No, that's not opium. That's prescription embalming fluid!"

George frowned. He really wanted to lie down. The tentacles of his headache were being peeled away from his skull one by one by the medicine, and it was so helpful. If he could lie down, and sleep, perhaps with his face nestled in the crease between Irene's breast and her upper arm, that would be even better. It actually was all perfectly legal. There had been doctors involved at all levels of the operation. Doctor, I have a terrible headache. What, again? Yes, and nothing seems to help. Here, let me get you this nasal spray. Take it if you need it, but by all means don't take it and then break into a crematorium.

"Come on, George," said Irene. "You have to boost me."

"OK," said George. He unfolded himself from her bitty little car and stood up and stretched. Immediately he felt better. He felt he could boost her, and steal these ashes. "Come on," she said. "This is the part of the building with the crematorium. See the chimneys? Plus, you can't get into this wing from inside, so you know. They must be doing something in there."

George nodded and followed her. There were no other cars in the lot on this side of the building. There was one car in the lot on the other side, possibly a security guard or another early mourner or someone who had just cheated and parked here while headed to a restaurant, a theater, a bar, and then they had too many drinks, and they were like I can drive, and their friend was like no you can't, and they were like where did I even park?

"George!" Irene was saying. He tried to listen to her very carefully, but she had walked all the way across the parking lot and was standing under one of the windows.

It was high on the wall, possibly to prevent onlookers from viewing the furnaces being stoked, viewing the corpses being loaded into them, viewing the whole morbid spectacle. When George made it all the way across the parking lot and found he was standing next to her again he felt like crying with relief. Just to be near her, this familiar person, who felt like a warm, satisfying piece in his puzzle, shaped just right. His only disappointment was that he wasn't kissing her.

"Boost me," she said. She was holding a long piece of metal and another small device that looked like a battery.

"What are you going to do?"

"Apparently scale this brick wall by myself or go get a ladder," said Irene impatiently.

He boosted her onto his shoulders. She sat there, fiddling with the piece of metal and the battery. Her thighs pressed against his ears. The back of his head was pressed into her lady bits through the black jeans. He could not resist bouncing her up and down a little bit. No one could have.

"Quit it," she said, and dug her heel into his ribs. But then she put her hand on the top of his head and ran her fingers down through his hair, curling around his ear in the most pleasing, soothing, maddening way. He knew that if nothing else happened, and he just felt the magic sensation of that hand running its way down through his hair, he would have lived for a reason. He looked up at her, and she was threading the long piece of metal through the bottom of the window frame. It was like a yardstick. Once she'd got it through, she applied the little battery to one end and flipped a switch.

"It's a shape-memory alloy," she said. "Nickel titanium, to be exact."

"You mean *Terminator* metal?"

"Yeah."

"Where did you get that?" he asked.

"I got it," she said. "It's commercially available."

"For this particular application?"

She didn't answer, but used the device on the end of the metal stick. When she applied the current to the metal, the part inside the window began to twist and shape itself into the form it had previously known. There was a reason for making metal like this, George knew, and it had to do with heart surgery and engine diagnostics. It did not have to do with robbing crematoriums. When she was satisfied with the shape of the memory metal, she gave a few quick jerks and the latch of the window swung free.

"I'm guessing it's not armed," she said. "The ones in the front weren't, and that was where the money was kept. Back here is just dead people."

"Great," said George.

Irene lifted the window and flung herself up and through. For a minute her feet were dangling, and then she was inside. George stood on the green grass around the building, looking at morning bursting onto Toledo, hoping not to be too conspicuous against the brick wall.

"Come in," he heard her call. "I'll throw you out something."

George leaned against the cool bricks. In a few seconds, she said, "Stand clear of the window." But before his addled brain could figure out what that meant, there was a stool hurtling over the ledge and onto the grass. George picked it up and set it against the wall, using it to climb up on the ledge and through. Then they were both inside.

The crematorium was like an operating room, all brushed metal and shining tile, and in the dim light it had a bluish and sparkling tinge to it, as if it had all been recently wet. There were gurneys draped in white cloth, and there were instruments in racks, overhead lights in trapezoid shades, and two desks near the door. The minute he swept the room with his eyes, he knew that something here was very bad. There was a lurking presence, a gap in the air, a shadow in his vision. This was not a good time for his gods and goddesses to show up. Or, it was a very good time for them to show up, but not this one. This felt terrible. He was afraid. Apart from that fear, he found the crematorium was very much like a lab. It had the same look, but not the same feel.

"Come on," said Irene.

The only door in the room was operated by one of those "panic bar" pressure handles, and George assumed the door was locked. There was no way out but the window, and he'd fallen six feet down to the floor. In a blaze of forethought that he paused to notice with pride, he grabbed another stool and set it by the window.

"Escape stool," he said to Irene. "This is very important."

She nodded. She was walking through the room quietly, her hands touching lightly on the gurneys as she passed each one. There was a clipboard with a few papers clipped to it hanging off the front of each gurney, but none were occupied. Irene examined the clipboards. She did not lift the cloths that were left on top. There were no toe tags lying around, discarded. Maybe the morgue had upgraded to wristbands, or forehead tattoos, or earrings. Left is right, right is dead. George examined a list on the wall, and Irene read over his shoulder.

Things to check for before using the retort:

1. **Pacemaker**
2. **Liquor bottles placed in the coffin by friends of the deceased**

Either can cause an EXPLOSION. Please mind the clients are properly prepared for the retort.

"This must be the retort," she said.

George looked at her, hoping to make a joke. About the word "retort." And how, in death, there is no retort, or something. However, behind Irene, he saw a dark shape move between a filing cabinet and one of the desks. It was not blurry, but flat and black, in the shape of a human, but possibly made of coal. The worst problem about it was that it had no face. He knew, without knowing quite how he knew, that this thing was disease and death. It was the god of death: Hades, or Satan, or Ereshkigal, or whatever you wanted to say: this was the modern American version of that. The stripped-down version. No horns, no blue skin, no pagoda on its head. No romance. No fire. The thing walked on tiptoe. He couldn't tell where it was looking. He closed his eyes and opened them again. Irene was looking at a row of machines that looked like front-loading washers. On top of them, in a metal tray, were a number of shining metal balls. George had to watch as this crusty, blank Osiris put its elbows on a gurney and jutted its chin toward Irene. Its face elongated, and it brayed. George jumped, bumping into a tray of instruments and sending a pair of forceps clattering to the ground.

"What's wrong with you," Irene barked.

She had found the ovens. Each had a metal clasp and was the height of one of the gurneys. There were three in all. Irene moved from one to the next, touching her hand to each one as if checking the temperature. The dry black thing came behind her, touching each one, too, mimicking her movements. George frowned. "Stop that," he said.

"I want to know which one she was in," said Irene.

"There's no way to know that," said George. "It was cool, or they wouldn't have taken her out."

Irene opened one of the doors. It opened with a hiss, and they saw inside the oven. It was very clean, a brick tube with a trench in the far end to collect the ashes. There were no bits of tooth and bone, no piles of dust in the corner. It all looked very sanitary. She shut the door again. Outside the door, there was a small peephole. She looked through it.

"Of course," she said. "They wouldn't want to mix up the people."

Her voice sounded strangled. He thought he should get her out of there, but she was moving again, around the wall. She had found a wire shelving unit that had small black boxes lined up on it in rows.

"Here," said Irene. "See here?"

George went to stand next to her and face the boxes on the shelves, shuddering to be so close to the death thing that kept walking around after her, but wanting to keep it away. He saw it go so close to her, but he didn't know what to do.

"Haven't you ever sat on a garden hose and said, hey, this is what it's like to get fucked by Poseidon?" it hissed into Irene's ear. George heard it clearly, but Irene seemed not to notice.

George put his arm around her. The dead

thing put its arm around her on the other side. George couldn't feel where their arms brushed together but he could feel Irene being pulled away, being pulled toward that black dryness. "She's got to be here," said Irene. "Look at the names. The dates."

Each black box had a plain white rectangle on the end and the name of a person printed there. Irene ran her finger down over the names.

"Haven't you ever sat on a vacuum cleaner and said, hey, this is what it's like to get eaten out by Aeolus?" it hissed again.

"We have to go," said George.

"I know," said Irene. "I know."

George pulled her sharply toward him. She looked up at him and smiled, so bravely, so sweetly, and behind her head he could see the black shape of the dead thing's head, trying to tilt at the same angle.

"I'm sorry," said Irene. "We'll go. Here she is."

Irene reached out both hands, hesitated, and then pulled one of the boxes off the shelf. "Heavy," she said. "I didn't expect that."

The death thing was climbing on the shelf now, rattling it, shaking it like an agitated monkey.

"Popped her cherry, did you George?" it

said. There was no mouth to move, no ears to hear an answer.

"Come on," said George. "Climb through the window. I'll hand the box out to you."

"You can't drop it, though." She laughed nervously. "That would be too horrific."

"Naturally," said George, trying very hard to pretend to be amused. "I'm allergic to dusty clouds of dead mothers-in-law."

"She's not your mother-in-law," said Irene quietly. She climbed up on the stool and heaved herself out, sat on the ledge, and then swung her legs out, dropped away.

Now George was alone with the thing and its black breath. The thing is this: there had never been anything all that bad in his life. No one had died. No one had even been very sick. His mother had laid waste to every problem in his path. She spread out the world, easy for his taking, tuned to his key, ripe for his harvest. No grandmother to wither, no teacher at school, no college chum, no one would have come to end up here or anywhere else where death could find them. His mother had kept that all from happening, from the sheer force of her human will. And now George stood, one foot on the stool, one hand on the window ledge, the black box of ashes tucked under his arm, and the bad ugly god said one more thing to him.

"I'm coming for you," it said. "Believe it."

18

Irene had no memory of the time before the fire. No memory of the fire itself. Irene's first memory of her mother was an incorrect outline of the mother's face against the white ceiling in the dark. It was bedtime and Irene was getting rocked to sleep. As she lay in her mother's arms, she would look up at her mother's face now and again and then close her eyes. She could remember looking up once, and instead of seeing the flatness of a face with a small nose poking out and glasses shining in the light from the hallway, she saw a sharp point jutting out of the forehead and a smooth recess where the face should be. She lay there for a minute, staring. In her memory, she couldn't place what she thought about it. But she remembered relief at realizing the sharp point was a chin, the smooth recess a neck. Her mother's head had fallen back against the chair because she was asleep, and Irene was seeing the bottom side of it. Then she felt like laughing. On subsequent nights, when she observed this shape against the ceiling, she was not disturbed. Because she knew it was just a chin. *Mommy,* she would say, *Wake up, please.* And feel a quiet smugness that her mother was looking undignified in the rocker.

She was always two years younger than her classmates. And always seemed to be a foot smaller. For this she was tortured on the elementary school playground, and later came the impossibility of dating in high school. None of the showio-boobio that was going on in other girls' lives. Irene could remember a little boy in her third grade class who chased her around the sandbox in the playground, trying to sit next to her and touch her legs. That was the last time she was pursued sexually until she was in graduate school.

To make matters worse, her mother read aloud every night from poems and novels that glorified love. Love of the ages, a penetrating, everlasting love of eternal proportions. Love you find once and cling to forever, even if the person you love is decapitated in the process. Love fraught with difficulty. Jane Eyre and Mr. Rochester love. Heathcliff and Catherine love. Love on the moors, love with a capital L. Cleopatra love, and Romeo and Juliet love. Love in uncomfortable costumes, with death at the end of it. It was like her mother's Bible. It seemed to be her mother's creed.

Irene didn't drink or have any sex in college, and when she graduated she was still twenty and went on to Bowling Green for a master's degree in math. In Bowling Green she loved a music graduate student who composed for a tuba ensemble. Or, more specifically, a euphonium ensemble. He lived in an apartment in a tower, and she took an elevator up. She sat in his bedroom on a chair and worked on her work, and he sat at his desk and worked on his, and they listened to Sting. From time to time he would come over to her and put his head in her lap or on her shoulder. He kneeled in front of her chair and she put her arms around him and patted his back. Periodically, he pressed his lips into her neck. He was cute, and had long hair. In her mind, Irene had been calling him Percy Bysshe Shelley, before they met. It was shocking to her that he wanted to date her. Once, she'd had a nonlucid dream where a kiss on the neck became pretty sexual, awakening feelings in her that led her to want to replay the dream again and again. But in real life it didn't happen that way. It just led to a wet spot on her neck.

When he first kissed her on the mouth, it was her first kiss. She was sitting on a radiator in his apartment with her back against the window and he came at her, with the obvious intent to kiss. He said, "Irene, I know you have been kissed before." She hadn't said no. She noticed he licked his mouth right before he came close. Eventually, they had a careful, feeble attempt at sex. Looking back later, she thought it might have been his fault, because he was terrible at it. He didn't even take his pants off or her clothes off, just pushed and pushed at her, and then eventually said, with a gasp, "I did it."

At the time, she just felt tired, like she wanted to go to her own bed. Nothing came of it thereafter. There was no further attempt. She started getting bored and dumped him. He was a good guy and very smart about music, but after he had been pressing himself on her leg through his pants, she never felt good about him anymore.

After that, she was getting her Ph.D. in Columbus, and she dated lots of men but didn't have sex with them. She learned instead how to do very good blow jobs, to the point that she felt quite masterful about it. She stopped dating academics and fell in with a man in a nightclub who didn't tell her his last name until she finally ripped his driver's license out of his hand and found out it was Wiener. He was handsome and funny, and he was also dealing drugs, which Irene didn't realize until later. They would walk up and down Park Street while he said scornful things about the liberal arts majors she pointed out. But sometimes, he would be in her apartment and he wouldn't talk and he'd appear to be watching television but would lose the ability to respond to questions. So Irene rolled him off the couch and into bed and then the words would come out, encouraging words. She realized later that he must have been tripping during these catatonic times. She thought back to cuddling next to him on the couch, while he stared blankly before him, and felt that it hadn't been so bad. In times of lucidity, he argued about his need to give Irene an orgasm with his tongue. But he failed to convince her it would work.

The relationship ended one night at a club. They ran into another guy she had dated a few times, a smart guy, a physics fellow. She was surprised to find that when she turned to introduce her boyfriend to this smart guy, she had forgotten the boy-friend's name. "This is uhhh," she said. The smart guy laughed. The boyfriend didn't. The next week he moved out to her neighborhood and bought a kitten, and said, *Look what I did for you.* But she couldn't face him ever again after that night. She wanted to go to his new apartment and see his kitten, but she broke up with him instead. It just hadn't felt good to stand there and forget his name. There had been no way to cover that up.

So in her mind the main history looked like this:

1. Mother's face as a chin.
2. The boy on the playground touching her legs.
3. Percy Bysshe Shelley's wet lips on her neck.
4. Drug dealer staring at the television.

The only thing next was Belion. And then George.

"Here we are!" said George.

Irene turned the corner into a rutted dirt road flanked by encroaching trees, each with leaves turning a different shade of brown. They had been on the main drag of Sylvania, a western suburb. Monroe Street was Vegas-wide and lined with neon, oversize restaurants, and gift shops. Then they had turned onto a blacktop highway, rolling over hills and through some woods. Now the road had narrowed and decayed.

"Just keep one wheel up on the middle thing, and one wheel over on the side. If you let yourself down into the ruts, you won't get through."

"You live here?" asked Irene.

"Well, my mother has a city apartment. My dad lives here. We used to live here. This is where I grew up. Yes, I live here. Sometimes."

Irene took her eyes off the ruts to give him a powerful stare. "If you're sure." He smiled back and she laughed.

The house was ramshackle-quaint. A tumbledown well in the center of the yard gave it a haunted feel. There was a two-story garage with wide, carriage-house doors, and cragged oak trees spread their gnarled limbs over everything.

"Wow," said Irene. "Picturesque."

"Yeah," said George. "My mother used to have her psychic shop set up out here. It used to be even worse than this — prayer flags and a llama. Over there in the side yard they had a crystal maze, where they'd buried crystals in the ground in a labyrinth shape — you were supposed to be able to get to the center by feeling your way along the crystal energy."

George pointed to a little meadow adjacent to the house, where rosebushes were sending out their fall offerings around the edge.

"Or you could just walk there, to the center," said Irene. "Not much of a maze."

"Yeah, you should try it," said George. Irene started laughing with sound coming out. Actual sound.

"Are you OK?" George asked. He smiled at her.

"I think you fucked me silly," she said. "This is me silly."

"OK, silly, you can just park here next to the garage."

When they got out, she picked her way across the lawn and sat down in the porch swing. She let out a long sigh and looked around.

"So this is why your hands feel like longshoreman hands," she said.

"Gardening," said George. "I do it a lot. And how do you know what a longshoreman's hands feel like?"

"Conjecture," said Irene. She pulled her feet up on the swing and hugged her knees, making the swing move but not rock.

"You do not look right at home," said George, pointing to a hand-lettered sign on the wall that said MAKE YOURSELF RIGHT AT HOME.

"How do I do that?" Irene asked.

"Probably with some of Dad's weed," George told her.

"Is your dad here now?"

"No one's seen Dad since the banquet," George responded. "But if he does show up, we're not supposed to . . ." George appeared to be trying to remember what he was not supposed to do.

"Let him in?" Irene guessed.

"Yes, or give him any money. Mom likes to keep the reins tight."

"Shit, I forgot the ashes!" Irene jumped up off the porch swing and the chains jangled.

"Where are you going to put them?" George asked.

"I don't know," said Irene. "I want to get them, though." She walked toward the car.

"We could scatter them here," George offered. "Around in the woods, on the crystal labyrinth, down the well."

"Down the well? How could you even suggest that?" Irene said.

"There's no water down there!" George

insisted.

"So much the worse," said Irene. She pulled the black box out of the backseat of the car and slammed the car door.

"Sorry," said George. He grinned at her, and she felt, looking at him, a flush of something blooming out of her face and out of her skin all over. A good feeling bubbling up through her skin, making her feel like giggling was a real thing that happens to people, instead of just something people do who don't read books.

"How about the crystal labyrinth then?" George was saying. "That might be a nice place to get sprinkled. All those vibrations."

"We can't leave her here at all," said Irene. "Why would she want that? She had no connection to this place."

"People have no connection to the cemetery either, and that doesn't stop them from being buried there in droves."

They went inside, and for now Irene put her mother's ashes on the kitchen table.

"Something about this place seems familiar," said Irene. "Like I saw it in a movie or something."

George frowned. "Let's go to bed," he said.

Irene lay next to George on a big bed.

346

George was asleep. The bed had a curling iron frame and there was enough room on it for two Georges and several Irenes, but she was tucked up close to him, so that their bodies were touching all the way down. In his sleep, his face was turned toward her, as if they had just now stopped talking. His eyes were closed, the lashes lay long on his cheeks. His arms were thrown out wide. Her head rested on one bicep, and his other arm was up on the pillow on the other side. She leaned into him and smelled the scent of his body, feeling she had smelled it before, had been this close before to his skin, to the hair under his arms, to the three small freckles on this side of his neck. It was just hard for her to remind herself that he was new. There was no sense to the idea that he was somehow old. Irene breathed deeply and sighed. Was he dreaming? Was he aware?

She saw his rib cage stretch and deflate, a low, slow rhythm of his life, and in the soft skin of his stomach she could see his heartbeat tapping at the surface.

"This is love," she said in her mind. "Love, love, love. This is love."

She laid her hand on top of his stomach, as if she was planting a flag. *I love you,* she thought. But the thing was, unfortunately, if she were to love him, she could never sleep again. As long as she stayed away from the inside of her mind, from her mother, from her Dark House, from the spiraling center at the black heart of her, she could try this love. She could lie down with this man in the middle of the day with no clothes on and put her mouth around him sweetly, and when she was done she could let him put his arms around her and fall asleep clutching her like a life preserver, his lips pressed against her hair. As long as she didn't sleep, this could happen again and again, every day here in the house in the woods, and she would lose her last name, and take his, and forget where she came from, and how it was clouded with piss, and gin, and unfortunate accidents.

Irene turned over and put her other cheek against George's arm and pressed her back against him, the backs of her legs, the soles of her feet. Her eye came to rest on the box of her mother's ashes, and she felt her heart lurch. Physically she could feel it beating, racing, under her arm.

She closed her eyes and began to put herself to sleep. She was dreaming, and aware, in her mind, of her mother's house, of the shelf of bells, of the sound each one made, and the final ring of the bell that told her she was in.

Asleep, I see that the Hinterland is changed, has become trees and bushes, and wild grass and a blue sky of fall. Directly across from my mother's porch is George's country place, where I am really sleeping now, with its own porch and its rambling pieces tucked under the spreading trees and behind the bushes turning red. I run across and go inside. There in the bedroom I see him stretched out still, the quilt tangled around his knees. He is so dear, and so sweet to me. I could devour him all over again, but I don't want him to wake up either, and anyway, my dreamspell is so embarrassing. I don't know if he would even want to see it. I am embarrassed of how dear I find him. I am embarrassed that I find him when I'm asleep and picture the angles of his elbows, his long feet, his absolutely beautiful face.

What is love? A contract for keeping us together, making things legal, perpetuating the species, a droopy butterfly wing of invented sap for the masses, a drug for idiots. That's what love is. I want to say that what I feel is desire, just sex, an animal firing itself up over another animal, but I know I have felt that before. Love makes me want to spread my legs. Love makes me want to put his hand down my pants. That's my version of romance.

The box of my mother's ashes is heavy in my dream, super-heavy, like it's going to kill me to carry this box through the house and out the door. How much did my mother weigh? How much did she weigh after her bones had been put through the pulverizer? This box is not my mother. It has her ashes in it, but it's heavier than that, it's heavy like heavy, dude. Meaning weighty.

I lug my mother's box of ashes into Dark House: the parlor, the library, the theater, the back room, the props room, and I know I'm coming to the center.

There's nothing inherently scary about a ruined room, a broken floor, and a hole that leads down. Or maybe there is. I don't know, because what this particular broken floor has always done is push my face away, so that it is perpetually in the periphery of my vision, and just looking at it sideways fills me up with paralyzing fear. I am the girl that has a solid plan for suicide in every city I am likely to visit, involving bridges of a particular height, water of a particular depth, and gravity. I face the side of a bridge with my toes curled, my breath let all the way out, my hands open like *catch me.* But that broken floor, that whistling dark, those beams sticking up through the floor, down through the ceiling, that causes me a fear that goes deep, all the way back to the little child's brain I had when I was six, and this whole thing started.

I'm afraid of the hole in the center of Dark House, but I walk straight over to it now, and I open up the box. Inside the box is a plastic bag. I open up the bag. Inside the bag is a thick powder, interspersed with bits of her. In the dream, it is the purest white. There is a wind coming at me from the back, a firm strong breeze behind me sucking straight down into the hole in the floor. The hole is big and draws everything to itself: the air, the people ground up into powder, the ideas in my head. I know that when I turn the box upside down the dregs of my mother will spiral into the hole and make a beautiful shape, like the curve of a snail shell, like the inside of a nautilus. It will spread out from my hand in a sparkling arc and make something so perfect as she floats away from me.

So I don't do that. I throw the whole damn box down the hole in one whoosh. And it is gone.

I feel dizzy, like I do when I stand too close. Then I'm running like a child up the basement stairs having banged the lid of the clothes dryer closed, and I burst through the door and out onto the porch, and George's country house is straight ahead of me and I run, run, run across to it and up onto the porch of it, and there's George again, and he's sleeping still. I lie down next to him in the bed, put my cheek on his arm, and curve my spine into him, and it's warm.

I'm looking at the place where my mother's box of ashes used to be before I threw it into the center of Dark House, and I know that now I can't wake up, because if I do, I will open my eyes, and it will be back there, that black terrible box. So I'll lie here, and sleep forever.

19

George woke up. His first instinct was to not open his eyes; the headache was that bad. He gently extracted his arm from under Irene's face, replaced it with a pillow, and left her sleeping there on the white cotton. He pulled the sheet up around her body and padded across the faded carpet and out of the room. In the bathroom, he closed the door so that it would be dark. He opened the medicine cabinet and by feel identified and took out a spray bottle, which he squirted into each nostril, sharply inhaling. He shut the medicine cabinet and looked at where he knew the mirror was, except that he was in the dark.

"This is a love story," he said. "Act one, boy meets girl. Act two, boy loses girl. This is act two."

He could feel the painkiller entering his headache and wrapping it up in cool plastic, pushing it back into its container, closing the lid. He stood there in the bathroom in the dark until he could roll his head around on his neck and not feel like he was going to pass out. Then he opened the door and went out. He pulled some jeans on from his dresser, thought about making a sandwich, and leaned over Irene and kissed her on the temple.

"Sweetheart," he said. She opened her eyes and stared straight across the room as if she'd seen a ghost.

"Are you OK?" he asked.

"Yes," she said. "Yes." But when she turned to face him, she was pale.

"Come and let me make you lunch," he said. "I have a way with meat and bread. We need to get going, because I have something at the institute I'm dying to show you before my lecture."

She nodded. She reached for the sheet and pulled it up around her chin.

"Come on, don't you want to see your supercollider?"

Irene and George stood in the elevator, going down. There were only two buttons on the wall: M and S. They'd started out in main and they were going to sub.

"This is the world's biggest scientific instrument you're about to see," said

George.

"I managed alright with one the size of a large bathtub," said Irene.

"This one is bigger than the one you had," said George. "Therefore better."

"Hmm," said Irene. "That remains to be seen."

Once they stepped foot on campus, Irene had gotten tough again, as if her combative exterior went on like a uniform when she was near science. George looked at her now, her jaw set and her eyes seeming to try to pierce through the elevator doors. She was a little dynamo. He felt a pang of love for her, watching her cross her arms and tap the toe of her ugly boot. *This is a love story about astronomy,* he thought. Twin souls collide and love each other forever. And no one ever goes crazy. And no one ever dies. And the universe folds back on itself and clicks into place, and the pylons holding up the electrical wires are really trees. And the trees are really gods.

When the elevator stopped and they stepped out into the cavern, Irene's eyes got wide, and she said, out loud, "Whoa." It had astonished George, too, when he first saw it. A tunnel, several stories high, was lined and laid with brightly colored wires, plastic tubes and disks, and it echoed amazingly, like a never-ending tiled bathroom, or a canyon, or a cave. Halfway to the ceiling was a tube, where the supercollider was being built. All around the opening on each side of the cavern were bright tiles, scaffolding, wires, and lights.

Dr. Bryant rattled down a flight of metal steps he had been climbing and came toward them with his arms open.

"Welcome, Dr. Sparks," he said. "Welcome to your new domain. I've got several appointments for you this afternoon, with engineers and fabricators, electrochemists and a couple of structural guys — I think your designs are going to fit right into our model."

Irene shook hands with Dr. Bryant and then turned to George. He knew immediately that she wasn't going to kiss him or give his crotch a good-bye pat or smooth his hair away from his face and look longingly into his eyes or anything. She was going to work, and she had probably said, if he had been paying attention, that at work they wouldn't be allowed to be together. Not yet. Dr. Bryant was looking at him expectantly, as if he wanted George to leave.

"Have you?" said Dr. Bryant.

"Have I?" asked George.

"Have you seen her?" said Irene.

"No," said George. "Unless you mean her?" George pointed to Irene.

"No, George, I mean Kate — Dr. Oakenshield. Your friend? Have you seen her? She didn't show up for her class this morning, and she hasn't tweeted. I thought maybe she had spent the night with you?"

"What?!" said George. "Of course not! Because fraternizing with other astronomers is both wrong and terrible."

Irene's face was inscrutable.

Dr. Bryant winked knowingly at George. "We all know you've been trying to get next to Dr. Oakenshield for months," he said. To Irene he added, "Of course as a policy we don't encourage our faculty to intermingle, but we work in such close quarters, there are some inevitable relationships that develop. I'm sure it was the same at your old lab."

"No," said Irene sagely. "We never fraternized. We also thought it wrong and terrible."

"Dr. Sparks," said Dr. Bryant, "this world is merciless. You must take love where you can find it."

Irene stared at him. He went on, "Anyway, George, I'm sure there's nothing to worry about. But I'm afraid there might be trouble at home for her, if you know what I mean.

I'll give you a ring when I've gotten to the bottom of it."

Then George walked away. It felt like there was ripping, like anyone could have heard it, when they separated. He didn't want to separate from Irene. It felt really wrong.

George's class was over. He waited another hour, doing some paperwork. He made some calls, looking for Kate Oakenshield, then dialed the Euphrates Project switchboard and got through to Irene.

"Sparks," she growled.

"Hey," he said. "There you are." The sound of her voice was like a hand on him. He felt it.

"It's amazing down here, George," she said.

"Great," said George. "I'm glad you like it."

"But I've had a lot of meetings this afternoon, now some things have to get done before we can proceed . . . if you want to . . ."

"Yes," said George. "I do want to. I need you, for something that might be a little awkward —"

"Can't be more awkward than stealing my mother's ashes from the funeral home."

"Right," said George. "Can't it be? Maybe. I'll come and get you."

George's car seats were awash with papers and books, and the floor was covered in empty Coke cans and coffee cups. In the back, an incredibly large ivy plant spread its many limbs around the trunk and over the backseat's headrests, having no trouble breathing.

"Mites?" said Irene, pointing at it before she entered the car. "You don't get mites?"

"I get oxygen," said George. He swept the front seat clear for her and then swept the backseat clear as well as she got in.

"Are we picking up a hitchhiker?" Irene wanted to know.

"In a manner of speaking," said George. "We're going to need your boyfriend for this errand, see? We're going to need Enkidu. For backup."

"What?"

"I need a heavy, to be honest," said George. "We're going on a rescue mission. And I'd feel better if I had some muscle on our side."

Twenty minutes later, Belion was glowering in the back, Irene and George were sitting in front, and the Volvo was on the freeway, headed west. Picking up Belion had

359

been awkward for George for several reasons.

First there was the fact that when Irene directed George to her mother's house, she had instructed George to drive straight to the house of the drunk psychic who had advised him to wait for a dreaming astronomer with brown hair. Irene's mother's house was the psychic's house, which meant that Irene's mother was the psychic. George had almost said something. It was at the front of his mouth, waiting to spring out, "Hey, you know what? I've been here before!" But he stopped himself. After her freaky reaction to the fact that they shared a birthday, George felt doubtful that Irene would embrace the information that her own mother had counseled George over a crystal ball, had recognized her daughter as George's future spouse.

It was the kind of information that George could tolerate but Irene could not. He was finding out all about Irene, and this was one of the main things: when confronted with a bizarre coincidence like this, Irene was not one to shake her head and comment on the mysteries of the universe. She was one to smack someone, deny having ever had a mother, and never speak to George again. So he kept his mouth shut.

Then there was the awkward moment while George was inside the car and Irene and Belion were outside the car and Irene was explaining something very firmly to him and used the words "penis sex" and pointed to George, and then clapped her hands together in Belion's face. George had emerged from his car, looking hopeful and inoffensive, he thought.

"Come on, Belion," he heard Irene say. "It'll be just like your game — you the strong warrior, saving the damsel in distress. We need you. We need the Archmage of the Underdark. It's a mission, Belion. Come on! There might even be weapons."

Now Belion was in the backseat and looking none too happy. That was OK, George thought. George needed Belion to be a bit riled up, for what they were going to do.

"Ever been to Sylvania before, Belion?" asked George.

"He's been to Sylvania," Irene speculated.

"It is Belion, isn't it?" said George.

There was a pause, and then Irene prompted, "Belion, say it's Belion."

"It's Belion," he said.

George went on. "So, you've been to Sylvania before, then? Lots of times?"

"Tell me, again, what has happened to this girl?" Belion asked.

George put on his turn signal, and they got off the freeway. "Well, she's been kind of kidnapped by her father. You know, he raised her as a mute."

"She's Kate Oakenshield, the girl who was raised mute. You may have seen it on the Learning Channel," Irene explained further.

"Oh, you saw that?" George asked her. "Did you see me?"

"No," said Irene. "My mother sent me a video once, but I didn't watch the whole thing. It was quite the news item, here in Toledo."

Belion growled. "So, again, I'm asking, what has happened to her?"

"Well, her father raised her mute, right, to develop her math brain. You know, no language, just music and, you know, noises and stuff," George said.

"Did it work?" Belion asked.

"Oh, did it," said George. "Yes, all the way. She's a freaky genius."

"So what's wrong then?" Belion asked.

"She was raised mute. No talking," Irene emphasized. "That's not normal, Belion."

"Not normal for you, fancy madam."

George laughed. "Fancy madam! I like this guy."

"Well, thank you very much," said Belion.

The Volvo rolled past the Spuyten Duyval

Country Club and into the wooded valleys of the Irwin Prairie State Nature Preserve. After a few more turns deeper into the woods, George pulled in to The Cedars and followed a circular drive around to park in front of a large brick manor house. He pushed the car into park and unfolded himself from behind the wheel, strode around the front of the car to take a fighting stance outside the front door.

Irene got out of the car and stood on the gravel of the driveway, still holding the door between her and the house, but Belion did not emerge. *Good,* George thought. *Secret weapon: giant hairy guy. This is how we bring Oakenshield down.*

George shouted at the front door. "Alright, Oakenshield, I'm back. And I brought reinforcements. You let Kate out of there now, or we're coming in."

There was no answer.

Irene said, "Belion, you should get out."

Belion emerged from the backseat bit by bit: first his meaty hand, then his arm and leg, then the rest of his body, leveraged out by his hand on the door frame.

George yelled, "Take a look, Oakenshield. And kindly remember, you're the guy who couldn't even take my elderly mother in a fair fight. How'd you like to go up and down the block with our young friend here?"

"Your penis sex friend is a fruitcake," said Belion calmly to Irene.

"Belion," said George. "Can't you roar or something? Wave your arms threateningly?"

"Well, like what?" Belion asked.

George demonstrated what he meant, cantering about on the portico in front of the door, swinging his arms like a mad gorilla. But Belion was unmoved.

"Well? Aren't you going to?" George asked.

Belion shook his hairy head. "No, but I enjoyed watching you do it."

Upstairs on the second floor, a window creaked open, and a dark head emerged.

"Emma!" cried George. "That's the housekeeper," he explained to Irene and Belion.

The housekeeper poked her head out the window. She pointed up, mutely, to a balcony on the third floor. George looked up. A curtain fluttered. And Kate Oakenshield stepped out onto the balcony, violin in hand. She was wearing a strange silver robe that George had never seen before, and it covered her so completely that George wasn't even sure it was her until she removed the hood, set the violin on her shoulder, and began to play Brahms. She cast a mournful eye down at her visitors as the melody soared.

Belion barked out a laugh. "Silvergirl? You have got to be kidding me," he said, as if to himself.

"Picturesque, isn't she?" said George.

Belion did not reply, but walked purposefully to the door and opened it, closed it gently behind him, and was gone.

George called up to Kate on her balcony. "Nevermind, Kate, Belion is coming!"

Kate continued to play her violin. George saw that eye-contact time was over. But he still called again, "This is Irene." He pointed at Irene, and Irene smiled a wan smile. "You'll see her lots when you come back to the institute. She's very nice."

"Looks like she's back to not talking," Irene said to George.

"Yeah," said George. "She kind of regresses when he convinces her to spend any time here. I think they've got a whole ballroom full of finches, puts her into some kind of twittery epileptic state."

"Lucky she has you," Irene said. He couldn't read the look on her face, but he felt it might be jealousy.

"Yes, well, I can't leave her out here, can I?" he pleaded.

Upstairs on the balcony, a door opened.

Belion emerged, picked up Kate and her violin, and carried her inside. The door closed.

"Well, that was better than I expected!" George said.

Irene nodded. "He must like her. He must like you. Otherwise, he wouldn't have come out here."

"Maybe it's just that he likes you," George said.

Irene smiled. The sight of it sent a spear through George's heart. The smile said that everything was OK. "He really is very smart."

"And Kate, too," George added. "Very smart."

"I've lived with him for three years. Three years I've been living with Belion."

George shook his head. "Well, we're not going to be messing around with them much anymore."

"Really? Are you sure? You came out here for her —"

George smiled now. "I can't honestly stand the sight of her anymore, sweetheart."

"It's me you want?" said Irene. "I mean, out of all the girls you —"

"Yes," he said.

Belion banged out the front door carrying Kate, her violin, several other instrument cases, and a couple of birdcages, too.

"Hey!" George leaped away from the car and Irene and clapped his hands together. "Excellent, well, you got her. Very nice. A fine job."

Belion opened the car and set Kate down like a baby in the backseat, tucked her silver robe in neatly, and then raised the hatch on the wagon. He flung the overgrown ivy onto the gravel drive without even looking at it and replaced it with Kate's possessions.

"That's all she pointed to. Should be enough," said Belion.

"Hey, my ivy! That plant is forty years old!" George protested.

"Don't grow plants in your car anymore, fruity," Belion told him. "Then you won't have to worry about people getting rid of them."

"I need more oxygen than other people," said George.

At this juncture, Father Oakenshield fluttered out of the front door waving a shovel.

"This is illegal! This is kidnapping! I'm calling the police!" he complained.

"Good," George told him. "Call the police, you ass. They'll love taking another trip out here to Birdybird Farm."

"Police!" the old man yelled. "Emma, call the police!"

The housekeeper poked her head out her window again and waved off George and the rest of them silently, rolling her eyes. She glared at Father Oakenshield and withdrew her head.

Belion closed the trunk and came around to the side of the car where Father Oakenshield was staging his little attack.

"Hi," said Belion, "I'm Belion."

Father Oakenshield was silent, and Belion went on. "If you ever approach her, breathe on her, call her, think of her, or even remember her, even in the night, even in the dark, I will be there, standing over you, and I will kill you before your heart takes its next beat."

"He's the Archmage of the Underdark," Irene added.

"I'm beginning to see that," said George.

Father Oakenshield retreated to the portico, dropping his shovel. Belion slid himself into the backseat beside Kate, and George and Irene took their places in the front.

"Drive, George. Drive," Belion commanded.

Toledo, the Glass City, sparkled on the edge of the Maumee Bay. In the harbor downtown, boats bobbed around the marina and the calls of gulls echoed across the water.

Citizens walked along the waterfront, their glasses rosy in the late afternoon sun, their laptop bags bathed in reflected light from the tall glass buildings. Down farther south, by the industrial docks, machines clanged and cranes swung wide over container ships. Little puffy clouds hung pink against the deep blue sky in arrays and arcs, bisected by jet trails.

George's boat was a cruising trawler. The hull was navy blue, the pilot's cabin glossy bright wood with white trim. The boat cut briskly through quiet lapping waves, creating a sharp white wake. George stood at the helm, one hand on the wheel, one hand on the throttle. He wore a captain's hat. Irene and Belion sat politely at the stern on a seat that stretched across the back of the boat. Irene hung over the side, trailing one hand in the water.

"Everyone alright back there?" George called.

He heard Belion say, "Great."

"Irene? You alright?" he asked.

"Never better," he heard faintly from the back.

Kate Oakenshield emerged from the cabin, wearing nothing but a loose, strapless white dress, gathered at the top with several rows of elastic over her breasts and just long enough to cover her butt. Her hair was a tangle of chestnut curls, falling down everywhere. She hung over the side of the boat, gazing intently into the water as it moved past.

Irene pulled her ponytail out and unbuttoned the top button of her shirt.

"Let's go out on the lake, away from the city lights a bit, so when the stars start coming out —" George began.

Kate gave a little gasp and then dove into the water. George instantly cut the throttle but did not seem alarmed. Irene, however, jumped up and rushed to the side of the boat. George switched the motor completely off, and the sound stopped. The boat drifted.

"Is she alright?" Irene asked. "Should we —"

"She's fine. She must have seen something."

"I didn't hear her beep or twitter or growl or anything. She just . . . kind of draped herself over," said Irene. "And then she fell in."

"Yes, yes, don't get worried," George urged her. "She does this kind of thing all the time. I promise you she'll be back up in three seconds."

They stood next to each other by the railing, watching the waves for signs of Kate's resurfacing. Belion started to take off his shoes.

"I'm going in after her," said Belion.

"Now hold on a minute, there, knight in shining T-shirt," George began. "Just because I signed you on to muscle her father doesn't mean I need you scouting for peril around every corner. Testing everyone's food for poison. You know, plucking us from —"

Belion threw his meaty leg over the side of the boat.

"Oh, alright, are you going in?" said George. "Fine, dive in and see what you can see."

Belion splashed into the water just as Kate resurfaced, holding tight to the horn of a narwhal. She was beaming, rubbing its horn, patting it on the face.

"Are you kidding me?" Irene asked. "Is that a fucking narwhal?"

"Yeah," said George. "She's one of those, you know, St. Francis of Assissi types. Twitter-dee-twoo and then you've got an orangutan for a pal, a Yorkshire terrier for a copilot, right? Especially birds but also, you know, the Erie narwhals."

"But I thought no one could catch them alive, they're so dangerous," said Irene.

The narwhal began to dive, and Kate let go of it. When she came back to the surface, she had shed the dress. It floated to the surface. Belion picked up the dress and, without looking at it or the boat, balled it up and hurled it back onto the deck.

Belion said, to Kate, "Are they dangerous? The —" Then Belion made a pretend angry face and a motion with his hand to indicate a narwhal horn.

Kate shook her head, smiled radiantly, and dove down under the water again. Her feet kicked up, and she was gone under the surface.

Another narwhal came up for air, and Belion gingerly, hesitantly touched it. It lashed around and dove. Belion looked up at Irene and George, amazed.

"Narwhal!" Belion trumpeted.

George laughed. He said to Irene, "Do you want to go in?"

"No," said Irene. "Let them."

"Come on up here then," he told her.

George took the key all the way out of the ignition and went up a few stairs to stand on the bow. He gave Irene a hand coming up and then leaned against the side of the pilot cabin comfortably, one bent leg crooked against the rail. Irene leaned against the rail, facing him, where she could still watch Kate and Belion cavorting with the whales.

"River dolphins," she said. "Like on the Amazon."

"They're actually whales, not dolphins," George said. "And don't tell me you've been on the Amazon."

"Actually, yes, my mom took me to Brazil when I was in high school."

"No, that is not true! I have been there, too!"

Kate made a screeching, burbling sound, putting her face in the water. Belion orbited her like a big polite buoy.

Irene said, "I bet she's a screamer in the sack."

"I wouldn't know," said George.

"Really?" said Irene.

"You don't need to be jealous," said George. "Really."

"Am I good at it," she said. "You know, am I good at it?"

George felt his body tighten up like a spring.

"At sex?"

"Yes," Irene said.

"You are the best," said George, "that I have ever had. But that doesn't mean we shouldn't practice like ten times a day for the rest of our lives. Because you never know. You could get even better."

She smiled and stretched. "It's just that, I don't understand how you could want her, and everything that she is, and then turn around and want me, and the person that I am —"

"Sweetheart, I only wanted her because she was a bad approximation of you. Don't you see that?"

"No," said Irene.

"Irene." George pulled her into his side and put his hands around her, clutched her to him. "We are soulmates."

"I don't understand that," said Irene into his chest.

"It doesn't take you understanding it," George explained. "In fact, if you'd stop understanding it so much, it might be a lot easier."

"But I'm not — like her," said Irene.

"You mean crazy?"

"I mean sexy." Irene's voice caught, and she coughed. "She's like you, like all plants and freedom and music and such an artist, a dreamer, like you are."

"You're a dreamer," said George.

"I am not," said Irene.

"Well, OK," he conceded. "If you say so." He moved his fingers up and down her spine, going up into her hair and then down,

down, into the waistband of her jeans.

"The truth is you're not like her at all," he said. "You're prettier than she is. And you're smarter. And when I'm with you, she seems like she's made out of paper and feathers, and you, I'd like to take down into the cabin, and treat you in ways that only wild bears can treat each other."

She smacked at him, and it felt good.

"George!" she said.

"You're the faery that I imagined when I was six," George went on, "I know what faeries look like. This is it. Why don't you just try loving me? It might be really easy."

"I —" Irene began. But George wasn't done.

"You're all I want, but you have to believe it, too."

"I'm not a believer."

"But you want to be," he said. He knew that he understood, and he tried to make her see it. "You want to believe, and yet you want to be honest. You want us to be great, but you want us to be real. I want those things, too. This is where we are the same."

She put her arms around him and held her face up sweetly to be kissed. He leaned into her, and their lips came together. It was as if George was spinning through her and back into himself, more rapidly than he could track. When she pulled back, he was dizzy.

"I love you," he said to her.

"Love isn't real, George," she said, her voice low and strange. "It's not real. It doesn't make any sense. Not for me. I don't believe in it."

"Then this must be science," said George.

"I don't believe in marriage either," said Irene.

"Fine," he said, trying to make her smile. "Then we'll be in science, and we'll perform a futuristic sex alliance instead of getting married."

"George! I just can't do it," Irene said. She looked sorry. Sorry that she couldn't do it. "I'm not good enough."

"We're soulmates — look at everything we know, everything we've done. It's like we were made for each other. That weird old folk music, what are the odds we would both have that same album? We've memorized the same poetry, you play the flute and I play the hand drum, you went to Brazil and so did I, we both loved Philip Pullman to the point of making Halloween costumes *before* it was a movie . . . For chrissake, you have one of my dad's paintings in your house."

"I don't believe in fate," said Irene. "Or

destiny or things like that."

"But it's more than that, Irene," he urged her. "What do you want, what do you want most of all, for yourself?"

He knew it was not fame, or to be right about black holes, or to be somewhere locked in a lab. He knew her better than this. But would she say it? Would she give this to him?

"To be loyal," she said slowly. "I want to be loyal. Loyal like my mother never was. Or my father. I want to be loyal for my whole life. I think that would be great."

"I want that, too," he said.

"But that doesn't mean we are in love," said Irene. "That doesn't make it true."

He kissed her again. "You're wrong," he said. "You're wrong about love. Maybe it's not true, but it's real. And it doesn't have to be true to be real. Can you see —"

"What if I do give up," she said suddenly. "What if I say, OK, I give up. What if I say I love you. I don't know what to do after that."

"I love you, too," said George. "There's nothing you have to do. It's done."

"George." She held onto him, but turned to look at Belion and Kate, who were swimming out some distance away from the boat, as the sunset turned the water to gold. "I feel stupid. I have this really stupid feeling in my brain."

"That's not stupid," said George. "That's happy. You're feeling happy."

Irene smiled and he picked her up and held her, leaning back against the wall of the cabin. She put her legs around his waist and pressed her face into his neck where he could feel her breathing.

"OK, I'm happy, George," she said. "I'm happy."

And then it was done.

20

The phone in the underground cavern rang. Sam Beth picked it up.

"Toledo Institute of Astronomy," she droned. Then she rolled her eyes and covered the receiver. She called out, "Dr. Sparks?"

Irene came riding down the walkway in the tunnel on one of the mopeds that the physicists used to traverse the sections of the collider between the insertion hubs and detectors.

She parked the vehicle and took the phone from Sam Beth's resentful hand. It was an irony that in the vicinity of some of the most specialized and technologically advanced equipment in the world, they had to use phones plugged into wires because their mobile phones could not communicate from four hundred feet belowground, around so many magnets.

"Sparks," she said.

Then she listened. Then she said, "This is unacceptable. How do you just lose a person from the face of the earth? I gave her to you. You were supposed to give her back to me, all burned up and stuff."

"This has never happened before," said the funeral home director.

Irene said, "That doesn't make a damn bit of difference."

"You're right, you're right," said the man.

"You're in big trouble, mister," Irene told him. "You don't just erase a person from the world. You don't just twiddle your thumbs and throw some glitter in the air and whoops, she's gone. You just can't do that, do you understand?"

"I do," said the funeral home director. "I do understand. I'm still hopeful that we will find her. It's still possible."

"See that you do," said Irene. "She was my mother. She was not just some box of dust that you don't know what to do with. She was all I had."

She slammed the phone back into the receiver and turned around to find that Sam Beth was looking at her with her mouth hanging open.

"What happened?" said Sam Beth.

"I stole my mother's body from the funeral home," said Irene. "Her burned up, post-cremation body. And now they can't find her, and I am blaming them for losing her."

"Wow," said Sam Beth, seeming to be genuinely impressed. "What are you going to do with her?"

"That's the thing," said Irene. "I don't know. I can't just randomly plant her in some flower garden."

Sam Beth narrowed her eyes and blew air out gently between her lips. She inflated her lips in this way, tapping one finger gently on the desk.

"I know what to do," said Sam Beth. "There is a ceremony that the Daughters of Babylon can perform. I think I can help you."

"You would do that?" said Irene.

"When you just stood there and said you stole your mother's ashes from the funeral home, my opinion of you kind of changed. I mean, I still don't think you're right for Dr. Dermont. But I think what you did was pretty badass."

It was summertime, 1986. Bernice and Sally had planted a flower garden, trying to attract as many hummingbirds as possible to their kitchen window, because the two-year-old George and Irene found them so interesting. They planted phlox, bee balm, tried to get a trumpet vine to riot over an arbor installed by Ray and Dean. The two men had stayed friends, in spite of the situation, and they often did projects around the house together, Ray coming in to visit for a few days or taking Dean off hunting in Michigan in the fall. Bernice avoided him when he was around, but came to grudgingly appreciate his continued interest in Irene. He was a wild character, but they had underestimated him.

Of course he later became a felon and a gambler, but this was still the golden summer when they were all together, and Bernice could pretend it would always be this way. The babies would sit in their high chairs, side by side, and eat their breakfast watching little birds hover over the flowers while the women drank tea, Bernice resting between sessions, Sally serving up applesauce, scrambled eggs, peach slices, and ripe tomatoes to the kids.

"We need to separate them soon," Sally said one morning.

"You said when they're three," said Bernice, her hands around a mug of tea. They had been making applesauce and had kerchiefs on their heads.

"I said when they're verbal," Sally corrected. She used a rag to wipe off the counter and replaced George's spoon with a new one from the drawer.

"Does it really matter?" Out of habit, she loosed the tea from the tea ball and swirled the contents around in the remaining liquid, then upended the cup on the saucer.

"Yes, it matters," said Sally. "We don't want them to be like cousins. We want them to meet as adults. Don't be weird. If they know each other too well, they can't fall in love."

Bernice slowly turned the teacup back over and peered inside.

"What is it?" asked Sally.

"You're not the one that's got to move out," said Bernice. "And lose her job."

"Yeah, you're not the one who's going to have to get a job. Without you here, there's no astrology practice — it's just smoke and mirrors."

"I'm smoke and mirrors," said Bernice. In the cup: a whirlwind, a broken chain. Sometimes there was a bell, a bridge.

"You're not smoke and mirrors," said Sally. "You have real talent, whatever your personal feelings about it are. I've seen you predict stuff, like spooky accurate."

"It's all science," said Bernice. "You know that. Charts, lists, books, technique. The fact that it happens to work has nothing to do with me, any more than the fact that you're affected by gravity has anything to do with you."

"What's in the teacup?" said Sally. "Is it more plane crash?"

"No," said Bernice. "I mean, yes, but it means nothing."

Sally pulled a large ceramic bowl out of the sink and set it on the kitchen island. She began to hum as she wiped it with her towel.

Irene said, "All done," and Sally swept her tray clean with the rag and replaced the food with some paper crayons for her to play with.

"Can't get down yet, darling," she said. "Mama's still resting, and I'm going to finish putting away the dishes we made the applesauce in. Then I'll take you outside. If only Uncle Dean would get back, he could take you kids for a while and let us finish."

Then Dean came through the door, pulling his flannel coat from his shoulders, "Hello, family!"

Bernice saw Sally's mouth drop open, her head jerk up. Her eyes met Bernice's eyes. "Wait, this is that moment. Applesauce," she said. "From our own orchard. It's happening. And here he is. It's him. He's about to do it."

"What, me?" Dean asked. "Brave, handsome me?"

Dean turned and swung his arms out wide, and the bowl, knocked off the counter, fell toward the ground. But Bernice was already there, standing, and caught it before it shattered on the floor.

"Yeah, right," said Sally. "You're smoke and mirrors. You don't know anything. But you predicted this moment, ten years ago. Down to the pot in your hands. And you know it."

Irene laughed in her high chair. George threw a tomato. Both the women turned then and looked straight at the children in their high chairs. George was holding Irene's hand.

Maybe Bernice did not realize that the moment of separation would ever come. Maybe she thought she could keep on tossing herself onto the sofa next to Sally, pulling her friend's head into her lap, or brushing Sally's long hair while she was on the telephone. "Oh, that feels good," Sally would say, hanging up. "It gives me goose bumps. Don't stop." Maybe Bernice imagined she would keep on hugging her behind the stove, rubbing her temples with arnica, doing her toenails and laughing. Never mind that she would fall into the arms of Dean, say "Hey, baby," and kiss him. Never mind that she would fall so eagerly into his bed, laughing into the night. Shitty as it was being third wheel, Bernice could go on forever.

But after that day in the kitchen, with the bowl that dropped and the children holding hands in their chairs, Sally seemed to never stop lecturing that they must raise the children separately to be compatible, so that they could find each other, so that familiarity would not breed contempt. They would train them independently to be magnets, north and south, that would click together when they met, years later, at the appointed time. Maybe Bernice had forgotten this part of the deal, in her happiness. Dean was gone from their lives so much, either in the studio or traveling, that it was almost like old times. Sometimes the mothers even slept together in the same bed. For Bernice, ignoring the possibility that they'd separate the children also meant turning her back on the idea that they'd separate from each other. Yet that's exactly what Sally had in mind.

They finally decided Bernice would leave on the children's third birthday. She would live in her old house in the East End, she would continue to work as a tasseomancer, an astrologer, a psychic, and Sally would get a job to supplement Dean's erratic income. The bags were packed and moved bit by bit, the furniture at the old house dusted and prepared, the utilities restored, and they were leaving. They had let the babies fall asleep in the same bed one last time, and Bernice was to leave as soon as they were truly sleeping, so there would be no sad good-bye to remember, only something sweet. Bernice sat on the bench near the door, hesitating to go and get her sleeping daughter, hesitating to leave her friend.

"It's only for a little while," said Sally.

"Twenty years," said Bernice.

"We can visit each other in our dreams."

"That's not enough. I'll miss you. This is a terrible idea."

"Well, terrible or not, it's not a new one. And you agreed to it."

Sally began to straighten up the entryway, folding a scarf and smoothing the sleeves of a jacket, putting shoes in a line: George's shoes, Sally's shoes, Dean's shoes, even some flip-flops that belonged to Ray, left the last time he'd popped in.

"This isn't going to work unless we separate them, Bern," she said as she cleaned. "And really separate — no playdates, no field trips. If we're still hanging out together all the time, they're not separate. This has got to be a cold cut."

Sally stopped fidgeting and put her hand on Bernice's shoulder. "And after they get married, why think of how much life we'll have to live together? We won't even be fifty! We can still get adjacent suites at the old folks' home, BERN-iss! It'll be just like we always planned. But our kids will be happy. And that'll mean we can be happy. Right? Come on. The grandchildren will be here in like five minutes. And then we can tell them everything. As soon as they're safely in love."

For three years they maintained the separation. For three years, Bernice was able to maintain the sobriety she had kept for the three years she'd lived with Sally and Dean. Sally would send her letters, sometimes, detailing the ways they'd put the children's lives together: what music they'd love, what countries they would visit, what poems they'd learn. She made a map for them to find each other, through the study of the stars. Every letter was signed, "I love you! Don't forget that!" Bernice kept these letters in a locked box, and read them over and over.

And then one night, alone, afraid, tired,

and restless, Bernice broke. There was no special reason for it: just a dissolution of will. Breaking meant drinking. Drinking felt terrible and wonderful and like going home again and like being cast out of home into the fire, and when she was good and drunk she called Sally, on the telephone, something that Sally had specifically forbidden.

"Hello?" said a voice. The voice of a child.

"Is your mother at home?" Bernice said, as best she could.

"What?" the child said. "What did you say?"

Bernice was mustering the courage to try again, do better, when Sally spoke, "Give me the phone, George. Who is this? What do you want?"

"Sally, it's me."

Sally arrived at the front door thirty minutes later, and the first thing she did was to grab Bernice by the wrist and pull her out onto the porch. She shut the door and the screen door and peeked into the window, where Irene was watching television.

"What's wrong with you?" Sally asked through clenched teeth.

"What's wrong with you?" Bernice responded.

"Are you drunk?" Sally was aghast.

"No. I'm not drunk. But I'm going to be a drunk if you don't call off this deal. I'm done. I'm done with the thing. It's stupid anyway, and who cares, and this is not right. I think what we are really doing is ruining my life." Bernice let herself drop into the porch swing.

Sally clutched her face with both hands and sat down next to her. "You're drunk! I've never seen you like this."

"I'm. Like. This." Bernice said it very slowly. "I. Always. Am."

Sally took Bernice by the hand. "We've got to get you some coffee," she said. "It'll be OK. We'll get you coffee and aspirin. It'll be fine. You just went a little crazy."

The touch of Sally's hand on hers made her begin to cry. "I'm so lonely," she said. "I'm lonely and I don't know what to do."

Sally smiled her big wonky smile. "Maybe you just need a boyfriend!" she said. "You could find someone. Someone like Dean. He may be gone a lot, but he's so —"

"He dazzles you," Bernice cried even harder. "I know."

"Is that it? Do you need to, like, date?" Sally frowned. "It almost seems like the last guy you had a date with is Ray."

"Irene's father."

"Don't call him that. He's George's uncle."

"That's what he is."

"What's going on with you? I mean, I get that you weren't dating when the kids were little, but why now? Are you, like, some kind of nun? Are you pouting?"

Bernice knew that what was going to happen next would be something she remembered forever, good or bad. In her mind, she would reach out and brush Sally's hair away from her face, place her palm alongside her friend's cheek, and say, "It's you, Sally. It's you, and it's always been you. That's why I can't bear this separation for the children. It's separation from the only one I've ever loved." She would see a light of understanding in Sally's eyes, and she would lean in and kiss her, first on one cheek, and then on the other, and then Sally herself would turn her lips to meet Bernice's. It would be something she would remember forever.

But what happened was different. Bernice said something Sally didn't understand, and then she reached for her friend and hooked her around the ear. She came in for a kiss, and Sally stopped her by pushing back on her shoulder and standing up.

"What are you doing?" Sally asked.

"I love you," said Bernice.

"You really are drunk," Sally laughed nervously.

"I like girls," said Bernice. "Girls, not boys. I like girls not boys. NOT BOYS."

Then Sally whispered, "What? You're GAY?" Her whisper was loud enough to wake the neighbors, loud enough to overcome the television, loud enough to rock the foundation of the house, loud enough to echo down the years of Bernice's life, and all the casual touching, and all the friendly hugs, booming with the secret. Bernice could see a light dawning in Sally's eyes, but it wasn't love. Sally understood very well what was happening. It was aggravation, and anger, maybe betrayal, and she felt as if Sally was seeing her for the first time, and she was seeing a monster.

"Why didn't you tell me?" Sally snapped. "I'm not an asshole. I would have been cool with it."

"Because you're not!" Bernice yelled back. "You're not gay and I am. That's it. That's what happened. Nobody twinned us, nobody set us up for a lifetime of happiness, we just happened to be two girls, one gay, one not, and what am I supposed to do, loving you? What am I supposed to do about it? You won't even let me see you anymore."

"You love me?"

"I'm really in love with you," said Bernice. "Really. I am. Since high school."

"No, you're not," said Sally. "You're not. You're over it. You got over it."

"I AM."

Sally came very close to her. Bernice could feel her breath coming in and out, landing on her face. Her face was numb. She could feel the heat from Sally's breath. That was it. Sally took a sharp breath in, and she glared at Bernice. When the words came out, they came hard and low. "Are you telling me that this whole thing has been you trying to get in my pants? Is that what you expect me to believe?"

"No," said Bernice. "Not the whole thing."

"When I think" — Sally put her face inches from Bernice, and it was terrible to see the rage in her friend's face — "about the ways I have let you touch me. You are disgusting."

"You don't mean that," said Bernice. "You're just mad. You're just surprised."

"Surprised is not what I am," said Sally. "I am not surprised you are gay. I'm unsurprised and unimpressed. Lots of people are gay. Lots of people I know, people you know, so it's not even news. It's not even interesting."

"Good," said Bernice.

"Not good," said Sally. "Because the lies you have told have been back to the beginning of our lives. If you love me."

"I do," said Bernice. She felt very quiet and small. She felt like a lot of things had been taken away from her that were protecting her, and now she was naked without them, small and cold. Sally stood up and began to pace the porch. The heels of her boots snapped against the floorboards. The light filtering through the blinds from the television streaked across her face, across the back of her head and her golden hair.

"What kind of mother are you," Sally said with precision. "What kind of mother are you, letting a stranger knock you up, just to get — just to get your breast into my mouth?"

Bernice put her hand over her mouth, and bit into her finger. Sally remembered that night. Remembered it with accuracy, all the ways that it had happened. She had hoped that Sally remembered it, in some way, but not like this.

"It was for the children," said Bernice. "I love them. I do. Even yours."

"Your breast was in my mouth!" cried Sally. "How dare you not tell me. How dare you?"

Bernice felt herself stiffen. She felt herself begin to fight. She fought for the memory of that night, for it not to be something wicked that she did, something small and deceitful, her deceiving both of them, for that brief second of contact, for that encouraging smile, that voice humming into her flesh, those eyes flashing encouragement at her: "It's working!"

Once, when they were kids, when Sally's breasts were just coming out, and they were still playing with Barbies, there had been a moment in Sally's bedroom. Making two moments, in all. Two, forgetting all the girls she had drawn into her bed, all the nipples she had rolled around in her mouth, all the tit fat she had smacked with the back of her hand, all the places she had put her cheek and slept. That day, they were putting on their bathing suits. Sally was having trouble with her ties, and the triangles of her bikini were laid down on her belly as she stood there, fighting with a knot, and her new little breasts sprouting. Bernice had said, "Can I touch them?" And Sally had said, "Yeah, sure."

Bernice, just another young girl with curiosity in the palms of her hands, put those hands over the place where the triangles would go, feeling Sally's skin cool under her hot palms. "Weird, right?" said Sally. "Come on." The knot was untied. They never talked about it. Never mentioned it. When they were in bed together, so many countless times, for sleepovers, for college overnights, for whatever reason, Bernice petting her endlessly on the back, never trailing her hand those two inches more down past her tailbone. Suntan lotion on the collarbones, the neck, but never inside two imaginary circles drawn around her breasts. For other girls, her hand slamming into the most unforgiving places. But for Sally, a map of forbidden zones. This body she knew so well. Better than her own.

"How dare YOU?" she demanded, shouting at Sally now. "How dare you not know? You have been my best friend for twenty years, twenty-five years, how dare you not know who I love?"

Sally hesitated, said nothing. Her face was a blank. Bernice was reminded of her expression in that moment, her hands pressing into the cool breasts before the swimming suit was applied, and it was as if Sally's face turned to hers, her eyes suddenly aware, locked on Bernice's eyes, saying, "It's you." Then Bernice swallowed.

"You knew," Bernice said slowly. "You did know. How could you not know?"

"No, I did not know. Because you lied!" Sally growled, her teeth bared. "You lied to me. Don't you turn this around, you liar."

"You knew," said Bernice. "You knew and you used me, you knew and you let me follow your bait. My breast in your mouth. You did that. On purpose. Like a prize you were giving me."

She could feel it there still, stiff under her friend's tongue, still feel her hands itching to crawl over Sally's rib cage, dig into her back, draw her down on top of her, never let go.

"This is over," Sally said. She stood up. She brushed off her shirt, pulled down her skirt.

"No," said Bernice. "I'm sorry. I'm sorry."

"You're drunk, may I remind you. And you're the one that wanted this to be over. So it is. I don't want you in my life, and I don't want your daughter for my son."

Bernice felt bad. She felt drunk and bad. And sorry. And like it was all her fault.

"It's not her fault," said Bernice. "It's not my baby's fault. Please, please. What is she, if we don't have this? What is she without him?"

"You sound like the town drunk," said Sally. "You are out of control. Get yourself together, and go find something else to do with your life. Obsessing over me, and prepping your daughter to marry my son, that's over now."

"No," Bernice begged. "Not like this."

"What's more," said Sally. Bernice, in her drunkenness, couldn't tell if her friend was angry, or tired, or excited, or dismayed. But she understood this: "What's more, if you ever come around trying to talk to me, or if you ever send her around to talk to him, I will fucking kill you. I'll kill you. I am not what you are. Remember that. I am not like you."

That night, Bernice set a fire. She set a fire but she did not die.

Here's what is known: one got pregnant and then the other. They took some herbal drugs to induce labor, and they had their babies at the same time. What else really happened? Who knows? What else can really be documented or understood? Why do some people fall in love with each other, and others don't? What is love? It's so, so, so stupid right up until it's real. And then it's the most important thing in the world, whether you believe in it or not.

Sam Beth was dressed as a Daughter of Babylon in all her ritual markings. Irene, uninitiated, was only allowed to watch and learn, but she wore a black robe with a long cowl that Sam Beth had provided. The procession started at the top of the ziggurat, at 10 P.M., when the moon was at its zenith. The dark rectangle containing the remains was draped with a black cloth, and Sam Beth carried it in her arms. She had a large diamond in her belly button, one shoved into her left nostril, and one hanging from her right ear. She had explained that the triangle created by the relationship between these three diamonds was also traced in coal around her right breast, and the parallax measurement described by the arc of the acute angle was reflected in the name of the star she claimed as her own talisman. They carried the dead woman's rectangle of ashes from the top of the ziggurat to the bottom and into the crypt that was generally kept for dignitaries in the world of astronomy and math, and they carried her past the person who created the lens that allowed the universe to be mapped and the person who hypothesized the particle that was created when two iron ions collide, and they laid her to rest in a very modest crèche and draped the black cloth across the entrance, and no one disturbed her at all forever. She was left entirely alone.

Bernice had tried to get into her daughter's dreams from the very beginning. From before she even gave birth she had tried to dream herself into her daughter's reveries. Before Irene could talk, before she could walk, Bernice was reaching out, reaching in, helping her discover how to release her body from her mind, and go where she would in sleep. All the while Bernice was dreaming and building a special place for her and her daughter to reside. It was a beautiful lake island, with a clay and wattle cabin, a bean garden, and beehives. She invited, and invited, but the girl never ever came. *Maybe when I am dead,* Bernice had thought, *this is where I will end up. Here on this lake island, with the girl I brought into the world. We'll hear the water lapping and the linnets swooping, and we'll drift through the rest of time this way. But if she never visits it with me now, how will she ever find me when I am gone?*

21

Irene and George stood on the porch of the country house, holding hands. In the field, the crystal maze hummed and flickered. In the well, nothing gurgled. Birds pecked at the dried remnants of summer berries, and a breeze puffed over the trees.

They had meant to go rushing inside and fall upon each other, and they were already laughing, but then Irene had put her hand up to stop. Now George paused, his hand on the doorknob, a floorboard creaking under his foot.

"Someone's inside," whispered Irene. "I heard —"

Then George nodded. He heard the voices, too. Still hand in hand, they tiptoed over to the window and peered inside. The big front room was empty and dark, but beyond that a light gleamed in the kitchen, and Irene heard a man's voice say, "You can't. I won't let you." Then there

401

was a crash.

Irene felt alarmed. Had they disturbed a break-in? Way out here in the woods? But George was shaking his head. "It's my dad," he mouthed to her, silently.

"I can do whatever I want," came Sally's voice, and then Sally herself came into view in the hallway.

"And my mom, apparently," George said.

She wore a long handkerchief dress and had no shoes on. Her hair was mussed and she had a wineglass in one hand. She raised the glass, drained it, and repeated, "I can do whatever I want. It's my property."

"But they were born here. This is where they played —"

Dean came into the hallway, chasing Sally, leaning into her. His shirt was open at the throat, his old painter pants rolled up to the knee and wet around the bottom, as if they had been wading. He sank his hands into her waist and pulled her to him.

"I don't care," Sally said. "That's as good a reason as any."

"*They* were born here?" George repeated into Irene's ear. *"They?"*

"Maybe you have a sibling," Irene wondered.

"Just wait," said Dean. "Wait. I'm begging you."

"I'm selling it, Dean," Sally snapped. "I want it gone. You can go live someplace else. Maybe I'll even let you come and live with me. If you change your pants."

"What, these pants?" Dean laughed, and began to undo his belt. Sally laughed. She actually laughed.

George shook his head, clasping Irene's hand tightly. He took two quick steps backward, fell into the porch swing, and then bounced backward into a bush. Both Sally and Dean snapped their heads around to stare at the window, and Irene waved feebly. Sally rushed for the door, trailing Dean behind her, and swung it open.

"What are you doing here?" she asked.

"I could ask you the same thing," said George from the bushes, swinging one arm up onto the porch.

"Are you alright, son?" Dean went to help George clamber back up, and when he was upright and had brushed himself off, Sally said, "I come here, sometimes."

"She does," said Dean. "It's true."

"I am the owner," Sally pointed out. "I own this. That's what I'm doing here."

"Yeah, you own this," said George. "But you haven't been out here in forever. And now you're here and . . ."

"Having sex," prompted Irene.

"Ugh!" George protested. "I was going to say wearing hippie clothes!"

"It's none of your concern what I'm wearing," said Sally, drawing herself up regally, which didn't work as well without her heels on. She turned to Irene. "And it's no concern of yours what I'm doing."

"Are you selling this place?" George wanted to know.

"No," said Dean. "She's not."

"I am," said Sally. "I should have done it years ago."

She shook her head sadly and set her empty wineglass on the porch railing. "Sentiment," she said to Irene. "It's such a bitch."

WARNING: Conveyor may start without warning. Moving parts can cut or crush. Keep hands and body clear of conveyor.

Irene was lying down flat inside the supercollider. Around her head, an array of trapezoids spread out in colorful arcs. She wasn't wearing any pants. The lights were bright in the wide cavern where her experiment was being built. Out there, you could walk around with a clipboard, nod and smile at passing colleagues, learn and use science facts. But inside the tunnel, where the beam pipes themselves would be, it was pretty dim. Pretty shadowy. If you're a pion, you don't need a lot of light to find and smash into another pion. You just do it.

It was George's idea to come here, after their failure to find privacy at the country house, after they'd made their embarrassed departure. "Such a college problem," George had said. "Madly in love and nowhere to be alone." So he had dragged a foam pad of high-density insulation into the pipe in order to lay her down on it.

"You're a proton," said George. "I'm a proton. Let's go in here together."

"Kind of a tight fit," said Irene.

"That way there's only room for us two," said George.

WARNING: Beyond this point: Radio frequency fields at this site may exceed acceptable amounts for human exposure. Failure to abide by all posted signs and site guidelines for working in radio frequency environments could result in serious injury.

When the construction team at the Ur insertion point had clocked out for the night, and the engineers from the Uruk detector were safely in bed, George and Irene entered the elevator together. They put their eyes up for the retinal scan. Then they were four hundred feet below ground, alone. Irene loved being with George. There wasn't anything going on in her mind right now except that there was no one else around. They could take their clothes off, and she could knock him to the floor, take his hip bones in her hands, and crouch over him. If she wanted to.

George climbed the bright green ladder that stood at the end of the pipe where the detector would eventually be mounted when it was built. He looked so small against the structure, against the scaffolding, so smooth against all the hard angles of the metal plates. He began to take off his shirt. They had deactivated the door. They had put a sheet of aluminum against the elevator window. The ventilation whirred and puffed, the light buzzed, the computer on the desk growled occasionally, making backups. There was no mood music. Irene imagined that George's face was changing shape, becoming more blurry, more smoky. Turning into animal George. Irene felt her body drawn to his as if there was a gravitational event happening inside her belly, and he was a nearby star, getting drawn into her, getting closer. She kicked off her boots, yanked off her jeans, unbuttoned her lab coat, pulled her T-shirt over her head, and stood there in her socks.

Then, as she watched, he put his feet inside the tube and slipped inside, like a kid into a water slide, and was gone. The last things she saw were his smiling face, the hair across his forehead, his fingers gripping the side of the tube, and then he went on in, feetfirst.

She climbed the ladder, put her hands on the lip of the opening, and peered inside. She could see him in there, looking out. His elbows, spread wide, reached across the tunnel. He was grinning.

"Come in," he said. He motioned with his hands for her to enter.

The air was cool in the tube and smelled slightly of oxygen. There was a light breeze coming up the tube from behind George. She put her arms into the tube, put her head in.

"Not headfirst, the other way," he said. He reached out his hands toward her. And that's how she landed on her back, with her head at the opening, her feet hooked over his shoulders and behind his arms, still in their white socks.

"No," she said. "I don't —"

"Yeah," he said. "You do. This is something you will like."

WARNING: Biohazard. Authorized personnel only.

While he was kissing her so softly, on her belly and the insides of her thighs, Irene could see the lights in the hard plastic shapes of all colors spread around the other opening in the tube, now dim but glowing. She could see the desk by the elevator with the computer on it, shining on the tile floor. She could follow the ropes of wires with her eyes, all their colors collected in bunches by huge zip ties, tied up to the ceiling and along the walls. She could see an emergency warning sign, mounted on the wall. A number of signs. Her eyes scanned them while his cheek pressed against her thigh.

"George," she said. "We're having sex in a supercollider."

"Shhh," he urged her. He brushed his hand over her body and she closed her eyes. He separated her slowly with his fingers and put his mouth against her, let his tongue come through.

Sometimes her life felt like one long inhale. This was like one long exhale, her air draining out, her whole self pushing down on him. Her knees were cold against the side of the tunnel, a cold dense metal stopped her legs from falling flat, and she could feel the bumps of her spine pressing down into the foam, making a row of indentations on it, as her body curled up. She put her fingers in his hair and felt the shape of his head, the surge of a deep, insatiable love for him, not because of what he was doing, or maybe entirely because of it. Because no one else could have done this. Because he had not tried to do it, but had simply accomplished it.

She thought, *This is a hot brush, pressed against me.* She felt she had never known what she had waiting in her own body until now. She didn't even know what it looked like down there, or what any girl looked like. It was as mysterious to her as another planet. In school they had been instructed to examine this piece of themselves in the bathroom, with a mirror, but she hadn't. Nor had she explored this strange nebula with her fingers. Not in the bathtub, not in the dead of night, not after reading a steamy passage in a romance novel. She didn't read fiction. She didn't abide stupidity. It wasn't her that made the noises like the ones she was making now.

WARNING: Keep all cylinders chained.

With her eyes closed she imagined the tunnel around her, the pipe she was in, when it was fully operational. The beam pipes would thread through this space, separate from each other, parallel and small. When the experiments were running, the temperature inside the pipe would be so cold that she would be instantly frozen, all parts of her body frozen except the part that was touching him. There would be particles whizzing by, and the two-ton magnets would be engaged all around her, dragging the particles from one insertion point to the next, past the detectors, so fast, so fast they could not be observed. The particles inside their pipes in the tunnel, never touching, never grinding into each other, only accelerating, and they would get faster and faster in their endless loop. Then, at the flip of a switch, remotely, from upstairs, a physicist — maybe even Irene herself — would change the path of the particles as directed by magnets, and they would intersect. They would begin to intersect here, in the detector. Here where she lay. Scattering gluons and quarks. Showers of decaying particles, shooting out in jets.

Inside the tunnel, there would be nothing

obvious going on. But secretly, everything would be going on. Black holes formed by colliding particles, spitting out energy until they were spent, dissolving back into space. A rush of particles like a rush of wind or a beam of light, charging around the circuit of the Euphrates collider like mad fish around a circular river, accelerating and accelerating, forever.

WARNING: X-rays. This equipment produces X-rays when energized. Film badge required in this area.

George's hands moved against her thighs, and he pulled her gently apart a bit further. She felt her head swing backward out into space, knock against the side of the pipe. She felt a little bit of pain where her skull hit the metal, but she didn't really mind. She said, "George," and it came out strangled, came out tight, and George said "Mmm hmm," in a very calm way like it was all fine. She shifted her hips, pressed herself into him, felt urgently like there was an intersection coming, an arrival of one particle and another particle in the same nanomolecular space, where they would touch, there would be a brief exchange of gravity, and then a sucking sound, a singularity, and all of herself would be drawn down into it. It was dangerous, and frightening, but it was all she could do not to yell out, "Do it."

Who cares if it's dangerous? Who wants to be the person who doesn't touch two bells together to make a sound, who doesn't hit a baseball with a bat, doesn't grind an orange against a knife. In life, there is only collision to keep us from dissolution, and there is only love to keep us from death. In this bumping into that, there is salvation and sacrament, an end to the endless falling, a wall between us and oblivion. Where she could have slid, helpless, through the tunnel, her face engaged in terror, her hair flying wildly behind her, body freezing, fingers broken, she was now stopped and jutted up against him, and the collision of their bodies was the best thing she had ever felt in her life. In the quiet place there in the tunnel, in the pipe, with no room for anyone else or anything else between them, she pushed her hands against the edges of the pipe, and her hips began to shake. She felt prevented from the fall. She felt a hand come out and stop her as she dove away from the bridge into the water. She felt herself traveling through space at a million kilometers per hour, and then a halt, a warm embrace, a pair of strong arms.

WARNING: Ultraviolet light. Wear eye protection.

Why not? Why shouldn't she have this love? Was she really so terrible, so defamed, so ruined in her soul that she did not deserve to be loved by a man, to be stopped from annihilation, to have this mouth pressing, this hand probing, and all the parts of her opening to it and rising up against it. *Against, against, what a beautiful thing,* Irene thought. To be opposed, to be stood up to, and not to free-fall, uninhibited, and die. As she felt herself begin to come apart and release all the energy churned up by this collision, she thought she might be turning to lavender, and sending out her plume of X-rays into the world, and making her statement against a radioactive plate: *Here I am. Here is he. We made this intersection, and it was good.* She clamped his head between her thighs, her fingers finding their way to his jaw, his arms, and she was pulling him up to her, where he gratefully came up through the pipe, and sank inside her, his face buried in her neck and his body now arcing over hers. The feeling of being filled, of being whole, of never again having to save herself from death, of never having to wait, alone, through dry years of work, was a more wonderful feeling than she would have thought herself capable of having.

When it was over, George lay next to her on the foam in the tunnel, her head again on his arm, their bodies locked together. No longer lavender, no longer exploding, just drifting, as if a breeze had picked up strong and carried them along through the tunnel, or down the river, in a little boat. Irene's swelled mind imagined them in a little skiff, on a lazy river, passing primitive irrigation systems, and palm trees, and wild grasses, animals you find in Iraq, and other skiffs, all empty, all safely moored. They would float down this river until they fell asleep, and when they woke up they would look up and it would be all stars, all ancient constellations, and they would laugh.

She knew that this love wasn't only the sweetest thing that had ever happened to her, but that it was the sweetest thing that had ever happened to anybody.

I didn't even know how to want this, she thought. And in the end, it didn't even matter, because he came to her, whether she wanted him or not. It didn't even depend on her in the end, what she wanted or didn't want, because what happened happened, and it was so easy and simple that it made her giggle.

"I love you," said George.

"I love you, too," said Irene.

"I'm glad you said that," said George. "I wasn't sure you would."

"Yes, it's been five whole days since we met. What a holdout I am. You've been through such endless torments," she teased.

"I have," said George. "I thought I would never find you."

"What do you mean," Irene said. Her eyes were closed. "Wait, are you about to say something about destiny? I might need you to shut up. I'm feeling very happy in my body, and if you wake my brain up, it might disapprove."

"I want to tell you something," he said. He turned to face her and propped his head up on an elbow. She did the same.

"Are you sure? With the talking? We can't just lie here?"

He put his hand on her rib cage. "I'm going to say something about destiny."

"OK," she said. "Get it over with. Pull the Band-Aid. Then I'm going to climb down and rummage in that desk and see if there are any salty foods."

"You are destined to be mine," he said.

"Here it comes." She smiled at him and

rolled her eyes. "Like in the stars?"

"In a crystal ball. I went to a psychic. She saw you."

"You know when those astrologer types catch TIA faculty outside the safety of academia they like to play all kinds of jokes on you, right?"

"On you. You're TIA faculty now, too."

"On us then. Nothing gives them more pleasure than to torment us with oogly stories about fate and prophecies."

"Yeah," said George. "I'm sure nothing gives them more pleasure than that."

He sighed, and then she felt a little bit bad. Not really, but at least she felt a little bit sympathetic.

"OK, go on," she said. "Tell me about this psychic you went to see, that saw me."

"I wasn't going to tell you, because I thought you'd think I was ridiculous."

"Right, that was wise."

"And I thought it would bother you."

"It does bother me. Things that are silly bother me."

"But now . . ."

"Now you've invaded my girl parts with your face, you can come clean with all your strange and mystical leanings."

"Right."

"Fine! I told you to go on." Irene laughed,

and settled in on her back again, desultorily stroking at the side of the pipe. There were no seams. There was no out.

"Well, I went to see this psychic, to find out, you know, if I was ever going to find you."

"True love, impending death, and whatever happened to Grandma," said Irene wryly. "The top three reasons to visit a psychic."

"She looked into her crystal ball." George went on.

"Where did I put my thingawhatever," said Irene. "Reason number four."

"She said you would have brown hair and would be an astronomer," George began.

"And that I would also have two legs and a ciliated lining in my intestine?" Irene asked.

"And that you would be a dreamer," he told her.

"Well, there you go," said Irene. "I'm not a dreamer. Obviously. I'm the opposite of a dreamer. I reject dreaming in all its forms."

I'm a dreamer, thought Irene. *I visit other people in my dreams, and I have a house in my dream that threatens to eat me.* Irene suddenly had an uncomfortable feeling, like itchy feet. The psychic's prediction was stupid but eerily correct. Well, not really.

Vague wasn't correct. Psychic predictions are always vague in the client's first visit. It was one of her mother's most important rules. You only need to give the client enough to get them feeling good and coming back. Save the specificity for when they've divulged a bit more about themselves.

"I think you are a dreamer," said George.

"You wish," Irene murmured. She rolled over and put her arms around him.

"Doesn't matter," said George, pushing his face into her neck and holding her close. "The thing is, Irene, she was your mom."

Irene heard the word "mom" like a clang of metal banging into metal. She pushed him off her so hard his skin made a smacking sound against her hand.

"What?" she barked.

"I saw when we went to pick up Belion that it was the same house —"

"Where did she live?" Irene asked.

"On Bancroft," said George, his forehead now wrinkled in concern. "I was going to tell you."

"Shut up," said Irene. "Shut up, shut up."

Remember when I told you my mother was an astrologer? Irene wanted to say. *Remember when I told you that she was a psychic?*

Irene pounded up the stairs in her mother's house. Belion had cleared out, and she was glad. Belion's scant possessions were gone from the bedroom, no evidence of him in the bathroom. Perhaps Belion and Kate Oakenshield were still out on George's boat, or had dived down to live with the mer-people at the bottom of Lake Erie. Why should they not? Obviously, they were in love. Simple, uncomplicated love between two people. The simplest thing in the world.

Irene pulled the rope that brought the at-tic stairs down and began to climb up. There were boxes and boxes up there. Boxes and boxes of everything her mother had touched, every piece of paper that had come through the front door, every session she had ever had, recorded on tape, and duti-fully cataloged alphabetically into lettered crates. If her mother ever had repeat cus-tomers who left long spaces between their appointments, she would need to listen to the previous session in order not to contra-dict herself. Her methodology was program-matic, but at times it yielded different results. It wasn't like she was listening to the stars, and the stars would not remember what she had said. It wasn't like she was actually psychic. It was a skill, a learned behavior, and the documentation of every session was part of what made the business work. The stealthy documentation. Tapes in the attic.

Irene located the D crate and began to paw through its contents. She felt darkly sure that she would find a tape with the name GEORGE DERMONT on it, and she did. She held it in her hand. George Dermont, and a date that matched the month he said he'd visited her mother. Irene came down the stairs slowly, slowly, thinking, just as she did every time she descended this staircase, about the fall her mother had taken. Which step represented the point of no return? And had her mother been fighting? Or had she just been falling?

A woman on a bridge has two choices: jump or not jump. A woman standing over a tape player has two choices as well: play or not play. Know or not know. A woman falling through the air has no choices. A woman listening to information from a taped recording of something that happened three years ago has no choices either. She already knows. There was no one there to push Irene, no hand on her finger clicking the PLAY button, no encouraging voice saying "Do it!" Was there a hand on the back of her mother, pushing her off that top step, taking all prevarication out of the equation, sending her to her death? Irene sat in her dead mother's chair and listened to her voice coming out of the machine. She'd clicked on the recorder surreptitiously toward the beginning of the reading; Irene could tell they were just sitting down. And then the words came out: *I see her. I love her. She is your true love. I cannot help but love her, too.*

What had her mother been on about? The wild, insane hope charged through Irene that maybe her mother was really a psychic. Maybe her mother had tapped into something cosmic, and George was right, and the stars were speaking, and it was possible that the universe could select her to receive love, could identify her as a worthy candidate, could be such a beautiful place.

Irene sat still and listened to the recording as Bernice let George out the door and said good-bye. And then she heard her mother's voice from very close to the machine. The voice was calm and low.

"Fuck you, Sally," she said.

22

"I need to talk to my mom," said George. His head was throbbing again.

"We'd like to speak to Sally Dermont," said Irene. George stood beside her, his hand on her waist.

"Who may I say is here?" the receptionist said.

"It's me, Rebecca," said George.

"But who is she?" Rebecca wanted to know.

"Irene Sparks," said Irene. "I work with George."

The words coming out of Irene's mouth were clipped and taut, like she was angry. The receptionist pushed a button on the phone and said a few quiet words into her headset. They sounded angry, too. George didn't know what was going on, but he was a little afraid to talk to Irene in her current state. He coughed into his hand and then regretted it. His head felt awful, and coughing seemed to send pain thumping through his skull.

"Come get me," she had said to him. "We need to go talk to your mother. Immediately." George had asked why, and Irene had hung up the phone.

"Ms. Dermont will be with you shortly," Rebecca said.

Irene and George took seats on one of the luxurious chairs in the waiting area. George tried thumbing through his e-mail on his phone, but Irene just sat rigidly beside him, her knee bouncing up and down, her teeth clenched. There was no good e-mail. Some data from the old orbiter on the Gould cluster. Some interdepartmental bullshit.

"What's wrong," he tried asking her at one point. But she just shook her head and said, "I don't even know yet."

They waited there for a full thirty minutes, and George had resorted to playing chess with his phone, when finally he heard the sound of high heels tapping down the hall, and Sally Dermont emerged in the room.

"Mom," he said. "Hey."

Her ice-blond hair was sculpted like a helmet around her head. No more hippie dress today. She was wearing a perfect pantsuit in a muted rose, with an ivory scarf wound around her neck. She carried a piece of paper in her hand.

"Yes?" she said curtly. George felt like he was in trouble here, too.

"I want to talk to you," said Irene.

"About?" asked Sally.

"About George and," said Irene. "And about Bernice. Bernice Sparks. My mother."

"I don't believe I know you," said Sally. "Who are you again?"

"Mom, she was at the cottage the other night, on the porch, remember? And also at the banquet at the institute," George explained. "This is Irene Sparks. We're dating. You met —"

"I don't even think the banquet was our first time meeting, actually," Irene cut in. "I am pretty sure I have seen you before. I don't know where, but I think that when I figure it out, I will realize that I was not awake when it happened."

George saw Sally's jaws clench together, and she turned as if to go directly back down the hallway without responding to Irene at all. Then she turned to look back over her shoulder for a brief second, locked eyes with George, and said, "Come on."

In Sally's office, Irene sat down in one of the chairs set up on one side of the desk for consultations, square and low, leather and cool metal. Sally stood behind her desk.

"What can I do for you, now, specifically?" she said. She set the piece of paper down on the desk, facedown. "A friend of George is a friend of mine, I suppose. However odd the circumstances." She forced a smile. "And a bonafide scientist always has my respect. I do remember meeting you now, at the banquet, of course. And on the porch. You are dating my son. I guess."

He had seen his mother acting like this before. It was the way she behaved to his father sometimes, when he'd been blissed out on pills for three days or had forgotten where he parked yet another car in the city. She'd hate him, she'd rail at him, and then it was as if she'd swallowed a pill that allowed her to tolerate anything. Then she would adopt this horrible, taut politeness. Thinking of pills made George stand up and cross the room so he could rummage in his mother's cabinet. He located a bottle of painkillers, uncapped it, and knocked two into his palm, slapped them into his mouth. Turning around, he saw his mother and Irene squaring off across the desk.

"I want to know," said Irene, "if you knew my mother. She seems to have known you. She seems to have known George as well."

"No," said Sally. "I don't know her. I never did know her." Sally smiled, showing

425

those two rows of perfect teeth. She tapped her fingernails on the desk. "I'm very sorry for the confusion."

"But you're lying," said Irene flatly. George stared at her. Her hair was yanked back into a ponytail, her shirt was buttoned incorrectly, with one extra buttonhole at the collar on the left side. One leg of her jeans was tucked into a white sock. He wanted to take her in his arms, fold her up, press her against his body. Gorgeous creature, how dared she to speak this way to his mother? He was shocked and turned on at the same time.

He went to stand behind her chair, put his hands on her shoulders. And from this position he could see through the windows out onto the balcony. There he saw that the goddess of love, in a beautifully tailored pantsuit, was standing at the railing and looking out over the city.

"Why? Why are you lying?" Irene pressed on.

Sally paused for a long moment with all her fingers spread out on the desk, and then she turned to the window and looked out over all of Toledo. On the outside, on the balcony, George saw the goddess of love tip forward without warning and spill over the balcony. His mother did not see this. She

426

knocked her knuckles against each other and pursed her lips together.

"Mother," George said. "What's going on?"

Then Sally finally turned, passing over George and looking straight to Irene.

"I think I know why you're here," she said. "But you should know you're in way over your head with me. I can prove exactly where I was at every minute of the day your mother died. And you don't want to fuck with me. I'm an attorney. I know what I'm talking about."

"The day she died? How do you know the day she died?"

Out on the balcony, the goddess of love stood back up at the railing. And she tipped over the edge. Her legs disappeared. Her shoes disappeared. And she stood up again, ready to tip. The balcony was high above the city of Toledo. The goddess of love tipped over the balcony and fell far, far down. And stood up again.

Sally was silent.

"Who are you?" Irene said. "Who were you to my mother? Why was she talking to George as if she knew he was going to fall in love with me? And why was she talking to you on her recording? Was that you in Dark House on the night she died? Were you there, too, looking for my mother?"

"She was nothing to me," said Sally, but Irene went on.

"How do you know her? What did you do to her? Why should I care where you were on the day she died. On the day she died? Were you THERE?"

"George, you need to leave," said Sally. "And take that with you."

"Mother, that is my girlfriend. She is actually . . . she is my fiancée," George began.

"No, I'm not," said Irene.

"Get out!" his mother snapped at Irene. Then she shook her head to George. "I'm sorry, baby. I'm sorry."

"Come on, George," said Irene. "It's OK. It's alright. I'll figure this out on my own."

George was distracted. He had a hard time pulling away. He was watching them tipping over the railing, in rows, in columns, the goddesses diving off the balcony again and again, without ever showing a face.

I am dreaming but I am not aware. I am riding on my moped between the Akkad site and my experiment site in the collider, and everything feels smooth. Like there's nothing but pure air, and there's nothing but cool breezes, and someone has shifted the visible spectrum five nanometers to blue, and the world down below looks cleaner, and brighter, and I don't even question why and I don't know I'm asleep.

If I could figure it out, I would rip the lid off that tunnel and float out of there, and I would go back to Pittsburgh, or to the moon, or somewhere, anywhere but where I am headed. But I don't know anything so I go on.

I get the first sense of foreboding when the lights go dimmer, and then in my dreaming heart I am aware that I am approaching the same old thing that I fear the most. I see wires broken, the ones that feed the magnets. They're twisted and blackened and broke. Then the tunnel itself begins to fail around the edges — a tile here, chunk of concrete there — and I am afraid. I see the familiar mess ahead of me, fading in from the blackness, the broken floor, the crashed-in piece of the world. It's whistling and gaping, but instead of being peripheral to me, and instead of creeping in on the edge of what I see, it is straight ahead, and I am heading toward it, and I can't stop the moped now, because it's just going on its own. The center of Dark House is here.

I try to wake myself up. I count my fingers clutching the handlebars: four and six. I shut my eyes and will myself into my mother's house. My mother's bathroom. My mother's basement. On my mother's porch, sitting on the swing. Somewhere across the world from this, but instead I'm on the moped and I'm flying down the tunnel, kilometer by kilometer, toward the broken floor, the twisted pipe, and my fear is that I will go hurtling into it. I'm so afraid that I turn and bite myself on the shoulder but feel nothing. I smash my face down onto the handlebars and do not feel it. I grab at a broken sheet of metal that has sheared off the tunnel beside me, and it slices through my hand but leaves no mark and I feel nothing.

Then I see her, standing in front of me: tall and sure. George's mother is here. She puts out her hand, and my vehicle stops. She's suddenly so familiar, but I remember seeing her with long hair and a happy face. I remember her from when I was a little girl, before the fire. I remember her hugging my mother. I shake my head back and forth, and everything gets clearer. I have never been able to remember anything that happened before the fire. I have always assumed that what happened before the fire was too bad to even remember. I don't mind forgetting bad things, but here she is — part of this thing that I forgot.

Now I am really aware that I am in Dark House. I am standing in a bedroom. My rocking horse is there, charred just enough to remind my mother of the fire, but still able to rock.

"I had to come and see you," Sally thunders, towering over me. "There are things you should know that I can't tell you in front of George."

"What things?" I ask.

"We thought it was a good idea!" she yells.

"Who?"

"Me! And Bernice!" she says. "And it was a good idea. It would have been good for both of you. But she fucked it up. She fucked everything up."

"My mother? My mother? Where is she?"

"We made you for each other," she says. "You and George. Everything, everything, everything was made for you and him. We gave birth to you, together. We planned for you to be together."

"But I don't know him. I don't remember. What happened?"

"We were best friends, do you get it? We wanted our kids to be in love, and safe, and for it to be easy. So we made you, together."

"And you thought that would work?"

"You were never supposed to know! You were supposed to grow up, meet, and fall in

431

love. It would be easy, after everything we had done to make you perfect for each other. We had a plan, but your mother fell apart," she says.

It was easy. I fell in love with George as easily as anything that has ever happened to anyone.

"What did you do to my mother?" I ask.

She comes toward me, and she almost looks like she wants to be sweet.

"I didn't do anything to her but help her, and you too. Don't you understand?" she says. "I loved you, Irene, from the moment I saw you. And I always meant to keep loving you. But because she made such terrible mistakes — I had to throw you away instead."

"What are you talking about?"

"She lost her mind. She burned down your house! She was a — drunk!"

"I know that," I say.

"You are damaged. I made a mistake! You are made from a drunk and a — loser. That is your makeup. It's unfortunate, but it is real. George is not for you."

"I'm dreaming," I say. "You can't be here."

"I know it's hard," she says. "But you can always say that you are not to blame."

"Who came first, me or George?" I want to know. It seems important.

"You were born together," Sally reminds me impatiently.

"Who. Got. Pregnant. First." Because I know what I mean.

"I did," Sally snaps. "And then we got her pregnant. Together. With you."

"What did you do to me? What did you do to her?"

"Don't you know who your father is?" she says to me. The world around her ripples, as if I am already underwater and sinking toward the bottom of some cold bay. But I concentrate to listen, because this is important. "I'll tell you now. I know she never would. It's Uncle Ray. It's George's 'Uncle Ray' — no, he's not my brother or Dean's brother. That man who shot himself playing roulette? That's your father."

"That's not true!" I say.

"I chose him for three reasons," she goes on. She puts up three fingers, and I count them: one, two, three, four. "One, he was available. Two, he was willing to turn his back on you and never look back. Three, he was born in June. There. Your father. The composition of you. I made you for George out of him and her, and I planned it for you to be perfect. But then she turned out so, so bad. It's not your fault, Irene. You came from two bad things. What could you do?

What could you do to help yourself? There is badness inside you. I thought that your mother was good. But she wasn't."

I'm fighting off images and skips in what I see: I see my life before the fire.

I see warm-weather picnics, and cold-weather mittens in a blue basket, and I see my rocking horse standing in a different room, a room with trees outside. It is the room in George's cottage, where I have slept with George. I see two high chairs together, and I know I usually sit in one of those chairs. I see pancakes on a platter, and two mothers cooking in the kitchen. I think very hard, and I see George, and I see George's mother, and she's smiling at me so kindly, so encouragingly, and I want her to love me. I do not want to disappoint her. But I know that I have.

"When I put you in her, I didn't know she was a drunk!" she is saying. "I didn't know she was a liar! I thought it would be different. But I'm sorry, but you can't have him now. I cannot let that happen."

"It's all fake?" I say. "Our love? It was all a trick? All a scheme?"

She is nodding her head. She is shrugging. "If you want to call it that. I tried to get her to stop, but she kept going. I tried to pull the plug, but she wouldn't leave us alone. All those years, she kept at it. She wouldn't stop spying on him, trying to get you two aligned. Everything we did, she did with you. It was so annoying! As if she didn't realize, wouldn't realize — I'm not like her!"

"We're not in love?"

"It was only science," she says. "It was a good plan. But she wasn't worth it, and now here we are."

She fades in and out as I stop looking directly at her. I hold my hands out in front of me, and I look at them. They look like monster hands. I know that if I saw a dream mirror, I would see a monster face looking back. Everything I have ever worried about myself, coming out the mouth of this put-together woman and her big bossy mouth. I am worthless. I am the most insignificant blob of cells, of all the cell blobs there are walking around. I am unwanted. I am a creature formed for a purpose and I am failed in my purpose and there is no purpose left for me. I feel the most terrible despair.

I get off the stalled moped and I begin to walk, and I walk past her where she is still standing there, so tall and still. She keeps making words come out of her mouth that I cannot hear. She is shrieking. She is calling to me. She is saying STOP STOP or she is saying YOU ARE FILTH ANYWAY SO JUST GO AND BE SAD or she is saying YOUR MOTHER IS YOU or whatever she is saying. She can't grab me or touch me at all. When I am past her I can't tell anymore what she's saying, and it doesn't matter, because I'm going where I have always belonged, and to the place that I see I have created for myself long ago, to use when I most need it, which is now. I walk to the edge of the hole in the middle of Dark House, and without waiting or thinking, I lean forward, and I fall in. And I am gone. It doesn't even feel terrible.

The first thing I remember, falling into the hole in Dark House, is my mother standing in the basement next to the ironing board, throwing clothes into a bag. I am ten. I am crying, saying, "Please, don't go." But my mother fiercely, angrily stows things in this black garbage bag, storming around the basement like she is cutting her life apart with an ax. "I would kill myself," says my mother in this memory. "I would kill, kill, kill, kill myself if I wasn't afraid to go to hell. After all this time, I think I'm actually afraid to go there!" And then my mother laughs a dry, humorless laugh and marches up the basement stairs. I remember reaching out to grab her by the elbow, begging her to stay, and now she swings around and snaps, "Don't you touch me! Don't touch me!"

The second thing I see is a moment when I was older, maybe twelve. I had been prescribed a dental retainer to wear during the day and at night. But it got left on my lunch tray at school, and I threw it out with the garbage. Twice. I see myself walking upstairs to find my mother lying in bed with her arm over her face. I remember standing inside the door, telling her about the thrown-away retainer really fast, and then slipping out into the hallway. In seconds, my mother is on me, her teeth bared. "You ungrateful, arrogant arrogant arrog." My mother's breath, her body, her hair, even her skin smell of gin. "This is the limit, the limit," she says to me. "I will take your model rockets, and I will melt them down. It will be plastic for plastic on the kitchen stove: you throw away your plastic, I throw away your plastic, plastic for plastic, for plastic, for plastic." I can feel her hand grinding into the meat above my elbow. Her feet, bloated and mottled, sticking out from below her flannel nightgown.

The third thing I remember is new: from before the fire. A fog has been lifted between me and my own mind, and I can see this for the first time:

I am standing on the road outside George's country house. I am young, almost three, and my mother and I are taking a walk. The fire hasn't happened yet. I am falling forward, rushing down through the hole in Dark House, terrifically afraid, but I can't stop myself from remembering it. I am afraid to think, afraid for what horror might be waiting for me, what painful memory from the time that I forgot. What have I been hiding from my own brain for all these years behind the wall of the fire? But I cannot pull away. Because I am holding my mother's hand.

"Look, mother," I say. "It's the naked hairy ape!"

"Irene," says my mother. "Shhh. Let's go into the house."

In front of us, on the other side of the street, there is a neighbor clipping his long rows of hedges without his shirt on. Clipping and clipping hedges, with all his gray hair curling up from under his arms, out from his chest, up his back and into the back of his head. I remember this man. He lived next door.

Back in the house, my mother is, laughing, talking to someone.

"I've called him that a thousand times just talking to you!" My mother laughs. I am looking at the back of her head and I cannot see the other person, but I hear laughter. "Of course I didn't realize she was picking up on it! She just called him that to his face!" The two people convulse with laughter. They cannot stop.

I remember violets. Violets in my hand, picked from the cracks of the patio bricks. A wave of violets. I remember these violets were before the fire. Before the fire, I remember a boy in the other high chair. It's George. He is looking right at me.

And then I understand that the reason I could not remember the things that happened before the fire was not because these memories were so sad, but because they were so happy. I was so, so happy back then.

23

"I am going to San Francisco, George," said Irene. "To that conference where Lebernov invited me to sit on a panel. Then I'm moving to Bowling Green. I already found a place, on Clough. Some poor idiot already dropped out of school. Parents desperate to sublet."

He sat at his desk. She stood in the doorway to his lab. They hadn't spoken in days. There was, ridiculously, a disco ball hanging from the ceiling. In the floor, scratch marks and shavings outlined the holes that had been freshly drilled. Poles of varying heights stuck into the holes, and on the poles were mounted galaxies, nebulas, the major landmarks of the near universe as George knew it, set up in a 3-D model.

"I don't understand," said George. "I thought you weren't going to that thing. I thought you wouldn't fly."

"They're trying to apply my substrate to

radiation detectors in nuclear power plants. I just got off the phone with Lebernov, and again he strongly encouraged me to go."

"So go," he said grimly. "But moving to Bowling Green is a little extreme."

"Ask your mother about it," said Irene.

"I did ask her," said George. "You were there. She said a bunch of crap that doesn't matter."

"Don't you get it?" Irene said. "They were friends. They planned the whole thing, George. Your mother and mine. All those little things you thought were fate? No. Plants. They plotted and organized it. All those things my mother said to you, you thought she was reading from the stars? No. She knew you when you were a baby. Probably if she hadn't been so wasted by alcohol and you hadn't been so tipsy and heartbroken, you would have remembered her, too. But whatever. You're right; it actually doesn't matter. We've been played."

"I don't care," said George. "It's not important. It doesn't change anything."

Irene let out a dry laugh. "It changes everything. Whatever we thought was happening wasn't happening. The Yeats poem? They decided when we'd both memorize it. You went to Thailand on vacation — my grandmother lived in Thailand for years.

Kismet? No. Thoughtful planning. Joke's on us. You're right — it never mattered."

"Stop saying that. You're being wrongheaded," said George.

"You're wrongheaded!" she yelled. "I'm the one that got made for you, like some custom pair of pants or a sauce recipe. I'm the one that got born for you. You can't possibly understand what that feels like."

"I'm sorry!" said George. "But it doesn't matter."

"You can say that because it's not the same for you. I didn't get to choose what I wanted to do. I always had to do what would make me better for you, because my mother was so committed to this — these lies — she wouldn't stop. I never got to choose! Anything!"

He sat there behind a pile of student papers. He was wearing his reading glasses and looked utterly adorable. But for all Irene knew, she had had the idea planted in her head when she was a toddler that tall guys with brown hair and pink cheeks and reading glasses were proper mating potential. She had it planted in her head, and then she had her head discarded by the people that planted it, before they even harvested the idea. Here it was, come to fruition, and she had nothing to do with it. She only wanted to retreat. Retreat, retreat, retreat, before there was more embarrassment and more grief.

That morning she'd hired a real estate agent to list her mother's house, and she'd hired a Dumpster company to come and park a big one in the driveway. She would empty out the house. Maybe Kate and Belion would help her. Then she would move to Bowling Green and commute. She would see George at work sometimes, maybe, but the Toledo Institute of Astronomy was a big place. She wouldn't run into him that often, and when she did she would be professional. She would see him married to someone else, someone he could pick in the usual way, where you look around and notice someone you like, and you don't get all hectic, throwing the word "love" around right away like a crazy person. She would work tirelessly at the Euphrates Project. She would finish setting up the experiment. If once in a while on her way home over the Anthony Wayne Bridge she stopped her car and got out, wavered a little on the edge of the river, no one would blame her for touching the railing. And when the project was up and running and the beams were firing, the detectors detecting, she would let herself fall forward, smack into the water, crush into a broken thing. Maybe they would name a particle after her. The George's Constructed Wife particle. How glorious.

What she knew, what she knew with utter clarity, was that if she could not have George, she could not continue. She could not go through life whizzing through a pipe unhindered, endlessly whizzing and whizzing, a proton in a circuit, a hamster in a wheel, with no one to intersect, nothing to stop her. She would stop, meeting water, meeting concrete, meeting whatever would break her apart into whatever particles were no longer recognizable as her.

"You won't do this," said George. "You won't leave me. You think you will, but you won't."

Irene bridled at this. She almost told him to go to hell. But then she felt sorry for George, too. It wasn't just her who'd been duped. Poor man, he'd bought the long, sick story even before she had.

"You don't know me, George. You think you do, but you don't."

"I do know you," he said. "I recognize every part of you. I knew you when I first saw you, before we figured out about all these stupid intersections they planned. I knew you when I first saw you in the banquet hall. Just because our mothers did some stupid crap back in the eighties. Come on. Two people meet and fall in love. Then they're happy forever. That's the story. That's the whole story."

"That story is not real!" she screamed at him.

"What in the time we've known each other has not been real? What about me is not real? What about you?

"Forget all the schemes and the intersections, all these little coincidences they planned. They also made us, on some deep and basic place, to work together. You're the lover, I'm the fighter, you're the believer, I'm the pragmatist, you're the heart, I'm the head. They built that. We can't ignore it — it's who we are.

"Then let's not ignore it. Maybe that is love."

"Of course you still believe that stupid crap! It's you that believed it this whole time! You're the believer, George, right? And I'm the scientist. We fit together like a puzzle! Except now, surprise! The thing you believe in so much means that our big fancy 'true love' romance story is bullshit, just a bunch of planted ideas, manipulation, hypnosis, whatever!"

"Irene, what if it's even lower than that, even deeper, beneath all that stuff? We're not the believer and the scientist. We're not the folk music and the travel and the birthday. We're two people who are loyal, and ambitious, and honest, and we *both* are scientists — hello? We *both* are believers — don't deny it. The girl who believed she could create a black hole in a lab? The guy who documents the location of distant stars — with actual math, thank you very much. We aren't puzzle pieces. We are actually the same."

She listened to him, her breath coming hard. He must feel such a fool, having sat with her mother, her drunk and devious mother, listening to a ridiculous prophecy of a girl with brown hair, astronomer, dreams, and nonsense, who was really hardly worth the use of a pregnancy test. How long had the mothers' plot survived, even six years? And then it fizzled. They were too crazy. They were too drunk. Or somebody changed her mind, and somebody else was too drunk to argue.

"Why are you trying to ruin everything? Why can't you just be happy?" He sounded so sad. She felt so sorry. She wanted to fix it. But how could she?

"I don't even know what happiness is," said Irene.

"I do," said George.

She should have let her mother burn their house down with both of them in it. She should have taken a deep, cleansing breath of the smoke and rolled over in her bed to pass out and expire right there. Then George would be with Kate Oakenshield right now. Or George would be with Sam Beth. And Sam Beth would take care of him properly. She, Daughter of Babylon, would know what to do with George. She was an astronomer, a brunette, and a dreamer in the most literal sense of the word.

"You don't belong with me," said Irene.

"You're not in your right mind," said George. He carefully made a mark on one of the papers in front of him and set it off to the left.

"Maybe you belong with Sam Beth," said Irene.

"Who?" said George. "Patrice?"

Irene began to move distractedly between the pieces of his universe model. She touched a galaxy with her left hand, a galaxy with her right hand. She stepped carefully around a single star, though she had no idea what it was doing out all on its own. She had seen George's calculations, his attempts at solving for a plane of symmetry in the universe, his attempts to fold it back on itself across a single plane and find that each half had a match on the other side. She felt the magnetism in his body, felt it pulling on her, making her try to find his words sensible, convincing. She felt she could almost let go, just nod, smile. She had to fight.

"Now you're being crazy," said George.

"No, you're being blind. Maybe Patrice really loves you," said Irene. "Just by chance. Real love. Not by design."

"You love me," said George.

"No, I don't." Irene corrected him sharply. "George. It's not how we thought. I am conditioned to feel something for you, but it's not love. It's training. Maybe Sam Beth loves you for real. Reach out to her. Why not? She's smart, and she believes in you."

"So do you," said George.

"I believe in nothing. No, correction," she added. "You're right. I believe in my experiment. Which is the only thing that's ever been what it's supposed to be. That's what I believe in. Observe. Collect data. Record that data. Make conclusions dependent on the data and nothing else. Absolutely nothing else."

George shook his head. "I'm not going to fall in love with Sam Beth just because you tell me to," he said. He smiled and she felt her heart lurch. She could just say OK. She could just laugh and forget the rest. But then, but then, there was still the fact of who her father was, who her mother was, who she was. She couldn't just laugh and forget that.

"At least give her a try. You'd be stupid not to."

"Not stupid, just happy," said George.

"Don't embarrass yourself," Irene admonished him. "You embarrass yourself and you embarrass me. Don't you understand that we're fools? We're tricked. We're misled. You're gold and I'm dross. You're teak and I'm fire. The fact that you don't know that is an embarrassment to both of us. It was a trick, George. It is. A trick."

"It doesn't matter what it was or what it is. It only matters what it does."

"This is what it does," said Irene. "This is how it ends."

"No, it's not!" He slammed his hand down on the desk and glared at her, eyes full of fire. "You think you know yourself, but you don't. I know you. I see you."

"No, you don't!" she screamed back at him, suddenly ferocious. "You see nothing. I am just the ruins of their plan. I am the hopeless residue of everything that they did wrong, George. I'm not worthy to be yours, and if you weren't brainwashed by them to want me, you would see it. I can't drink, because I'm too scared of falling down drunk. I can't have sex — I am too scared of falling in love. I stand on bridges, stand there and stand there, scared to death of falling. I can't even fall asleep without controlling my dreams. Dreamer? Oh, yes I am. I'm falling, falling, falling all the time. I'm half an inch from suicide, whichever way I turn."

"You adorable idiot," said George, now quieter. "Is that what you think?" He stood up from his desk and came toward her, but she held her hand up for him to stay away, and he stopped.

"You've had sex, if you didn't notice. You've fallen in love. Done."

Irene said nothing. Her jaw worked back and forth.

"You think you stand on bridges because you are afraid to die? Baby, you're the least afraid to die of anyone I have ever known, and the place you stand up on that bridge, that's the place where you should know that more than any other time. Suicide? Hell, no. That bridge is where you know *your impulse is to live.* Walking around in our normal lives, on sidewalks, on floors, on the ground, we don't have to make that decision to live or die. But on the bridge, you're making that decision: LIVE. With your whole body. That's where you show how strong you are, Irene. I get that the bridge is where you meet your demon, yes, but that's why you go there, to *kick its ass*."

Irene was breathing heavily. She said, "Well, I'm still afraid to drink."

"Drink or don't drink," he said. "I promise you, it's got nothing to do with us."

She leaned against the door frame, trying to think about everything he had just said.

"My head hurts," said George. "I just want things to go back to how they were."

But Irene turned and walked away.

When she had gone, George felt sick. He believed that she would come back. But he would miss her in the interim.

He picked up his phone and used a remote to switch off the light in the room. Instantly, his head felt better, and he felt less worried about encroaching visitations. He felt his way over to the middle of the room and lay down on the cool concrete floor in the center of his universe model. He looked up through the pieces of his model and saw nothing. One benefit to being in the basement: total darkness. He swiped a finger across his phone and dialed his mother, the bright screen lighting up his face and the poles right around his body.

She picked up on the first ring.

"Hi," she said.

"Mom," he said. "You have to fix this."

"I did fix it, baby," she said. "This is it after it's fixed."

"No, this is wrong," he said. He felt so tired.

"I'm sorry you are having a hard time," she said. "But this is right."

"I want her back," said George. He felt like he might be five years old. How could she have gone? How could she have left him? "You did this. You fix it. I miss her!"

"George, let's not go back over the same territory."

George pressed his hand around his forehead and squeezed.

"I don't understand," he said.

"Of course not. But it's OK. You don't have to understand everything. Just let me fix it, and move on."

"But you're not fixing it. You're ruining it."

"George, you think you love her, but you don't. You've had your head turned by some crazy woman with a crystal ball. I know you like that sort of thing, George, but it's just irresponsible to make your life decisions based on some fortune-teller."

"She cared about me. I felt it. She knew

452

me. She was Irene's mother."

"She didn't know you, and she wasn't capable of caring about anyone. I'm sorry she was Irene's mother. That was a mistake I made that I will never forgive myself for."

"A mistake?"

"I used to be kind of an idiot, George. But I was young, and I won't apologize too much for it, because I was only trying to love you, to save you."

"Save me from what?"

George heard his mother's voice tighten up. "You're better off free from this entanglement, darling. Let's just say I acted in your best interests, then and now."

"I want to talk to Dad. Is he there? Are you with him?"

"Actually, no," she said.

"Where did he go?"

"George, forget about your father right now! He has been nothing but a disappointment."

"To you, Mom. He was a disappointment to you, never to me."

She stopped talking.

"Let's return to the point, OK?" George said firmly. "When were you acting on my best interests, exactly? When you trained up this girl to fall in love with me, or when you told her it was all a trick and made her leave me and go to California?"

"George . . ."

"As if she couldn't love me on her own? Am I so broken —" He coughed and realized he was about to kick something. He sat up and scootched across the floor, away from his model. He didn't want to kick it or punch it.

"Don't say broken. That's not what you are," she said.

"You didn't believe that she could love me without you making her do it?"

"I was wrong," she said. "I said I was wrong then, but I have fixed it now."

"It doesn't feel fixed!"

George felt his hand clench together as if he was going to punch something immediately.

"And I'm going to punch something!" he added.

"Well, go ahead and punch something," his mother said. "Do it. I dare you."

"Fine!" said George. He pointed his phone around the room like a weak little flashlight and lit on a pile of folded cardboard boxes, the remnants of his move down to the basement from his lab upstairs.

"Fine!" his mother said. George made a fist and slammed it into the pile of boxes. They slid around and crushed beneath the weight of his arm.

"I did it," said George. "I punched something. I'm serious!"

"George, you need to punch everything! And start with yourself! Look, we just need a reframe. You can see this as a positive, eventually, and you're going to end up thanking me."

"Bullshit," said George. He punched the boxes again. He felt strong and angry. Almost like he might stand up on his feet, turn on the light, storm around.

"You're free, George!" she said. "You know everything now. You know what happened, what I planned for you, what I did. So hate me. That's fine. Hate me all your life. But now you're free to find someone you can love that's not all tied up with that nightmare. Someone good. Someone new. Think of how many girls are out there, George: smart, pretty girls with no skeletons in the closet. This girl's not worth it, George. You think she is, but she's not. I tried to make her something worthy of you, but I failed. So now you try it. Find someone on your own — I promise to stay out of it. George, you're a handsome boy, so beautiful and funny, and you've got everything you need to find a wonderful wife and have a happy life. Happiness, George. Not with some crazy, twisted, little accident from Toledo."

"I want her back," said George. He punched the pile of boxes one, two, three, four times, one for each word. "And I'm going to have her. This has nothing to do with you. Do you hear me? Nothing to do with you."

Irene sat on the plane in a window seat. The flight would take four hours. She had never been on an airplane before in her life, but now that her mother was dead, she felt released from her solemn promise that she would not fly. She had a young man next to her in a coat and tie, a woman in sweatpants next to him on the aisle. They were both reading magazines. They had been in the air for thirty minutes when someone announced that drinks would be served. The flight attendant stopped her metal cabinet in the aisle next to Irene's row and asked if they would like anything to drink.

"I'd like a gin," said Irene.

"Gin and tonic?" asked the flight attendant. She was a redhead, her bright hair pulled back into a stiff bun, her lipstick very crisply applied, a dull burgundy.

"No," said Irene. "Just gin."

Irene passed over her credit card. The

business-suit guy next to her was having tomato juice. The woman in sweatpants was having Diet Coke. So they didn't have to pay anything, but Irene had to pay because she was having gin. The gin came in a little bottle, and the flight attendant gave Irene a clear plastic cup with five rounded, hollow ice cubes in it. Irene twisted the knob and let the tray fall from the back of the seat in front of her. She set the cup with the ice on it but kept the gin in her hand.

"I'm going to drink this," she said to the man next to her.

"OK," he said. He was reading a magazine about running and competing in triathlons. The article he was looking at talked about how it was a good idea to finish every run really strong because it would give you a good feeling about starting up your next workout.

"I've never had a drink before," she said. "Not even wine. Not even Communion wine."

The man next to her turned the page to read more of his article, and then reached into the pocket of his suit coat to retrieve some earbuds, which he applied to his ears without bothering to turn on any sort of music-playing device. The woman in the sweatpants was sipping her Diet Coke and reading *In Style.*

Irene twisted the cap off the gin, the noise from the plane making a low hum in her head. She put the little bottle to her lips and paused, knowing that a whole life of keeping herself in check was about to end. She had not wanted to be like her mother. She had never had a drop to drink, never taken a puff on a cigarette or a lick of a line of coke, even after it had been sniffed away, and never hovered, breathing deeply, around a group of people smoking pot. She had not wanted to lose control.

Her lips parted and the gin went in. It didn't taste like much. She swallowed it, and it felt warm inside her esophagus, like it had left a trail of heat down it that could be detected by an infrared camera applied to Irene's chest. This is where the alcohol went. With the second swallow, Irene had a black realization and understood herself a little. *I thought it was the same as sex,* she thought. *I thought drinking was the same as sex, and it makes you lose control, and that's why I didn't ever want to do it.* She emptied the rest of the little gin bottle into her mouth and then followed up by crunching the ice in the cup between her teeth, letting it slide in slivers into her throat. *This is why I wanted to stay a virgin,* thought Irene. *It's because drinking is like sex. Except it's not. Is it?*

There were no effects. The plane landed safely. She had flown for the first time in her life, and nothing bad had happened. Her mother had been terribly, wonderfully wrong about the plane crash predictions. When she got off the plane, she only felt a little tired. She registered for the conference at the hotel, checked in to her room, undressed, and went to bed. *I drank alcohol,* she thought. *I had sex. I'm just like my mother. I'm just like everyone.*

In that moment, Irene felt sorry for her mother. What if, after all, she had only been trying to do something good? What if she had always been working for Irene's benefit, even in her drunken way, and Irene's success? Irene had judged her harshly, and that was fair. But if it was fair, it was also cold. In the shadow of the gin in her body, Irene felt a bud of warmth for her mother, a bud of something she might someday recognize as forgiveness.

I lie on the ground in the Hinterland. The sky is pale over Dark House. Since I threw myself into that broken hole, it has closed over. My mother's house, Dark House, and the wishing well stand like silent sentinels on the square. The buildings are crumbling and fading, and I know they'll soon be gone, along with all the evidence that I had ever shared this dream with my mother or allowed her to collaborate in its shape. I lie there on the scrubby, dry grass missing her, missing George, missing everything I have lost, gained, and then lost again in such a brutally short amount of time. I want to sleep, but I am already asleep.

I sit up and look around the town square of this place that I've built. I'm the only resident of it now. I'm the only resident of my entire life. George is gone. He was my love, and I his golem. I was built for him by a stranger and then yanked away from him by that same heartless stranger. Now even Sally is gone. I had not realized she was even there, but she was, moving the pieces around on her stupid chessboard. I was not even a pawn. I was a red checker chip, invading the black-and-white board. I resent her. That's an understatement.

Now I'm all alone. What do I want?

I stand up to play Mother's old game with the wishing well. I close my eyes and say, "Show me something pretty." I pull out a handful of brightly colored fall leaves. I toss them into the air and they float away, dissolving into puffs and fragments. "Show me something funny," I say. I reach deep into the well, and my hand touches something rough. I pull out a carrot that's grown two knobs and a peg, so it looks like genitals. This makes me laugh. I toss the carrot up as high as I can, and it dissolves as well. I reach my hand back into the well. "What do I want?" I say. "What do I want? Show me what I want."

My hand brushes against something soft, like fabric. I tug on it, and I pull it up out of the well. It is a shirt, and it is attached to a man. George. George is here in the Hinterland with me, and I lift him out and set him down. He is sitting on the side of the well. He's wearing a T-shirt and jeans, and no shoes, and he's smiling, but his eyes don't focus.

"George," I say.

He doesn't answer.

"George," I say. I take him by the arms, pull at him, shake him a bit. Then I feel that his body is so close to me, and I press myself into it. I put my arms around him and pull him close, and I feel how big he is, and how alive, and how good he feels being there with me, just another human being that I happen to love. He puts his arms around me, too, without saying anything, as if it is an autonomic reflex. He doesn't even need to engage his brain to do it.

"Are you dreaming, George?" I say, my chin tucked over his shoulder and my chest against his. He is sitting on the well and holding me close. He says nothing.

I run my hands up his back, stroking him. I feel the length of him, up to his neck, his head, and I bury my hands in his soft shining hair, and my face in his neck. He is so dear, so precious. How can I ever give him up? Then my hand touches something bad. It is wet and spongy, and I pull away. I stare at him and really try to focus through the dreamspell, and get some clarity in my eyes. I see that something is coming out of George's head. I examine him. I pull apart his hair. There on the side of his head is a terrible wound, a deep aberration in his beautiful head, and it is spewing ganglion and bloody membranes and bits of something that I don't understand.

"George, something is wrong with you," I say. "Something is wrong with your head. Are you OK? Are you OK, George?"

He just smiles and sits there, with this hideous blob coming out of his brain, and I become frantic and try to shake him and pry his mouth open. But he doesn't listen. I hit his face.

"George," I say, and I am crying. "I need

you to understand me. There is something wrong with your head. Please listen. Wake up, George. I see something. I need you to listen."

But George does not wake up, and neither do I. We just stay there holding each other in the Hinterland, and I know that the well has not failed me, and that this is what I want, for sure, forever. The terrible fact is, however, that I cannot have him. And in the Hinterland my dreaming self knows this. And I'm crying by the well, holding my boyfriend, and he's got bloody brains coming out of his head, and there's nothing I can do.

24

George sat on the edge of the examining table with his legs dangling off the side. He wore a hospital gown, tied in the back, and his feet looked odd sticking out from beneath it, like they were someone else's feet, someone bluer, older, thinner. He could see all the weird little veins in them. *How can I not even recognize my own feet?* He thought. *The world is changing, and I don't like it.*

"My feet look weird," he said.

"It's the light in here," said Sam Beth. She was standing next to him, leaning back against the examining table, her little hips and shoulders shifting back and forth occasionally like she was dancing. She was listening to something on her phone through earphones, and thumbing through messages, too.

"I thought you weren't listening to me," said George.

"I can hear you," she said, without lifting

her eyes from the phone. Her ponytails waved back and forth.

"How old are you, Sam Beth?" said George.

"Twenty-four," she said.

On his other side, the goddess of the race sat fidgeting. She wore a tracksuit with the hoodie pulled up. Inside the hood, her pale, silvery face was tense, and she was biting her lip. George patted her on the leg. He could smell her eucalyptus gum.

"It's alright," he said. She snapped her head around to look at George, and the piercing eyes met his.

"Yeah, are you alright?" asked Sam Beth.

"I'm alright," said George. He put his other hand on Sam Beth's shoulder, reassuring them both. "I've just got to get some better drugs."

They were all three waiting for the doctor to come back. She had given George a cursory examination, moving a finger in front of George's face, asking him to walk heel to toe across the room, in a straight line on the tile floor. She'd checked reflexes and examined George's pupils at length. During this time the goddess of the race had done standing jumps, where she'd touch her knees to her elbows by leaping into the air and bouncing them off each other in midleap. When the doctor left, she sat back down next to George and seemed to want to huddle against him.

George's phone rang. His pants were across the room, but Sam Beth went over to them and fished his phone out of the pocket.

"It's her," she said, looking at the screen.

George snatched it out of her hand. "Irene?" he said into the phone.

"It's me," said Irene. "George, listen."

"Hi! How are you?"

"George, listen," she repeated.

"Listening," he said. He couldn't help but feel his face stretch into a grin. He wanted to squeeze Sam Beth around the shoulders until she popped. He wanted to cheer the goddess of the race to victory, pumping his fist in the air. He was so happy that Irene had called him on the phone.

"I know this is going to sound odd, but you need to take this seriously, George. What I'm about to say."

"I absolutely will," he said.

"I can tell that you're not, though," said Irene.

George laughed. "Of course I am," he said. "If it's something you want to say to me, then it's serious to me."

George was ready for her to talk. He was ready to hear that she was sorry, that she never should have left him, that she'd been impulsive. He knew that these answers were coming. He just wanted her to say them and get it over with. He needed to hear her say she was coming back, and he could say that all was forgiven. "We never have to see my mother and father again," he had prepared himself to say. "We can pretend we fell out of trees or arrived in a spaceship or grew from the swamp. Nobody has any mothers where we come from. We don't even believe in mothers."

"You need to go to the doctor," said Irene.

"OK," said George. "Is that the thing you wanted to tell me?"

"Yeah," she said. "That's it. I think — this is going to sound really weird, but bear with me — I think there is something wrong with your head."

George said nothing. He pulled the hospital gown lower over his knee.

"Can you hear me?" Irene said.

"Yes," said George. "I just thought, I thought that you were going to say something else."

"What else?"

"I thought that you were going to say —"

He felt embarrassed, in front of Sam Beth, in front of the goddess. They both knew so much about it already. It was shameful, what was happening to him. It was embarrassing.

"Did you think I was going to say that we were getting back together?" Irene wanted to know. Her shrill voice cut into him. He had been thinking it was a beautiful voice, so clear and direct. But now it just sounded awful.

"No," said George. "Well, yes."

"We can't, George. You know that. We can't even think about that."

George said nothing again. He had no response. His head was throbbing. The goddess of the race put her hand on his back and rubbed back and forth over his spine, her blunt fingers with their short pale nails scratching gently over his skin.

"So, what then?" he finally said.

"Go to the doctor," she said. "Get your head looked at. It's important. I can't explain why. But it's important. I think there might be something badly wrong with you."

George gave a little wry laugh. "OK. OK, I'll go to the doctor."

"Don't blow this off," said Irene. "Don't snort painkiller up your nose and wait another day. Please. For your mother, if not for me. For Sam Beth."

"OK, Irene. I said OK," said George. He cut her off before she asked if Sam Beth

468

was with him. She was with him. She had asked to come with him. She was tapping away on the screen of her phone, sending messages, maybe finding strength in quotations found online.

"OK," said Irene. "Promise me, though."

"I promise," said George. "I promise."

"Good-bye George," said Irene. "I won't call you again, and I'm sorry for this. But I had to tell you. You don't have to check back with me. I know you are mad. But just go."

The phone chimed and George knew she had disconnected. He knew she did not think he was aware that something was wrong with his head. She did not know he was present in the dream she'd had, that he was there, dreaming with her, sucked out of some addled version of a can't-get-ready-for-work dream and into her bleak nightmare. And all he had thought, while he was listening to her talk about the missing parts of his head, was how beautiful she was, even in the blurring back-and-forth of dreaming, she was so beautiful, and even with a bloody mess falling out of his skull, he was just happy to be in her arms.

When the doctor came back in she had a frown on her face. Sam Beth whipped her phone into the back pocket of her jeans and said, "What."

George felt a cold fear sink into his chest as if a snowball had landed on his sternum, dissolved, and flowed inside.

"George, we're going to do some tests. I'm going to be honest with you now. Because of the severity of the headaches you are experiencing and some of your other symptoms, we are a bit concerned. Please don't worry yet, but let me do what I can to get a clear picture of what's going on so we can get you on the road to feeling better, OK? I want you to be patient with us today as we are going to try some different things, and know that it is worthwhile, finding out as much information as we can."

"What tests?" said Sam Beth.

"Well, we'll start with an MRI. The nurse will be in shortly to give you an injection, some contrast dye that will go right here, into a vein in your arm."

"He just wants medicine for his head-aches," said Sam Beth.

The doctor smiled at her, crinkling up the skin around her eyes until they almost disappeared.

"Of course, that will come later," said the doctor. Then she reached out and put her hand on George's knee and patted it firmly. "I'll be back," she added.

Sam Beth took her phone back out but just held it idly in her hand. "I don't like the sound of that," she said. "Contrast dye."

"Maybe I'll be radioactive," said George. "You can put me in the detector and say, there he is."

The nurse helped him to lie down on the curved table that would feed him into the MRI. The room was bright white, dominated by a huge beige machine with a round opening in it and a table sticking out of the opening, which he could lie down on. When he was in place on the table, he could see the machine above his head, its tube waiting for him.

"We're just going to stabilize you," the nurse said. George's head was pounding with pain, and he acutely felt her fingers touching him around his skull, brushing his hair aside, and aligning him on the table, then applying a brace to his head that made it impossible for him to move his neck or rotate his head. His hand went up to scratch his eyebrow and knocked into a piece of this head cage, making the nurse chuckle.

"Itch?" she said.

"No, I'm fine," said George.

Inside the tube, he tried not to think about Irene. He concentrated instead on the clicks

471

and whirs the machine was making around him, on keeping his eyes closed, on inflating his lungs and deflating them rhythmically, on the feeling of the cage on his head, and then the clicks and whirs again. But it was hard not to remember being with her, inside the space where the proton collider would go. The burning urgency of her hands on him, every touch of her mouth like a little singe, of her voice telling him things, never shutting up, just egging him on and on until he was maddened by it, and lost track of himself, and lost the headache, and the visitations of the gods, and just surrounded himself in her, and found her there for him, very simple, very close.

In the imaging machine with its grumbles and whines and its lights moving strangely across his face, he wondered where Irene could be and how if you folded the United States on a central line of symmetry between San Francisco and him, then you would fold it in Kansas, and Louisiana, Nebraska, and when the angle of the line was just perfect, then he would be reflected onto her, and she onto him, perfectly asymmetrical, a transformative equation where the left does not equal the right but is the right. Where the night doesn't mirror the day but is the night, and the day is the day, and they're both the same thing.

"Irene," he would say. "I didn't get the idea of the Gateway of God from my own brain."

"Oh, OK," she would say. "Where did you get it?"

"I was visited by a god, and the god told me about it."

She would wait.

"Then other gods visited me, and they further confirmed and explicated the idea. It all came from them."

Then she would say, "But that's crazy."

And it was crazy. George was very, very afraid that it was very, very crazy.

"I know," he would say. "I know it's crazy. And I'm afraid that because it's crazy that I'm crazy."

"You are. You're totally nuts if you think gods visited you and explained physics concepts to you."

"That's just it."

"But don't worry. We can fix it." Irene would want to fix it. She was a doer. She was a fixer.

"That's just it. I don't want it fixed. I'm actually more afraid that if I'm crazy, I might someday have to stop being crazy."

George halted his imagination in the middle of this hypothetical conversation, before Irene would say something insulting like "Don't be stupid. Of course if you had the choice to be crazy or not, you'd choose not." Or she might say, "Don't worry, being crazy is great." But probably not.

He wanted to say that losing his faith was terrifying to him. That if he did not have the gods, and he did not have Irene, then he would have nothing. If he thought very hard, in the middle of the MRI machine, with his brain elevated beyond itself by the whirs and clicks and whines and lights of the imaging mechanism that was mapping his brain, he could almost believe that she would say, "Babe, if you lose your faith, you can use mine. Mine is better. I believe in machines, remember? They'll never call you crazy for believing in that."

Would she ever say that? Would he ever be brave enough to tell her all about it?

"You have a tumor," said the doctor. "I'm sorry to say. In your brain."

George had his street clothes on again and was sitting in one of the regular chairs in the examination room. The doctor had sent Sam Beth out of the room, after determining that she was not his sister or his wife.

"A brain tumor?" said George. He could not hear the doctor properly because the goddess of the race was standing behind the doctor, putting her silver hands over the doctor's wide mouth, and occluding her speech as much as she possibly could. She gritted her teeth with the effort. She squinched her eyes together. The doctor was mumbling.

"A brain tumor," she said again. "George, are you having difficulty hearing me?"

"No," George lied. "I'm just tired."

"I need to ask you some questions," said the doctor. "I'm afraid your situation is quite serious and we must act quickly. There is a severe amount of pressure from this tumor encroaching on several very important areas of your brain. I'd like to show you a picture."

The doctor wheeled her chair over to a flat-screen computer monitor and, with a few clicks of the mouse, opened a file so that George could see it.

"Your tumor," said the doctor, "is here." She pointed to an area in George's brain that George believed to be near the front.

"It is shaped like a barbell," the doctor pointed with her finger to show the two sides of the tumor. "Part is here in the frontal lobe, and then part is over here in the temporal lobe, both on the left side of your brain. Do you see?"

"I do," said George. George thought, *People with brain tumors have hallucinations. That's what they have. They have hallucinations. They don't have visitations from gods who explain physics concepts. They have hallucinations of visitations from gods who explain physics concepts. A much different thing.*

"So, to our questions. I know you have had headaches for quite some time now. And they were diagnosed as migraines, and you've been taking narcotics to control the pain. But do you ever see things that aren't there? Smell anything odd that doesn't make sense to you? Hear things?"

George looked up at the goddess of the race, who was standing behind the doctor still but was now gesturing eagerly, waving her arms in front of her as if to say *no, stop, don't.* George looked at her and felt as if he was being torn apart by inches on the inside. He didn't want to lose her, didn't want to lose the goddess of love, and the coy sex goddess, and even the god of wealth, and the god of war, the mermaid, the goat, the mistier ones like Quetzalcoatl and Osiris, the firm ones like Philanthropy and Revenge. These familiar figures, present in his life for such a long time.

"If you take out the tumor, all that will

stop?" he asked the doctor.

"All what?" said the doctor. "All what?"

25

Irene stood on the Golden Gate Bridge. The red metal of the railing was cool under her hand and very solid, but there was a fog over the bay hovering just below the bridge itself, so that the bridge seemed truly suspended. It was a dream bridge floating over nothing, as if one could just fall off the edge of it and be buoyed up by the air.

So many people had jumped off this bridge that there was a plaque next to Irene on one of the girders, advertising a crisis hotline, with an emergency phone under it that you could call if you were feeling sad. The plaque told her the consequences of leaping from the bridge were fatal and tragic. The first she could not dispute. The second, she pondered as she leaned out over the fog, was not so clear. Maybe death was not so terrible. How could it be, when she had practiced it so many times? What was waiting for her on the other side: A leafy island? A new, more cheerful Hinterland? George?

Irene listened to the dampened sounds of the seabirds, the hiss of the cars passing behind her over the bridge. There was no city, and there were no mountains. Only fog and the strangely transmitted few sounds: water lapping, a ringing bell, the thump of her heart under her armpit. She thought about what George said about inhabiting the transitional point between life and death. Did she do it because she was a suicidal coward, as she believed, or because she was victorious over the weak impulse for death, as George suggested? Empirical evidence suggested she was not a jumper. She had never jumped. The data supported George's hypothesis.

Irene's phone barked. She took it out of her pocket and looked at it as if it were an artifact from another world. At the conference, physicists were walking around, going out and in the doors of the different meeting rooms at the hotel, along with the businesspeople who gave physicists their money. Maybe she was late. How long had she been standing here? The area code was from Toledo. It could be someone at her lab, someone with a problem. Maybe one of the pieces had come back from the fabricator already. Maybe it was ready to be installed.

"Sparks," she said. Her voice echoed a little bit.

"Irene," said Sally. "It's Sally. George's mother. You know."

Irene imagined Sally standing in her office in Toledo, perfectly groomed. She pictured her standing on a pedestal, clothed in a drapey robe, blindfolded, holding up a set of scales. She pictured her presiding over Sam Beth's marriage with George. She would wear the clothing of a high priestess of Babylon, and it would be pretty strange on such a Norwegian-looking lady, but then Sam Beth was Korean and seemed to pull it off alright.

"Hello," said Irene. "Is everything alright?"

"Well actually, it's about George."

"Did he go to the doctor? Is there something wrong with his brain?"

"How did you know that?" Sally asked, her voice suddenly sharp and accusing.

"Never mind," said Irene. "Is he sick? What did the doctor say?"

There was a long pause, and Irene chewed on her lip. She reached into her pocket and found a pen there, began stabbing it into the railing of the bridge, making a very small blue mark there.

"Irene, it's actually . . . George has a brain tumor, the doctor said."

She paused, and Irene scraped the railing with her pen. "It's threatening —" began Sally. Irene could hear panic leaking into the older woman's voice, and felt horrified that she might start to cry. But Sally didn't. She went on to explain the tumor, its shape, its slow rate of growth.

"They can do a needle biopsy," she said. "They can drill down into his — head" — her voice caught but she continued — "and pull out a piece of it and see what it is. Or they can do an open biopsy, where they go in to take out the tumor and biopsy it during the operation. Right there at the same time."

"That sounds better. The open biopsy. When are they going to operate?"

"That's the thing," said Sally. "He doesn't want them to operate."

"Why not?" Irene asked. "Why would he not want that?"

"He says the symptoms have been steady for so long, it cannot be growing at a dangerous pace."

The consequences of jumping from this bridge are fatal and tragic. A person falling from this bridge would surely die. In her mind, she had always felt she would die in

Toledo, in the Maumee River, like an Ohio person. But the feeling she got from inhaling deeply on this bridge, so tall the biggest ships could pass beneath it, made her feel that something else was possible. She could do a world tour of suicide bridges. She had never seen the Brooklyn Bridge, the Gorge Bridge above the Rio Grande. She could explore the possibilities of not jumping from every vantage point in the world. The towers of Europe, now that she could fly. The minarets. Everywhere she could find to not die.

After falling asleep so many times, she could only die once. After slipping under every night of her life, she could only crash into one water.

"He has a brain tumor!" Irene screeched into the phone. She turned and leaned her back against the railing, kicking at the barrier with the heel of one shoe. A young couple passed in front of her on the walkway, and the woman looked at her with a concerned frown, as if to say, *Are you alright?*

"Calm down," said Sally. And the crying sound was gone from her voice. She was all business. "You don't know everything about this. OK? So listen."

"Fine," said Irene. She was pacing up and

down beside the railing now.

"The tumor is in two parts," she began. "And the operation is dangerous. He could forget who he is, a little bit or a lot. Forget who he knows, or what he knows. Or not, it just depends on what happens in the surgery. So he doesn't want to. He doesn't want to lose anything."

"But that doesn't matter, does it? Could he die?"

"The doctors would like to operate immediately, as apparently the pressure on his brain is serious."

Sally stopped talking, and Irene could tell by her breathing that she was choking down another crying jag. "But he is refusing treatment," she clipped out. "He wants to continue as he has been. He's in a lot of pain, and they won't give him his drugs. They don't want him on the opiates when he goes into surgery."

"Who's with him?" Irene said. "Where are you, and who's with him?"

"Sam Beth is with him," said Sally. "But she doesn't —"

"Oh, I see," said Irene. "Sally, what do you want, from me? Why are you calling?"

"I want you to come home." The words came out in a rush. "I'm sorry I shouted at you. I'm sorry I treated you so badly. Come back."

"You're sorry for how you treated me?" Irene pushed on. "Not sorry for what you did to us? To me and George?"

"I'm sorry for what happened to your mother."

"My mother was a drunk and a suicide," said Irene. "I don't know what you ever knew of her, or what she did to you to make you hate her, but to me she is —"

"She's what?"

"She's the reason I'm standing here!" Irene snapped. "She's what I am: worthless, expired, a golem, a suicide. This is what we are. Used up, and then too shamed to go on."

"No," said Sally. "She wasn't a suicide."

"She was," said Irene. "She killed herself! I know! You don't know where I am right now. You don't understand anything."

"No, she didn't kill herself, Irene."

"How could you possibly know? *Were* you there? Will you tell me the truth?"

"Irene, I was there. I was there!"

"Why?" Irene asked. "Why?"

"I was there for George," said Sally. "I was there to yell at her, because she wouldn't leave him alone. Stalking him, feeding you information about him, tailoring your life to his. After I had told her no!"

Irene swallowed. "Did you push her? Did you kill her?"

"No. And she did not kill herself. She was drinking, and she fell, and she died. We were talking, arguing, and she just fell."

Sally coughed and went on. "I didn't ignore her, you know. All those years. I looked in on her, you know, only to make sure she was alright."

Irene took a deep breath in. Just a drunk. Just a fall. This must have been the client Mrs. Betty had seen. Just an old friend, an old fight. Nothing more complicated than that. "That's fine, that's fine. She needed all the help she could get. And look at me," she said. "I'm just like her. You know I don't belong with him. You said it yourself: I'm ragged. I'm ruined. I'm not for him."

"You stop that," said Sally, her voice savage. "And you listen to me right now. You worry that you're just like her?"

"I do," said Irene. "I came from her and I am her."

"Of course you are. Of course you're just like her," said Sally. "And you should be. Your mother died drunk, Irene. And that was horrible. But Bernice lived beautifully, and she loved forever. You'd be lucky to be as good as she was, but damned to be so unlucky. It was not her fault, falling down those stairs."

"Then whose was it?" Irene sobbed. "I couldn't do anything more than what I did. I did everything I was supposed to do."

"I should have helped her," Sally cried. "I should have been there, not to yell at her, but to be her friend. But I was a coward, and I left her all alone. It was me. I did it, twenty years ago. I made this happen. And I will pay. I'll pay whatever you want, but please come home. He needs you here, and I need him to be well."

Irene paused.

"Don't bear the weight of this down on his head. I'm begging you," Sally said. "I am so, so sorry. You have to forgive me. I wanted to help you. I wanted to save you! Both of you, don't you see, we were a family. I —"

"Why did you leave her? Why did you leave us?"

But Sally was silent. Irene chewed furiously on her lip, and with the phone still stuck to the side of her head, she began to march off the bridge. All she could think about, suddenly, was Sam Beth. She thought, *How dare she? How dare she stand there where I should be standing? How dare she, with her little gold snake armbands and her weak understanding of string theory and her dark eyeliner? I belong there. I belong with him.* And she could say it was her doubt and her fear that kept her away, or her loathing for herself or her desire to die or not die or her mother's awful failings. She could say whatever she wanted, and stand on whatever bridges, and take whatever positions she wanted, but that was all bullshit. Who cared about being right?

She was bound to him, heart and soul, and had been for as long as she had been alive. As she ground her teeth into her lip and felt the skin break and tasted the iron in her own blood, she realized what a stupid idiot she would be, to keep on punishing herself, and him, for their mothers' crimes. Their mothers didn't care. One was dead and one was crazy. There was no score to keep, no justice to be served. There was either a life of loneliness with death at the end, or love and happiness, and Irene was in control of which she had. She resolved at that moment not to be stupid about this any longer.

"Alright, I'm coming," she said. "And I don't care what you have to say about what happened. And I don't care who you are, or who my mother was, or what happened twenty years ago, or on those stairs, or what star was in what sky, or what planet was orbiting what star, or what lunatic was standing on what landing. It doesn't matter. I'm coming home."

"Please come," said Sally. "Please come. I need you. Please forgive me, and come. You have to know, in all of this, I only wanted to help George. And that's what you want, too, isn't it? Isn't it?"

"I'm coming on the first plane I can get on."

"Don't fly," Sally said. "She always said —"

"Now come on — pull yourself together," Irene growled. "And don't be ridiculous. Don't you get it? All of those plane predictions, all those dreams she had about a plane, are really about George! His plane, his symmetrical plane in the universe, all of his research — this is what she must have been seeing. She just had the wrong kind of plane."

"I don't know," Sally said.

"I flew out here, nothing happened, and I'm flying home. But I don't know how easy it will be for me to get out of here, how long it will take. If you can't get him into surgery, you find someone who can. Where is Dr. Bryant?"

"He won't see anyone from the institute

except Sam Beth."

"What about his father? Where is his father? Have you told him about this?"

"I don't even know where he is. We were fighting —"

"Find him," Irene said. "Find him, and get him to the hospital, and get him in the room. Tell him he must convince George to have this surgery. And I will be there as soon as I can."

As Irene marched off the bridge she was filled with an emotion she could only identify as sympathy, and the target of this emotion was her mother. Or maybe it was pity. Or respect. It was too unfamiliar to properly understand, but in the forefront of Irene's mind, a phrase pounded in time to her heels tapping on the sidewalk: it worked. Her mother had created her to be a golem, a monster. She was the Bride of Frankenstein. And she should be angry about that; she should hold on to the rage that made her frown, the resentment that made her hate. *But in the end, I do love George,* she thought. Could she argue the path that brought them here? Could she blame her mother now? Maybe, in the end, it had all been motivated by love, and love had been the result. After all the murky circumstances, and the trials and failures and right and wrong moves, she loved him. And as she flew to him now, all she could think to say to her mother was: thanks.

Whether love, or faith, or science, or machinery, it worked, and they loved, and that's all that mattered.

George's father entered the hospital room where they were waiting to begin preparing George for surgery, if only he would consent. Dean was wearing gray pants stained with red and orange paint, work boots, a checked shirt, and a tweed jacket. He had a slouch hat on his head, which he took off as soon as he entered the room. He set it down on the bedside table next to George with a reverent gesture.

"George," said Dean.

George started, as if he hadn't seen Dean properly, or hadn't expected him to speak.

"Dad!" George said. "It's great to see you."

"Your mom asked me to come, actually," said Dean. "She asked me and then she drove me here. It was really astonishing. I was wondering if it might be your mother who has the brain tumor."

George smiled. "So they told you about it."

"They did," said Dean. "Well, she did. Did

you want to tell me what you know about it?"

"No," said George. "I'm sure she presented an accurate picture. There's a tumor. It's got to come out because it's pressing on my brain. If they take it out and anything happens while they're knifing around in there, I could wake up thinking my name is Diana and parading around in high heels."

Now Dean smiled. "Was that really presented as an option?"

"It's a possible side effect of going insane."

Dean sat down on the side of the bed and took George's hand in his, in a way that was gentle, paternal. George remembered feeling his father's hands on his when he was learning how to paint, or how to push a seedling into the ground, or cut rootstock, or hold a charcoal pencil. His father had never hit him, never yelled at him, never told him what to do, never been that interested, George thought.

"I want you to be completely honest with yourself right now, George," said Dean. "And I want you to really think about what you're doing here. Why are you refusing to let them help you? You can't keep on living like this forever."

"I know, but I can't change what I am either," said George. "If I change what I

491

am, then what do I become? What happens to the me that was?"

"You'll stay the same," said Dean. "You just won't have these goddamned headaches all the time."

"You don't know that I'll stay the same," said George. "And by the way you don't know the tumor won't come back."

"Its rate of growth is slow," said Dean. "I'm ashamed, ashamed that your mother and I never realized it was there. We really let you down. I'm sorry."

"Yeah, but I never realized it either, and it was in my head."

"It's just your symptoms were so obtuse, son," said Dean. He patted George on the head. "And then there's the fact I wasn't really paying attention."

George was taken aback, but his father seemed undisturbed, just patting away at his head and smiling warmly.

"I'm sorry about that, George," said Dean. "You couldn't help it. Mom kept you away."

"Well, I'm more powerful than your mother," said his father mildly. "In fact, I'm really powerful. It's my fault."

George let his head sink back into the pillow. He closed his eyes and opened them again, and there was his father, paint-stained, crazy-haired, wrinkled by the sun.

"It seemed like you said you were really powerful," said George. "That's funny."

"Would be nice to have an all-powerful father around, wouldn't it?" Dean's eyes twinkled. "Might almost make up for missing out on visits from those other half-assed deities that have been pestering you all your life."

George sat up quickly, his head pounding. "What?!" he yelped.

"George, I know about your visions, remember?" said his father. "You told me. And now I'm here to tell you — I see them, too. I see them because I am one of them. Do you understand? I am one of them."

As George watched, his father's teeth began to straighten, his skin to smooth and pull up out of its folds and stretch firmly across his bones. He saw the paint stains on his father's hands fade away, and then he said, "Whoa, Dad. What the hell is going on?"

"I want you to have this surgery done now, Son," said Dean. "And if you lose the visions you've been having, just let them go. You will never lose me. Never. Shit as I've been, distracted as I've been, worthless as I've been, I will never let you down again."

"You're a god, too?"

Dean didn't have to explain — George could see it in every hair on his head, every pore of his skin, and he understood his mother, and his visions, and himself.

"I don't want to lose them," said George. "They tell me things, things I need for work! They have given me all of my ideas, and everything I've done in astronomy is because of them."

"I know you are afraid to let them go. But you should never let yourself make decisions out of fear," said his father. "Fear is a bad reason to keep a tumor in your head. I think you should pass on, pass on to what is next."

"What if I die?"

"Then that's next," said his father.

"I met that girl, Dad," said George. "I can't lose her. She's so great, she's really mouthy and smart, but she's kind of shy and she's really good at math."

Dean laughed, and folded his hands over one knee.

"George, I know her. You know this. You two grew up together, when you were small, so of course I know her."

"Right," said George.

"And I've known her father forever. Like literally forever."

George felt like his head was about to pop

off, tumor and all. "What? Uncle Ray is a god?"

"Just another holy shitbag," said Dean.

"You have got to be kidding me," said George. "I thought he died!?"

"Yeah, that's his out, for now. Deadbeat. Now, listen, let's not waste time on this stuff. Let's get your head fixed, Son. And then we can find that girl and set everything straight."

"I have so many questions for you," said George.

"I already promised I would be around for you more, from now on," said Dean. "You can ask me whatever you want."

"But what if I don't remember? What if I don't even remember this, that's happening right now? What if this is just another vision, and it all goes away?"

"George," said Dean. "I'm sorry I can't fix it. If I could, I would."

"I could die, Dad. I could die. I'm afraid to die."

"I don't think that's going to happen."

"What if it does? What will happen?"

"If you die, you will just dream. The best dream. A dream that never ends."

Within hours, George was on his way under. He was immobilized, his head shaved, his body loose and drugged, and he felt better and worse than he ever had in his life. His mother and his father were both with him. He was not alone. But he felt as though he needed just a bit more time, just a bit more practice before he went to sleep. The surgeon would peel back his scalp, would take out a piece of his skull, would operate via monitors with little radioactive knives, and take out the thing that was causing him so much pain, but also the thing that was causing him so many ideas, so much insight, the thing that made him who he was. And the reason he was sitting here doing it, instead of back in his room, or at home, or anywhere else but here, stubbornly refusing, was because his father had come into his hospital room and claimed to be a god.

The bad thing about having a brain tumor is that you can't trust anyone, including yourself. But ultimately, it wouldn't matter, because he would probably wake up not remembering anything, except that his name was Diana, and that he preferred thongs to bikinis. *At least if I wake up empty,* thought George, *then I can fall in love with Irene again, and this time she will believe that I love her, not because of what I remember or how I was taught, but because of who I am.*

■ ■ ■ ■

Irene sat on the plane on the last leg of her journey from San Francisco back east. It was a little plane, hopping from Chicago to Toledo, and Irene was again in a window seat, but with no one sitting next to her. The curved hull of the plane made an arc around her body. Irene refused a gin in favor of an orange soda, and quickly read two article abstracts written by people she'd met at the convention. Her heart felt sick, her head thick and clouded. She found as the plane made its way east and the night deepened that she could not take her eyes off the window, could not help but look ahead to where she knew that he would be. She leaned her forehead against the cool plastic of the window and looked out into the night.

Up above, she saw all the fixed stars. The same ones Aristotle had seen when he imagined them lodged in perfect crystal spheres, hung sparkling above the dead, decaying earth. How beautiful they were, these perfect points of light, spread wide over the messy, fragile humans down below. How perfect were the gods. Irene looked down toward the earth and saw the bright streets outlined in shining lights, the clusters of houses, buildings, long stretches of parking lots, and here and there a lonely beam, a point of light in an expanse of darkness, like a single star. It reminded her of standing with George on One Seagate and looking down over all of Toledo, when he asked her how to tell the difference between the stars above and the earth below. Now it made sense to her, looking up at the sky rippled with constellations, and down at the black earth crisscrossed with roads and sparkling towns. And she knew the answer to the question: what is the difference?

Irene closed her eyes and felt the movement of this little plane. A bump, a silence, and then a shift, a deep shuddering. She felt herself slipping under that familiar fog of sleep, letting go of her senses as she crossed that grand chasm that was really as quick as a breath, as light as the flutter of a wing, between herself and what lay beyond, that stunning outerwhere: she lost herself, the plane thumped, shook, and she began to dream.

She was outside the plane and falling, falling into the city of Toledo. It was lit up and alive, cars buzzing along, boats motoring up and down the river, little clumps of people on the sidewalks, crossing streets, running to meet each other in the dark. And when she turned her head up, looking into the night sky, and all its distant perfection, all the majesty of its timelessness, its immeasurable depth, she knew. This is the difference between gods and humans. This is the difference between divinity and what exists on earth: Toledo is moving. It's alive and changing. The myths, the stars, the fixed stories — these are static, measured only by math and memory. The men, the science they make, the roads they travel — these move, they change and grow, they cannot be mapped. It moves, she wanted to say to George. That's the difference between Toledo and the night sky. It moves.

I love it, thought Irene. Her heart froze with happiness. Her arms spread out, as she fell down through the air, her body the shape of a star, plummeting, sailing downward into Toledo. *I love what I am, this human, even if this is where I cross over, bleed, and die. This is where I become human. This polluted, human town, this love, this is what I am, more than the stars, even though they are so big, and so vast, and so perfect. They're just so far away.*

Irene fell down into the orange constellation that was Toledo, that shape that was moving, dirty, changing, alive. She closed her eyes, and passed through.

26

Irene's eyes were closed, and her head was on George's stomach. She could hear his stomach noises, gurgling and popping. That made her feel a little bit better about his prognosis. His face was still, completely still, and his whole body seemed dormant and strange. From the side of his head, a drainage tube emerged from the bandage on his wound and looped around into a small reservoir. There was also a tube coming out of his nose that ended in a bag, and there was a tube taped to a needle in his arm, where they were dripping things into him. His head was neatly shaved.

Irene had been sitting here for hours, leaning against him. The nurses had come in to check him, to take readings from his body, measuring his pulse and looking at the readings on different machines around his bed. He was in the ICU. This meant to Irene that he was going to be fine. The care he was getting was intensive. His life, at Toledo General, had meaning and was being intensely cared for. There had been no discussion of throwing Irene out, even though in the ICU there were severely limited visiting hours. No one would have thought to make her go. She was so sad and serious, so deeply attached to him. It was as if they hadn't noticed she was there.

The important thing to her was that she stayed focused on him, so that any little movement in his eyelids, of his lips, would not escape her, and she could shout for the nurses, shout for the doctors, alert the authorities that he was back. What he was back for, they would not know. If he was back for starting over fresh from the beginning of his life, if he was back for stepping in exactly where he had left off, or if he was back for being a pants-wetting vegetable from now on, no one knew. Irene hoped, and Irene imagined, that George would open his eyes, look up at her, and say, "You came back." This would mean that he knew her, that he remembered everything, that he forgave her, and that he was going to get better. Or maybe he would just say, "Irene." Or maybe he would say "Ouch" and then vomit. Really, Irene had started to believe that anything he said was better than him just lying here silently, retreated into his own head.

The nurses coming in and out seemed progressively less cheerful. The doctor had come around and had checked George several times. He did not respond to having his feet scratched sharply. He did not respond to having light shined in his eyes. He was unresponsive. Irene wished the doctor would pat her on the shoulder and say, "He's going to be fine. The tumor is gone. I think he will make a full recovery." But the doctor said nothing to her. No one said anything. She was invisible. So much sadness, concentrated into one person, can make a darkness no one wants to touch. So it was with Irene, miserably pressed against George, believing so much that he could come back to her.

The doctors and nurses waited to see whether his brain was ruined. Whether he would be himself, or wake a total stranger. Irene lay across him, holding his hand, stroking the sleeve of his hospital gown, and crying a little bit now and then. She did not eat or drink. She didn't answer phone calls from her lab. She stayed and waited, and George's mother came and went but did not disturb them. His father came and went and did not say a word. The ICU was bright and quiet. It seemed to go on forever.

Then Irene felt George take a big breath in, like a man coming up from deep underwater takes a gasp of air that fills his lungs with life.

"Curvature," said George. He said it loudly, urgently. Irene sat upright, still clutching his hand.

"What?" she said. But George said nothing else, and when she examined his face, she noticed no change. Then his brow wrinkled up, his hand grabbed hers tight, and he said, again, "Curvature."

"Curvature?" she said. His eyes were still not opened.

"It's curvature!" Now he was smiling, and his chest was shaking with laughter, as if he was having a beautiful dream.

"George, what's curvature! Be still! You have tubes all over you!"

He opened his eyes. He looked at her and their eyes met, and he said, "It's curvature. That's why I can't find the plane of symmetry."

"OK," said Irene. She was beginning to laugh, too. She didn't know if he recognized her or if he knew his name, but his brain was clearly working, and he was trying to sit up. "Lie down, George," she said. "Lie down. You have to rest."

He lay back obediently, but turned his head to face her, and with a very George-like twinkle in his eye, he told her, "The reason I can't find the plane of symmetry is because it's not a plane; it's a lens. Babe, it's a lens. A lens! Why did you not see this? Why did I not see this? If we're so smart, why in the hell did we not see that it is a lens! A LENS!"

He was getting loud. The nurses were coming in. The machines around were beeping and blaring. Doors flew open and doctors barked orders. But George was past all that. He had his hand behind her head now, and he was pulling her in for a kiss, and when she kissed him she knew that he knew her, and that he remembered everything, and that it was all going to be fine.

Spring had wakened up Toledo with flowering trees like lanterns and lights across the city. On a beautiful morning in April, George and Irene were taking a walk through the quad, as they habitually did for George's health, once a day. Irene did not allow him to bury himself in calculations and models, imaging and sketching, nor did she let him work himself to death on the satellite telescope that he was still pouring his time into. She forced him out into the air, because this is what she knew that he should do, to rest his brain periodically, like a man who'd had a thousand concussions waits in the dark, in the quiet and calm for his mind to heal before he can try on something new. George wasn't waiting, but he was taking breaks, following Irene's orders.

They walked together hand in hand around the quad, looking at the tulips that were emerging from their bulbs, bulbs that had been planted last fall. They were trying to talk about nothing. Taxing his brain was the opposite of what they were supposed to do during his rest periods. So sometimes they recited poetry they both knew well, or hummed songs they both had memorized, or just walked in silence.

Irene's work in the collider was just beginning to take off. Construction was nearly finished on her experiment site, and when the other teams were up and running and the collider was set in motion, the world of astronomy could expect big things of her and her detector.

"I'm so glad you had your surgery," she said to him. "This day wouldn't be as beautiful if you were still doped up on opium nasal spray."

"I'm glad, too," said George. "Because

now I get to constantly laugh at you for do-ing things like appreciating a beautiful day."

"I'm a new woman," said Irene. "Now I do things like that. Why not?"

"Why not is right." George squeezed her hand. "I've never loved you more."

"What was it that your father said to you that made you decide to do it?" She had asked him this before, many times, as if she thought she could trick him into a different answer. But he always came up with the same one.

"I can't remember," said George. "I can't honestly remember much that he said to me at all."

"Would you tell me?" she asked him. "Would you tell me what he said, and what else you forgot? It seems like that's the only thing that you forgot."

"I don't have any secrets from you, Irene," he said. "I do recall him saying that if I agreed to it that he would try to be a better dad. And he has been. He really has been."

They walked on in comfortable silence for a while. Then Irene spoke up.

"You know what I just now noticed, George?"

"What?" George wanted to know.

"This is stupid, but it's going to annoy the piss out of me now."

"What is it?" he said. "Nothing mathematical now — you know my synapses are in rest mode."

"It's nothing mathematical. In fact, it's the opposite of mathematical. These tulips are all so randomly planted, there are clumps of red and white all scattered around this quad, in no apparent order."

George looked at the tulips and nodded. There was a ring of them, all around the quad, and the arrangement of white to red was neither symmetrical nor a regular repeating pattern. It appeared to be random.

"Wow, that is true," he said slowly.

"What idiot did this? I mean, obviously, whatever. It doesn't matter, right? They couldn't have known. But really they're going to be there for years now, all clumped and irregular. What the hell? I'm tempted to just tear them up."

"Strange," said George.

Irene kept walking, her arm through George's arm, but now her pace was more brisk.

"Maybe we should walk over in the ruins from now on," she said. "Avoid this mess."

"Maybe it's Fibonacci," said George, looking at the tulips. Irene stopped in her tracks and frowned, glaring at the tulips. She put her hand up as if she was counting, arranging them differently in her mind.

"No, it's not a Fibonacci sequence," she said. "Look at it — come on, that's not even a good guess. Go back to sleep, synapses."

She began to walk again, dragging him along, but then she stopped again and said, "Wait a minute."

She looked at the tulips, all around the ring, moving her finger up and down as the color changed from red to white and back.

"Oh, for Pete's sake," she said. "It's not some random dumbass gardener; it's a very specific dumbass coder. I know what it is now."

"What is it?" said George.

"It's Belion!" she told him. "That foolish, stupid oaf must have been trying to work out a way to propose to Kate Oakenshield, the girl who was raised mute, for months now. And I think he has finally done it. Or he did it last fall."

"What are you talking about?" George asked.

"Well, look at the tulips. No, don't look at them, because that's like counting or whatever. Rest your brain, but I'll just tell you they're planted in binary. Like Morse code, you know, red and white for one and zero. And it says 'Marry Me.' Cute. Very cute. I mean, it's super dorky and obvious, but she'll fall for that kind of shit like it was wine and roses, you know? Dork that she is. Sorry, but she is."

"Irene," said George. "You have no idea how relieved I am you finally noticed those lousy tulips."

He reached into the pocket of his khakis.

"I've been carrying this thing around for weeks, hoping you would figure out that binary before the petals rotted off and I had to start over with azaleas or pansies or something."

"What?"

He went down on one knee, there in the quad, and she put her hands on each side of his face. He smiled at her, a perfect smile.

"Irene, will you marry me?"

"You did this? You did this tulip thing?"

"I did the tulip thing. Will you marry me anyway?"

"George, yes!" she said. She threw herself into his arms. "Yes, yes, yes. I will marry you, you dork. I will marry you forever."

"I'm so happy," said George. He lifted her off the ground. "I'm so happy, I must be dreaming. I must be dreaming."

All around, the people of Toledo found their own happiness, with or without parental machinations, or they made terrible mistakes and rectified them, and went to

510

sleep and woke up. They pulled out stupid things and wise things from their wishing wells. They learned the truth and forgave each other, or they never figured out how to do that at all, and died without redemption. Sometimes they looked into the stars with rulers and wrote down evidence, and figures, and used a straight edge to measure out their lives. And sometimes they stared into crystal balls, and found true love is a miracle, one they could never understand.

AUTHOR'S NOTE

Thirteen years ago, I sat with my dear friend Kristen in her mom's living room in Ohio. On the floor, my one-year-old son played with her one-year-old daughter. As we watched them, we talked jokingly about how great it would be if they got married, how we would love to be grandparents together, and how many potential problems would be averted if they had cool, evolved in-laws like us. "They'd be perfect for each other!" we joked. "We could make them be!" Obviously the idea never left me, so I thank Kristen for the inspiration and for letting me name my strange, repressed heroine after her beautiful, exuberant child.

Second novels are difficult. Without the encouragement and ass-kicking of my friends, this novel would not have been written. Joshilyn Jackson, this is your book. Thank you for loving it when I couldn't, for sticking up for the characters, and for staking out that ending. Susannah Breslin, thank you for your relentless drive. When I whined about revisions, you said, "If one of your kids had pooped all over the floor, would you stand there complaining about it? No, you would roll up your sleeves and clean it up. So clean it up." One would think that comparing a novel to a diaper leak would be paralytically insulting, but instead I think I should do this quote in cross-stitch.

To my brilliant agent, Caryn Karmatz Rudy: You are every author's dream. Thank you for working so hard and so long on this book. To my brilliant editor, Hilary Teeman Rubin: I am so grateful to have you in my corner. Your insights and ideas were invaluable in creating this novel. Loving thanks to my wise and helpful publicist at St. Martin's, Dori Weintraub.

Thank you to my writing group: Veronica Porterfield, Antonia Giordano, and Layla Denny, and to my early readers: Sherene Silverberg, Kristen DeHaan, and especially Andrea Kinnear, who told me I could write about a brain tumor. A particularly urgent thanks to Christian Kiefer for wading into an early draft and saying the true, hard things. Thank you to my friends online, especially my friends at Book Pregnant, and to my friends out in the real world: You bought my book, you invited me to your book clubs, you linked, you tweeted, you shared. You are incredible.

The booksellers I have met in the last two years are some of the most marvelous, intelligent, driven, and charming people I've met in my life. I'm so thankful for the work you all are doing to connect books and readers!

My wonderful children, Benny and Sadie, are a cheerful, needed balance to the darkness in my brain — more than a distraction from the work, they are my salvation from the work. My husband, Dan, is an endless source of happiness for me, as well as a good listener with a deft hand at untangling plot problems. I am grateful for my family above everything else.

ABOUT THE AUTHOR

Lydia Netzer was born in Detroit and educated in the midwest. She spent many nights, dark and bright, in Toledo, Ohio, but now lives in Virginia with her husband, her homeschooled children, two Boston Terriers and a Morgan horse.